Children of the Siege

DINEY COSTELOE

HEAD of ZEUS

First published in the UK in 2019 by Head of Zeus Ltd

9 7 5 3 1 2 4 6 8

A catalogue record for this book is available from the British Library.

ISBN (HB): 9781784976200
ISBN (XTPB): 9781784976217
ISBN (E): 9781784976194

Typeset by Divaddict Publishing Solutions Ltd.

Printed and bound in Great Britain by CPI Group (UK) Ltd, Croydon CRO 4YY

Head of Zeus Ltd
First Floor East
5–8 Hardwick Street
London EC1R 4RG

WWW.HEADOFZEUS.COM

In memory of my great-grandmother Adele Perraire, who according to family legend was carried into Paris on her father's shoulders at the raising of the siege in 1871.

FRANCE
FEBRUARY 1871

Chapter 1

The cold was bitter. Biting wind swept across the grey-green fields under a leaden sky which promised more snow. Patches of earlier snow still lingered in the hedgerows and sheltered hollows by the wayside, and icy puddles crunched and cracked under the horses' hooves and carriage wheels. The road, such as it was, was ridged, rutted and iron hard. Furrows of frozen mud, which on a warmer day might have clutched at the carriage wheels, bogging them down, remained unyielding, so that every turn of those wheels jarred the occupants of the carriage, shaking them mercilessly despite the most modern of springing, until their heads ached and their teeth rattled and every inch of their bodies felt bruised and battered.

Eleven-year-old Hélène St Clair huddled against her mother trying to keep warm, for despite the fur-lined travelling cloaks and rugs, the piercing cold penetrated the jolting carriage and chilled her to the core. When would the journey be over? When could she escape the freezing, rattling carriage and feel warmth seep back through her body? The blinds were drawn down to help keep out the cold, so Hélène could not even watch from the window to pass the time. She longed to ask, 'How much longer, Maman?' but she did not speak. It was no use asking, her mother did not know.

The journey from St Etienne usually took two days in the carriage, but they had already spent three on the road and in such conditions, with the horses struggling through the wind, who knew how much longer it would take? How cold Papa must be, thought Hélène, and wondered why he chose to ride outside the carriage instead of travelling more comfortably inside as he usually did. She turned to ask her mother, but as she glanced up at her, she saw in the dim grey light which filtered through the blinds that Maman's eyes were closed, her face drawn and pinched with cold and fatigue. Even as Hélène looked, the carriage jarred violently on a stone. Rosalie St Clair's eyes flew open in alarm, and her arms tightened round the fur-cocooned child on her lap, Hélène's younger sister Louise. Louise shifted uneasily in her sleep, but did not waken. The carriage jolted on its way and Madame St Clair smiled reassuringly over Louise's head at her other two daughters. Clarice, Hélène's senior by three years, shivered and drawing her hood more closely round her face, said petulantly, 'How much further, Maman? Aren't we nearly there?'

Madame St Clair lifted the blind a little and looked out through the window. The bleak countryside had given way to a scattering of houses as they approached a village, and as they turned into the main square the coach drew to a halt.

'There,' said the fifth occupant of the carriage who was huddled in a corner beside Clarice. 'We have arrived.'

Marie-Jeanne, the children's nurse, peered out from her enfolding blankets, her face lined and old but her eyes as bright as black buttons. Marie-Jeanne was nearly as dear to Hélène as Maman. Her comfortable face, so familiar and unchanging, always reassured the child, and in times of uncertainty or distress her arms were always warm and sure.

'I'm afraid not, Marie-Jeanne,' replied Madame St Clair. 'We're at an inn. Still, we should be able to get warm and have something to eat, which will make us all feel better.' Gently she woke the sleeping Louise, who complained miserably at being disturbed.

The carriage door swung open and Emile St Clair looked inside. He glared at Louise who was still moaning and immediately the child was silent.

'We'll stop here for a meal and then move on,' he said to his wife. 'I want to be in Paris tonight.'

His family disentangled themselves from their rugs and clambered down from the coach. The bitter wind made them gasp and Marie-Jeanne shepherded them hastily across the cobbled yard into the shelter of the inn. Monsieur St Clair engaged a private sitting room on the first floor and as they crowded into it his daughters cried with delight at the sight of the roaring fire which had been kindled in the grate. Cloaks and muffs were discarded and they clustered round the fire, stretching their frozen fingers to the heat. Hélène sat down on a tuffet by the hearth to bring her nearer to the flames, and extending her feet towards the blaze felt a delicious though painful prickling as the numbness left her toes and warmth crept back into her body.

'We can't stay long,' her father warned them as he found them thus grouped round the fireplace a moment later. 'It may snow again and we don't want to travel far in a snowstorm. We could really run into trouble then.'

Madame St Clair thought privately that if it were about to snow again, it would be far better for them to stay at the inn overnight than hurrying onwards with no idea of what they might find at the end of their journey. Suppose the house was no longer there? After all, Paris had been bombarded. This fear had nagged her ever since they had set out from St Etienne. The world had changed irrevocably since they were last at home in Paris, and she wished Emile had waited for answers to the letters he had sent before removing the family from the comparative safety of their country house. She had said as much to him, but he had remained adamant in his determination to return.

When they had left the capital for St Etienne in early July last year, it was merely to escape the summer heat in the dirty city. Even in the more fashionable quarters, like Passy where they lived, the smell could become oppressive in August. They had expected to return in September as usual and their house was left in readiness, with Gilbert and Margot, the butler and his wife, staying to look after it. But events had overtaken them. The declaration of war against Prussia a few days later, followed by the dramatic advance of the Prussian troops and humiliating defeats of the French armies sent to halt them, had kept the family in the safety of their country home. When Paris was besieged, entirely encircled by German troops, Rosalie and Emile St Clair thanked God they had taken their annual trip to the country as always and thus escaped the horrors of being trapped in Paris. Rumours flew through the countryside; Parisians were dying like flies from starvation and disease, and the city's defenders, after abortive attempts at a sortie, could do little but tighten their belts and wait for relief from outside. That relief never came. The French armies had surrendered, leaving Paris to fend for herself, and the disgrace of those surrenders weighed heavily. Rosalie and Emile felt it as much as any. Their two sons were both with the army and had been, as far as their parents knew, in the disastrous battle at Sedan when Emperor Napoleon himself had been taken prisoner, but since then they had heard nothing. They did not even know for sure that Georges and Marcel were alive.

Fear for the safety of her sons was another thing that haunted Rosalie. It was with her day and night like a nagging pain and though she knew Emile was afraid for them too, emotion seldom showed on his face. He never shared his fears with his wife and so she lacked the comfort he might have given her. Emile was a good husband and father, but his feelings for his family were never revealed; he would have considered that weakness, and so the children gave him respect rather than affection. Rosalie had loved him and still did, but when he made it clear that he considered displays of that love unbecoming, she had lavished her affection on her children and received theirs in return. The days after the surrender of the army at Metz and Sedan had turned into weeks and then months and there was still no word from either son. Thousands had been killed, thousands more taken prisoner, and Rosalie, with no news of her sons, ached for them both.

At last the siege was ended and the armistice was agreed. Emile St Clair was eager to return to Paris. He was a man who hated inactivity and the normal family holiday of two months in the country always tried him to the limit. When the quiet life there threatened to engulf him, he would visit Paris for a few days, leaving the family to enjoy St Etienne without him. Because of the war, the two months had elongated to almost eight and had kept him in a fury of frustration. Like a caged lion he paced the house and garden, longing to return to his beloved Paris and his all-consuming work, the rebuilding of that city.

Louis Napoleon had had great plans for the city and had cleared the ground, pulling down cluttered housing and slum tenements to clear the way for wide, tree-lined boulevards and gracious buildings. This meant that though some slums were cleared away there was greater crowding in those that remained, but for Emile St Clair, architect, it meant that he was more than fully employed. He designed with simple grandeur and though none of the major public buildings were his, the new comfort of apartments and houses spreading at the western end of Paris owed much to him. As a consequence, he and his family were soon well established in a tall, grey stone house in a quiet avenue, Avenue Ste Anne, in the Passy district, while retaining several properties in Montmartre which added to his income if not his prestige.

He was thankful that his family had not had to suffer the dangers and privations of existence in a besieged city, but now there was peace, Emile lost no time in arranging his return. He had written to the housekeeper to announce the family's arrival and to his office to announce his own. Although the war was over, the country was not free from German occupation.

'I have decided we must all go back to Paris,' he told Rosalie. 'I cannot possibly stay away longer and neither can I leave you and the girls unprotected at St Etienne. With Prussian soldiers on the loose in the countryside, it is far too dangerous; you will all be safer in Paris.' He spoke with conviction, believing himself to be right in the matter; Rosalie had not been so certain, but having made a small protest which he swept aside, she accepted his decision.

Her place was at his side and the family should not be divided in such uncertain times. She longed for news of Georges and Marcel, and it was the thought that she was more likely to hear of them in the city than buried in the country that went a long way to resigning her to their return to Paris.

Emile had ridden alone to the headquarters of the German Army corps whose troops barred the way from St Etienne and requested permission to remove his family back to Paris.

He had been treated with stiff courtesy by Major Schaffer, to whom he had made his application. The major had pointed out that many Parisians such as himself were making every effort to leave Paris now the siege had been raised. Emile was undeterred, even when the major had gone on to discuss the dangers of such a journey from the comparative safety of the country to the war-torn capital – particularly as the railways had not resumed normal operations and they would have to travel by road – but at last Major Schaffer had shrugged his shoulders and signed the necessary paper.

Emile had ridden home triumphantly with it in his pocket.

'It's all arranged,' he cried when he returned. 'We leave for Paris in two days.' But as the carriage swayed out of the gates at St Etienne and security and comfort were left behind, Rosalie could not restrain a sigh for what she was leaving, nor repress the creeping fear that all would not be well in Paris when they arrived there. Now she was only a few miles from the city and she longed to put off the moment of truth.

'Don't you think, my dear, that if it is going to snow again, it would be as well to spend the night here?' she ventured as she glanced anxiously out of the inn window at the louring sky. 'If we should get caught in a snowstorm we might all freeze to death.'

Her husband's lips tightened into a straight line. He pulled his gold-rimmed glasses from his pocket, set them on his nose and looked coldly at his wife above their rims. It was a habit he had when he felt his authority questioned, and when faced with this bleak expression, his wife seldom pressed her argument.

He said, 'I hardly think there is much chance of that. You know we are nearly there and I'm sure the children would be better in their own beds than spending a third night in a village inn.'

Before Rosalie could reply, the door opened and a maid entered carrying a tray with hot chocolate on it, a plate of chicken pieces and some bread and cheese. She put the food on the table and withdrew without speaking. Marie-Jeanne poured out cups of chocolate and the girls took them gratefully, nursing the warm cups in their hands before they drank.

'It's snowing,' cried Louise suddenly, putting down her cup by the fender and running to the window. Hélène joined her and the two girls knelt up on the window seat, pressing their noses against the glass as they watched the huge white flakes come drifting silently from the sky to lay a white mantle on the cobbles of the inn yard and the slates of the stables beyond. With the snow came the darkness and it was with enormous relief that Rosalie heard Emile turn from his original decision to travel onwards at all cost, and bespeak beds for the night.

'Come away from the window and drink your chocolate while it's hot,' she said to the girls, and as they turned reluctantly back into the room, Rosalie went to draw the heavy curtains across to shut out the night. As she reached the window there was a sound of hooves in the courtyard below and a troop of soldiers rode up. With shouts and laughter they dismounted and clattered in through the inn door.

Hurriedly Rosalie pulled the drapes across and kept her children's attention from the commotion outside. Throughout the last few months she had tried to shelter her daughters from the news of the war and its activities, and now because of Emile's determination to return with all speed to Paris they were actually staying upstairs in an inn where German soldiers drank below.

Later, their supper finished, Rosalie and Marie-Jeanne took the girls to their bedchamber and tucked them into the enormous bed all three must share.

'Home tomorrow,' murmured Hélène as her mother kissed her goodnight.

'Yes, home tomorrow.'

And to the rhythmic sound of Marie-Jeanne in a rocking chair in the corner of the room, the travel-weary girls fell fast asleep.

They awoke next morning to a white and glistening world. The snow had not been as heavy as Emile had feared and the gleaming blanket covering the village, on which a wintry sun danced and sparkled, was in fact only an inch or two deep. The wind, so bitter the day before, had died away and as there was little danger of drifts blocking the road, Emile determined they should set forth without delay. The February sky was cloudless, a cold, pale blue, and despite the difficulties of the road yet to be faced, the whole family felt considerably more light-hearted and hopeful than they had on the previous days of their journey.

Emile had the carriage brought round and the horses stood snorting in the inn yard, their breath clouding the sharp morning air, as the girls, their mother and nurse climbed in once more and settled themselves amongst the rugs. This time they did not draw the blinds and the pale sun brought faint warmth into the carriage.

'Why doesn't Papa ride with us?' asked Hélène, as she saw her father mounting his horse once more. 'Why does he ride outside in the cold?'

Her mother said carefully, 'He can see the road ahead that way, in case there is any difficulty.'

'What sort of difficulty?' persisted Hélène.

'In weather such as this,' replied her mother, 'one must always take extra care. There may be drifts across the road, a fallen tree, or perhaps other vehicles which have crashed or even overturned in the snow. We don't want to have an accident ourselves.'

Hélène thought that at the slow pace they had been travelling so far it was unlikely that they would run into anything and was about to say so when Clarice said, 'He's keeping guard in case we're attacked. They say the people are still starving in Paris, and no traveller is safe. They'll kill you for a slice of bread.'

'Clarice, don't be ridiculous,' said her mother sharply with an anxious glance at Louise who was settling herself in the corner.

'It's true, Maman,' protested Clarice. 'I heard the patron in the inn tell Papa to beware of the citizens. They've even been eating cats and rats because they were so hungry. Ugh! Rats! I couldn't eat a rat even if I were dying!'

'That will do, Clarice,' snapped Rosalie. 'I want to hear no more about it.'

Clarice lapsed into silence, but she caught Hélène's eye and mouthing the word 'rats', pulled a face.

'Shall we have to eat rats, Maman?' enquired Louise. 'When we get home?'

'Certainly not,' said her mother.

'Oh, good.' And Louise snuggled back into the rugs.

'They might try to steal our horses,' whispered Clarice to Hélène. 'They could eat those...' but the frown on her mother's face stopped her from elaborating.

Emile looked in through the window. 'All right?' he asked.

'Yes, quite ready,' replied his wife, and at his word of command the carriage rattled slowly out of the inn yard and once more took the road for Paris.

Rosalie closed the window and they all sat back to endure the last few uncomfortable miles. Hélène, this time sitting beside Marie-Jeanne, thought over what Clarice had said. She knew Paris might be very different from the place she had known before, and she was a little frightened. One of the housemaids at St Etienne, Anne-Marie, had told her about the siege, giving all the lurid detail her fertile imagination could conjure up. 'And all as true as I'm standing here, Miss Hélène. Robert, my brother, he's been there. Walking skeletons them people are now, walking skeletons. And some of them Prussian soldiers, well, do you know they eats children? Boils them up and eats them.' Hélène's eyes had started from her head at this and well aware of the impression she was creating, Anne-Marie had lowered her voice to a chilling whisper and continued, 'They do say that some of them soldiers has got two heads, 'cos Prussians is different, see, not like us French, and of course no decent girl is safe within a mile of them. Robert says...' But Hélène had not discovered the latest saying of this fount of information, for Marie-Jeanne had come into the room at that moment and immediately summing up the situation from the gleam in Anne-Marie's eyes and the fear on Hélène's face, she sent the housemaid about her business and did her best to undo the harm that had been done.

In some measure she succeeded even though Hélène would not specify all her fears, but she laid to rest the myths of the two heads and the boiled children, and Hélène's terror at what she had been told receded a little, though she still puzzled over how a girl could be in danger from the Prussians a mile away from them. Had they got strangely long sight? And why girls only? Did Prussians hate girls more than boys? Afraid of the answer, Hélène did not dare ask the question.

The carriage rumbled its way forward and Hélène watched the country creeping past. It was not at all as she remembered it, but quite strange and rather frightening. In the outlying villages the houses and farms had been deserted, their owners fleeing to the safety of Paris as the Germans approached, and their homes had been taken over by the enemy to be used as billets. Peering white-faced from the window Hélène could see dugouts and ramparts with long trenches linking one place to another, turning the villages into one huge ribbon of fortifications.

'Maman,' she whispered, somehow not daring to raise her voice, 'why are the villages full of soldiers, are they Prussians?'

Tight-lipped her mother nodded, and Clarice gave a little cry. 'Oh, we shall all be killed.'

'Be quiet, Clarice,' Rosalie said sharply. 'The war is over. We have nothing to fear from the soldiers. Your father has a permit to travel in his pocket.' Her own fear was not stifled however, as they drew nearer to the walls of the city and saw the devastation caused by the war. Trees and houses had vanished, destroyed to ease the defence of Paris, to give the huge guns mounted on the city walls a wide field of fire, and all that was left were ugly stumps and pieces of rubble; indeed in many places the road on which they were travelling disappeared altogether and the carriage had to proceed at a snail's pace over rough and stony ground, in extreme danger of losing a wheel or even overturning.

Hélène clung to Marie-Jeanne's hand as they bumped and swayed along the frozen track and stared fearfully out at the desolation, its starkness increased by the mantle of snow which robbed the countryside of colour and left it etched in black and white against the slate grey sky.

No one else travelled the road that day, the eerie silence which surrounded them was broken only by the sound of their own progress, and so when he did see a troop of horses coming towards them Emile St Clair signalled to Pierre, the coachman, to stop and let them pass.

For a blessed moment the bumping, swaying motion of the carriage ceased and peering once more from the window, Hélène saw the troop approaching, heard the hooves of their horses clattering on the frozen road.

The officer leading the troop called a halt and rode forward to speak to her father. Everyone within the coach waited in silent fear after Hélène had whispered, 'It's soldiers. One's talking to Papa.'

Emile produced the permission to travel he had obtained from Major Schaffer and after a few moments' conversation the German officer shrugged his shoulders and waved his men forward. They trotted by on either side of the coach and the girls watched them pass the windows. Louise, wide-eyed with wonder, waved her hand and to their astonishment one of the German soldiers smiled and waved back.

'Louise,' cried Clarice in horror, 'those are the enemy!'

'That one was nice,' remarked Louise, unconcerned. 'He wasn't an enemy, was he, Maman?'

'He was a German, Louise,' replied Rosalie, 'but he may have been a kind man. Perhaps he has a little girl like you.'

'Do Germans have little girls?' asked Louise, much interested.

'Of course they do,' said Hélène scornfully, but despite her assertion, the idea that the Germans had families was an entirely new one to her and something which she found difficult to accept fully. Germans or Prussians to her meant rampaging armies, invading France and taking her brothers away.

Emile St Clair came back to the window, Rosalie lowered it a little and he said, 'Everyone all right? We're not far from the gates now.' His wife replied that all was well and so he called to Pierre to drive on and the carriage began its lumbering progress once more.

Hélène continued to watch from the window half fascinated, half terrified to see the walking skeletons Anne-Marie had described, but she saw none. At length the carriage rolled to a halt and for a long moment Hélène was only glad that the jolting had ceased. She looked out of the window to see why they had stopped and saw that they had reached the walls of Paris and were waiting outside the gate. Then raised voices from outside the carriage brought the attention of all five occupants to an argument that had arisen. They could hear Papa speaking angrily and another man shouting in reply. Both Hélène and Clarice craned their necks to see what was the cause of the dispute, but were pulled up by their mother.

'Sit back, please, girls, and wait until your father has finished speaking to the gatekeeper. If there is anything you should know I have no doubt he will tell you.' Afraid, she spoke more sharply than she had intended, fear sharpening her tongue as she too strained her ears to discern the cause of the trouble.

They were not long left in ignorance, however, as Emile St Clair appeared beside the carriage and opened the door. His face was white with barely suppressed fury and he spoke in the low, tight voice that always betokened his rage.

'My dear, I must ask you and the children to step down from the carriage for one moment, please.'

He stood aside and handed his wife down the steps, then with unusual care lifted each of his daughters down and set her on her feet beside her mother.

'You too, Marie-Jeanne,' he said, glancing back into the carriage, and even gave his hand to the old nurse as she clambered awkwardly to the ground. Then he turned back to the soldier who lounged at the gate and said angrily, 'There. Now I hope you will be satisfied. You have our permission to travel in your hand, you see the complete party standing before you and now, if you please, we would like to enter the city and go peacefully to our home.'

The soldier stepped forward, the St Clairs' permit to travel still in his hand. Remembering Anne-Marie's tales, Hélène edged closer to her mother and clutched hold of her cloak. Instinctively Rosalie drew the children towards her and stared at the approaching soldier, her head raised proudly and her pale face brave and calm. Hélène stared at the soldier. He must be a Prussian, she thought, he looked fierce enough, his face dark with unshaven stubble, his uniform filthy and needing some repair. Hélène shrank away from him as he approached and stretched out his hand towards her. He did not touch her but as she recoiled he dropped his hand and spoke to her mother.

'Ah, madame. Your children? Please tell me their names.'

Rosalie spoke the names and the man made a show of consulting the permit.

'Thank you, madame. Be so good as to wait for one moment.' He called another man and together they made a leisurely search of the coach. The family stood in the cold, waiting. Suddenly the cumulative fatigue of the past few days overcame Louise who began to cry, and even a sharp call to silence from her father could not quieten her. Rosalie gathered her into her arms and hushed her like a baby, ignoring the studied insolence of the scruffy soldiers as they rifled through the travelling rugs to discover anything or anyone that they might conceal. Not content with looking inside the coach, they made Pierre, the coachman, come down off the box and then unloaded the two travelling trunks which were strapped to the back of the carriage. These they opened and searched thoroughly, making much of the search, tumbling the St Clairs' possessions into the dirt or tossing them into untidy heaps until the trunks were empty. Emile St Clair stood motionless in icy fury as he and his family, shivering with cold and humiliation, watched their most intimate garments and private possessions discarded carelessly onto the road. At length, the soldier turned back to them and growled, 'You may proceed.'

'Put the children into the carriage, Rosalie,' said Emile very softly as he struggled to hold his temper, 'then you and I and Marie-Jeanne will repack the trunks.'

Rosalie turned back to the carriage, only to be halted again by the guard who had not yet finished with them.

'But your horses are requisitioned. We need those. You may proceed on foot.'

The curb on Emile's temper finally snapped at the cool contempt with which the man spoke and he exploded with rage.

'How dare you steal my horses? What right do you think you have? You interrupt our journey, despite the written permission we have to make it, which, no doubt, you can't read, you search our carriage, ransack our possessions and now you think you can steal our horses. We need these horses to continue our journey.' As he spoke he moved forward and laid a hand on the bridle of his own mount which was standing patiently beside the carriage. From nowhere five more guards appeared and Emile found himself in the centre of a ring of rifles. For a moment there was an absolute silence, for all the world, thought Hélène viewing in a strangely detached way the unreal scene of her father degraded and held at gunpoint, like a photograph; then slowly her father dropped his hand from the horse's head and stepped back.

'What about the carriage?' he asked in a low voice, his temper once more under control; raging could only bring his family into more danger. The soldier shrugged. 'We have no interest in that,' he said, and ordering his men to unharness the horses which drew the carriage, he turned away, leaving the little family group standing forlorn, outside the gate.

Emile, still fighting to control the anger his humiliation had caused, turned to his wife.

'I'm afraid we must walk,' he said shortly.

'What about the luggage?' Rosalie glanced at the two trunks standing empty, their contents disgorged on to the cobblestones.

Emile answered with controlled calm. 'Don't worry, my dear, I will arrange something. Now, come along, children, sit back in the coach and keep warm until we are ready to leave.'

As if in a dream the three girls moved back to the stranded carriage and climbed in out of the coldness of the street. A handful of people had gathered and were watching the strange group speculatively, eyeing up the strewn luggage. One braver than the rest, a skinny girl, darted out and snatching up a shawl of Rosalie's which lay on top of one of the piles of clothes, made a dash through the little crowd and disappeared in through the city gate. With a bellow, Emile discharged his pistol in the vague direction of the thief, which did nothing to hinder her, but had the effect of dispersing the others and causing cries of alarm from the carriage. But the scavengers would not stay away for long. Emile knew there was no time to be lost if they were to salvage anything from this disastrous episode. He turned abruptly to the coachman who was standing at a loss beside the now horseless vehicle and called out, 'Pierre.'

'Yes, monsieur.' Pierre crossed over to join them.

'Go quickly into the city and find someone with a handcart. Bring him here and we'll load the trunks on to the cart. We'll take them to the Avenue Ste Anne that way. Give him this,' Emile handed the man a gold coin, 'and tell him he can have as much again when he delivers the trunks unopened to the house. Stay with him all the way.' He gave the coachman a push towards the city gate. 'Go quickly. We will clear up here while we wait for your return. Hurry or I have no doubt everything else will disappear as the horses have done.' Pierre went unwillingly towards the gate and crossed without hindrance into the city.

'Try and keep warm until Pierre gets back,' said Emile, turning his attention to his daughters shivering in the carriage. 'Wrap up warmly, he may be some time.'

If he comes back at all, thought Rosalie to herself as she tucked the girls into the travelling rugs once more, and Marie-Jeanne and Emile began stuffing the clothes back into the trunks.

Hélène, feeling less frightened now that they were back in the illusory safety of the carriage, said, 'Why did the Prussians want our horses, Maman? Have they no horses of their own?'

'Prussians?' Rosalie looked across at her daughter and laughed bitterly. 'Those men weren't Prussians, those men were French. They were from the National Guard.' The expression on her face halted the flow of Hélène's questions and the girls sat in silence watching their parents and Marie-Jeanne at their task and awaiting the return of Pierre.

Return he did in a comparatively short time. Emile, who had mounted guard on the reassembled luggage, his pistol conspicuously in his hand, arose from the trunks as the coachman appeared with a scruffy urchin wheeling a ramshackle handcart.

'Says he'll do it, but wants double,' said Pierre, jerking his head towards the boy.

Emile looked at the youngster and said solemnly, 'You shall have double, providing nothing is missing or damaged when we get there.'

The boy grinned and his grin revealed that he had several teeth missing. Despite the bitter weather, his bare legs, thin as sticks and bowed outwards, protruded from ragged cut-off trousers, over which he wore a much-patched jacket. Perched on his thick matted hair was a filthy cap. It was clear to Emile that this child had been inside the walls of Paris throughout the siege, but he spoke up perkily enough.

'All right, m'sieur. We'll make it, you'll see.' He had survived the bombardment and the starvation of the siege, and the offer of so much money for such an easy job made him throb with excitement. The food that money could buy! Food and warmth too!

'What's your name, boy?' demanded Emile, hating to trust their possessions to this boy, but knowing they had little alternative.

'Jeannot, m'sieur.'

'Well, Jeannot. How do you propose to get the luggage to the Avenue Ste Anne without losing it to some marauding thieves?'

'I will show you, m'sieur, and if you all walk with me, none of you will be touched. But first we load the trunks, *hein*?' He spoke with such confidence that Emile nodded and between them he, Jeannot and Pierre lifted the trunks and manhandled them on to the rickety cart.

'Now blankets, m'sieur,' and unquestioning, Emile fetched them from the carriage, telling Rosalie and Marie-Jeanne to get the girls out now.

Jeannot took the blankets and covered the trunks with them; they lay side by side, two long rectangular shapes discreetly draped, completely concealed. Then he turned to Rosalie. 'Keep the young ladies at your side, madame, and follow behind me. You walk behind them,' he continued, turning to Emile, 'and you,' he said to Pierre, 'help me push. I can't manage on my own.' This last was all too obvious – his strength was in his character, not in his emaciated body, and it was Pierre who would do most of the pushing, but the coachman did not question the command.

Without argument they all took up the positions he had indicated, the adults suddenly aware of the urchin's superior knowledge, aware that they were about to enter an alien city, no longer the Paris they had left so cheerfully eight months earlier, and the girls too frightened and numb with cold to do anything but obey dumbly and wait for it all to be over.

Ignored now by the National Guardsmen, the little procession passed through the gate, leaving the carriage standing deserted outside the walls at the mercy of the scavengers who were already creeping back.

And so it was that the St Clair family returned to Paris, tired and on foot, pushing their possessions before them on a handcart.

Anne-Marie's stories came flooding back to Hélène and she clutched her mother's cloak as they followed the boy, Jeannot, along the narrow cobbled streets, sometimes so enclosed by the tall buildings on either side that it was like walking down a gloomy, noisome corridor. The road was slippery and foul underfoot, slimy with ordure, human and animal, giving off an indescribable stench which on occasion threatened to overcome them. Only by following Jeannot, trudging ahead with the rattling handcart, did they keep moving. Hélène found herself fighting not to be sick, concentrating her attention on the man and the boy ahead of her, keeping her eyes away from the filth around her feet, clutching Marie-Jeanne's hand for strength. And all the time she knew she was being watched; she felt unseen eyes staring at her from doorways, spying from windows and shadows.

Strange people loped along the street, ducking into buildings, emerging from alleys, and every time someone approached Jeannot cried in alarm, 'Beware! Keep away! Fever! Fever! The sickness is here.' And a pathway cleared before them and they kept on moving. But at last, one group braver than the rest, or more driven by hunger or greed, barred the way and did not retreat at Jeannot's cry.

'Well now, *mon brave*, what have we here then?' The leader stepped forward and made to draw off the blanket. Jeannot tugged the scruffy cap from his head and turning it agitatedly in his hands, cried out, 'Only two coffins, m'sieur. So far only two of us have died, but already my grandmother,' he waved a casual hand at Marie-Jeanne, 'has begun the shakes and may be in the cart herself before the journey's end.' The man drew back a step, but still very suspicious, pointed at the St Clairs.

'And these? Who are these so fat and well-dressed? They never lived in Paris these last six months.'

Emile fingered the pistol he carried under his coat, ready to fire at the man if he made a further advance, but young Jeannot, determined to keep the money he had already received from Pierre and to collect the rest as promised, knew that his fortune was, for the moment, inextricably linked with this well-to-do family so foolishly returning to the city, and he was prepared. He gave a thin laugh.

'You're right,' he squeaked, 'but they'll surely die as well, for we've been locked up in the guardhouse together these last three days. The guards only let us out 'cos Ma and Pa died of the fever and they'm afraid of taking the sickness from us. See how pale that child is.' Jeannot pointed a grubby finger at Louise who once again burst into tears and buried her face in her mother's skirt. The thief gave a little ground and Jeannot said cheerfully, 'Would you like to see in the coffins? They stink something powerful 'cos we'd no way to lay 'em out proper when they died. Still, I 'spect you'll want to be sure.' He reached for the blanket and there was a moment's pause, then Hélène, entirely overcome by the foul-smelling midden beside her, lost her battle against her stomach, retched and was violently sick all over the cobbles. It was enough and the thieves lost their nerve. To a man they melted away into the shadows, their avarice overwhelmed by their fear of the sickness.

Marie-Jeanne comforted Hélène and wiped away the vomit from her face and clothes, but the child was horrified by her lack of control, knowing she had disgraced herself and that she must have incurred the anger of her father. But strangely Papa did not seem at all angry at the exhibition she had made of herself in the public street. Indeed, when her face was wiped clean he patted her cheek in a rare display of approval and said, 'Clever little chick. Brave little girl.' Bewildered at his reaction but somewhat comforted by it, Hélène reattached herself to Marie-Jeanne's hand and once more the little procession continued, this time unhindered, until they came out to the wider streets and boulevards nearer their own district of the city.

Rosalie gasped in dismay at their strangely denuded aspect. Gone were the spreading trees which had lined them; only ugly stumps remained in the ground to show where they had once stood to lend their gracious shade.

'The trees,' she whispered. 'What happened to the trees?' It was strange, but of all the horrors they had seen and experienced in the last hour, it was the remains of the trees that finally cracked her iron control and silent tears crept down her cheeks.

'Firewood,' said the boy laconically and moving a little faster now on the broader thoroughfare, at last trundled the handcart into the Avenue Ste Anne, which had also been stripped of its trees, and turning to Emile he said, 'Which house?'

Chapter 2

The Avenue Ste Anne was deserted. As the St Clairs walked along it towards their home, their feet echoed eerily on the paving and the squeak of the handcart seemed magnified in the surrounding silence. Nobody spoke, but all stared round at the changes that had occurred. Two of the houses had been destroyed by fire and remained only as blackened shells, unsightly gaps like rotten teeth; and many others presented only blank exteriors, their windows shuttered and their doors barred.

As the family reached their own house they discovered it too was closed up, and for a long moment they stared at its shuttered windows and barred door with very varied emotions. Rosalie experienced a vast, if premature, relief; the house was, after all, still standing, it had been destroyed by neither the Prussian bombardment nor the French occupation, and she thanked God fervently that they had not survived the journey from St Etienne only to discover their home was a ruin. Emile also was relieved finally to have reached the house, for at last he was seriously beginning to doubt the wisdom of his decision to bring his family back to Paris, but he was amazed and angered by its air of desertion. Why was it shuttered and barred? Where were Gilbert and Margot? Why was nothing prepared for their homecoming?

Clarice and Louise, hardly taking in that the door was not wide in welcome, were far more interested in getting warm and having something to eat, and Hélène longed to remove her soiled dress and wash herself free from the smells of the back streets and the taste of her own sickness which lingered stale and unpleasant in her mouth.

Marie-Jeanne was old enough to remember revolution in Paris before. She was realistic enough to know that the declaration of the Third Republic in September last year, when the Emperor Napoleon III had been taken prisoner and subsequently returned to England, was going to have wrought an irrevocable change in Paris, and she knew very real fear as she stared up at the blank exterior of the house. Her eyes ran along the empty street where few houses showed any signs of life. The axed tree stumps were a stark reminder of the very recent and extreme needs the people of Paris had had to withstand and the gas lamps standing along the edge of the pavement did nothing to relieve the new austerity of the avenue. Marie-Jeanne shuddered as the cold fear came creeping.

'Well,' remarked Jeannot, cheerfully impudent, 'they haven't exactly rolled out the red carpet, have they?'

His sharp little voice broke in on their individual thoughts and Emile said shortly, 'Wait here while I get the door open.'

The front of the house, guarded by large iron gates set in a railing-topped wall, looked across a paved yard with stone urns to be filled with flowers in the summer and shrubs to lend colour from November until spring. A wide flight of shallow steps led up to a huge front door, flanked on either side by shuttered windows and topped with a gracious fanlight splayed wide like a rising sun.

All was quiet and still and wrapped in a melancholy air of desertion and neglect. Emile went up the steps and pounded on the front door with the fine brass knocker, but even as he did so he realised the knocker was not as fine as it had been; both the knocker, wrought in the shape of a dragon, and the heavy brass door handle, were sadly dull and discoloured. It was clear that neither had seen polish or cloth for a very long time. There was no reply to his pounding and he knocked again, aware that his original unease at finding the house closed was increasing to alarm. What had happened here during the long months of the siege while they had been away? Where the devil were Gilbert and Margot? The echoes of the dragon knocker died away once more but there was still no sign of anyone answering its summons.

'No one at home,' remarked Jeannot helpfully and ducked to avoid a box on the ear from Pierre.

Rosalie approached her husband. 'I still have my keys,' she said and pulled a heavy key ring from her pocket. It was attached to her waist on a chain and she struggled for a moment to release the key he needed. Emile waited impatiently with his hand extended and when at last she proffered the huge key of the front door he almost snatched it from her. Inserting it in the keyhole he turned the lock and tried the handle. The door remained immovable, and Emile realised with a jolt that the massive night-time bolts were drawn across inside. He turned back to the family, who were waiting expectantly beside the disreputable handcart.

'It's bolted inside,' he said. 'Pierre, go through the stable yard and try there.'

Pierre disappeared to the carriage entrance in the lane that ran along behind the house but was soon back. 'I can't get into the stable yard, monsieur,' he said. 'The *porte cochère* is chained and the door in the garden wall is locked as usual. From what I can see above the wall, the house is shuttered at the back as well. It is all closed up.'

For a moment they all stood there at a loss and flakes of snow began to drift silently down; the fragile illusion of spring which had come with the morning had disappeared with the afternoon, the sky was once again leaden and the reality of winter returned. Hélène shivered. She stared up angrily at the barred front door and then, suddenly, an idea came to her. Taking her courage in her hands, for she seldom spoke to her father uninvited, she ventured to his side and said timidly, 'Papa, the sunshine window.' She pointed to the fanlight above the door.

Her father turned, irritable. 'Well, what about it?' He looked up at the semicircular window above the dark door.

'It has no shutters, Papa. Perhaps if you could break the glass and lifted me up I could…' Her voice, uncertain of her suggestion from the start, trailed away as she saw incredulity in her father's face. She felt the colour flood her cheeks and said in a whisper, 'Sorry, Papa.'

But her father was not angry, he was just amazed that Hélène had seen a solution to the problem that he had not. For the second time that day he patted his surprised daughter on the cheek and said, 'Well done, Hélène, but not you.' He glanced up at the little window again and said, 'Jeannot, if I break that window can you wriggle through and draw back the bolts on the front door?'

Jeannot grinned and said loftily, 'Well, breaking and entering isn't really my line, of course, but I reckon I could manage that all right. As long as you're the one what breaks the window!'

Using the butt of his pistol Emile reached up and with a sharp blow shattered the glass, then Pierre tossed the feather-light Jeannot up on to his shoulders and the child peered inside.

'Break away more glass if you have to,' ordered Emile and unwilling to hand over his pistol, he picked up a piece of stone and passed it up to the boy.

Balancing easily on Pierre's shoulders, Jeannot broke the remaining shards of glass and with a cheerful, 'Here I go then,' hoisted himself up on to the window frame and started to slide through head first, drawing his legs in behind him to swing them round and drop down on the inside. He made the move with such practised ease that Emile, watching him, thought wryly that there was no doubt the boy had completed this manoeuvre on many occasions before. But just as Jeannot was preparing to drop nimbly down into the hall he suddenly froze and then with a tremendous scuffling re-emerged from the window and leapt down from Pierre's shoulders. As he landed there was a loud report from inside the house and a bullet whistled through the broken window.

'Good God,' ejaculated Emile. 'What the devil…?' He looked at Jeannot, white-faced and poised for flight but firmly held in Pierre's massive grasp.

'There's an old biddy in there with a pop gun,' explained Jeannot, his voice quavering a little at his narrow escape. 'Just standing in the hall shooting.' As if on cue there was another bang from inside the house and they all instinctively ducked away.

Rosalie came to her senses first and raising her voice clearly and commandingly called, 'Margot? Is that you?

It is I, Madame St Clair. Open the door at once, Monsieur and the children will take cold standing in the street in such weather as this. You hear me, Margot? It is I, Madame St Clair, speaking to you.'

A tremulous voice called from behind the locked door, 'Is it really you, madame?'

'Indeed it is,' cried Rosalie. 'Now look sharp and open the door, for it is snowing again and we wish to be indoors immediately.'

There was another moment's pause and then to their relief they heard the bolts being dragged back and the door at last eased open to reveal the pale and frightened face of Margot Daurier, the housekeeper. At the sight of Emile and Rosalie standing on the step her face crumpled and she began to wail. With a muttered oath at the terrible sound Emile led his family indoors, instructing Pierre and Jeannot to find Gilbert and get the cart unloaded. At the mention of Gilbert's name Margot's wailing intensified and Emile said angrily, 'For heaven's sake, Rosalie, find out what's wrong with her and stop that appalling noise.'

Rosalie, once safely inside her own home, felt immeasurably restored and took immediate charge.

'Marie-Jeanne, please take the girls upstairs and get them changed into warm, dry clothes. Margot, stop that crying if you please and tell me what has been happening here.' She spoke firmly, her tone rallying the distraught woman a little, and her wails subsided to quieter sobs. Marie-Jeanne bustled up the stairs, chivvying the girls before her, while Rosalie continued to calm Margot.

'Now,' she began, but looking at Margot she suddenly saw how old and shrivelled she had become, her face like parchment stretched over her skull, and her clothes hanging off her as if they were not her own. She softened her voice. 'Now, Margot, tell me, where's Gilbert?'

'Gilbert is dead, madame.'

'Dead!' Emile had just returned from below stairs where he had been unbolting the back door. 'What happened?' he barked.

Margot shrank away from him and said, 'He went for food, m'sieur. He did not come back.'

'How do you know he's dead?'

'Emile,' remonstrated Rosalie, but he ignored her and repeated his question.

'Because I found him, m'sieur. We'd nothing left to eat, not a crumb in the house. Then we heard that food waggons were coming into Les Halles so we went to buy food, but so did all of Paris. As they began to unload, the whole crowd surged forward, pushing and shoving, fighting to get the food. We were separated, Gilbert and I, and I lost him. People were grabbing at the food, screaming and cursing each other as they fought to snatch a chicken or some vegetables. Eggs were smashed on the ground – those precious eggs.' Margot began to weep again and her story became less coherent. It seemed she had escaped the mob clutching a chicken and a cabbage. Concealing them beneath her cloak, she had made her way fearfully home to wait for Gilbert. When he did not return and darkness fell, she ventured out to look for him, but an angry mob was still seething round Les Halles and afraid for her own safety she had run back home. Next day, when there was still no Gilbert, she returned to the market and in a narrow alley she had found him a crumpled heap, still clutching half a loaf of bread. 'They'd smashed his head in.' Margot's voice had become almost normal once again and then she cried, 'but they didn't get the bread. He was holding it still, clutched tight in his hand. A loaf of bread, that's what they killed him for, but he didn't give it up even then. He kept it. For me. I found it. He gave it to me, that's what he died for.' She began to laugh, a shrill hysterical laugh which rocked her frail body and echoed terrifyingly in the lofty hall.

A glance up the stairs showed Rosalie three pairs of horrified eyes peering through the banisters and she acted at once. She dealt Margot a sharp slap across the face and as the awful laughter ceased abruptly, hurried her away to the privacy of the kitchen, where to her relief she found the embers of a tiny fire in the grate. Gently she pushed Margot into a chair and looked for wood to rebuild the fire. There were two sticks in the basket and no sign of more, but recklessly Rosalie put them both on the fire and poked the embers to coax a flame.

'There, that's better,' she said, turning back to Margot who sat quietly rocking herself in the chair, her thin arms clasped round her, hugging herself for warmth and comfort and crooning tunelessly.

'Is there any more wood?' Rosalie asked, but Margot did not reply. Her eyes stared, unseeing, into the middle distance as if she had not heard her mistress speak. With a tut of irritation Rosalie gave her attention to the kitchen, opening cupboards and then going into the stone-floored pantry. She stared in horror at its emptiness. It should be filled with hanging meat, there should be vegetables and bowls of eggs, cheeses stacked on the stone shelves, and chickens waiting to be plucked; crocks of bread and butter and fruit grown at St Etienne and brought into town. Today it was empty except for two turnips and an apple. The sight of the empty shelves panicked Rosalie for a moment. What would they eat? Here they were, a hungry household of eight – or nine if she was to feed Jeannot – and there was nothing in the house but two turnips. Of course Paris had been besieged, of course people had gone without food, died of starvation and, if Margot's dreadful tale were true, been murdered for a loaf of bread, but the siege was over now, had been for two weeks. The gates of Paris were no longer closed, there must be food and fuel coming into the city, why had Margot not gone out and restocked the store cupboards? Why had she not re-engaged the necessary servants when she had received notice of their homecoming? Rosalie turned to Margot to demand these things but as she did so her anger faded. It was clear Margot had been incapable since Gilbert's death, only fetching enough food to keep her from starving. Terrified and alone, she had barred herself into the house and as she lived in perpetual fear, her mind had cracked. She was of little practical use to them now, and leaving her huddled in her chair, Rosalie hurried from the kitchen to acquaint Emile with the situation.

She found him assisting Pierre and Jeannot to carry the trunks up to the bedrooms.

'Emile, I must speak with you,' she said. Her voice was sharp and brooked no argument, and caused her husband to lift his head in surprise. Rosalie had never addressed him in such a tone before.

'Very well,' he said and turned to dismiss Pierre and Jeannot.

'Tell Pierre and the boy to wait here,' said Rosalie. 'We shall need them in a moment.'

Even more surprised, Emile said, 'You heard Madame. Wait here for a moment.'

Rosalie led him into the drawing room and closed the door

behind them. The shutters were still drawn across the window and the room felt cold and damp in the dim light that filtered through the slats. Rosalie shivered despite the fact that she had not yet removed her travelling cloak.

'Well?' demanded Emile. 'What is the matter?'

'Everything,' said Rosalie shortly. 'There is no food in the house and I doubt if there is any fuel either. I don't think Margot can have got your letter; it's obvious she wasn't expecting us and anyway her mind has softened. There are no other servants and I should imagine little likelihood of obtaining any at the moment, so we shall be cold and hungry if we don't fend for ourselves.'

Emile listened and then said, 'Well, we'll keep Jeannot on for a while, he seems an enterprising boy and he'll probably be glad to stay for some warmth and regular food.'

'When we've got some to offer.'

'Precisely, when we've got some. Now, if you will be so good as to make a list of what you need I will send Pierre and Jeannot out to get it. I think it will be better if they keep together. Jeannot will know his way around all right and Pierre can deal with the money.'

Rosalie nodded and feeling a little less desperate, said, 'I'll go and talk to Marie-Jeanne, she'll know what to get,' and leaving Emile to speak to Pierre and Jeannot she went up to her daughters' rooms to find her old nurse.

'Madame,' cried Marie-Jeanne as she entered. 'I was coming to find you. We must have fires lit at once, the house is cold and damp. We shall all catch our deaths.' At the comforting sight of the old lady Rosalie felt suddenly tired. She sank on to Hélène's unmade bed and said, 'We have to get food and wood for the fires. We have nothing in the house. Monsieur St Clair is sending Pierre out to get things. What shall I tell him to bring? What can we cook to feed us all?' Her news was greeted with cries of consternation from the three girls, but she hushed them saying Marie-Jeanne and she would soon have everything planned, and in the meantime they could help by removing the holland covers from the furniture. With the children busily employed, Rosalie gave her attention to Marie-Jeanne.

Between them they concocted a list of basic necessities and when it was complete Rosalie took it downstairs. Jeannot was standing with Pierre, grinning from ear to ear, and at her approach he cried out, 'Don't worry about food, madame. I know where to buy food, as long as you've the money. Rich folks don't starve!'

Pierre aimed a cuff at the boy's ear which was dodged neatly and said gruffly, 'If you're going to work here, young 'un, you learn not to speak till you're spoke to.' Having asserted his authority over the boy, Pierre said to Rosalie, 'Monsieur St Clair has given us money, madame, and the lad here knows where to go to get what we need.' Rosalie nodded and turning to Jeannot asked, 'Will you stay with us, Jeannot, after today?'

'Yes, madame.'

'Then when you come back we must find you some better clothes – perhaps I have an old suit belonging to one of my sons.'

The boy's eyes gleamed and tugging his appalling cap from his head, he said, 'Yes, madame. Thank you, madame.'

Undeceived by this action Rosalie smiled and handed Pierre her list. 'Well, off you go or we shall all be hungry and cold.'

While they were away in search of provisions Rosalie organised Marie-Jeanne and the girls into making the house habitable again, and Emile searched the attic, finding several old packing cases which he brought down to the yard and chopped for firewood. They decided that only two fires could be lit: the kitchen range which would be needed to cook their food and would warm the lower region of the house, and the one in the drawing room where the family would congregate and for the present, take their meals.

'The bedrooms will be very cold, I'm afraid,' said Rosalie, 'but there are plenty of bedclothes and everyone can have extra to keep warm.'

Hélène and Clarice were set to unpacking the trunks and shaking out the crumpled clothes which had been so hastily bundled back into them at the city gate, and Louise helped Marie-Jeanne shake out the feather beds and draw the curtains against the encroaching darkness. The lamps were lit and the mellow lamplight gave an added illusion of warmth.

Pierre and Jeannot arrived triumphant, Pierre carrying two baskets containing vegetables, bread and cheese, and Jeannot trundling his squeaking handcart laden with two sacks of coal and some green logs. They were greeted with cries of delight and Marie-Jeanne soon produced some hot, thick soup and hunks of bread and cheese after which everyone felt considerably better.

'Not the dinner I had imagined on our homecoming,' remarked Emile in a rare moment of family companionship, 'but I've never known a meal more welcome or taste better.' And taking the relaxation of his mood from him everyone agreed, and for a short while the whole family enjoyed the content brought on by full stomachs and a warm fire.

Below in the kitchen, Jeannot, resplendent in trousers two sizes too big for him and a warm woollen shirt, regaled the company with horrific tales of Paris under siege, describing his life in the streets where he slept rough and lived on his wits.

'Haven't you any family?' asked Marie-Jeanne.

'No,' replied Jeannot breezily. 'Never knew my pa, and Ma died a long time ago.' He glanced round the kitchen and knew he had struck lucky. Warmth, food, clothes and wages. He was made for life, but even with these wonders all in prospect he already regretted his loss of freedom and wondered how long it would last, this living in a posh house. He eyed Margot, still huddled in her chair, and wondered if them upstairs would turn her out. It was clear she had gone barmy. He shrugged and turned away. Not his problem. He would stay for a while anyway, see how things went; he might get to like it.

Margot had not moved from her chair; she still sat rocking herself, apparently unaware of the activity about her. Her pitiful fire had died, but the kitchen glowed with heat from the range; even so she looked shrivelled with cold. Marie-Jeanne had coaxed her to swallow a few spoonsful of broth and spoken to her softly, but Margot had made no reply and at last Marie-Jeanne left her to retreat into her private world and went upstairs to put the girls to bed.

Alone in the drawing room, Rosalie spoke to Emile about their unexpected situation.

'Should we get the staff to come up from St Etienne, do you think? Or engage new servants? Poor Margot, Gilbert's death and the siege have quite turned her brain. I think we should send her to the country.'

Emile looked up from his contemplation of the fire and replied, 'It is as you wish, my dear – I leave the running of the house to you, as always. I shall return to the office in the morning to see how they have fared there.'

'We'll need another governess for the girls,' went on Rosalie. 'When Mademoiselle Germaine left in July I had several applications for the post, but as we decided to leave it open until we returned from St Etienne, perhaps they are no longer available and I should advertise again.' Rosalie fixed her mind determinedly on the normality of these problems to keep at bay the fears she had for their future. Suppose there were no servants any more? Suppose there was no food; had they to live indefinitely from hand to mouth as they had today?

'What about the boy, Jeannot?'

'I've told him he can stay and help Pierre,' said Emile. 'He's glad of the food and a roof over his head, I should imagine. Scruffy little urchin. Still, he knows his way about and we'd have been in trouble without him today.'

Rosalie shuddered at the remembrance of their walk through the back streets. If they had been in the carriage they would have followed the main roads and avoided all that squalor. She looked round her comfortable drawing room and knew that whatever privations they might suffer in the immediate future, her life was immeasurably better than the sordid lives of people in those streets and she was not ungrateful.

Upstairs in the chilly bedroom, Hélène lay and listened to the regular breathing of her two sisters. She was too cold to sleep; she curled her legs up and wrapped her arms round her body in an effort to get warm and fall asleep, but she seemed as cold as ever and her brain whirled with the events of the day. She had seen places today that she did not know existed. She had seen the walking skeletons promised by Anne-Marie and had smelt the condition of their lives. Even in the chilly freshness of her own room, wearing a clean nightdress, her face and hands scrubbed and her mouth rinsed, she could smell the stench of the street and taste the foulness of its air. She had known fear in herself and seen it in the eyes of others and Hélène knew this day would be with her always, for the rest of her life.

Chapter 3

Normality returned gradually to the house in the Avenue Ste Anne. A housemaid and cook were engaged and food became more plentiful and varied. Though there was as yet no governess, a daily routine was established with lessons set by Maman, meals in the schoolroom supervised by Marie-Jeanne, sewing with Maman and piano practice for an hour before the evening meal. Very occasionally they were allowed to go for a walk in the gardens nearby, but only if escorted by Pierre as well as Marie-Jeanne. These excursions were few, however, and became increasingly less frequent, finally ceasing altogether as the air of unrest in Paris increased and returning soldiers began to bivouac in the parks and gardens. It was considered far too dangerous to allow the possibility of young girls encountering the sullen defeated soldiers.

Hélène, who disliked the schoolroom and missed the freedom she had grown to enjoy at St Etienne, hated being cooped up in the house, but there had been demonstrations against the new government at Versailles and people had been murdered by angry mobs. Her parents were adamant, there was no question of any of the girls leaving the house except under the strictest supervision.

A new cook reigned in the kitchen now, a cheerful, dumpy woman called Berthe. She wore a huge blue apron and her arms were strong and floury. Berthe always welcomed the girls to her kitchen and allowed them to help her with pastries and pies. Rosalie was aware of their expeditions below stairs and did not altogether approve. However, she recognised her daughters' need for diversion, and the nice brisk walk around the gardens which she would have recommended against boredom being in the present circumstances inadvisable, she did not forbid them to visit the kitchen for a short while each day. Emile might have taken a far less lenient view, but he was unaware of their visits. Scarcely at home, he spent all day at his office trying to gather the rags of his business together. He had returned there the day after his arrival in Paris to find the building deserted, cold and dank, with the air of having been so for many months. Obviously his letter warning of his return had not arrived and his draughtsmen and clerks imagined him still in the country and the office closed. The business of setting things in motion once again kept him from home all day and often into the evenings so that his daughters were already in their beds before he came in to dinner.

Often, when the girls were making gingerbread and custard tarts, Jeannot would linger in the kitchen in the hope of sampling their cooking, until Berthe noticed his idleness and assisted him back to his work with a box on the ear and a piece of pie. She had a soft spot for the boy and was seldom really angry with him and so Jeannot was often about the kitchen. Gradually, a friendship grew between him and Hélène. Clarice regarded him as dirty and kept herself fastidiously away from him, Louise was as unaware of him as she was of anyone who was not immediately concerned for her comfort, but Hélène was intrigued by him and by the fact that he had been in Paris throughout the war and the siege. They were probably much of an age, though in worldly knowledge and experience Hélène was a babe in arms compared with Jeannot. She loved to talk to him, pouring out questions she would never have dared to ask anyone else.

'Where are your parents?' she asked one day. 'What happened to them?'

'Don't know where they are,' Jeannot said. 'Don't know who they are, neither.'

'But haven't you got *any* family?' asked Hélène, wondering how that might feel.

Jeannot gave brief thought to the elderly couple, Tante Edith and Oncle Alphonse, who'd given him shelter during the siege. But they weren't family.

'Nah,' he said. 'I'm on my own.'

Berthe put a stop to their chatter if she thought it unsuitable, which was often, sending Jeannot to his work outside, but Hélène slipped away, following him out into the yard where he was splitting logs or pumping water, and while he worked, or more often while he leaned on the axe or pump handle, he told her about the city he knew, so different from the one known to her. And she believed his tales, for she had seen for herself on the fateful day of their arrival. He told her, too, about the riots that were going on now.

'There was a huge meeting at the July Column in the Place de la Bastille the other day,' he told her importantly, 'to keep the anniversary of the last revolution.'

'And did you go there?' asked Hélène.

'Of course, I support the Fédérés.'

'Fédérés?' Hélène had never heard of them. 'Who are they?'

'They're our people,' replied Jeannot importantly. 'The people of Paris. The National Guard. They're going to throw the Prussians out and run Paris for the people.'

'How will they do that?' Hélène was unconvinced.

'Us Fédérés...' began Jeannot.

'But what *is* a Fédéré?' demanded Hélène.

'National Guard!' Jeannot informed her.

'You're not in the National Guard,' objected Hélène.

Jeannot gave her a withering look and repeated, 'Us Fédérés will fight.' He waved his skinny arm in the air and cried, 'Vive la République. Vive la Fédération.'

Hélène was impressed despite her lingering doubts. 'So, what happened by the July Column?'

'The people of Paris came, thousands of them, all marching past the column. The National Guard led the way and...' Jeannot dropped his voice dramatically, 'there was a spy there. He was counting...'

'Counting? Counting what?'

'Just counting,' Jeannot said, nodding his head judiciously. 'Going to report back to the government.'

'What happened?' asked Hélène again.

'They caught him. No government spies get away from us. People were shouting, yelling what was to be done with him!'

'And what was?' Hélène was wide-eyed.

'Trussed him up and chucked him in the river!'

'But he'd drown!'

Jeannot nodded again. 'Course he would. That's the whole point! That's what you do with spies... kill 'em.'

Hélène, silenced at last, stared at him. A picture of old François, the gardener at St Etienne, drowning a litter of unwanted kittens in a barrel flashed into her mind. He'd just tossed them, mewing, into the barrel of water; they couldn't get out and they'd drowned, but how could you do that with a man?

When Hélène remained silent Jeannot went on, 'Never mind him! I'll tell you something else…' and he gave her the most exciting news of all. 'The Prussians are coming to Paris.'

Her heart contracted with fear and she cried out in horror, 'Oh no. Not into the city, we'll all be killed.'

Jeannot laughed. 'No, we won't,' he said. 'They're not coming to fight again. They're coming to parade – so's we can all see them. So's they can show us they've won.'

'But we know that already,' pointed out Hélène, her fear subsiding now she knew it was only a parade.

'Course we do,' agreed Jeannot, 'but they want the world to know, see. Their emperor wants to ride in and make believe he's our emperor too. They want to show they can walk in and out of Paris just as they please.' He laughed again and added in a whisper, ''Less, of course, they'm stupid enough to come by theirselves.'

Hélène's eyes widened again. 'Why? What do you mean? What happens to them?'

Rolling his eyes, Jeannot drew a dramatic finger across his throat and then with a strangled gasp collapsed in a heap on the ground.

'You mean…?' Hélène stared.

Jeannot nodded and got to his feet. He might have said more, but Berthe appeared from the kitchen to call Hélène in out of the cold and the boy snatched up his axe and began enthusiastically splitting his pile of logs.

Hélène considered this news and when working her

embroidery later in the day in the company of her mother, she said casually, 'Maman, will we see the parade?'

'Parade?' Rosalie looked up in astonishment. 'What parade?'

'On Wednesday. The Prussians. Coming into Paris. The Emperor's leading them in.'

'Where did you hear of this?' asked her mother sharply. 'Who told you?'

Anxious to protect Jeannot and to keep the secret of their friendship, of which she knew her mother would not approve, Hélène said she had heard Pierre mention it to Berthe in the kitchen.

'I see. Well, you should not listen to the idle gossip of the servants.' She appeared to be going to say no more but Louise, intrigued by the idea of a parade, asked, 'But will we go, Maman? To the parade, to see the Emperor?'

'Certainly not,' replied her mother firmly. 'And I wish to hear no more about it. Your father would be very angry to hear you discussing such a subject.'

At her mother's reaction to the news of the Prussian parade, Hélène decided not to ask the other question which intrigued her, so she did not speak of the National Guard, and the 'Fédérés' of whom Jeannot had told her. But despite Rosalie's warning not to listen to the servants' gossip, she did not forbid the girls to go into the kitchen.

Next day Hélène was able to talk to Jeannot again and immediately pursued the subject of the coming parade.

'When is it, Jeannot? Will you be going to look?'

'You bet,' said Jeannot. 'I'll be there all right. I got some rotten vegetables saved up ready. We've been up the markets and picked up the garbage. Them Prussians may have won, but me and my mates aren't going to let them march in here without showing what we thinks.'

Hélène looked at him admiringly. 'You are brave. Are you really going to throw old rubbish at the Prussians? What will you do if you're caught? Will they shoot you, or send you to prison?'

'We shan't get caught,' said Jeannot confidently. 'They've got to keep marching, see, so even if they wanted to they couldn't come after us. And if they did we could lose them, no trouble. We know the streets, they wouldn't get far.'

'When is it?' asked Hélène again.

'Tomorrow,' said Jeannot. 'You come down here tomorrow evening and I'll tell you all about it.' He paused and then added generously, ''Less you want to come too.'

Hélène stared at him. 'Come too?' she repeated incredulously.

'Why not? I'm s'posed to be working here, but I'll slip out of the yard in time to meet my mates. You could slip out with me.'

'But how? I'd be seen. Maman would miss me.'

'So she would,' agreed Jeannot. 'Of course, if you're afraid to go…'

'I'm not afraid,' snapped Hélène.

'No?' Jeannot was scornful. 'You daren't, that's what! Because your papa will be cross when you get back.'

'I dare,' cried Hélène, angry that her courage should be called into question, yet afraid it might indeed fail her at the thought of Papa's fury on her return, for she knew there was no way such an escapade could go undetected. 'You'll see,' she said resolutely, closing her mind to her father's anger; after all, such an adventure would be worth a day's bread and water, or even a beating. 'I'll come. Now, tell me what to do.'

Jeannot thought for a minute and then said, 'You'll need a dark cloak to cover up them fine clothes,' he said, 'and your walking boots, not your indoor pumps.'

'I can put my boots on,' said Hélène, considering, 'and probably no one would notice, but I can't come into the kitchen in my cloak.'

'Tell you what,' said Jeannot, 'leave your cloak at the top of the stairs and I'll fetch it down to the yard. Then you come down early, before breakfast, and off we'll go.'

'But I've got lessons in the morning,' objected Hélène.

Jeannot shrugged. 'Then don't come,' he said. 'If we go later we'll miss the parade.'

'I'll come,' said Hélène. 'Don't go without me.'

'I'm not waiting long,' said Jeannot. 'If you don't come straight down first thing, I'm off.'

'All right,' agreed Hélène, and suddenly afraid of her own daring she turned on her heel and went back into the house.

It was incredibly easy, for no one had considered the possibility that Hélène might attempt to leave the house to watch the Prussian parade. Emile was still unaware that his children knew anything about it, and apart from mentioning to Rosalie that there appeared to have been some National Guard activity in the Champs Elysées the previous evening, he did not give it much thought. Such gatherings of both soldiers and civilians had become too commonplace to give particular alarm and he had held himself aloof from them. Of course, he would have been a great deal more than alarmed had he realised his younger daughter was contemplating venturing out by herself into the city at any time, let alone on the day of the Prussian triumphal march, but apart from deciding to remain at home himself that day, an intention of which Hélène was unaware and which itself might have made her think again about her escapade, he gave little attention to the parade.

'It's quite mortifying enough that they should have the right to march into Paris with banners flying, without the need for Parisians to turn out to watch,' he remarked to Rosalie at dinner the evening before. 'It's an insult to the honour of the capital!' Then considering the matter closed, he dismissed it from his mind.

Hélène had hidden her cloak as arranged and having donned her walking boots in secret she crept down the stairs to the hall, and hearing Arlette, the housemaid, laying the table for breakfast in the dining room, slipped along the passage to the kitchen quarters. Berthe was working at the kitchen stove, but even as Hélène peeped through the crack in the door the cook disappeared into the pantry and the child was able to dart across the kitchen and out through the scullery unobserved. Jeannot was waiting by the yard gate and with one hasty glance behind her Hélène was across the yard and out of the gate into the lane beyond.

'Here's your cloak,' he hissed, tossing the dark bundle to her. 'Put your hood up and keep close to me.' Hélène did as she was told and the two children emerged from the lane into the street beyond. Turning away from the house so that they would not have to pass under its windows, Jeannot set off at a quick trot along the road and Hélène followed, terrified of losing him in the warren of little streets.

'This isn't the way to the Champs-Elysées,' she called to him, catching hold of his jacket as soon as she was able.

'Got to meet my mates first. Come on.' He plunged down a cobbled alley and emerged into another slightly wider street and after several twists and turns which left Hélène completely confused as to where she was and which way led home, they arrived outside a tall tenement which looked to Hélène exactly like all its neighbours.

Jeannot went through an archway which turned out to be a covered way between two buildings, and gave a long shrill whistle followed by two more. Out of the gloom a pale face appeared, its cheeks hollow, its eyes staring.

'Jeannot?'

'Yes. Ready to go?'

'Who's that with you?' The voice was sullen and suspicious.

'Hélène. She's all right.'

'From your 'ouse?' The voice was incredulous. 'What d'you bring 'er for? You must be crazy!'

'She wanted to see the parade. She's all right.'

There was a sniff from the darkness and a second voice spoke, making Hélène jump as it was right beside her.

'If you say so.'

'I do,' said Jeannot fiercely. He turned to Hélène. 'These are my mates, Paul and the Monkey.'

Hélène peered through the gloom, trying to fix the faces to the names, but the one who Jeannot had pointed out as the Monkey said impatiently, 'Come on then. Here's yours.' He thrust something at Jeannot who nodded at Hélène and said, 'Give it to her.' Hélène felt a greasy bag being pushed into her hands and on investigating it she found it filled with rotting vegetables.

'Keep it hidden,' instructed the Monkey and Hélène tucked it under her cloak.

'Come on,' hissed Jeannot, and the little quartet left the dark passageway and threaded their way through dingy streets and alleys until they reached broader thoroughfares and at last the Champs-Elysées.

Amongst the shifting crowds the four street urchins occasioned no comment even though there seemed to be more soldiers of the French National Guard than there were civilian spectators. Hélène followed close behind Jeannot and the other two, who had, on emerging into the dull daylight, been revealed as two more hungry street boys looking as pale and underfed as Jeannot had on that first day by the gate. They pushed and scrimmaged their way through the lines of people until they had succeeded in reaching the front of the crowd. Even so they were forced to remain behind a cordon of National Guards and were some way from the roadside. Hélène, standing between Jeannot and a tall man, became aware of a strange and unpleasant smell. Cautiously she glanced round her but was horrified to discover that it seemed to come from herself. Then she remembered the bag she had been given and was still clutching under her cloak. Once again she opened its neck and closed it immediately.

'Here,' she said, giving it to Jeannot. 'You'll be a better shot than me.'

Jeannot grinned. 'Front line here,' he said, and with cheerful impatience they awaited the parade, Jeannot whiling away the time by removing the odd handkerchief and pocket book from the surrounding spectators and secreting them in his capacious pockets.

In the main, Paris had stayed away from the triumphal entry, preferring to ignore the ignominy imposed on them by the Prussians. The most common attitude was the one Emile St Clair had adopted, a haughty disdain about the whole affair, but amongst those who had suffered most in the siege, fury at the humiliation of Paris seethed and all round Hélène could see gaunt, angry faces ready to jeer the parading army. She felt a knot of fear inside her as she saw them waiting there and felt herself caught among them. Supposing there was a riot like there had been the other day in the Place de la Bastille? Jeannot had told her all about that and it had sounded exciting and patriotic until now, when she was trapped in the middle of it all and was afraid. She looked anxiously about her, wondering if she could creep away before the riot began, but she was afraid of getting lost or crushed in the crowd. Perhaps she would be safer staying with Jeannot. She clutched hold of his jacket so as not to lose him and he turned, irritated by her action.

'Won't be long now. Can you hear the band?'

And suddenly she could, loud martial music, and despite her fear, Hélène felt excitement rise within her. She, Hélène St Clair, had dared to come out to show her displeasure at the Prussian invasion of Paris.

They came, music blaring with trumpets and drums led by a young officer and six mounted troopers, their horses high-stepping as they passed along the Champs-Elysées followed by the rest of the parade. Hélène stared round-eyed as column upon column of soldiers passed by; some were mounted, carrying spears from the top of which flew blue and white pennons, fluttering in the wind. These were followed by others in light blue coats, and yet more in ceremonial white jackets and plumed hats, marching riflemen and yet more cavalry, horses prancing with excitement.

Hélène was amazed at the variety and splendour of all the uniforms, none of which conveyed anything to her, but all filling her with wonder at their dazzling array. The steady flow of noise and colour continued as the columns of men came by in an apparently endless stream: marching feet, clattering hooves, clinking harness enough to bemuse the hostile crowd which lined the road.

There were few cheers to greet them – they were an invading army – but there was an angry rumble in the crowd as the people watched them swagger towards L'Etoile and actually march through the Arc de Triomphe. Those lining the street felt themselves betrayed by their own government, a government not yet even returned from exile to govern from Paris. The mood of the crowd was ominous and there were shouts of anger and abuse, but these were submerged in the general roar of disapproval and the din of the parading men. Hélène caught the mood and shouted her disgust too, her voice high-pitched, using a new vocabulary she had learned from those around her, but her insults were drowned by the rumble of the artillery being drawn past her.

Suddenly there was a scuffle near Hélène as one of her companions hurled a stinking cabbage and an egg in the direction of the passing soldiers. It was a signal and, as one, all three boys, careless of the consequences, attacked the hated Prussians, pelting them with the garbage they had brought. Jeannot, grinning wolfishly, held out the bag to Hélène. She delved into it, pulling out two rotten apples which she hurled with all her strength at the passing soldiers. Several people nearby cheered the children on, encouraging them to greater deeds until it became clear that it was not the Prussians who were taking the brunt of the attack, but the National Guardsmen standing on sullen duty between the crowds and the conquerors. Even then the cheers did not diminish, for some of the National Guard had been making themselves fairly unpopular of late. Full of excitement now, Hélène snatched more apples from the bag and continued her onslaught. One lucky throw hit a guardsman on the back of his head and giving an angry roar, he spun round and advanced angrily towards them. One glance at his red glowering face was enough for Jeannot.

'Run for it,' he bellowed and grabbed Hélène who, unaware that in her frenzied throwing she had actually managed to hit anybody, was hurling yet another apple in the direction of the parade. Jeannot dragged her into the crowd, which parted and swallowed them, separating them from the irate guard. The tall man who had been standing beside Hélène closed ranks and the guardsman found himself facing an angry crowd ranged against him instead of the vagabond children who had thrown the refuse. He turned back, defeated, to watch the rumbling Prussian artillery drawn by heavy horses trundling by in the wake of the procession, a fearful reminder of the power of this German army.

Unaware of the crowd's protection, Jeannot scuttled through the crush of people dragging Hélène behind him, Paul and the Monkey having disappeared in different directions. But as they wriggled free of the immediate area, others grabbed at them, taking them for pickpockets or snatch-purses, and one man succeeded in holding on to Hélène who was less used to escaping through crowds than Jeannot.

'Now, now, young lady. What's all the hurry, eh? Somebody after you, are they? Got their wallet, I'll be bound.' He kept her firmly by the wrist while holding her at arm's length to see more clearly what he had caught.

'Bite!' bellowed Jeannot from the shelter of a doorway. 'Hélène! Bite his hand.' In the uproar she heard his voice and needed no second bidding. She bent her head and sank her sharp white teeth into the back of her captor's hand and closed them as hard as she could. She tasted blood on her lips as with an outraged cry of pain the man let her go and for a moment she was free. Instinctively she spat, hating the taste of his blood in her mouth. The man grabbed at her again and clutched her cloak, but twisting sharply once, she left him with the cloak in his hand and ducked away without it to get lost in the throng. Jeannot was at her side and again they were running until they left the crowds and disappeared into the comforting anonymity of the myriad of alleyways beyond.

Once she slipped on some rubbish and fell into the ooze in the gutter, but Jeannot dragged her to her feet and hurried her on before she could complain. And she did not complain; somehow she knew that in accepting his challenge to go out into the city she had also accepted his codes and standards. Mud and slime meant nothing, not being caught, everything. As she stumbled along behind him, Jeannot glanced back with new respect in his eyes at her brave determination, and at last ducking through a gate, stopped in a tiny courtyard where they found Paul and the Monkey waiting for them.

'Took your time,' growled the Monkey. 'Thought they'd snaffled you.'

'Not likely,' laughed Jeannot, but Hélène shuddered at how nearly they had been caught.

'Have any luck?' asked Paul. 'I got two—'

'I'll see you later,' interrupted Jeannot with a frown in Hélène's direction. 'I did all right. See you later.'

Hélène, still entirely unaware that her companions had had any purpose for being in the crowds other than showing the Prussians how they felt, watched the Monkey and Paul melt into the shadows and then said wearily to Jeannot, 'I want to go home. Will you take me home now?'

Jeannot nodded, saying, 'Yeah, all right. Come on.'

Hélène felt her heart still pounding and her legs weak beneath her as she followed Jeannot at a quick trot along streets very similar to those they had travelled on their first day back in Paris. Then they had been stared at, now they were given no second glances, just two more scruffy street urchins, probably up to no good, but occasioning no interest.

As they reached the better quarter, however, Hélène began to prepare herself for the reception she knew would await her; Maman's tears and recriminations, and when he returned from the office, Papa's anger and possibly a beating. But on their approach to the house it was not a tearful Maman who greeted them as they stole in through the courtyard gate, but a white-faced Marie-Jeanne and an angry Pierre who had just that minute returned from scouring the streets of the city in the vain hope of finding them. Marie-Jeanne let out a cry as she saw Hélène, cloakless with her dress covered in mud, her hair loose, tangled and dirty and her face smudged with dirt where she had brushed the hair out of her eyes.

Leaving Pierre to deal with Jeannot, Marie-Jeanne grasped Hélène by the arm and without a word propelled her none too gently into the house and up the stairs to her father's study where her parents were waiting.

Chapter 4

Hélène looked across at her parents and the force of their anger made her shrink away, her hands trembling with fear. She had thought she was ready to face them and the punishment they would undoubtedly inflict. She had seen her father angry before but it was nothing compared with the tight-lipped, white-faced, closely controlled fury that she faced now. And her mother was not weeping, though her face showed traces of earlier tears; she too was angry beyond anything Hélène had seen in her before. When her father spoke, it was in a low, tight voice far more frightening than any angry shout.

'How dare you?' he said. 'How dare you disobey my orders and cause your mother such distress?' Rosalie did not speak, she just stared stonily at her daughter, and if Hélène had hoped for clemency from her, she was unlucky.

'I wanted…' she began, but knowing no explanation would be of any use, she stopped.

'*You* wanted,' repeated her father. '*You* wanted… Who are you to put your wants against the wishes, no, the *orders*, of your parents? Out there,' he gesticulated vaguely in the direction of the city, 'out there is a revolution. Out there people are fighting and dying, murdering and looting. The city is crammed with soldiers who'd think nothing of grabbing a child your age to satisfy them. As for that boy Jeannot, how dare he lead you into such danger after all I've done for him...'

Hélène plucked up her last pinch of courage and said, 'Jeannot didn't take me there. I went by myself. I wanted to show the Prussians they couldn't just walk into Paris and none of us do anything, so I went and threw some rotten apples at them. So they'd know we didn't want them here.' She stood with her head held high and, as her remarks were greeted with an astonished silence, added, 'Jeannot found me. I got lost and he found me and brought me home.'

She was not beaten, as she had truly expected to be, but was confined to an attic bedroom which contained nothing but an iron cot and a chamber pot. Marie-Jeanne had removed her stinking clothes, scrubbed her from head to foot, washing and brushing out her matted hair, and then had returned her to her father. Without speaking he led her upstairs and thrust her into the tiny room, locking the door behind her. There Hélène was left to ponder on her conduct on a diet of solitude, bread and water. She did not see the second parade of German soldiers as they left Paris after two days' token occupation, nor hear of the patriot Parisians on their knees scrubbing the streets so defiled by the invaders' feet. She remained locked in the attic for a whole week before she was received back into the family and treated, by her parents at least, as if the adventure had never occurred.

With her sisters, however, she was something of a celebrity and they plied her with questions about her escapade, shivering with delicious fear as she described the angry face of the National Guardsman whom she had hit with the apple, and crying out in shocked delight as she recounted how she had bitten the man who had tried to catch her. They demanded descriptions of the parade, the proud, marching soldiers, the cavalry riding their splendid horses, the cannon drawn behind, and these became more and more graphic at each telling.

Though the matter was never referred to again by her parents, several things happened as a direct consequence of her action. First, she discovered Jeannot had disappeared. Her denial of his involvement had not saved him and after receiving a hiding from Pierre and a tongue-lashing from Emile St Clair, he had been turned out into the street with his handcart and the tiny bundle of his possessions, and a piece of cheese in a twist of paper slipped into his hand by Berthe who, despite the enormity of his crimes, was sorry to see him go.

'He went quite cheerfully really,' she told Hélène one day when the girl had slipped down to the kitchen to see her. The regular visits to Berthe were no longer allowed, but Hélène had taken advantage of her mother retiring to bed with a headache to creep below stairs to ask about Jeannot. 'Said he didn't like being cooped up here. Trouble was they found he'd been thieving too.'

Hélène looked up in astonishment. 'Thieving? From us?'

Cook shrugged. 'Can't say about that, but he had some bits and pieces in his pockets when Pierre searched him, which he couldn't explain.'

'Poor Jeannot,' said Hélène as she thought of him once more living rough, scavenging food and in the company of Paul and the Monkey.

'Don't worry about him, Miss Hélène,' said Berthe, and lowering her voice added, 'I see he gets a piece of pie or a lump of cheese from time to time, and Pierre sees him too. He's got fond of the lad.'

Hélène's face lit up. 'Does he come here?' she asked. 'Tell me, so I can see him.'

Berthe looked severe. 'Certainly not. You and he've caused enough trouble as it is. Your papa would throw me out too if he thought I'd told you as much as I have. You're not allowed down here now, you know. We'll both be in trouble if you're caught. Go on up now, before your ma misses you.'

Hélène went back up to the schoolroom where her sisters were dutifully learning a poem to recite to Maman later, and though she too settled down with a poetry book in her lap, her thoughts were far from the enclosed warmth of the schoolroom. She gazed out over the walled garden in which she and her sisters were allowed to play, and thought of Jeannot. He had never joined their sedate games of ball and hide and seek in that garden; he had been confined to the courtyard behind the kitchen, but now even that was forbidden to him. He had the freedom of Paris, the streets were his world, not the cloistered life Hélène must lead, and despite the dirt and hunger she knew he faced, she envied him his freedom. She longed to talk to him again and wondered if Pierre might tell her when he came, as Berthe would not. She thought it was worth a try and decided to watch for an opportunity to ask the coachman.

This opportunity presented itself a few days later, on a chilly but sunny afternoon when the girls had been sent out into the garden for some fresh air. They decided to play hide and seek and Hélène, covering her eyes, counted to one hundred while her sisters hid. As she began to search for them she noticed that the door in the wall between the garden and the courtyard was open. Wondering if Clarice had dared to go there to hide, Hélène peeped through. The yard was empty but the door to the stables was open and Hélène realised that this was the chance she'd been looking for. With a furtive glance behind her, she slipped through the door and, running across the courtyard, went in to the stables to see if Pierre was there.

If anyone asks what I'm doing if I get caught out here, she thought, I'll tell them we were playing hide and seek and I was looking for Clarice.

Quietly she crept along, peering into each loose box; they were all empty so she moved on to the tack room at the end and there she found them.

Her approach was so silent that she was able to stand in the doorway for several seconds before they saw her. Jeannot, sitting on the floor beside the old iron stove, was devouring bread and cheese from a tin plate, and Pierre, perched on an old saddle horse with his back to the door, was asking him about the street fighting on the previous evening.

Jeannot glanced up to answer and saw Hélène standing at the door, half-poised for flight. He grinned at her cheerfully.

'Hello,' he said.

Pierre spun round and relief spread over his face as he saw who it was.

'You didn't ought to be here, Miss Hélène,' he said gruffly. 'Your pa'll be after you for running off again.'

'I haven't run off,' said Hélène indignantly, approaching the stove to warm her hands. 'We're playing hide and seek and I'm looking for Clarice.'

'Well she's not here, so you'd better get back into the garden, sharpish, before they all start to look for *you*,' advised Pierre.

'But I want to talk to Jeannot,' said Hélène. 'I was going to ask you to tell me when he came to see you, but now I don't have to, he's here already.'

She was about to join the boy sitting in the dust by the stove when Pierre said testily, 'Well, don't sit down then, or you'll get that dress dirty.'

Hélène, seeing the wisdom of this, remained standing and asked, 'Are you all right, Jeannot? They locked me up for a week.'

'Good thing they didn't try nothing like that with me,' said Jeannot darkly. 'Don't like being shut in, I don't.'

'I'm sorry they sent you away,' said Hélène. 'I told them it wasn't your fault. I said you brought me home when I was lost.'

'Did you?' Jeannot seemed impressed. 'You always was a game kid. Not like most prissy misses. Don't worry, I'd had enough of this place anyway.'

'Jeannot!' protested Pierre, uneasy at the boy's casual conversation with a member of the family. 'Take no notice of him, Miss Hélène, he was grateful enough to your pa at the time he was took on, I can tell you.'

'So I was,' agreed Jeannot with his mouth full, 'but I don't like being tied down... do this, do that. I like to come and go as I please.'

'But how do you live?' asked Hélène. 'How do you buy food?'

Jeannot winked at her knowingly. 'I get by. I always have, always will. I'm a survivor, me.'

'There's someone calling you,' said Pierre tersely. 'Go back to the garden quickly, or I'll be out on the street like young Jeannot.'

Solemnly Hélène held out her hand to the boy, and he,

getting to his feet, wiped his grubby hands on his grubbier clothes before taking it in his and shaking it.

'Go on, Miss Hélène,' said Pierre urgently, 'or we'll all be found.'

'Don't worry, it's our secret, Pierre,' said Hélène and darted out of the stables into the sunshine. She was only just in time. As she reached the gate in the garden wall she met the new governess, Mademoiselle Corbine, coming through to look for her.

'Hélène, where have you been? Why were you in the courtyard? You know you are not allowed to leave the garden.' Mademoiselle Corbine spoke crossly. She had been afraid Hélène had slipped away again and knew the responsibility would have been hers this time.

'Sorry, mademoiselle,' said Hélène meekly. 'Only I couldn't find Clarice in the garden so when I saw the gate open I thought she might have hidden in the yard.'

'Clarice knows she's not allowed to leave the garden, the same as you do,' said Mademoiselle Corbine tightly. 'You will learn three extra stanzas of your poem tonight as a punishment for disobedience.'

Hélène hung her head and murmured, 'Yes, mademoiselle.' But she was not dismayed, three stanzas would be no trouble; Hélène learned easily enough, and it had been worth it to see Jeannot even if only for a moment or two. He was her link with the world, the real world, outside the regulated confines of the Avenue Ste Anne.

'Come inside now,' said her governess, 'your mother wishes to see you.'

Mademoiselle Angèle Corbine had been a second consequence of Hélène's day out with Jeannot. A young lady of refined but reduced circumstances, she was hastily engaged to become the girls' governess, while Hélène was in the attic, paying the price for her adventure. On her return to the family she discovered Mademoiselle Corbine already installed in the schoolroom.

Angèle Corbine was kind and she was sensible and she made her charges work hard. Clarice grumbled about their lessons, but Hélène enjoyed them. She had an enquiring mind and was interested in the other countries that Mademoiselle Corbine showed them on the globe, the movement of the planets in the sky, the stories she told them from history, and her explanation of how numbers worked. During the day the girls were seldom out of her sight and after they had spent a comfortable hour with their mother in the evening, Mademoiselle Corbine handed them over to Marie-Jeanne. There was never a moment when they were unsupervised, and though they did not know it, this was entirely intentional. Hélène's excursion had terrified her parents. They were under no illusions as to the worsening situation in Paris, there was increasing unrest in the streets of the city. The killing of the 'spy' in the Place de la Bastille during the demonstration at the July Column had been bad enough, and soon after, some of the rioters had dared to break out prisoners from the Ste-Pélagie gaol. But none of this had occurred anywhere near their home, and though Rosalie was anxious to leave the city once again for the safety of St Etienne, Emile would have none of it.

'I need to stay in the city to protect our interests,' he maintained.

'We need to leave to protect our children,' countered Rosalie.

'Provided they remain in the house they are in no danger,' Emile said. 'The unrest is in the slum quarters of the city, not round here. We have nothing to fear provided we are careful where we go. We shall not run away at exaggerated news of the squabbles of a rabble.'

There was no moving him on this point and for the moment Rosalie held her peace. She was used to his intransigence and usually managed to soften it in time.

The days passed and it seemed that Emile was right. The continued unrest and outbreaks of violence were elsewhere in the city. Gradually he began to gather the reins of his business, and though the rebuilding of the city after the pounding it had received during the siege was yet a long way off, he was determined to keep his other sources of income safe in his hands.

With this in mind, Emile set out one Saturday morning to collect some of his rents.

He would go and visit the several houses he owned in Montmartre. They were only small, each comprising two rooms, huddled together as if for mutual support, built in a tiny lane that wound up the hill, the homes of street cleaners and washerwomen. Nothing to fear from them, but as Emile approached, entering the winding lanes that led up the hill, he heard the rumble of a gathered crowd, like the growling of a large and predatory animal. Pausing, he contemplated turning back, recognising that something extraordinary was going on, but then decided to press on. He was only going to visit a few houses, after all, so what was there to fear?

As he continued to make his way up the hill, he considered his approach. He knew that he was going to have trouble collecting the rents after such a harsh winter. During the siege the back rent had accumulated, but there had been no one there to collect it. Normally, Marc, a lad from Emile's office, went weekly to each house to take the few francs Emile charged for this very minimal housing. During the siege, when he had been at St Etienne, this had not happened and Emile had been afraid that he would never be able to claim the money owed to him. But now the newly elected government had passed two laws, one declaring all debts, on which there had been a moratorium during the war, must be paid within forty-eight hours, and the other, that a landlord could now demand payment of all back rent accumulated during the siege. Because his tenants would be reluctant to pay, Emile realised he must collect these monies himself. Marc would have neither the authority nor the courage to demand such payment. Emile actually considered that forty-eight hours was too harsh a timescale for the people who lived in his properties, and he was planning to offer them a week, say, or possibly two, to find the back rent, for as he said to Rosalie over the breakfast table that morning, 'I'm a reasonable man. These people will have to have a chance to find the money, and so I will give them time to pay.'

His thoughts were unexpectedly interrupted by the rattle of gunfire, shots ringing out across the hillside, which brought him to an abrupt halt. More shots and a triumphant roar from the throats of a mob. Emile turned to flee, but he was too late. Moments later he was engulfed by a tide of humanity sweeping down through the lanes.

Emile had not reckoned on the increasing power of the National Guard. Since the siege had ended and the French Army was being reduced in numbers by the unpopular Peace Treaty, the Paris National Guard had become more and more powerful, banding together to form their own Central Committee. Determined not to give up any of their armaments to the victorious Prussians who were about to occupy the city, they had moved the two hundred cannon within its walls and dragged them up the hill into the Republican stronghold of Montmartre. Here they were determined to keep them from the clutches of both the French and the German armies. The new government led by Adolphe Thiers, however, had other ideas and sent a force under the command of General Lecomte to retrieve the stolen artillery. At first all went well and the cannon were soon back in the hands of government troops, but due to an incompetence which had dogged them throughout the war, the army had failed to bring the horses needed to tow the cannon away.

Alerted to what was going on, it was all the opportunity the revolutionary Fédérés needed, and before they knew it, the inexperienced French troops were surrounded by angry National Guardsmen and an irate local populace. Many of the young soldiers refused to fight, throwing down their weapons, and mob violence took over. Lecomte was pulled down from his horse and beaten up, but this wasn't enough to satisfy the madness of the mob, who then grabbed and attacked a much-hated former general of the National Guard, dragging both him and Lecomte through the streets into a garden where they were both set against a wall and shot out of hand.

The mob were fired up now and burst back out into the streets, shouting and yelling, carried forward by the lust for blood that the executions had unleashed, and it was this surging crowd erupting down the hill that engulfed Emile, dragging him along amid the screeching swirl of people, unable to break free, at risk of being trampled if he tried. Keeping his head down and allowing himself to be carried with them was the only way he was going to survive. If the rabble had not been so incensed by the invasion of their territory, their Montmartre, their revolutionary fury whipped up into a frenzy, they might have noticed from his dress that Emile was not one of them; that he was one of the hated bourgeoisie, and he might never have reached the safety of his home again. As it was, after what seemed to him an age of being pushed and shoved by men and women, some armed with sticks and clubs, a few with guns, others waving their fists, all shouting invective, crying down curses on the government and all those who supported them, he managed to ease his way to the edge of the churning horde and slide sideways into the mouth of an alleyway and escape from the mania of the crowd.

Without looking back, he scurried to the end of the lane, ducking round the corner, hurrying along another narrow passageway leading to a third. He had no idea where he was, but by always heading downhill, Emile managed to find his way through the labyrinth of lanes and alleys, back to the river and the wider boulevards that led him eventually to his own neighbourhood. He had lost his hat and his cane in the crush, but once back into civilisation, he straightened his dishevelled clothes, drew a deep breath and set out for home. That he had been afraid, he had to admit. Never an emotional man, the mob hysteria he'd just encountered frightened him more than he would have believed possible, but it was a fear he would never admit to anyone but himself. He walked slowly to the Avenue Ste Anne breathing deeply, and by the time he stood outside his own front door, the first rush of fear had dissipated somewhat, and he was able to enter the house without it being apparent that he had passed anything but a normal day. It wasn't until he was back in his own bedroom that he realised his wallet was no longer in his pocket.

Later that evening, when the news of the disturbances began to find its way to the more prosperous neighbourhoods, he was told of the mob violence by Pierre. Emile made no mention of having been caught up in it. He simply shook his head in apparent disbelief, remarking, 'We've more to fear from our own countrymen than the Germans now. The Prussians will sit snug in their encampments and watch us tear ourselves to pieces.'

Once again Rosalie suggested removing the family to the comparative safety of St Etienne, but Emile dismissed the idea. If he had admitted how close he'd been to that violent mob, she would have insisted, but as he made no further reference to the events in Montmartre, Rosalie simply accepted it as another exaggerated rumour and said no more.

The following morning Emile walked out into the town, simply to take the air, he said, in answer to Rosalie's raised eyebrows, but he wanted to see what reaction there was to the Montmartre riots. He walked towards the centre of the city and strolled along the left bank of the Seine. Surprisingly, it seemed to be a normal Sunday. There were National Guardsmen about, but there was nothing threatening about them, and people were taking their usual Sunday promenade in the warm spring sunshine. Emile met several acquaintances, neighbours from nearby, a couple of business associates, and none of them seemed in the least anxious or expressed any surprise at seeing him out and about.

The news that the government had lost its nerve after the confrontation in Montmartre and had left Paris for Versailles had not yet reached his peaceful neighbourhood. He had not been to the Hôtel de Ville, the City Hall, and seen the red flag flying from its belfry. During the night the last of the government ministers had decided that Paris had become too hot for them and had quietly left the Hôtel de Ville through an underground passage, and the building had been seized by some of the dissident National Guard, but Emile had no knowledge of this and returned home relaxed.

'There's no need to make a dash for the country yet,' he assured Rosalie at luncheon. 'Indeed, if you and the children would care to take a walk in the park this afternoon, I'd be happy to accompany you.'

Rosalie smiled and agreed it would be very pleasant to get out of the house on such a beautiful day. Walking along by the river they saw a small band of National Guardsmen, causing Hélène to shrink against her mother as she remembered the furious face of the guardsman who had tried to catch hold of her at the Prussian parade.

Seeing her reaction Emile said bracingly, 'Chin up, Hélène, nothing to fear from those gentlemen, they're not Prussians.'

'Yes, Papa,' she whispered, but she held tight to her mother's arm nonetheless.

Unbeknownst to Emile, Rosalie had also felt a frisson of fear at the sight of the swaggering guardsmen. She remembered only too well their behaviour at the city gate. This bunch looked harmless enough, but you never knew, did you? Even now Rosalie wished with all her heart that they had never returned from St Etienne; at least she and the girls should have stayed in the country where there were no National Guards, no shouting mobs and where the Prussians lived quietly in their encampments. She said nothing more to her husband, there was no point in upsetting Emile unless she had to, but she decided to begin making plans for their removal. It would be a long and arduous journey by train. They still had no carriage and no horses. Pierre had returned to their carriage the day after their arrival in the Avenue Ste Anne and found it stripped of every removable part. When Emile had heard, he merely said that they did not need a carriage for the time being, the light chaise was still in the coach house if required and he could always take a cab to the office. But from the rumour of violence and riots yesterday, it was clear to her that the city wasn't safe for anyone and Rosalie made up her mind to take the girls back to the country as soon as possible, despite Emile's opposition if necessary. Quite aside from the dangers of Paris, seething with unrest, it would do them all good to get back to the clear fresh air of the country where the children could quite safely ramble in the surrounding meadows. Apart from their surprise excursion this afternoon, they had been cooped up in the house for too long. Hélène was beginning to look decidedly pasty, and had complained of occasional headaches, and all three were bad-tempered and peevish.

Marie-Jeanne and she would take them on the train, Rosalie decided, accompanied by Pierre if Emile was really unable to leave, and they would stay in the country until life in Paris became settled. Mademoiselle Corbine should come too, of course, so that the girls' schooling should not be interrupted. Relieved at having made a decision, Rosalie waited for the right moment to tell her husband.

Her plans came to an abrupt halt next morning, however, when at last the long-awaited letter arrived from Georges, her eldest son. Her joy at hearing he was alive and well overcame her natural reticence and she ran up the stairs clutching the letter and rushed unannounced into Emile's study.

'Georges is here in Paris!' she cried, waving the single sheet of paper at her husband. 'This was brought by one of his men. I've sent him down to the kitchen for a meal. Oh, Emile, isn't it wonderful? Georges in Paris and he's coming to see us! Not for a few days, but in the next week. Perhaps he'll have news of Marcel.'

Emile's pleasure in receiving news of his son was probably as great as Rosalie's, but his expression of it was far more restrained. Reaching for the letter he carried it to the window to read for himself.

'This is indeed good news, my dear,' he said, turning back to her with a smile. 'We must thank God he's safe.'

'Will he be able to come here to live?' asked Rosalie, as excited as a child. 'Will he be back with us for good, do you think?'

'I doubt if he will live at home,' returned her husband. 'He says here that his troop are bivouacked in the Luxembourg Gardens waiting for billets. Have his man brought up here when he has eaten and we'll ask him what's happening.'

The corporal knew no more than where the battalion was camped and that Lieutenant St Clair had been called to Versailles and would be back in Paris in a day or two.

The following days were full of excited anticipation in the house in Avenue Ste Anne; everyone listened for the doorbell, and should it sound, the household held its breath until the caller had been admitted and was discovered not to be Georges. There were, in fact, few visitors these days. Gone were the social comings and goings of visits and morning calls, drives through the Bois and evening parties. Much of Paris society and many of the well-to-do had not yet ventured back to the city, and those who had remained, or returned early like the St Clairs, kept very much within doors as the outbreaks of unrest and violence grew more persistent.

Mademoiselle Corbine kept her charges busy, but she was equally unwilling to leave the house and so the tasks she set were confined to the house and its secluded walled garden.

Hélène found this forced seclusion particularly irksome. She had loved the freedom of St Etienne and grown used to it during their extended stay. Cooped up in the house in the Avenue Ste Anne she was becoming bored and bad-tempered. Clarice dubbed her 'Cross-patch', and the two girls seldom passed a day without an argument which usually ended in tears and Hélène complaining she had a headache.

Of Jeannot there was no sign. He seemed to have disappeared back into his own world. Hélène wondered what he was doing and how he was passing his days, and envied him the freedom of being able to decide. Only the news that Georges had survived the war and was coming to see them made her world seem brighter.

Chapter 5

Marcel St Clair limped into Paris through the Porte de la Villette, and made his way slowly through the back streets towards Montmartre. He had walked all the way from the internment camp outside Sedan, the so-called camp of misery, where he and the remains of his corps had been held as prisoners after the battle of Sedan was lost.

Hundreds of prisoners had been herded into the bulge of land contained by the River Meuse. A canal made the fourth side of the area and two cannon faced into the camp across the only bridge, discouraging any breaks for freedom. The French soldiers were left for days with little shelter or food in the conditions that gave the camp its miserable name, before they were gradually led out company by company and marched to prison camps in Germany.

Marcel, young and still strong, was a survivor, and became almost feral as he used whatever means that came to hand to ensure that he remained one. As men around him in the camp fell ill, weakened by dysentery, starvation, cold and unattended wounds, Marcel had no compunction in relieving them of any morsel of food they had managed to find. Occasionally baskets of bread were sent in by the local townspeople, but if they managed to get them past the guards at the gate, it was only the strongest of the prisoners who got hold of any. It was every man for himself and Marcel soon determined that he was not going to miss out. He held himself aloof from his mates, many of whom lay dying on the ground as they sought shelter amongst the trees and bushes, but as evening fell each day and they lay exhausted, he would slip down among them in the darkness and take anything which might be of use to him: a coat, a hat, a scarf, a better pair of boots, even the last few francs from a dying man's pocket.

He's got no use for these things any more, Marcel reasoned, and I have.

Dysentery was rife, but Marcel stayed alone, determined not to succumb, so that when his platoon were called he still had strength to march out of the hellhole where he'd been confined for nearly two weeks, with a pair of boots that nearly fitted him, a piece of old blanket that he wrapped round him over the tatters of his uniform and a small-bladed knife he'd retrieved from the body of a dead comrade the previous night. His entire focus had been on survival and he had made it. His next goal was escape.

As they marched towards the German border, many of his companions fell by the wayside, literally collapsing into the hedges and ditches that lined the road, but that was not a means of escape, as these were often dispatched with a bullet in the head or the plunge of a bayonet into the back. Marcel watched and waited, trying to work out when and how to make a break for it. He had no weapon but his knife, little money and his clothes were in rags, but his resolve was unshakable. He would escape from the Prussians, return to Paris and destroy the officers who had led them so disastrously into humiliation and defeat. The Emperor had fled with his enormous baggage train, and left his countrymen to face imprisonment or death. Marcel had no intention of submitting to either and was bent on revenge.

Each evening on the march, the dwindling group of prisoners was herded into a barn or a cowshed. Bread was issued, the doors were closed and guards posted. There appeared to be no way out of these buildings, but Marcel searched for possibilities even so. On one evening as the twilight was darkening to night, he heard a hoarse whisper in his ear.

'Hey, you! St Clair!'

Marcel turned his head but could see little but the shadow of a man in the darkness.

'Who's that?' he hissed, bunching his fists ready to defend himself.

'Durand,' came the whispered reply.

Marcel recognised the name, could even put a face to it. Gaston Durand was in B company, a small but muscular man, with a strong growth of beard and a shock of black hair. An unpopular man with a vicious temper who always decided an argument with his fists or, if he had one, a knife. He carried an arcing scar above one eye, the souvenir of one such fight, and men tended to steer clear of him. He too had decided that he wasn't going to be locked up as a prisoner in Germany, and he'd recognised the same resolve in Marcel.

'What do *you* want?' Marcel demanded, his own voice gruff with menace.

'Same as you,' returned the other. 'Time to get out, don't you think?'

'Oh sure!' agreed Marcel with sarcasm. 'Shall we leave now?'

'Could do,' Durand replied, 'if you've the stomach for it.'

'For what?' Marcel failed to keep the note of intrigue from his voice.

'You got a weapon?'

'No,' Marcel replied, even as he fingered the little knife in his pocket.

'Me neither,' Durand said, 'but this barn's falling to pieces. I did a recce when they first shoved us in here. There's old, rusty farm stuff at the back. Easy to make a weapon.'

'Yeah? And who're you going to use it on?'

Marcel couldn't see the other man's face but he could hear the excitement in his voice as he answered, 'There's a door at the back that looks pretty old and rotten. I reckon we could bust out there with no trouble.'

'Yeah? And onto the bayonet of a Prussian sentry?'

'There won't be one.'

'What do you mean there won't be one?'

'We'll create a diversion.'

'Diversion? What sort of diversion?'

'There's a load of straw in here,' Durand said.

Marcel said nothing. He'd already seen the straw and earmarked a patch in the corner for his own bed. It was days since he hadn't had to sleep on the cold ground.

'Well,' Durand went on, eager to keep Marcel's attention, 'we make ourselves a couple of weapons from that old farm stuff and then we wait by that back door. A match to that straw will cause a blaze and the fuckers'll have to open the doors to let us all out. There'll be a stampede, and in the chaos we can make a break for it. We'll be armed and any bloody Kraut in the way's a dead man.'

'Supposing they don't,' said Marcel.

'Supposing they don't what?' demanded Durand.

'Supposing they don't open the doors? Supposing they decide to let the fire burn and all of us with it?'

Marcel felt the man shrug. 'They won't,' he said dismissively. 'Not even these German bastards will do that.'

'They'll do anything,' Marcel said. 'You saw them after Sedan, shooting the wounded.' He thought for a moment. 'Still,' he said, 'I like the idea of making ourselves some sort of weapon.'

'I'll show you,' said Durand, and taking hold of Marcel's arm he pulled him through the barn. Marcel's eyes had gradually adjusted to the darkness, and he realised that there were holes in the aged roof where glimmers of moonlight offered a faint grey light. He could make out shapes now and decipher what they were. Bodies littered the floor, exhausted men lying where they had fallen as sleep overcame them, and Marcel and Durand met with anger as they pushed their way through those already bedded down on the straw for the night.

'Look out where you put your fucking feet.'

'Christ! Get off me!'

'Mind my bleedin' legs!'

Ignoring such cries, they reached the back of the barn where Marcel could just make out the outline of the door frame.

'See,' whispered Durand, 'easy enough to break out there.' Then he bent over and picked up a curved piece of rusty iron from amid the straw. 'And this'd give a Kraut something to think about,' he added, hefting it in his hands. 'Wouldn't wake up from a bash with this. Feel around,' he said to Marcel, 'see what you can find.'

Marcel was already searching through the straw and moments later he too had found something, a piece of piping, maybe the handle of an old plough. He didn't know what it was, but that didn't matter, it felt good in his hand. With that and his knife he might stand a chance in a fight.

'Right,' Durand said. 'Ready?'

'Ready for what?' demanded Marcel.

'Our diversion,' said Durand. 'Remember?'

'Christ, Durand, you can't!' cried Marcel, his horror of what he thought Durand was going to do making him forget to keep his voice down. 'You're mad! You'll kill us all.'

'Not if we're quick I won't. When we break out of here the others will follow.'

'But they're all asleep!'

'It'll soon wake them up,' snapped Durand. 'Are you with me?'

Marcel had become ruthless on the battlefield, but even his ruthlessness did not go as far as killing anything up to a hundred of his comrades in cold blood, just so he himself could escape. 'No!' he cried, clutching his knife in his hand. 'Not in this. This is plain murder!'

'Thought you had more balls!' snarled Durand, and with no further warning he swung his makeshift weapon at Marcel's head. Although he couldn't see the sweep of it through the darkness, instinct made Marcel throw up an arm to protect himself, and the curved metal smashed against it. With a cry of pain he staggered sideways, but managing to keep his feet, he launched himself at his attacker, thrusting viciously upward with his knife and feeling it bite into Durand's shoulder. With a roar of rage, Durand dropped his weapon and Marcel thrust again, this time at his face, laying open his cheek. Ignoring the pain, Durand flung himself at Marcel once more, grabbing him round the neck and crashing them both to the floor. Marcel was winded and before he could regain his feet, Durand was on his. With one final kick at Marcel's head, he struck a match and tossing it into the straw, turned his attention to the rotten door.

For a moment Marcel must have blacked out, for the next thing he knew there were screams of 'Fire!' and the exhausted prisoners were scrambling to their feet, fighting their way through dense smoke to where they thought the door might be.

The flames took hold extremely quickly and there was blind panic among the confined men. Durand had been right about the strength of the old door and it only took moments before its rotten wood and rusty hinges gave way before his onslaught. As the door burst open the rush of oxygen gave new vigour to the flames and the panic escalated as the terrified captives struggled and fought to escape the inferno. Many, those further in, were almost immediately consumed by the fire, hopelessly beating at their burning clothes, rolling on the floor in their efforts to put out the flames and only succeeding in setting light to even more straw.

Men struggled past Marcel as he got to his hands and knees and began crawling towards the open back door. From the other end of the barn came a yell as the German guards opened the main doors to discover the inferno within. Many of the prisoners had now seen the broken door and there was a stampede away from the blaze towards freedom outside. Marcel, crawling, was almost trampled in the rush to safety, but as he reached the door he managed to regain his feet and stagger out into the blessed fresh air. Outside, men were milling in every direction, completely overwhelming the guards who had dashed round from the front of the barn when they realised that there was an escape from the back.

Shouts of 'Halt!' went unheeded as the French soldiers scented freedom, and despite the outnumbered guards firing into the crowd, very few obeyed the shouted order in their bid to escape into the night.

Marcel had been horrified at Durand's plan to achieve the escape, deliberately causing men, his own fellow countrymen, to be burned to death so that he might go free, but once it was in motion, he wasn't going to miss the chance to make good his escape. He pushed his way through the press of prisoners, shoving men aside as he ran, deep into the night. The fitful moon aided the escaping men, disappearing behind a bank of cloud, thus plunging the scene into darkness, leaving only the barn, a blazing beacon, a funeral pyre to light the sky.

Since that dreadful night Marcel had made his way slowly westward back to Paris. On the way he had stopped in tiny villages, working a day's labour in the fields for an evening meal. He divested himself of the rags of his uniform and dressed in smock and gaiters provided by a farmer in return for chopping wood. The area was full of Prussian soldiers, camped outside towns and keeping watch for the remnants of the French army trying to regroup, but the local population were ready to help any French soldier continue his escape from the hated Prussians and he was often given food and shelter.

It made for very slow progress. He heard that Paris was now besieged, entirely surrounded by the German army. The only escapes had been made by balloon, the only means of communication by carrier pigeon. Marcel gave little thought to the fate of his family; he was not worried about them for surely they would be safely at St Etienne. He had left them there last summer before going to join his unit and he couldn't believe they would have gone back to Paris in the autumn.

There was no way to let them know he had survived and since the dreadful night of the barn fire he knew he would never tell them how. He was haunted by nightmares of the fire. Night after night he awoke shouting, running with sweat and shaking with fear as he dreamed of the fire, of burning to death. In some of his dreams it was he who struck the fateful match and he would wake, shaking, his eyes staring into the darkness, afraid to go back to sleep. He had no idea if Durand, the true author of that night's misery, had survived his own escape attempt. He hoped he had not, but as he was the only one who knew what was about to happen, and apart from Marcel the only one who knew there was another way out, Marcel had little doubt that the cruel, callous man had made good his escape. If he ever came across the man again, Marcel vowed he would kill him and avenge his murdered comrades.

Over the winter months Marcel had found work in a brewery, and when the siege had been lifted in January he had continued to work there until the spring warmed the earth and new growth appeared on the trees. Rumours of the National Guard defying the government spread into the countryside. An unpopular peace was signed with the Germans and there was great unrest in the city. Then and only then did he return to Paris to take up arms against the authorities who had sent him, and thousands like him, to face the Prussian guns, generals whose incompetence and confusion amongst themselves had led to the humiliation of defeat after defeat and the decimation of the French army.

Now, as he came in through the La Villette gate, Marcel knew there was no point in going back to his family home. If he reappeared now, they would expect him to re-enlist in the French army and put down what was fast becoming an insurrection in the capital city. Nothing was further from his mind. He intended to join that insurrection; nothing would make him fight for the government again. This time he would be ranged alongside the rebellious factions of the National Guard, defending its takeover of the city. He wondered if Georges had survived the war so far. Their paths had crossed once in the course of the fighting, almost passing in the night a week before Sedan; time only for a brief exchange of news and a handshake, neither knowing if he would ever see the other again.

Back in Paris at last, Marcel climbed the hill to Montmartre which he had heard was the National Guard stronghold, determined to volunteer as a foot soldier, but as he reached the cemetery he found himself caught up in a tumultuous crowd. Hundreds of people pushing and running and shoving and shouting. There were chants of 'Long live the Republic!' and 'Death to all traitors'.

'What's going on?' Marcel grabbed the arm of a young woman who was yelling obscenities into the air. 'Tell me what's happened?' he demanded. 'What the hell's going on?'

'They tried to take our cannon,' she screamed, 'so we shot them! Two generals dead! Long live the Republic!' And with that she pulled free and disappeared into the baying crowd. Two generals dead! Dragged along by the swell of excited people, Marcel allowed himself to be carried forward, cheering with the best of them.

It was then that he saw his father. Emile was also being swept along in the mob, but he took no part in its exuberance. He was clearly terrified, his face grey with fear. Marcel dropped back into the crowd, not wanting his father to see him, though it would have been unlikely that Emile would have recognised his younger son even if they had bumped into each other, face to face. Gone was the attractive, laughing-faced boy he'd last seen almost a year ago, replaced by an angry and bitter young man, gaunt, bearded, with a harsh expression and cruel eyes, out to avenge atrocities that no man should ever have to see.

What on earth is Papa doing here, Marcel wondered, caught up in this roiling crowd? Why is he in Paris at all? Surely he and Maman and the children were safely in St Etienne! Surely he had taken them to safety as soon as the fighting had broken out.

Moments later he could no longer see him. His father had disappeared into the throng and Marcel began to wonder if he'd seen him at all; maybe his eyes had deceived him and it was someone else of similar face and build. Marcel dismissed him from his mind and continued up the hill to volunteer.

The sergeant at the command post on the heights of Montmartre accepted Marcel's services with alacrity. More and more of the government soldiers were changing sides, deserting the army and joining the dissident National Guard. Marcel was one of many such, and with his return unknown to his family, he disappeared into the chaos of the city, just another deserter, pitted against the government forces on the brink of a bloody civil war.

Chapter 6

Georges came home on a sunny morning two days after his message and his coming brought excitement and laughter into the house. His parents greeted him with delight while his sisters mobbed him and he had to fend them off like so many boisterous puppies. Even Clarice forgot her dignity and hugged and hugged him, crying, 'Georges, Georges. You've come back. You've come home,' while Hélène and Louise climbed one onto each knee and clung to him as he laughed and hugged them in turn. Hélène and Georges had always been particularly close despite the disparity in their ages, and though she was happy to share him with her sisters for now, she was determined to get him to herself for a while before he left.

Berthe, on instruction from Hélène, had prepared Georges's favourite food and the celebration dinner in his honour was a gay and festive affair, for which even Louise was allowed to stay up. When at last the girls were collected for bed by Marie-Jeanne, they were all tired, their faces pink with excitement and their carefully dressed hair awry from the party games in which everyone except Papa had joined; and even Papa had watched with an indulgent eye instead of returning to the peaceful seclusion of his study.

Left alone with his parents at last, Georges sat back with a glass of cognac and told them of the past nine months. Of Marcel he had heard nothing since before the Battle of Sedan, when the Emperor had been vanquished and thousands of his men had been killed or taken prisoner.

'It was dreadful at Sedan,' Georges said quietly. 'The whole army was in chaos and the German bombardment never stopped. No one knew what was going on and when we did get any orders they were in complete conflict with the ones we'd had before. The Emperor was there, and somehow he managed to move from place to place trying to encourage the men, but no one took any notice of him. He's a pitiful little man.'

'Georges!' expostulated his father. 'That's no way to speak of the Emperor.'

But Georges was unrepentant. 'It's the truth, sir, he was an incompetent, and the army was better off without him. He ordered a white flag to be flown before the battle was lost. General Wimpffen had it hauled down, but the damage was done. Morale was gone and in the end defeat was inevitable.' Georges sipped his cognac and his parents waited in silence for him to continue his tale. Neither could imagine the horrors of such a battle where civilians and soldiers alike were subjected to continual bombardment, where fear ran like fire through the streets consuming not only the fighting men desperately trying to break through and come to grips with the enemy, but also the civilians, men, women and children cowering in their houses, homes which might at any moment come tumbling about their ears.

'When the white flag was finally allowed to fly and the guns stopped it was quiet, but frightening. There seemed to be a total silence, though of course there wasn't – there were too many people wounded or dying for that. After the surrender we officers were offered a chance to give our parole and never to fight against the Germans again. Several of the fellows took up the offer and went free but I couldn't believe that I wouldn't be able to escape, so I refused. I was sent to the internment camp – the camp of misery we called it. It was just a piece of land in a huge loop in the river, where we were herded in like animals. There was no shelter and almost no food – and as it turned out, no prospect of escape. Several tried jumping into the river to swim to freedom, but the Prussian soldiers camped on the opposite bank used them for target practice. I doubt if anyone made it to safety on the other side and if they did, I doubt if they got very far with so many Germans in the surrounding countryside.'

Silence again lapsed between them as they contemplated the horror of what he had described.

After a moment or two, Rosalie asked, 'Was Marcel a prisoner too? Did you see him?'

'No, Maman,' said Georges gently, and added as he saw the hope fade from her eyes, 'But there were thousands of us there. I did look for him, of course, and I found some of his company, but no one had news of him.'

'He must have been killed then,' said Rosalie flatly.

'He may have been, Maman, it's something we must face up to, but on the other hand no one had seen him killed, and even now men are filtering back into Paris and many of them have come to rejoin their old regiments.'

What Georges said was in effect true, but the numbers of

such men were few and he himself held out little hope of news from his brother now.

'What happened to you then?' asked Emile, anxious to turn the subject away from Marcel.

'Well, I was there in the camp for about a week. It was so bloody awful, I beg your pardon, Maman, it was so awful that I lost track of the days. Existing was the most any of us could do. Anyway, at last our company was called and we were marched out – not that any of us were really in much condition to march. Some food had been brought in by the citizens of Sedan, but there'd been little enough of it and with the cold and the wet none of us had much strength. Anyhow, we were moved out on our way to Germany as prisoners, and I watched for a chance to escape. The guards were well prepared, however, and the two men who I saw make a break as we passed through a neck of forest were shot in the back.'

Rosalie gasped and at the sight of her pale face Georges slid over the events of the few days that followed.

'We were lucky,' he said. 'We were exchanged for Prussian prisoners taken at Metz and so suddenly I was free again' – he smiled wryly – 'free, that is, within the besieged fortress of Metz.'

'And that was a shameful defeat for France,' put in Emile bitterly. 'A complete fiasco. General Bazaine was a traitor and should have been shot.'

'He should have made a break in the early days of the siege,' conceded Georges, 'but in the end he had no alternative but to surrender – he'd left it too long and we were starving. Food was rationed but even that wasn't enough. Some of us got out. I managed to get hold of a woman's dress and shawl and slip through the lines.'

'But how?' asked Rosalie, pressing her hands to her mouth in agitation. 'How did you get away?'

'Well, food was so desperately short, we used to creep out into the fields beside the city and grub for potatoes. Occasionally the Germans fired over our heads to discourage us, but often they turned away and left us to search. Anyway, this time I carried a basket and was wearing my dress, so hoping they wouldn't shoot a woman, I worked my way towards the edge of the field. It was early in the morning, and very wet and misty so the visibility was pretty poor. I knew there was a clump of bushes in the far corner of the field, so scuffling along, I made for that. Once there I lay down and pulled a covering of leaves over me and waited for dark. It poured with rain all day and I dared not move an inch in case a German from one of the outposts spotted me. I lay there for nearly eight hours…'

'Eight hours!' echoed Rosalie in horror.

Georges gave a rueful grin. 'I couldn't come out in the daylight, Maman, so I had to wait until evening. When at last it was dark enough to risk moving I was so cold and wet and stiff I could hardly stand. There was no moon and I couldn't see where I was going. Twice I fell flat on my face and I sounded like an elephant moving through the undergrowth. How the guards didn't hear me I don't know, except that the weather was so bad they were probably sheltering in their dugouts.' Georges shivered now at the recollection.

'Anyway, I did manage to stumble on and get clear of the immediate line of German guard posts. I had no idea where I was going except to put as much distance as possible between me and that fortress. I found a road and decided to follow that as I thought I'd make better progress than across country I didn't know. It was a mistake and I nearly ran into a German troop bivouacked at the roadside. They heard me and there was some shouting, but I hitched up the petticoats I was still wearing and took to my heels.' Georges laughed a little at the recollection of his undignified flight. But his parents did not smile, they just sat silently watching this tall soldier who was their son, who had returned to them so much older than his twenty-one years; so different from the young man who had left them in St Etienne less than a year ago. His face, though still handsome, was leaner and his eyes more serious; experience had left its mark both in the premature lines which creased his forehead, and in his bearing and demeanour. Georges was no longer an inexperienced youth, but a man grown to maturity and refined by war.

'It was after that that I knew I had to find somewhere to hide, or I'd be caught again at first light. So I kept going, hoping I was moving away from the actual German lines. It was pouring with rain and there was no moon or stars, so I couldn't actually tell. Still I was lucky. As it began to get light I reached the outskirts of a village and found a house with a hen coop in the garden.'

'A hen coop?' exclaimed Rosalie in surprise.

'Yes, and I can tell you Maman, I've never been more glad to see anything. I was soaking wet and freezing cold and just wanted to get out of the rain, so I crawled inside. The hens cackled like mad, but I was too tired to care.'

'My poor boy,' murmured Rosalie. 'You must have been exhausted.'

'I was, but there was plenty of hay in there and I simply fell asleep. After that it seemed like a miracle. When I woke up again I wasn't in the henhouse any more, but in a bed with white linen sheets and soft pillows. It was the first bed I had slept in since long before the battle at Sedan. I tried to sit up but I couldn't move. I was as weak as a kitten. There was a woman sitting by the bed and when she saw I was awake she asked me if I could understand her. I said I could and she cried out, "The Lord be praised," and rushed from the room. She came back at once with her husband, who smiled and asked me how I was. I managed a croaky, "Very well, thank you, sir," which made him laugh and tell me I was a brave fellow.'

'But where were you?' demanded Rosalie.

'It turned out,' replied Georges, 'that I had chosen the henhouse in the garden of a lawyer, Monsieur Claviet. The maid found me when she came to collect the eggs and had called her mistress. At first, of course, they thought I was a woman, until they pulled me clear and saw several days' growth on my chin. My disguise had only been for deception at a distance. Anyway, they guessed I was a soldier who'd escaped and it was very obvious I was ill so they'd taken me into the house, cleaned me up and put me to bed. They tell me I was delirious and shouted a good deal. In fact, one day when there was a German troop in the village they were afraid I'd betray them all with my cries – but at last the fever broke and I regained my senses. Madame Claviet and her daughter nursed me through a long illness and all through my convalescence. They kept me warm and fed and at last my strength began to come back. I was there for three months before they would let me consider rejoining the army. Three months – so that the siege of Paris was nearly over before I could begin to make my way back to find my regiment. Metz had fallen long before, Gambetta had just been defeated at Orleans and Paris was being bombarded.'

'But why didn't you write to us?' cried out his mother. 'Why didn't you let us know you were safe at least? We might even have fetched you to St Etienne.'

Georges looked across at Rosalie in surprise. 'I did write, Maman. Not to say where I was in case my letter fell into the wrong hands and endanger the Claviets, but I wrote saying I had been ill but was recovered now.'

'The letter never came,' signed Rosalie. 'The Claviets must be very good people,' she went on, suddenly taking Georges's hand between hers in a burst of affection. 'I will write and thank them for taking such care of you.'

'For saving my life, Maman,' said Georges simply.

His mother nodded and then said, 'Your father's letters did not arrive here either, nothing was prepared for us.' She paused, brooding for a moment, and then said, 'Perhaps Marcel has written too, and his letter is mislaid.'

'Perhaps he has, Maman. Don't give up hope,' said Georges earnestly, seeing how bravely his mother fought back her tears. 'So many prisoners were taken, there is no record of them all. Lots escaped and even now they are being released and sent back. We need them now to hold Paris against this rabble of a Central Committee.'

Rosalie looked fearful at the mention of the Committee. 'How bad will the trouble be, Georges?' she asked. 'There've been riots in plenty already, and when they brought the soldiers into Montmartre last week, I made plans to take the girls back to St Etienne.'

'And so you should, Maman,' said Georges seriously. 'Paris is a powder keg and already the sparks are flying. You should all leave at once before it explodes in your faces.'

Emile had said nothing as Georges had been telling his story, simply listening in silence, pale-faced. Georges turned to him now, noticing for the first time how much his father had aged since he had last seen him.

'You must take them back to St Etienne, Papa,' he insisted. 'No one in Paris will be safe. There's tremendous unrest in the army, and a great many of the men are slipping away because they won't fight against the people of Paris; many are lining up with the dissident National Guard. It'll be civil war before the situation is resolved.'

'Come now, Georges,' expostulated his father. 'I think you're being a little alarmist.'

Georges gave an inward sigh. How could his father, usually so astute, not see the dangers ahead? 'Sir,' he said patiently, 'I have been with the army; I've seen the men, those of them that have stayed loyal. The war and the surrender to the Prussians have left them demoralised and angry. They've no faith in the government, a government that has run away and doesn't even govern from Paris any more. It only takes a couple of fanatics, a couple of rabble-rousers, and all their pent-up hatred and resentment will boil over. It's already happening. Why couldn't the army take those guns from the Fédérés in Montmartre and Belleville? All negotiations with the National Guard failed and when we went in to take the guns by force, what happened? The men, our men, wouldn't fight. They were all lined up ready to carry out a pretty simple operation, but when it came to it few had the stomach to fight against fellow Frenchmen. Some made the pretence of obeying orders, others just marched away again and yet others were simply disarmed by the National Guard and then quite happily joined them, leaving us officers to do as we chose.' Georges looked wearily across at his amazed parents. 'Surely you heard how Lecomte and Thomas were murdered by the mob that day.'

His father nodded, but his mother looked confused. 'Murdered!' she cried. 'What are you saying, Georges?' And turning to her husband she demanded, 'What is he saying?'

Emile had taken care to conceal from his wife the extent of the violence that had stalked the streets that fateful day. Except for their family walk in the park the following afternoon, she had not left the house since, and though rumours had been brought into the kitchen by the new housemaid, Arlette, Rosalie had dismissed those as exaggerated backstairs gossip and told Arlette she wanted to hear no more of it.

'There was a mob that ran riot,' Emile conceded, 'but you don't have to worry, my dear, things have quietened down again now.'

'I beg to disagree, Papa,' Georges said. 'You have no idea of the situation that is brewing. I've been outside the Hôtel de Ville, the seat of government which the rabble have taken over. Whatever happens, one way or another there's going to be bloodshed.' He looked earnestly across at his father. 'But I mean it, sir, when I say that Paris in the next few weeks is no place for Maman and the girls.'

'But surely,' protested his father, 'the government troops will be more than a match for the rowdies of the National Guard. Surely not all the National Guard are involved in these insurrections.'

'At present the government troops are a match for no one,' stated Georges flatly. 'The whole army is in chaos. Battalions and regiments have all been reformed, and brought up to strength with undisciplined and unseasoned troops. Half the officers have never been in action and even in my own command there are so many new faces I don't know all my NCOs by name.'

'But that's terrible,' cried Rosalie. 'I should take the girls to St Etienne at once.'

Emile nodded, saying, 'You must do as you think best, my dear. Make what arrangements you will.'

'Yes, Maman,' reiterated Georges, 'you should make arrangements at once.'

When Rosalie retired to bed, Emile poured Georges another cognac.

'Your mother will have to take the girls to St Etienne alone.'

'Alone!' Georges sounded horrified.

'Well, of course she'll have Marie-Jeanne and Mademoiselle Corbine with her.'

'At least you should send Pierre with them, sir.'

'Perhaps you're right,' his father agreed with a sigh as he handed Georges the cognac and seated himself before the fire with another. 'I cannot leave Paris. There's no work coming in, and the war has completely disrupted business. The boom of the sixties is over. Many of the speculators have gone to the wall and I am left with accounts unpaid and little chance of seeing my money. I may manage to recoup some of my losses if I stay, but if I leave now all will be lost and we could well be ruined.' He sighed and Georges realised why it was that his father had aged. He had never discussed his business with his son before and in broaching the subject now it was apparent that a milestone in their relationship had been reached. At twenty-one Georges was no longer a boy, until this evening still considered so by his father, but at last he was being recognised as a man.

He looked across at his father and said, 'What about the property in Montmartre? You must receive some income from that.'

His father shrugged. 'You know how things there are at present. It's hardly the time to tour Montmartre collecting rent! I'd be lucky to get home alive.' Not even to Georges was Emile going to admit having been caught up in the Montmartre riot. 'No, we must wait out the troubles as everyone else must, and pray that we shall be able to salvage something at the end of it all. But when will it end, Georges? When will it end?'

Georges sipped his cognac and said quietly, 'I didn't want to frighten Maman, sir, but there'll be a full-scale civil war here in Paris before we're through. If I said that back at headquarters, I'd be accused of being alarmist, but the divisions are too deep to settle without bloodshed. Maman and the girls should leave at once and you too, Papa, whatever the state of the business. There is such feeling amongst the men that Paris could end in flames unless decisive action is taken now.'

But while he recognised that Georges was in a better position to know the situation within the army, Emile St Clair still hoped that his son was being over-pessimistic.

'I agree that your mother and the girls should leave as soon as possible,' he said, 'but I really cannot go myself.' No further argument from Georges was able to persuade him, and when they had finished their brandy they, too, retired upstairs.

Chapter 7

As he prepared for bed Georges considered what his father had told him about the state of his business affairs. Emile had never confided in his son before and he was so obviously preoccupied with his problems that Georges decided not to mention his other piece of news until a more propitious moment. He thought his mother would be pleased with what he had to tell them, indeed he was tempted to confide in her first, but he knew his father must be told before or at least at the same time as she.

Sylvie. Beautiful Sylvie. At the very thought of her Georges felt the blood drum in his head and knew a physical ache for the feel of her: the silky softness of her dark hair piled with demure correctness on her head yet from which a few tendrils escaped to curl so enchantingly at her ears: her smooth skin and her laughing eyes which teased and tempted him as he lay ill in her father's house. In his matter-of-fact account of his illness and convalescence in the home of the Claviets, Georges had done no more than mention Sylvie in passing; he had not spoken of his love for her nor that it was returned.

He had not told of her calm reassurance and understanding when, assailed by nightmares, he would wake crying aloud, covered in cold sweat and shaking. Gently soothing, she would be at his bedside to wipe his face and hands and soothe his fears. He had not told of the hours she spent reading to him while he still lacked the energy to read to himself; nor of the endless games of chess and backgammon they played when he was well enough to be propped up with pillows. Sylvie. Little Sylvie whom he loved with an intensity he would have considered impossible last summer. His previous loves, so many and varied, slipped from his memory and Sylvie filled his heart and mind. He had asked her father's permission to address her and when he had proposed, he was enchanted when she cried out, 'Oh, Georges, what a time you have been coming to the point! I was beginning to think you didn't love me after all.' She had held up her face to be kissed and he had pulled her into his arms with a passion which enflamed them both.

What his father would think of his marrying the daughter of a country lawyer Georges did not know, but he was sure his mother would not mind provided she knew Georges was happy. Sylvie had saved his life, that was all Maman would need to know.

Georges's reveries were interrupted by a soft tap on the door. He opened it to find Hélène outside on the landing, dressed in her nightgown with a shawl thrown over her shoulders.

'Can I come in, Georges? Can I come in for a while and talk?'

Georges smiled down at her. 'It's very late, Hélène.'

'Just a few minutes. Please? You'll be off tomorrow and goodness knows when we'll see you again.'

Georges let her into the room and installed her on the bed, wrapping an eiderdown about her.

'Just for a minute or two, then you must go back to bed. You look very tired.'

'Tell me what's going on in the city,' begged Hélène once she was comfortable. 'We're not allowed out any more, especially since I went to the parade.' And she recounted her adventure to Georges. Georges laughed when he heard about the fruit and vegetable throwing but he was serious by the end of her tale.

'I can see why you wanted to go, Hélène, but it was a very dangerous thing to do. No wonder Papa and Maman were so angry.' Safely at a distance now from their rage, Hélène was able to smile at it, but Georges went on seriously. 'It would be even more foolish to try and repeat the exercise,' he warned. 'There are so many soldiers with no barracks just living in the parks, it would be very dangerous for you to go out now.'

'I won't,' promised Hélène. 'But,' she confided, positive her adored brother would not tell her parents, 'Jeannot still comes here sometimes. I saw him one day. He'd come to see Pierre in the stables. He told me about the Fédérés.'

'Did he indeed,' replied Georges.

'Well, not since we went out,' conceded Hélène. 'Last time I only saw him for a few moments, but I'm going to ask him more when I see him again.'

'I don't think he should be coming here at all,' said Georges. 'Papa dismissed him for leading you into danger.'

'But he's nowhere else to go,' pointed out Hélène. 'He's got no home and no family. Pierre just gives him a meal from time to time, that's all.'

'Well, I don't think you ought to go down and meet him. Maman would be most distressed if she found out.' Georges's tone was severe.

'You won't tell, will you?' begged Hélène. 'I wouldn't have told you if I'd thought you'd tell.'

'No, I won't tell,' agreed Georges, 'this time. But you're to promise not to meet this boy again.'

Hélène hesitated, looking mulish.

'If you don't promise, I shall have to tell,' said Georges, 'and that will get Pierre into trouble too.'

'All right,' said Hélène grudgingly, and crossing her fingers under the eiderdown, added, 'I promise.'

'Good girl,' approved Georges and made a mental note to speak to Pierre on the subject of Jeannot. Anxious to turn to a more cheerful topic he went on, 'Anyway, you may not be staying in Paris much longer, you may be going back to St Etienne.'

Hélène's eyes lit up. 'Do you think we might? I hate being shut in here with nothing to do.'

'Well,' said Georges, 'I advised Papa that he should take you all, but—'

'You advised Papa!' Hélène gave a shout of laughter at the thought of anyone telling her papa what to do. 'Will he take your advice?'

'Hush,' grinned Georges. 'You'll wake them all. I don't know if he will, but as I shouldn't have mentioned the subject to you in the first place, you'll oblige me by being as surprised as the others if and when he makes the announcement. Now, tell me what else you've been doing apart from showing the German army your displeasure!'

Hélène sat cocooned in the eiderdown for another half an hour chattering on about her days, but even as she did so she became increasingly aware of an ache behind her eyes and an insistent throbbing in her head. She shivered suddenly and Georges said, 'Come on, back to bed, you're getting cold.' He picked her up in his arms and she nestled against him as he carried her along to the room she shared with Clarice. Clarice was sound asleep, a soft-breathing mound beneath the bedclothes as Georges crept into the room carrying Hélène. He put her into bed and tucked the bedclothes round her. Hélène reached up to hug him and he felt her cheek hot against his own.

'It's been lovely having you home, Georges,' she whispered. 'Be careful, won't you?'

Georges returned her hug. 'Don't worry about me, *chérie*, but you remember what I said – no more tricks like the Prussian parade, *hein*, and no more meeting Jeannot.'

Hélène smiled. 'I promise. And I'll be as surprised as anything when Maman tells us about St Etienne.'

Georges grinned. 'You do that,' he said, and stealing silently from the room he left her to sleep.

That night Rosalie lay in bed unable to sleep as she went over what Georges had been telling them. Two generals murdered by the mob! Surely the army would bring those men to justice, wouldn't they? Surely the mob wasn't completely out of control. Even as she lay there, alone in her bed, she thought she could hear distant shouting, then a shot rang out, and the sound of running feet. She felt a stab of fear. Had some of the rioters come into their quiet neighbourhood? She crept out of bed and peeped through the window. She could see no one, but the sounds in the night had heightened her fears. She went back to bed and pulling the covers up round her ears, tried once more to go to sleep, determined that whatever Emile said in the morning, she and the children would take the train and return to the country.

Chapter 8

The next day was a flurry of preparations. Marie-Jeanne sorted and packed the children's clothes, Pierre went to the station and bought tickets for St Etienne, while Berthe packed baskets of food for the journey.

Emile had remained adamant that he could not accompany his wife and daughters to St Etienne, but agreed to allow them to travel by train the following day with Marie-Jeanne, Mademoiselle Corbine and Pierre in attendance.

'What will you do?' Rosalie asked him anxiously.

'I shall remain here,' he replied. 'Berthe and Arlette will look after me and Pierre can return as soon as he has delivered you safely to St Etienne.'

'You make us sound like parcels,' complained his wife. 'Are you sure you can't come with us, just for a few days?'

'We've had this conversation, Rosalie,' Emile said coolly. 'I do not wish to have it again.'

Georges had heard their plans that morning before he left to return to his regiment. 'You've made the right decision,' he assured his mother. 'And I promise I'll keep an eye on my father.'

That night they all went to bed in a hum of excitement.

Hélène had kept her promise to Georges and shown surprise and delight at the news of their return to the country.

'Now don't forget,' he had whispered into her ear as he gave her a farewell hug before leaving, 'no more consorting with urchins, here or in the village when you get back!'

Hélène gave him an extra hug and said demurely, 'No, Georges,' her fingers crossed behind him, adding with a grin, 'Anyway, I don't know any urchins in St Etienne!'

'Well, you make sure it stays that way,' he said with mock severity.

All Rosalie's carefully laid plans were thrown into disarray next morning, however, when Marie-Jeanne went in early to waken the girls. Clarice was already wide awake, but Hélène was not.

'Wake up, lazybones,' Marie-Jeanne scolded, but when Hélène did not wake, simply muttered in her sleep, Marie-Jeanne reached down to shake her awake. It was then that she realised that the child was extremely hot. Quickly she turned away and said to Clarice, 'Here, put a shawl round you and go and fetch your mother,' adding when Clarice seemed about to protest, 'Look sharp!'

Moments later Rosalie was in the room, a robe thrown over her nightdress, her face full of concern. 'Marie-Jeanne, what is it?'

'Miss Hélène has a fever, madame. She's burning up and talking nonsense. We should keep the other two away from her and send for the doctor.'

Rosalie crossed swiftly to the bed and laying a hand on Hélène's forehead, felt the hot, dry skin under her fingers. As she did so, Hélène began muttering again, a stream of incomprehensible words.

At once Rosalie took charge. 'Clarice, get dressed and then go and tell Louise to do the same. Marie-Jeanne, fetch some cool water and a flannel and bathe her face. I must speak with Monsieur, but I'll be back directly.' Waiting only until Marie-Jeanne returned with the water and facecloth, Rosalie hurried down to find Emile. He was standing in the hall, putting on his overcoat, already preparing to leave the house.

He stared at her in amazement as she appeared in the front hall still dressed in her nightclothes.

'Rosalie!' he exclaimed. 'What is this?'

'I have to speak to you, Emile,' she said, laying a hand on his arm.

'What is it?' he asked testily. 'I'm late already.'

'It's Hélène,' she answered. 'She has a fever, we must send for the doctor.'

'Indeed,' returned her husband, 'then please do so.'

'You know we were leaving for St Etienne today,' said his wife, 'but I think she's too ill to travel, and...'

'And so she must stay here,' he finished for her. 'Surely you don't need to leave today.'

'After what Georges told us the other night, we really should go. Paris is no place for the children. We should never have come back.'

Emile's lips tightened at this implied criticism, but all he said was, 'It is your decision, Rosalie.' He relaxed a little and said, 'I agree from what Georges told us that you should go, but will it hurt to wait a couple more days until the child is fit to travel?'

'I don't know!' cried Rosalie wretchedly. 'But I can't go without her.'

'You could leave her here with Marie-Jeanne,' suggested

Emile. 'Take Mademoiselle Corbine and the other two out of town. Leave Hélène in Marie-Jeanne's care, it's probably just some childish ailment. Then, as soon as she's recovered, I will bring her out to St Etienne.'

Rosalie stared at him for a moment. 'If I did that, would you really bring her as soon as she is well?'

'I have just said so, madame,' Emile replied stiffly. 'Now, if you will excuse me?' He touched her hand in farewell and then opening the door, walked out into the street.

For a moment Rosalie watched him walking away from her. He was never one to show his emotions, but even so she knew he loved her as she loved him; she would miss him while she was in St Etienne and he remained in Paris. Suddenly remembering she was clad only in her nightdress and a bedroom robe, she hurriedly shut the front door and went back upstairs.

Dressing quickly, she returned to Hélène's bedside. Marie-Jeanne was gently sponging the child's face, neck and hands with cool water, but Hélène seemed unaware of her or her surroundings.

'I will send Pierre for Dr Simon, Marie-Jeanne,' Rosalie said. 'We'll see what he says. In the meantime, you stay here with Hélène until I come back.'

Dr Simon arrived within the hour and Marie-Jeanne took him straight up to Hélène's room where Rosalie sat sponging her daughter's face.

'Ah, madame,' he said, executing a small bow. 'And how is the little one?' He set his bag to one side and approached the bed.

'Very hot,' replied Rosalie. 'She doesn't wake and murmurs and mutters all the time.' She moved aside so that the doctor, a man she had known for years, the doctor who had brought all her children into the world, could move closer to see Hélène's face, flushed against the white of her pillow.

Approaching the bed he laid a hand on Hélène's forehead and then took out his pocket watch to take her pulse. 'Her heartbeat is very fast and she is indeed very hot.' He leaned forward and touched the collar of Hélène's nightgown, and then turned back to Rosalie saying, 'Please expose the child's chest.'

Rosalie unbuttoned the nightdress and pulled it away from Hélène's body. Dr Simon put on his spectacles and inspected the small frame.

'It is good there is no rash, madame, which could indicate typhoid fever…'

'Typhoid!' cried Rosalie.

'As I said, there is no rash, so I think it is unlikely, but one can never be sure. Has she complained of any ache or pain in the last days?'

'She said her head ached,' replied Rosalie, 'but we were not concerned. There's been a lot of excitement in the house the last few days.'

'No er-hem, no trouble… er-hem,' the doctor looked away as he murmured, 'her bowels? No diarrhoea?' There! He'd used the word… in front of a lady.

Rosalie had no such scruples. 'No,' she replied, 'no diarrhoea.'

'That is good,' said the doctor, allowing himself to meet her eyes again. 'I cannot say it definitely isn't typhoid, madame, though as I said, I think it unlikely, but in any case you would be wise to keep your other children away, and nurse her separately. I will call again later in the day to see how she goes on. There is a fever in the city,' he went on. 'From what

I've seen, the illness lasts for a day or two, and when the fever breaks the patient begins to recover quite soon.'

'And is there a treatment?' demanded Rosalie. 'Can you give her a powder or something that will bring her temperature down?'

'Give her plenty of water, boiled water, and I will mix a tincture to give her three times a day, but otherwise there is little I can do,' the doctor admitted. 'The fever must run its course. With a well-nourished and normally healthy child like your daughter, madame, her body is strong and will do the work. For a slum child weakened by starvation the outlook would be very different, very grave.'

'But where can she have got it from?' asked Rosalie.

'Anywhere,' replied the doctor. 'Since the siege, there is sickness all over the city.'

'But the infection, will it pass to my other daughters?'

Dr Simon shrugged. 'Who can say? Perhaps they have it already. If not, they should be safe if you keep them away from this child. Of course, you yourself may also be infected… or the nurse.' He indicated Marie-Jeanne standing quietly in the corner of the room.

'We were leaving Paris today,' said Rosalie wretchedly, 'going into the country.'

'Far healthier,' agreed the doctor. 'Away from the malodorous humours of the city.'

'But surely she's too ill to travel.' Rosalie glanced down at the still-muttering figure in the bed.

'Indeed it would be most unwise to attempt to move her when her temperature is this high. In a few days when the fever has left her, she will begin to recover. She will be weak and need much care, but then a gentle journey, comfortably in a carriage, will be safe, I think.'

'But suppose the other children…' began Rosalie, at a loss to know what to do for the best.

'It would be better to take the other children from the house, madame. One never knows which direction such fevers will take.'

'But you said she would recover!' cried Rosalie.

'And so she should, madame, but I cannot promise. All I can say is, keep the other children away. Take them to the country.' He glanced again at Marie-Jeanne. 'Surely the nurse can look after this child here.'

Dr Simon would say no more. He moved towards the door, picking up his unopened bag, pulling on his gloves. As he reached the door he turned and said, 'I will send my boy round with the tincture and call again myself later on.'

Rosalie went with him down the stairs, and as they passed the open dining room door he glanced in and saw Clarice and Louise still seated at the table.

'Take them to the country, madame,' he advised again. 'Paris is no place for such children. Soon it will run with blood.'

When he had gone, Rosalie went back up to the sickroom. 'You heard what the doctor advised, Marie-Jeanne,' she said. 'That I should take Clarice and Louise to St Etienne as planned.' She looked across at the woman who had been her own nurse before her children's. 'But what of Hélène?' she asked wretchedly. 'How can I leave her, so ill? Oh, Marie-Jeanne, what should I do?'

'I think you should do as the doctor suggests, madame,' the old nurse answered. 'It is a wise decision. I will stay here and nurse Hélène until she recovers. Then we can come to join you in St Etienne.'

'Monsieur St Clair said he will bring you,' Rosalie said.

'Of course he will,' agreed Marie-Jeanne, 'just as soon as she is better.' She smiled reassuringly. 'I will look after the little one and all will be well.'

'Oh, Marie-Jeanne,' Rosalie had tears in her eyes, 'what should I do without you?'

For a moment she was a child again, and allowed Marie-Jeanne to put her arms round her.

'Now then, Miss Rosalie,' Marie-Jeanne said comfortably, 'don't you take on so. The boxes are all packed. You get Pierre to call you a cab and you can all be off to the station.' Nodding reassuringly she went on, 'Mademoiselle Corbine seems a sensible woman, so you'll have her to help with the girls, and Pierre will manage the luggage.'

'But you? Will you be all right, while we're away?'

'Of course I will,' Marie-Jeanne assured her. 'I'm not alone in the house. Berthe and Arlette are downstairs, Pierre will soon be back and the master will be home at nights. We shall manage perfectly. When the doctor sends round the medicine for Hélène I'll give it to her, regular, no worry.'

Soothed a little by Marie-Jeanne's quiet common sense, Rosalie went down the stairs to find Pierre and Mademoiselle Corbine and to get the girls ready for the journey back to the country.

Marie-Jeanne sat with Hélène for the rest of the day. Berthe sent up her midday meal on a tray and a pitcher of cooled boiled water for Hélène, as instructed by Rosalie before she left. The doctor's lad arrived soon after with a flask of brown liquid and a note to say it should be administered three times a day. Hélène had not properly awoken from her restless sleep, but Marie-Jeanne had managed to get her to take a little water poured down a twist of cotton into the corner of her mouth. Dr Simon's tincture had been more difficult, but when Hélène had opened feverish eyes and looked unseeing at Marie-Jeanne, the nurse had managed to get her to take a teaspoon of the mixture, only half of which the child spluttered out again.

When the doctor returned as promised he simply took Hélène's pulse again, noted that the fever seemed as high as before and repeated the instructions he'd given the first time.

Emile came home as it was getting dark. He knew that Rosalie and two of his daughters would have left the house, but even so he wasn't quite prepared for the silence that had settled on the place after their departure. He let himself in with his own key and went upstairs to his bedchamber. He changed his clothes before making his way to the children's bedroom and quietly opening the door. The room was very warm, the windows having been kept firmly closed despite the warmth of the day outside. Infection had to be kept at bay and none must be allowed to enter the sickroom from the streets below.

Marie-Jeanne was sitting beside the bed, mending a pair of stockings by the light of a single candle. She turned her head as the door opened and setting aside her sewing, gestured with her hands that he should stay outside the door. She joined him in the doorway and reported what Dr Simon had said.

'So he doesn't think it's typhoid?' Emile asked, relief in his voice.

'No, monsieur,' she replied. 'He says there is a lot of sickness about in the city. He blames the siege; people being weakened by hunger.'

'But Hélène wasn't here during the siege!' Emile scowled as he went on, 'I expect it was brought to the house by that sewer rat, Jeannot.'

'Perhaps.' Marie-Jeanne had wondered about that herself. 'But,' she pointed out, 'you sent him packing weeks ago. She would have been ill before now, if he was the cause.'

'Well, whoever infected her, the important thing is to nurse her back to health as quickly as possible. Madame is very anxious to get her safely to St Etienne.'

'Have no worries, monsieur,' Marie-Jeanne said. 'I shall be with her night and day until she is better.'

Emile nodded. He had expected nothing less. 'I will come and see how she is in the morning,' he said. 'Pierre will be back tomorrow.' And with that he went downstairs to his solitary dinner in the dining room.

Emile had had a relatively peaceful day. The office was now up and running again, and though there were no new commissions coming in, he had set his draughtsmen to work, continuing the projects they had been involved in before the outbreak of war. When he retired to bed that night he realised the fact that Rosalie and two of the girls were safely out of Paris had released him from one, subconscious, worry. Hélène, though ill, was safe enough in her own home and so he had only himself to worry about. He would not return to Montmartre until everything had settled down again. Safe in a world of his own, he shut his eyes to what was brewing in the city around him.

Chapter 9

The doctor proved to be right. Within another twenty-four hours Hélène's fever had broken and though she felt weak, she begged Marie-Jeanne to let her get up.

'I'm better, Marie-Jeanne, really,' she insisted. 'I hate being in bed!'

'Of course you do, pet,' soothed Marie-Jeanne, 'but you were quite ill for a while, you know, and we have to take things slowly. Now, how about a spoonful or two of this broth Berthe has made you? Then when you've had another little sleep perhaps you can go into the schoolroom and sit by the fire. How would that be?'

Hélène accepted the compromise and had to admit to herself, if not to Marie-Jeanne, that when she did get out of bed her legs felt decidedly wobbly. But there was a blazing fire in the schoolroom and lying on the old sofa in front of it was better than being shut away in her bedroom. Though it was late March and the weather was clement, Marie-Jeanne was taking no risks with her charge. She insisted that Hélène stay by the fire with a hot brick at her feet and a blanket round her shoulders for another day before she was allowed out into the garden for half an hour to enjoy the sun on her face.

Each evening since her mother had left, Emile had come in to see her, though he stood by the door, afraid of infection. However, on the third day of her recovery he simply said, 'You'll be pleased to hear that we're going to St Etienne tomorrow, Hélène. Do you think you can manage the journey? Pierre is making the light chaise ready so that you can travel comfortably.'

Hélène was delighted. 'Oh yes, Papa!' she cried. 'I'm quite better now.' She was completely unaware of the reason for this hasty withdrawal from Paris, and even if she had known, she would not have understood the gravity of the situation. All she knew was that they were going to St Etienne where Maman and her sisters would be waiting.

Emile had finally realised that he had to get Hélène out of Paris, whether she was truly fit to travel or not. When he had told Marie-Jeanne of his decision she was concerned.

'She is still weak from her illness, monsieur,' she protested. 'Surely another few days' rest before the journey would be better.'

But Emile had been adamant. 'No, Marie-Jeanne,' he said. 'Have her packed and ready to leave first thing in the morning. You will accompany us, of course.'

Marie-Jeanne was still anxious that the journey would be too much for Hélène, and wondered what had caused this sudden urgency. Still, she could do nothing but give a bob and say, 'Yes, monsieur, we shall both be ready.'

Emile's decision had been prompted by a terrifying event that very day. The city was in a continuous state of flux and yet again Emile had been caught up in violence, the violence Georges had predicted, and finally he had accepted it was too dangerous to stay; that he needed to get his small daughter to safety before it was too late.

He had been doing some business in the city earlier that day and returning to his office, he turned into the Rue de la Paix, Peace Street, and found himself once again caught up in a crowd. A throng of people filled the street, heading as one body towards the Place Vendôme. He was surprised at their numbers, but he felt no alarm. They were nothing like the mob he'd encountered in Montmartre previously; they were clearly respectable, law-abiding citizens and they moved down the street with quiet purpose. Some were carrying placards asking for peace, and one banner announced that they were 'The Friends of Order'. No one carried weapons, there were no brandished swords or waved pistols; the Friends were marching peaceably to the National Guard headquarters in an effort to show that they were not happy with the way things were going since the Central Committee had taken control.

Emile had joined at the back of the crowd, more because it was going in his direction than as a sign that he agreed with its protest. The demonstration was clearly peaceful and its leaders were seized with dismay when they found their way into the Place Vendôme blocked by ranks of Fédérés. They halted, and there was shouting from both sides, as the officer in charge of the Fédérés ordered the demonstrators to disperse. His words went unheard in the general commotion, and unaware of what was happening at the front of the march, those at the back continued to press forward, pushing its leaders closer and closer to the waiting line of National Guardsmen.

For a moment, neither side gave way, and then from nowhere came the rattle of rifle fire and the street was filled with smoke; there were screams of pain and panic as the gunfire continued to rake the crowd, and when the order to cease fire was given and the firing died away, the street was strewn with bodies. The National Guards withdrew to the Place Vendôme, leaving the dead and injured lying on the ground to be cared for by their comrades.

Emile had recoiled in horror as he saw what was happening. He was far enough back in the crowd to be unaffected by the gunfire, but not by the panic. At the sound of shots he lost his nerve and was immediately caught up in the mass of demonstrators who pushed and shoved their way back up the street. Emile was almost knocked to the ground in the rush to escape, but with the strength of terror, he forced his way through the crush and away from the street. Once clear of the place he clambered into a cab and directed the driver to take him to his office. His heart was still thumping in his chest as he climbed the stairs to the safety of his own room and collapsed into a chair.

'Monsieur?' His secretary, Albert Forquet, followed him into the room, a look of concern on his face. 'What has happened?'

'Water,' Emile said feebly, and when Forquet returned carrying a glass, he snatched it and gulped it down. 'Riot,' he said. 'Massacre, Forquet!' And he proceeded to tell the younger man what had occurred in the Rue de la Paix.

'Things are getting much worse,' Forquet agreed. 'Paris will soon be at war with herself.'

'She already is!' Emile said. 'I think it is time to close the office for a few days. I shall take my daughter to her mother in the country, but I shall come back, and we will decide what is best then. In the meantime, Forquet, put up the shutters, lock the doors and tell the others that the office is closed until I return.'

Having given these instructions, Emile had taken another cab home and began making plans for their journey the following day.

He found Pierre in the stable, cleaning tack for non-existent horses since theirs had been seized at the gates, and told him they would need the light chaise next morning. He had considered trying to leave the city that night, but decided travelling in the dark through streets where National Guardsmen held sway was more dangerous than waiting until the following day.

'The chaise hasn't been used for months, monsieur,' Pierre pointed out. 'It will have to be cleaned—'

'Then clean it,' snapped Emile. 'Then first thing in the morning find us a horse to pull it.'

Pierre looked doubtful. 'That won't be an easy task,' he said, spreading his hands.

'Just do it, man. I don't care where it comes from.' Emile's anxiety made him unusually terse. The deaths in the Rue de la Paix had scared him even more than the riot in Montmartre.

'Yes, monsieur,' replied Pierre and set to work to make the chaise usable.

That evening Georges reappeared at the house. He was not wearing his uniform, just a simple coat over dark stuff trousers, workman's boots and a hat pulled down over his eyes.

'Georges!' Emile's face lit up when his son was shown into the dining room where he was eating his solitary supper. 'What brings you here? Will you have dinner? I'm sure Berthe has more of this pie in the kitchen.'

'No, thank you, Papa,' said Georges. 'I've already eaten.'

Emile pushed his half-empty plate away. In truth he was pleased to have an excuse to do so. Since his narrow escape in the Rue de la Paix, he found he had no appetite. 'So,' he said, smiling at Georges, 'what brings you here?'

'I've come to warn you again, Papa. You must get out of Paris,' Georges replied, his voice carrying a note of desperation. 'I thought you'd already gone.'

He was on an errand for his commanding officer, infiltrating the streets, drinking in the bars and cafés to report back the mood of ordinary people within the city, when he'd seen lights in the window of his family home and realised, to his dismay, that the house was still occupied.

'We're going first thing tomorrow,' Emile replied. 'Hélène had a fever and was too ill to travel when your mother left with the other two, but she's better now and I'm taking her and Marie-Jeanne to St Etienne in the morning.'

'Hélène's still here? Is she all right now?' Georges was horrified. 'You should leave at once, Papa. No one's safe in the city since the Central Committee took over.'

'The government shouldn't have run to Versailles,' returned his father.

'I agree,' said Georges, 'but they have, and things are going to get worse before they get better. The Paris National Guard are running out of control. There was some sort of confrontation in the Rue de la Paix today and they opened fire on an unarmed crowd. Several people were killed and many more injured.'

Suddenly Georges broke off, realising that he'd said too much. This incident was already being called a massacre, and he was to carry news of what happened back to Versailles.

'I know,' replied Emile. 'I heard.'

But he didn't say how he had heard. Again, he wasn't

prepared to admit to anyone that not only had he been caught up in the affair, but that he had run for his life.

Neither of them asked how the other one knew.

However, Georges was determined that his father should understand the gravity of the situation. 'There is more violence every day, people being attacked, kidnapped, hostages taken,' he told him. 'People are using the general chaos to settle private scores. When you get to St Etienne, you should stay there, too.' He knew he shouldn't warn his father of the imminent attack on the city by the troops now stationed at Versailles, but he gestured to his unusual garb. 'I'm disobeying orders even being here, Papa, despite the fact that I'm not in uniform. I'd be lucky to escape with my life if I was recognised.'

'Then why have you come?' asked Emile.

'I can't tell you, indeed it's better that you don't know. The most important thing now is that you should get out of the city as soon as you can… and Papa, don't come back until all this is over.'

'Don't worry, my boy.' Emile tried to sound reassuring. 'We shall be gone as soon as Pierre has secured us a horse to pull the chaise.'

'That'll be no easy task,' commented Georges.

'I know,' Emile agreed, 'but he's a resourceful man. No good finding it today, it would have been stolen by tomorrow. Better to put it straight between the shafts and set off at once.'

Georges nodded. His father was probably right there.

For half an hour father and son sat at the table and drank a glass of cognac together before Georges got to his feet. 'I must be off,' he said. 'I understand there's a curfew within the city walls now.' He put on his cap, again pulling it down over his eyes to shade his face, and led the way into the hall.

'I'll leave through the kitchen and go out through the yard gate,' he said as the two men awkwardly embraced. 'Suits my disguise better.'

'Take care, son,' Emile said. 'I don't want to know what you're doing, but don't put yourself in unnecessary danger.'

Georges gave a short bark of laughter. 'Difficult not to, these days,' he said, 'but I'll do my best!' And with a wave of his hand he disappeared into the kitchen. Emile watched from an upstairs window, but in the gathering dusk he hardly recognised Georges as he shuffled off along the road, just another scruffy individual haunting the night-time streets, out for what he could find.

Emile went into his bedroom where a small fire burned in the grate and got ready for bed. As he lay in the darkness he relived the terror of the Rue de la Paix, feeling again the chill of his fear as he'd run from the scene. Georges was right, they should all have left Paris sooner. Tomorrow he would make a quick visit to his office to ensure that Forquet had followed his instructions. There would be time for that while Pierre acquired a horse, and then they would set out for St Etienne, away from the madness that was Paris.

Chapter 10

The next morning dawned dull, grey and cold; a complete difference to the previous day, as if spring had changed its mind and winter had regained the upper hand.

Marie-Jeanne woke early and looked out of the window. Her heart sank to see the dank garden. If she'd had any say in the matter there would have been no question of exposing Hélène to such chilling weather, but she had known Emile St Clair long enough to know that once he'd made his mind up, he was not going to change it. She would have to ensure that the child was well wrapped up for the journey. She went into the kitchen where Berthe was preparing the breakfast to remind her to put up a basket of food and drink for the journey.

'Not to worry,' Berthe said. 'It's all ready. There's bread and cheese and some apples; a bottle of cold coffee too, and another of water.' She beamed up at Marie-Jeanne. 'And I've made some soup specially for Miss Hélène. I've put that in a bottle too, so she can drink it easily. It will taste just as good cold.'

Marie-Jeanne thanked her for her forethought and went to wake Hélène. The girl was already half awake when

Marie-Jeanne came into her room. Clearly better now, she sat up rubbing her eyes as Marie-Jeanne threw back the curtains.

'It's today, isn't it?' she cried as she scrambled out of bed. 'Today we're going to St Etienne. I can't wait to see Maman!'

Marie-Jeanne smiled at her excitement. 'Well, come here and get washed, Arlette is just bringing up some hot water.' She supervised Hélène's ablutions and then told her to get dressed in the clean clothes she'd laid out for her and come down for breakfast.

Hélène needed no second bidding, and was soon sitting at the table drinking hot chocolate and eating freshly made croissants. Briefly, Emile joined her there, but only took a cup of coffee.

'I have to go out for half an hour,' he said. 'By the time I get back, Pierre will be back with a horse and we shall be off.' He turned to Marie-Jeanne. 'Is everything packed?'

'Yes, monsieur.'

'Then we should load the chaise so that all is ready for our departure.'

'I will ask Pierre to do so as soon as he gets back,' said Marie-Jeanne.

'No,' replied Emile, 'I want the luggage on board straight away. I will carry it out myself.'

'You, monsieur?' Marie-Jeanne couldn't help the words escaping, she was so astonished.

'Indeed me,' said Emile. 'Do you think it beyond me to carry a few valises out to the chaise?'

'No, of course not, monsieur,' said Marie-Jeanne hastily. 'I will just close the clasps.'

Within ten minutes the three cases were strapped to the back of the chaise and Berthe had been told to load the basket of food.

'I will be back very shortly,' Emile said as he put on his hat and coat, and without further ado, he went out into the street.

'Where is Papa going?' wondered Hélène as she drank the last of her chocolate.

'I don't know,' Marie-Jeanne said, 'and it's his business not ours. Now, child, if you've finished your breakfast, let's go upstairs and make sure we haven't forgotten anything.' Though Marie-Jeanne knew this to be unnecessary as she had done all the packing herself, she wanted to keep Hélène occupied until Pierre arrived with a horse and her father reappeared.

As they reached the top of the stairs there came a loud crash and the front door shuddered from a blow from the outside, followed by another and then another. Marie-Jeanne looked over the banisters as Arlette hurried into the hall to open the door.

'Don't!' cried Marie-Jeanne. 'Arlette! Don't open the door!'

The maid hesitated, not knowing what to do, and before she could make up her mind there was a fourth crash and the door burst open, sagging inwards on damaged hinges. As it swung wide, three large and ferocious-looking men erupted into the house. Marie-Jeanne had never seen such men enter the house through the front door; men of the street, in filthy clothes and workmen's boots, the first waving a pistol and the other two carrying the metal piping that had been used as a ram on the door. Arlette gave a scream of terror and received a backhanded slap across her face from the man with the gun.

'Shut up, you little slut!' he snarled as Arlette fell whimpering to the floor, blood gushing from her nose. 'Get up and get out.'

Arlette managed to scramble to her feet and with one

terrified glance up the stairs at Marie-Jeanne, she bolted out into the street, her wails echoing behind her.

'And don't come back,' yelled the second man, shaking his fist after her.

Marie-Jeanne pushed Hélène along the landing, hissing, 'Go into your room and wait for me!'

Hélène didn't move immediately, simply stared down at the intruders with wide and frightened eyes.

'Go!' Marie-Jeanne gave her a push towards her bedroom.

At that moment Hélène caught sight of a face she recognised and her eyes widened. Jeannot was peering in through the front door.

'Jeannot!' she shrieked.

Jeannot's head jerked upwards and he saw her pale face looking down at him through the banisters.

Hélène! She wasn't meant to be here! His expression changed to one of dismay.

'Go!' Marie-Jeanne urged her with another push. She, too, had recognised Jeannot and knew at once that this was no random attack on a rich house. This was a planned invasion of a prominent man's home by an envious rabble.

One of the men grabbed the boy by the scruff of the neck and dragged him inside. 'I thought you said that the house would be empty!' he growled.

'I… I thought they'd gone. They was going away!' jabbered Jeannot. 'I thought they'd gone.' He tried to pull away from the man's grip, but it was too strong for him.

'So, boy, who else might be here, eh? Any more surprises?'

'Dunno,' stammered Jeannot, cringing away from him. 'I dunno, honest!'

'Better find out, hadn't we?' said the gunman. 'Jules, you search down here. Auguste, keep hold of the boy.' He looked up the stairs to where Marie-Jeanne stood, blocking the way up, arms akimbo. He gave a lascivious grin. 'An' I'll take the upstairs.'

The other two men disappeared, Jules heading to the kitchen. The other, Auguste, still holding Jeannot by the scruff of the neck, dragged him into the dining room. The third man, who was the obvious leader, put his foot on the bottom stair and looked up.

'Anyone else up there?' he asked.

'You can't come up here,' Marie-Jeanne told him, her hands clenched into fists so that he wouldn't see they were shaking.

'Oh? And why's that then?' The man climbed two more stairs.

'It's only me and the child... and... and she's ill.' Remembering how this ruse had worked on that first day they had arrived in Paris, she went on, 'She has a fever. She is infectious!'

It gave the man pause, but then he laughed. 'Good try, old woman,' he crowed, 'but she looks well enough to me. Pretty and young! Just as I like 'em.' And he took two more slow steps up the stairs.

'Hélène! Hide!'

This time the urgency in Marie-Jeanne's voice did get through to the girl and as if she'd been released from a spell, she scurried out of sight along the corridor and then a door banged.

'You can't come up here,' Marie-Jeanne said again. 'We'll call the police!'

'Doubt if they'll hear you,' sneered the man. 'And they won't come, even if they do.'

Marie-Jeanne knew he was right, knew that she couldn't

stop this man, but even so she looked round for some sort of weapon. There was an ornamental chair standing at the top of the staircase and she grabbed it, holding it by the back and jabbing its spindly legs at the approaching man. He gave another laugh.

'Out of the way, old woman. You can't stop me and you'd be a fool to try!' He had almost reached the top step, but he was still a little lower than Marie-Jeanne and with one last desperate effort, she swung the little chair into the air and brought it down as hard as she could on his head. It was an elegant piece, not built for such usage, and it disintegrated about his head and shoulders. He staggered, giving a roar of fury, but as he regained his balance he raised his pistol and pulled the trigger.

Marie-Jeanne slumped to the floor, blood spreading across her breast, the momentary look of anguish in her eyes almost immediately extinguished. Her attacker kicked her, pushing her body aside and out of his way with his boot. A call came from downstairs, and Auguste, having heard the shot, reappeared in the hall, Jeannot still held in an iron fist.

'Gaston?' he called. 'What's going on?'

'Nothing I can't handle, mate,' Gaston answered. 'You wait down there and watch the front door. Don't let no one in!'

He knew the shot could have been heard in the street and he wanted no inquisitive busybody coming into the house to see what was amiss. Jeannot had promised there was a haul of valuables just waiting in the empty house.

Well now, thought Gaston, as he thrust the pistol into the waistband of his trousers and went along the passage in search of the young girl, here's a 'valuable' we hadn't expected! What a hostage she'll make! What a ransom her rich family will surely pay to get her back… maybe slightly damaged… but alive, if enough gold is offered.

The landing was lined with doors, most of them open, and he glanced into each room as he passed. But he had heard the slamming of a door when the girl had run, and so he wasted no time searching those, he went directly to the two closed doors at the far end.

He opened the door of the first, and went in. The room, a man's bedroom, looked empty but it offered plenty of places to hide and he flung open cupboard doors, pulled out drawers and looked behind curtains and under the large bed. The remains of a fire lay in the grate, but they were cold and undisturbed. There was no sign of the child and so he moved on to the second closed door. When he opened that, he found himself in another bedroom, a much more feminine room, with a tidily made bed, a dressing table under the window, wardrobes and a tallboy. The fireplace was clean and obviously had not been in use for some days. Whoever slept in here had not done so last night. A quick search of the outer room produced no hidden child, but led him to a second door, tucked discreetly behind a screen. He pushed the screen aside and it fell with a crash to the floor, then he reached for the handle and flung the door open to disclose the 'cabinet', a tiny room housing a commode and a washstand. Crouching behind the commode, pale-faced and terrified, he found Hélène.

She gave a scream as he reached in to drag her out of her hiding place. His grip tightened on her arms as he pulled her back into the bedroom.

'Now then, missy,' he said, 'you're going to come with me and we ain't going to have no fuss, neither. All right?'

Hélène looked up into his cruel face and was terrified. Tears were streaming down her cheeks as she sobbed for her mother. Gaston shook her violently and shouted, 'Cut out that wailing or I'll give you something to cry about!'

Hélène knew enough to understand that she had to be quiet and go with this horrible man and she fought valiantly against her sobs as she was brought out onto the landing. Suddenly remembering how she had escaped the grasp of the man in the crowd in the Champs Elysées, she bent her head and sank her teeth into her captor's hand. Gaston gave a cry of pain and for a moment released her as he snatched his hand away. It was all she needed and she raced along the landing before coming to an abrupt halt at the top of the stairs where Marie-Jeanne lay like a discarded rag doll, her eyes staring unseeing at the ceiling.

Hélène gave a howl of anguish and flung herself down at her beloved nurse's side. She could see that pool of blood spread about her and knew Marie-Jeanne was beyond help.

Gaston was on her in an instant, grabbing her by her hair and yanking her to her feet.

'You've killed her,' shrieked Hélène, and unaware of the pain of her tugged hair, she beat him with her fists, pummelling his chest, his head, his face. 'Murderer! Murderer!'

Jules, Auguste and Jeannot, gathered below in the hall, stared open-mouthed as Gaston fought to hold on to the screaming girl, then with one blow he slapped Hélène so hard about the head that she was silenced and she collapsed against him. Immediately he hoisted her over his shoulder like a sack of coal and carried her down the stairs into the hall.

'Time to go!' he snapped.

'But what about the stuff here in the house?' demanded Jules, waving a hand vaguely about him. 'Weren't that what we come for?'

'An' what about her?' Auguste nodded towards the body at the top of the stairs.

'Leave her,' snapped Gaston. 'An' as for the other stuff, we can come back later. We need to get this one away from here and locked up before someone comes looking for her.' He grinned. 'She's our most valuable find!'

He glowered at Jeannot who was staring past the limp figure across Gaston's shoulder to the body at the top of the stairs. 'It's your fault she's dead, boy,' he said dismissively. 'You told us the house was empty.'

'It is now,' Jules told him. 'There was a cook in the kitchen, but she took off out of the back door like a scalded cat. She won't be back in a hurry.'

'Right, well, we'll go out the back way too. Don't want no busybodies asking about the child.' He turned again to Jeannot. 'Where does the back door lead to?'

'Just the stable yard and then out into the lane at the back.'

Was Pierre hiding in the stables? Jeannot wondered, hoping desperately that he wasn't. Pierre had been kind to him and Jeannot didn't want him to be murdered like poor Marie-Jeanne. How he wished he'd never mentioned the valuables in this house to Gaston and his crowd, but they were revolutionaries and he'd wanted to impress them with his knowledge and his daring. How could he have known the stupid St Clairs had stayed in the city? Pierre had told him they were leaving.

'Right,' Gaston was saying now, 'you can lead the way, boy, and no making a run for it, 'cos if you do I'll tell them it was you what shot the old biddy upstairs.' He gave a malevolent grin. 'After all, it was you what knew about this house and what was in it, so you was only getting your own back for being turned off!'

They passed through the empty kitchen, Auguste snatching up a loaf of warm fresh bread as he went through, and emerged into the lane that ran along the back wall.

Marie-Jeanne was left lying where she had fallen. The front door still sagged open, and the house was empty. Gaston and his cronies had been in and out in less than twenty minutes.

Chapter 11

Unaware of what was occurring at his house, Emile took a cab to his office and spent five minutes checking that Forquet had fixed the shutters properly before going inside. The draughtsmen's room was orderly, the drawing boards cleared of papers, instruments tidied away into locked drawers. He stood for a moment in the silence of the normally busy room and looked about. All was well in here, Forquet had made sure that nothing had been left out, so Emile went upstairs to his own office to have one final look round before leaving. He had considered taking some papers away with him, thinking perhaps he could continue to renew his business contacts from St Etienne, but now he decided against it. He would not be away for long, and there was the chance that something of importance might get lost.

For a moment he crossed to the window and looked out into the street below. It looked as it always did, with people going about their business, passing the time of day with acquaintances, hurrying by with bags and satchels, a truly ordinary day. Yet again Emile wondered how urgent the removal to St Etienne was. Normally a man of decision, he never vacillated, but now he still wondered, should he go or should he stay? Georges said he must go, and he'd said he would, but still he felt a certain confusion at the events taking place around him. Left to himself, he thought he might have kept his office open and kept his draughtsmen working on the projects that had been unfinished at the outbreak of the war, but the strength of the fear he'd felt in the Rue de la Paix the previous day had frightened him. He looked out into the busyness of the street beyond his window and told himself he was no coward, running at the first sign of trouble, but that was exactly what he had done, now on two occasions, and he felt a wave of shame.

'Pull yourself together,' he said aloud. 'You weren't the only one to run!' Somewhat reassured by the sound of his own voice, he continued, 'I will take Hélène to her mother and then I will come back into Paris. I will reopen my office and I will not be afraid of the rabble who inhabit the rough districts of this city.'

He closed his office door, locking it carefully behind him, and went down to the street. He locked that door too. His business would be safe until he came back to it. Paris was relying on citizens like him, moderate, professional men, to keep the wheels of business turning. He squared his shoulders and set out to find a cab.

As he reached Avenue Ste Anne, he saw Pierre walking down the street leading a bony nag beside him. Emile paid off the cab and hailed him.

'Is that really the best you could find?' he demanded, looking askance at the tired wreck of a horse.

'I could find nothing else, sir,' Pierre replied, 'and this one cost a pretty penny.'

'Ah well,' Emile shrugged, 'he'll have to do. Take him round to the yard and give him a feed before you hitch him up. I'll go and find Marie-Jeanne.'

Pierre disappeared into the side lane and Emile turned towards the front door. It was only then that he saw that it was already open, and not only open, but hanging off its hinges. He ran up the steps and paused for a moment on the threshold. The house was silent. Emile drew a deep breath and went into the hallway.

'Hello?' he called. 'Marie-Jeanne? Where are you?' The silence of emptiness settled back round him and he called again. 'Marie-Jeanne? Hélène? Are you there?' Receiving no reply he strode along the kitchen passage to find Arlette or Berthe, but the kitchen was empty, the scullery door standing wide to the stable yard beyond. Emile went outside. Pierre was giving the hungry horse a nosebag of oats. He looked up as his master came out, his face pale.

'There's no one here,' Emile said. 'Someone has broken down the front door, and the house is empty.'

'No one?' Pierre left the horse to his feed and turned to the house. 'Where is Marie-Jeanne? And Berthe? They must have gone for help when the thieves broke in.' He tried to sound reassuring. 'That'll be it, you can be sure.'

'Well, they certainly aren't here,' Emile snapped. 'And nor is Hélène.'

With one accord the two men went back into the house. 'There's nothing amiss in the kitchen,' Emile said as he stood by the big wooden table and looked round. 'See? There's even some fresh bread!'

'Could they be upstairs, monsieur?' suggested Pierre, and walking past his master he went into the hall. When he saw the front door still hanging askew, he said, 'They must have been robbers. Marie-Jeanne will have hidden Miss Hélène upstairs.'

'Of course,' Emile said, ready to clutch at any such straw, and he took the stairs two at a time, calling Hélène's name, before coming to an abrupt halt at the top where Marie-Jeanne lay, her eyes still staring sightlessly at the ceiling.

'Oh, my God!' he breathed. 'Oh, my God!' He stepped past her body and shouted, 'Hélène! Hélène! Are you there, little one? It's me! It's Papa. You can come out now! You're safe now!'

Pierre had followed Emile upstairs and he, too, paused in shock at what he found at the top. Then stepping past Marie-Jeanne he walked slowly down the passage, looking into each room, terrified that he was going to discover a second body. Emile followed him and together they searched each room, calling to Hélène to come out of hiding, but as their voices died away and they listened for an answering cry, they heard nothing. When they had looked in every room but Rosalie's bedroom, Pierre stood aside, unwilling to enter his mistress's private boudoir. Emile strode past him into the room. At once he saw the screen lying on the floor and rushed over to the cabinet. Its door stood wide and it was empty.

He stared into the tiny space as if he might still find Hélène crouching, hidden behind the commode, before turning back to Pierre with bleak eyes.

'She's gone,' he said huskily. 'They've taken her. Whoever killed Marie-Jeanne has taken Hélène.'

Pierre, relieved that there had been no second body, said, 'They will ask for a ransom, monsieur. They will keep her hidden and ask for gold.'

'We must find her,' Emile said, and suddenly leaping into action he hurried back towards the stairs. Once more he paused at the top and looked down at Marie-Jeanne's body.

'What shall we do...?' Pierre gestured helplessly to her.

'Nothing now!' shouted Emile as he catapulted down the stairs. 'We can do nothing for her. She's dead. Hélène's alive. Come along, man, we must look for her.'

Pierre looked down at the lifeless form on the floor and, bending down, gently closed the staring eyes before making the sign of the cross and murmuring, 'Rest in peace, Marie-Jeanne. You died trying to save her. Rest in peace.'

'Come on, man!' Emile shouted again and Pierre left Marie-Jeanne lying alone and followed him downstairs.

'Sir, we shall need the horse when we find her,' Pierre ventured. 'We should hide him somewhere else in case they come back!'

'The cowards wouldn't dare...' began Emile, but he saw the sense of what Pierre was saying and went on, 'Take him round to Monsieur Thiery's house,' he said.

'But they have already left Paris, sir,' Pierre said.

'I know that, but you may be able to hide him in their stable. Yes, take him there and then come back and we'll search for Hélène.'

Pierre did as he was bid and within fifteen minutes he had put the horse safely into the neighbours' stable. While he was away, Emile looked into his own stables to see if the chaise had been touched by the thieves. It appeared that in their hurry to leave with their prize, they had not been into the coach house and the chaise stood as he'd left it that morning, with the valises strapped to the back.

Perhaps Hélène had run away, Emile thought. Perhaps she had escaped while brave Marie-Jeanne kept the thieves at bay. Maybe Marie-Jeanne had paid with her life so that

Hélène could make a break for it. And where were Berthe and Arlette? Had they run away or – a thought brought him up short – had they been in on the whole thing? They were new servants, only hired since the family had returned to Paris in February. They had little loyalty to the St Clairs. Their bodies were not here; were they part of the attack or had they simply run away?

When Pierre reappeared Emile said, 'Did you manage that all right?'

'Yes, sir,' replied Pierre. 'The yard gates were closed, but there was no padlock and chain.'

'We must go out and look round the streets, calling,' Emile said. 'Hélène may have run away when the thieves broke in. Marie-Jeanne at the top of the stairs may have given her the time to get away.'

Pierre didn't think so, remembering the upturned screen in Madame St Clair's boudoir, but he could think of no other suggestion and so the two of them set out, hunting the surrounding streets, knocking on the doors of friends and neighbours in case Hélène had taken refuge with them, but several of the houses were already closed up, their owners having fled the violence of the city, and no one in those that were still occupied had seen or heard anything.

'They must have heard the shot that killed Marie-Jeanne,' Emile said in despair. 'Surely somebody heard the shot and looked out of their window. Somebody must have seen something!' But if they had, nobody admitted it.

They continued from house to house, and the only glimmer of hope they had was when a maid in the last house on the street said she had seen Arlette.

'I knowed her from when we was kids. Sometimes we spend our day off together,' explained the girl. 'She ran past here this morning, with her face buried in a handkerchief. I thought she was crying and I was going to call out to her, but she was gone that quick.'

'Are you certain it was Arlette, our maid Arlette?' demanded Emile.

'Oh yes, sir, quite certain,' replied the maid. 'It was me what told her Madame St Clair was looking for a maid.'

'Was there anyone with her?' asked Emile, the faint light of hope in his eyes. 'When you saw her?'

'Oh no, sir. She was by herself. Probably going home to her ma's. In a right state, she was.'

'What is your name, girl?' Emile asked.

'Mireille,' replied the girl.

'Well, Mireille, can you tell us where Arlette lives?'

The girl nodded. 'Yes, monsieur, in the sixth arrondissement.'

Emile thought of the narrow streets in that area. How would he ever find Arlette's home in that myriad of streets, even if she gave him a street name and number?

'Will you take us there?' Emile demanded.

'What, sir, now?'

'Yes, girl, now!'

'I'm sorry, sir, but I can't leave the house. Madame Jourdain would turn me off without a character.'

Emile could feel his frustration rising. 'Is Madame Jourdain at home?' he asked, his voice tightly controlled.

'I can enquire, sir,' came the reply. 'Who shall I say is calling?'

Stupid girl! he thought, but the niceties had to be observed, and even though Mireille knew perfectly well who he was, she waited for him to produce his card to send up to Madame, who was probably, even now, watching them from the window.

'Please will you give my compliments to Madame Jourdain and say I am sorry to disturb her so early, but I need to see her on important business.'

'Yes, sir,' agreed the maid, accepting his card. 'Would you care to wait in the hall?'

Exasperated, Emile stepped inside and said, 'Please hurry, this could be a matter of life and death.'

Mireille's eyes widened with the drama of the situation and disappeared upstairs to the drawing room. While they were waiting to be shown up, Emile turned to Pierre.

'Go back to the streets and keep asking. Who knows, someone could have seen her… or the men who broke into the house. Maybe someone saw them and knows which direction they took; knows if they had a child with them. I will visit Arlette and hope she can tell me more.'

'Yes, monsieur,' answered Pierre and let himself out of the front door.

Moments later Mireille returned to usher Emile upstairs. 'Where's the other man?' she asked, looking round anxiously.

'Don't worry about him,' replied Emile, 'he's gone.'

He followed the maid up into Madame Jourdain's drawing room. Madame Jourdain rose to greet him, but did not extend her hand. She was a tall, rather scrawny woman with a beaky nose, thin lips and hard, calculating eyes. She looked at Emile with some disdain. She knew the name of St Clair, but she had never met Emile or his wife and calling in this fashion was not at all expected.

'I am sorry to disturb you, madame,' Emile said and gave her a brief and edited version of what had happened. He made no mention of the murder of Marie-Jeanne. 'I don't want to alarm you, madame, but I need to speak to my maid, Arlette, who ran away from the attack. My daughter is missing and

I need to ask Arlette what happened. Your maid Mireille knows where she lives and I wondered if you could spare her for half an hour to take me there.'

'You think this Arlette will know something?' asked Madame Jourdain.

'Until I speak to her I cannot tell, madame,' replied Emile evenly, 'but I must try and find her. If my daughter ran away, we need to find her again. I was taking her to the safety of the country this very morning.'

'And she did not want to go. Perhaps that is why she ran away.'

Emile held onto the rags of his temper. 'She was looking forward to going. Madame, I think she may have been abducted, but until I speak to Arlette I shall know nothing for sure.'

Eventually Madame Jourdain gave a small shrug. 'You say Mireille knows where this girl lives. She may take you now, but I need her back before my husband comes home for his midday meal.' She rang a small bell on the table beside her, and the alacrity with which it was answered suggested that Mireille had been standing outside the door. Madame gave her instructions and moments later the maid had her shawl around her shoulders and they were back in the street. She led Emile to the end of the road and then took a small alleyway to the left, leading away from the prosperous area where he and the Jourdains lived, into the more run-down parts of the neighbourhood. Following her through the countless twisting lanes and narrow streets, Emile wondered if he would even find his way back into a civilised part of the city. At last she turned in through an archway and led him across a small yard hemmed in by dilapidated buildings and up a flight of stone steps. At a turn in the stairs were two doors, and then the steps disappeared into the gloom of the floor above. Mireille paused outside these before knocking on one of them.

'In here,' she said and banged on the door with her knuckles. The door didn't open but a reedy voice called out from within, 'Who's there?'

'It's me, Mireille,' answered the maid. 'There's someone to see Arlette.'

'She don't want to see no one,' said the voice.

'It is important—' began Mireille but Emile interrupted her.

'It is I, Emile St Clair,' he spoke the name imperiously, 'and I need to speak with Arlette… now. Please open this door at once.'

The door remained shut, but they could hear voices from inside the apartment. Emile was just about to shout through the door to them again when they heard the sound of a bolt being drawn back, then the turn of a key in the lock and slowly the door was inched open. An old woman's face, creased with wrinkles and the sunken cheeks of the toothless, appeared in the gap and she looked at both Mireille and Emile before she opened the door any further.

'Please, madame,' Emile said, his voice tight, 'I must speak with Arlette.'

Apparently having assured herself that the two visitors on her doorstep posed no threat to her or her daughter, the woman opened the door wide enough to let them in and then closed it quickly behind them, immediately sliding the bolt across to secure it.

Emile found himself in a dark space, too small to be called a hall. Two doors led off it, one of them closed. The old woman led them through the other into a tiny living room, crammed with an assortment of furniture. Grey daylight hardly penetrated the grubby windows and at first Emile didn't see Arlette, sitting curled into an armchair. When she saw it really was him she tried to get up, but he waved her back to her seat. Even in the dull light of the room he could see her face was very swollen, a bruise covering her left cheek and running upward to join with another around her eye. Her nose was swollen and red against the pallor of her face.

'Arlette,' Emile said, trying to moderate his voice to sympathy, 'I've come to talk to you about what happened this morning while I was out. I know some thieves broke into my house and I can see they hurt you very badly, but I need you to tell me exactly what happened before you ran away.'

Arlette looked up at him and tears began to flood down her cheeks.

'Come now, Arlette,' he said and handed her his handkerchief. 'I'm not angry with you for running away, I don't blame you, but I need to know what happened.'

Arlette dabbed at her eyes with the hankie and then held it out to him, but he waved it aside. 'Just tell me in your own words,' he said.

'I was in the dining room, clearing the table,' she began, 'and then there was this banging on the door. Not a knock, you know, real banging.' Emile nodded to show he understood.

'Mistress Marie-Jeanne was on the stairs, and she called down to me not to open the front door.'

'But you did?'

'No, monsieur, they broke it down, the men what come in. There was three of them, and one had a gun and the others some sort of clubs. The man with the gun hit me across the face and knocked me down. I screamed and he told me to shut up. Then one of the others yelled at me to get up and get out. And that's what I did, monsieur. I was out that door like light and I ran, all the way here. Ma barred the door in case they come looking for me.'

'You saw Marie-Jeanne on the stairs,' Emile said, 'was Miss Hélène with her? Or somewhere else in the house?'

'She was upstairs too,' replied the girl, warming to her story. 'She was looking down through the banisters.' She dabbed her cheeks again and added, 'I didn't stay to see what happened next, I can tell you. I legged it here and if you don't mind, monsieur, I ain't coming back. Those men might know who I am and that I work for you. They don't like people who work for people like you, so I ain't coming back no more.'

Emile ignored this and asked, 'You didn't see what happened to Berthe?'

'Berthe? No, monsieur, she was in the kitchen when they broke down the door. I didn't see her, but if she had any sense she'd've been out the back fast as you like. Them men wasn't joking.'

'So you haven't see Berthe at all?'

'No, I told you, I didn't hang around to see what happened.'

'And you didn't see anyone else.'

'Didn't stop to look. There was some kids in the street, I suppose, like usual.'

'Now I want you to think carefully, Arlette,' Emile said. 'What did these men look like? Was there anything special about them?'

'Big,' replied Arlette promptly. 'Two of them was big. They all had beards and whiskers, and the one with the gun had black hair on his hands. He weren't so big, but he had the gun and he was the boss.'

'And what were they wearing?'

Arlette shrugged. 'Just clothes,' she said, 'workmen's clothes...' She thought for a moment and then added, 'and heavy boots, workmen's boots.'

Emile could see he wasn't going to get anything else from Arlette, and suspected anything else she told him would be embroidery. All he had learned was what he had most feared: that Hélène had been upstairs when the men broke in. She'd had no opportunity to escape from the intruders and when Marie-Jeanne had been shot she'd had no one to protect her. He decided not to tell the girl that Marie-Jeanne was dead and Hélène was missing. He wanted no sensational version of events out on the streets, and he could see Arlette would relish the attention such a story would bring.

He put his hand into his pocket and pulled out two silver coins. 'Thank you for your help, Arlette,' he said as he handed them to her. 'We shan't be expecting you to come back, but I hope you get better very quickly.'

Moments later he and Mireille were back in the twisting lanes, heading back to Madame Jourdain. When they reached the house Emile extracted two more coins and slipped them into Mireille's hand. 'If you hear anything, anything at all that might help me find my daughter,' he said, 'there'll be plenty more where that came from. But please, do not speak of what you've heard this morning.'

The maid gave her promise and thanked him for the money before scurrying back inside to face Madame Jourdain, twenty minutes beyond her time.

Emile turned back towards his home with heavy tread and a heavier heart. Hélène had been kidnapped and carried off by some revolutionary ruffians, and it was all his fault. If he had left Paris when Rosalie first asked him to, Hélène would be safely at St Etienne. If only they had left earlier today; if only he hadn't visited the office first, they'd have been away. Hélène would be safe and Marie-Jeanne would still be alive. If only, if only...and it was all his fault.

Chapter 12

Pierre was waiting for Emile as he approached the house and each recognised his own hopelessness in the face of the other. There was no good news.

'Arlette was knocked down by one of the thieves, and told to get out,' reported Emile. 'So, she ran. She doesn't know that Marie-Jeanne is dead, and she knows nothing of Berthe. She said the men just broke down the door and burst in. They were big and had beards; they wore workmen's clothes and boots. She couldn't give a better description and that could fit half the population of Paris. What about you?'

Pierre shook his head. 'Nothing, sir. No one saw or heard anything.'

Emile's shoulders slumped. He had not expected anything, but even so he was disheartened. 'Come on,' he said. 'Let's go indoors and decide what to do next.'

They entered the house through the broken front door but in the hall Emile stopped short. He looked about him and knew that somebody else had been in the house. The dining room door was open and he saw at once that the silver candlesticks that normally graced the dining table had gone.

The drawers of the big mahogany sideboard were pulled out, their contents dumped on the floor, but no silver cutlery was to be seen except for one silver fork, lying forgotten on the hall floor.

'Looks as if they've been back,' Emile said bitterly. 'Isn't stealing my daughter enough?'

'Probably not the same thieves, sir,' replied Pierre. 'Just someone noticing the open front door, you know, and taking the opportunity.'

Pierre's probably right, thought Emile with a sigh as he made a quick tour of the downstairs to make sure no one was still in the house. It was opportunist theft. As he returned from the drawing room he was surprised to find Pierre had gone upstairs to the first floor and was standing on the landing.

'I don't think they came up here, monsieur,' he called down. 'And I think they left in a hurry.'

'And what makes you think so?' demanded Emile, surprised into anger. How dare Pierre go up to the family's private landing without permission?

'Marie-Jeanne is still lying here,' Pierre replied. 'If they came up here, I think they found more than they bargained for. They wouldn't want to be accused of her murder. I reckon they just grabbed what they'd found downstairs and got out fast.'

'Perhaps you're right, Pierre,' Emile said, his sudden anger fading. The testimony of the forgotten fork bore this out. 'But I don't care what they took. I can only think of Hélène.'

'Monsieur,' Pierre said softly, 'we also have to think of Marie-Jeanne. She cannot be left to lie here in this empty house. We must give her the proper rights.' When Emile said nothing, Pierre went on, 'She died trying to save your daughter, sir.'

Pierre had never spoken to his master in that quiet, authoritative tone before and Emile gave him a sharp look before acknowledging, with a slight nod, that he was right. He drew a deep breath and took charge again.

'We'd better try and fix the door so that no one else breaks in,' he said, 'then you must go to the priest and arrange to have Marie-Jeanne's body taken to the church. I will, of course, pay the necessary expenses. Have masses said for her soul and see that she is decently buried.'

'And you?'

Emile accepted the question as from an equal. Master and man, they were in this together now.

'I? I shall take the horse, if he's still in Thiery's stable, and go to find Georges. He'll want to help. He may even be able to bring some of his men, which would let us widen our search and maybe flush out the kidnappers.'

'His men were bivouacked in the Luxembourg Gardens,' Pierre said, 'but they may have moved now. Most of the regulars have been sent out to Versailles.'

'Well, I shall go and see, but he was certainly in the city last night, because he came here. Now, Pierre, the door!'

The two men managed to lift the front door and push it back into the frame. It was still lopsided, sagging on its hinges, but it was no longer hanging open and from the outside it was not immediately apparent that it was not secure.

'From now we'll use the back entrance,' Emile said, 'so we don't have to move that door again.'

Before he left to find Georges, Emile made a quick tour of upstairs, but there was no sign that anyone else had been up there. Pierre followed him, meaning to straighten poor Marie-Jeanne's body to a more respectful position, but rigor mortis had begun to set in and there was little he could do.

'When I find my son, we'll come back here,' Emile said. 'Wait for me here when you've made the arrangements for Marie-Jeanne.' With that both men left the house by the kitchen door and checking that they each had a key, Emile padlocked the courtyard gate.

Emile was relieved to find their horse still in his neighbour's stable. He found saddle and bridle hanging on pegs in the tack room and several moments later he emerged into the street, pulling the yard gate closed behind him.

He rode through the city, picking his way through the streets which despite the confusion in the city were busy with people going about their daily business. An ordinary day for the ordinary people. When he reached the Luxembourg Gardens his heart fell. They, too, were busy enough, but there were no troops bivouacked there, just the detritus left from the hasty evacuation of the camp being picked over by the usual scavengers. Emile dismounted and looked about him. A grey-haired old crone was sitting on the ground, her back to a tree, smoking a clay pipe. Held firmly between her knees she had a black canvas bag in which, Emile supposed, she had secreted the items she had scavenged. She watched him through rheumy eyes as he stared bleakly at the remains of the camp.

'You looking for the soldiers?' she croaked. 'They've gone, and good riddance!' She gave a cackle, but Emile ignored her. He could see they'd gone and it was clear they weren't coming back. They must have been ordered out to Versailles where the government had set up after it had beaten a hasty retreat from its offices in the Hôtel de Ville.

Emile remounted his horse and headed back to the Avenue Ste Anne. It would be far harder to find Georges among the numerous troops now mustering at Versailles. He felt he should go at once, but it was already late afternoon and it would be dangerous to travel alone in the gathering twilight, a lone man on a horse a tempting target for a wayside robber. And, he thought, even if he set off straight away, it would be well after dark before he arrived. He'd have little hope of finding Georges before morning and he'd have nowhere to lay his head in the meantime. As he retraced his way home he suddenly thought of Rosalie. Rosalie! He must send a message to Rosalie. She would have been expecting Marie-Jeanne and Hélène in St Etienne and would be worried sick at their non-arrival. When he got home, he'd send Pierre with a note, explaining what had happened and what he was trying to do. It would make grim reading but he knew she had to know what had happened. He considered going himself, but realised that first he must ride to Versailles, find Georges and enlist his help. Pierre must go to St Etienne.

Pierre was in the stable yard when Emile got back. He had visited the priest and Marie-Jeanne's body had been fetched and carried to the church.

'He will hold the funeral tomorrow,' Pierre said. 'She will not go to a pauper's grave.'

Emile told Pierre of his fruitless search for Georges. 'I'll ride out to Versailles tomorrow,' he said. 'You must go to St Etienne and let Madame know what has happened. I will give you a letter for her.'

'You want me to go tonight, sir?' Pierre sounded less than enthusiastic.

'If there is a train; if not, first thing in the morning. Whatever happens, you must tell her that on no account is she to return to Paris. She's to remain in St Etienne in safety with the other children.'

Reluctantly Pierre set off for the station carrying the hastily written note with which Emile had entrusted him, but there were no more trains tonight and before long he was back at the house and very relieved to be so.

'No trains until tomorrow,' he said.

Though he wouldn't have admitted it, Emile was relieved to see him. As dusk had crept into the city, darkening the evening sky and filling the empty house with shifting shadows, Emile listened to his home's nocturnal creakings, magnified by the deep silence around him, and he found he was loath to spend the night alone in the insecure house. He went into all the rooms, lighting lamps and candles in his effort to dispel the darkness in the house and the darkness in his mind. Suppose the vagabonds came back! He would be powerless against them if they came in numbers. He went back into the dining room where the contents of the sideboard lay strewn across the floor. Suppose they came back for more!

Emile poured himself a cognac for courage and having downed it in one swallow, poured himself a second and sat down at the table. He found he was hungry and realised he'd had nothing to eat all day, his breakfast coffee being all that he'd taken.

He was in the kitchen looking into the pantry to see what he could find when Pierre called to him to unlock the door, and slipped back into the house. He was carrying the food basket Berthe had packed and loaded into the chaise that morning.

'I thought you might be hungry, sir,' he said and placed the basket on the table.

The two men sat at the kitchen table where Pierre had unpacked the food Berthe had prepared for the journey, and as they ate each retreated into his own thoughts. Emile was wondering how he was going to find Georges the next morning in the multitudes at Versailles, and what they might be able to do when he did. He was at a loss to know what to do for the best. He must rely on Georges; Georges would know what to do.

Pierre was thinking of his errand to St Etienne. He wasn't looking forward to delivering the letter with the sad news it contained, and he knew he couldn't carry out his master's instruction, to forbid Madame St Clair to return to Paris. He thought of Marie-Jeanne, lying in the church awaiting her funeral mass in the morning. He had told the priest that he would be there. Should he take the train first thing as instructed, or wait until the service was over? There would be no one at the church unless he went. Would it make that much difference if he took a later train? Would Monsieur St Clair even realise he had?

Neither of them slept very well that night, Emile alone in his bedroom without the comfort of knowing Rosalie was in her boudoir next door, and Pierre in his loft above the stable. They slept fitfully, jerking awake at each night-time noise in the street, and though the house itself remained undisturbed, they were both glad when they saw daylight fingering the ceiling and they could give up on sleep and face the new day; Pierre to St Etienne and Emile to Versailles.

When Emile reached the Porte de Versailles, he was relieved to see that it was open to travellers, but they were being stopped by men of the National Guard and asked their business. Seeing one lone traveller being turned back, Emile paused out of sight, waiting, trying to think of an acceptable reason for leaving the city. Looking for a son with the government troops was not the answer to give a National Guardsman. As he watched and waited, a small family group appeared and were stopped by one of the two guards on duty. There appeared to be some sort of altercation taking place, with the husband waving his fists in the air and shouting. The second guardsman walked over to assist his comrade and Emile saw his chance. The road ahead was clear. He rode slowly towards the gate, as if prepared to stop when he reached it. The second guard looked up as he heard Emile approach and called out to him to halt. Emile raised his hand as if in acknowledgement, but did not stop, and as he reached the waiting guard, he dug his heels into the horse's flanks and crouching low over its neck, he almost rode the man down as he galloped out through the gate and along the road beyond. The guard leapt for safety and raised his rifle, but the bullets flew wide of the diminishing target as Emile galloped on into the morning mist. Only when he was well out of sight did he slow his exhausted nag to a walk. He was out, on his way to Versailles to find Georges, but he'd had a close shave. He dismounted and led the horse to a wayside trough to drink before walking him slowly along the road. There were few other travellers on the road, but twice he was stopped by outposts of government troops and questioned as to where he was going and why. Now at least he was able to give a truthful answer and say he had urgent messages for Lieutenant Georges St Clair with General Vinoy's regulars. It was afternoon by the time Emile finally arrived at Versailles and found the army camped in companies with men coming and going, bugles blown, shouted orders and the general hubbub of hundreds of men living in the widespread confusion which had dogged the army throughout the war.

Emile dismounted and leading his horse, made his way through the lines asking for Georges's battalion. Several men looked askance at him, a civilian walking amongst them, and he was challenged on several occasions, but at last he found Georges's unit and spoke to one of the officers, a captain with a haughty stare and an abrupt manner of speech.

'Lieutenant St Clair?' answered the man. 'He's not here. He's been seconded to General Vinoy for special duties.'

'Then where shall I find him?' asked Emile.

'You won't,' replied the captain tersely. 'I just told you, he's been seconded to General Vinoy for special duties and we have no idea where he is.' It was clear from his tone that the captain resented the fact that General Vinoy had sent for a more junior officer. 'What do you want with him, anyway?'

'Purely a family matter,' responded Emile. 'He's my son and I need to speak to him.'

'Well, he's not here, and he has no time for family matters!' With that, the captain turned away, his back telling Emile that he should not be there.

As Emile watched him go, a corporal edged up to him and said, 'Was you lookin' for Lieutenant St Clair, monsieur?'

'Yes,' replied Emile, 'I was. Do you know where he is?'

'No, monsieur, but if you wish I will pass on a message when he comes back to us.'

Emile was about to say that it would be too late when he thought better of it. Any contact with Georges would be helpful.

'Thank you, Corporal,' Emile said. 'I'd be very grateful if you'd tell him his father is looking for him as there is a family crisis.'

'I'll tell him, monsieur, just as soon as I see him, but as

Captain Ducros said, we don't know when he'll be back here with us.'

Emile thanked him again and led the horse back to the road. He went in search of a tavern where he could get some food and a drink and decide what he was going to do next. Having come this far he was determined to find Georges if he possibly could.

Pierre had made his decision. He would go to the funeral first and catch the later train. When he finally left the church and went to the station he was only just in time. He had Emile's letter stowed safely in the inner pocket of his jacket and as he settled himself into a corner seat of the carriage, he felt himself relax for the first time for days. Delivering the letter was going to bring horrific news to Madame St Clair and Pierre thought Monsieur St Clair spineless not to have taken the news to his wife himself. What good would it be to find Georges at Versailles? What could his son do that he could not? Looking for Hélène was like looking for a needle in a haystack. If the girl was still alive, which was a question in itself, she could be absolutely anywhere in Paris, hidden away in a cellar or an attic, and kept there for whatever reasons her captors chose. Pierre assumed it must be for ransom, in which case she would surely be kept alive and well, but if this were the case where were the demands for money?

Pierre had to change trains, but when the train finally steamed into the station at St Etienne, he was surprised to find Madame St Clair standing on the platform as if she had come to meet him.

'Madame!' he called and she waved a hand and hurried across to speak to him.

'What news?' she cried. 'What is happening? I had a letter from my husband to say to expect Hélène and Marie-Jeanne, but they haven't arrived. Has Hélène had a relapse? Has she taken a turn for the worse? I'm on my way to Paris now!'

'Madame,' said Pierre, his voice the level voice of a trusted servant, 'I have a letter for you from Monsieur. It will explain everything, but he did ask me to beg you not to return to Paris. He wishes you to remain here in St Etienne with the other children until he comes to you and—'

'A letter?' interrupted Rosalie, holding out her hand. 'Give it to me at once!'

Pierre hesitated and said, 'Perhaps it would be better, madame, if you read the letter at home.'

'Don't be ridiculous, Pierre,' Rosalie cried. 'Give it to me at once.'

Pierre reached into his pocket and pulling out the envelope, handed it over.

Chapter 13

Hélène drifted back to consciousness and for a moment she was completely disorientated. Where was she? She was very cold and her head ached. When she opened her eyes the world spun round her, and she closed them again. When it ceased revolving, she cautiously opened them again, but could see almost nothing. The place she was in was filled with thick grey light which obscured more than it revealed. For a moment she lay still, remembering nothing, but then the events of earlier in the day came creeping back into her mind. They had been going to go and see Maman in St Etienne. Papa had gone out, but he said he'd be back soon. She remembered going upstairs with Marie-Jeanne to make sure nothing they might need had been forgotten. Marie-Jeanne! A picture of her as Hélène had last seen her filled her mind and she gave a scream. The sound echoed round her and she sat up with a start. The sudden movement made her head spin again and she thought she was going to be sick. She clutched her head in her hands, fighting against the bile that rose in her throat as tears began to stream down her cheeks. Marie-Jeanne was dead, shot by a man with a gun.

She, Hélène, had run to hide leaving Marie-Jeanne to be shot by the man with the gun.

And then the man had come to find *her*. Memory came flooding back. He had found her hiding in the cabinet in her mother's boudoir and pulled her out. She recalled biting his hand, sinking her teeth into his flesh, biting him as hard as she could. The man had let go and she had run, only to find Marie-Jeanne lying dead on the stairs. The man had caught her again and held her by her hair, but she had hit him and hit him until he had hit her on the head and she remembered no more.

Now she was awake again, and shut in somewhere. But where? And why? What was he going to do with her? Was he going to kill her like he'd killed Marie-Jeanne? Hélène shivered with cold and fear. And then she remembered Jeannot. What had he been doing there? Had he brought the men to the house? She remembered looking down through the banisters and seeing him staring up at her, his expression one of horror, before she'd fled along the landing to her mother's boudoir. Surely Jeannot wasn't one of the thieves.

Carefully, Hélène eased herself upright, rubbing her arms to warm them up. She found a hankie in the pocket of her dress and blew her nose. That hurt. She realised that her whole face was aching, and running her fingertips across her cheeks she felt the swelling and the tenderness.

After a while she tried standing up. Her legs felt wobbly, as they had after her stay in bed, but she managed to get to her feet. Her eyes had become accustomed to the twilight of her prison and carefully she edged her way round the room. There was a pile of dirty straw in one corner, but no furniture, simply four walls and a barred window high up on one wall. It was through this that a faint grey light filtered. She couldn't reach the window to look out and there was nothing to stand on, so she had no idea what was outside. She remembered the dismal streets through which she followed Jeannot when they had gone to find Paul and the Monkey, streets lined with tall, dark tenement houses, so close to each other that they shut out the sunlight, leaving the street in gloomy shade even at midday. Was she in one of those houses?

She thought of the man with the gun again and shivered at the memory. He must have locked her in here. He would come back and find her and then what would happen? She was cold and she was alone and she needed the toilet. Misery flooded through her and she sat back down on the cold floor and wept. She wept for her mother, for Marie-Jeanne and for herself, but eventually she had no more tears and curled in a ball for warmth as an exhausted sleep overtook her.

She was woken by the scraping of a key in the door. She scrambled to her feet and backed away into a corner, terrified at who might be coming into her prison.

The door opened a fraction and a woman's voice said, 'I'm bringing you something to eat. Stand under the window where I can see you. Any funny business and I'll take the food away again and let you starve. All the same to me!'

Cautiously, Hélène moved to stand under the window. The door opened wider and a woman edged her way into the room. She was holding a flagon of water and a loaf of bread. As she stepped into the faint light cast by the window, Hélène could see that she was not old, though her face was lined and her hair, drawn back off her face, was dirty and tangled. A shapeless dress hung from her shoulders, a drab of a woman.

'Please, madame, I need to go to the toilet,' Hélène whispered. Although she was hungry and thirsty, it was at that moment her most pressing need. The woman gave a sharp laugh.

'Do you now? Well, you'll just have to squat in a corner like the rest of us.' She dumped the bread and water onto the floor and moved back to the door. 'I'll bring you a blanket,' she said, adding with a grin, 'Don't want to kill the goose before we've got the egg, now, do we?' And with this strange remark she backed out of the room. The door closed behind her and Hélène heard the key turn in the lock with a loud click.

Goose? What goose? What was the woman talking about? But Hélène couldn't think about that now, she had a more pressing need. She crept back into the furthest corner of the cellar, for that indeed was what it was, and despite the fact that there was no one there to see, she had tears of embarrassment in her eyes as she hoisted her skirt and crouched down to relieve herself.

She returned to the water and the bread and found she was suddenly very hungry. She pulled the loaf apart and though it was stale and dry, she stuffed the pieces into her mouth and washed them down with the water.

When the woman reappeared with the promised blanket, she simply tossed it in through the door without a word. Hélène grabbed it and wrapped it round herself, grateful for the minimal warmth it gave her.

She wondered what her father was doing. He must have come back from wherever it was he went this morning. He would have found Marie-Jeanne and would surely now be out looking for *her*. Surely Papa would find her. He would expect her to be brave. He would expect her to know that he was coming to find her, and that she must be brave until he did.

'I am Hélène Rosalie St Clair,' she announced to the room. 'And I am not afraid.' This last was certainly not true, but simply saying it gave her a modicum of courage. She said it again, several times. 'I am Hélène Rosalie St Clair. And I am not afraid.'

She thought again about Jeannot. Was he one of them? Perhaps he would come and see her and she could ask him what was going to happen to her. She hoped he would; she wanted to see him, a face she knew, an old friend.

He did not come. No one came. No one came again before the room darkened completely with the fading of the day. Wrapped in her blanket, Hélène curled up on the stinking straw, her only refuge from the cold stone floor, and finally drifted off to sleep.

When she woke again, it was early morning. A single shaft of sunlight found its way through the dirty window and for the first time Hélène could see the whole of her prison. It was a depressing sight, grey stone walls, dirty stone floor, completely bare. She stood up and clutching the blanket round her, went over to the window. Standing on tiptoe she could just reach the sill. Gripping the rough stone, she managed to grasp the bottom bar to haul herself up for a moment, her eyes above the level of the sill long enough to see that she was looking out at street level. There were feet walking past and she could hear familiar street sounds, voices shouting, the rumble of wheels, the clatter of a horse's hooves. The world was out there, but she was locked in here. Unable to hold on for any length of time she dropped back down to the floor. She stood in the shaft of sunshine, lifting her face to its feeble warmth, but it wasn't long before the sunbeam had moved on, leaving her once more in the gloom of dusty daylight.

At that moment she heard the sound of the key in the door again and then the woman's voice. 'Stand by the window. No funny business!'

Hélène did as she was told and the woman came into the room with more bread and water. Keeping a wary eye on Hélène, as if she feared she might attack her, she bent down and retrieved the empty flagon from the night before.

'Why am I here?' Hélène asked. 'I want to go home.' She had tried to sound brave but her voice trembled on the word 'home', and the woman laughed.

'That'll depend on your father,' she said. 'Whether he coughs up.' She gave another laugh and added, 'One way or another you won't be stopping here very long.' She closed the door with a bang and Hélène was left alone with the meagre ration of food. She ate the bread, but only sipped at the water, remembering from when she had been confined to the attic room after her jaunt with Jeannot that she had been thirsty again before she was hungry.

She thought of her mother and the tears ran down her cheeks. How she wanted Maman. She thought of her father and wondered if he was looking for her. Surely he would find her soon. Resolutely closing her mind, she did not allow herself to think of Marie-Jeanne.

Sometime later, she had no idea how long, she heard the scrape of the key and the door swung open. This time it was not the woman who came into the cellar, and Hélène shrank back in terror as she saw it was the man with the gun. He wasn't carrying a gun now, at least she couldn't see one, but that didn't make him any less frightening. She could hear her mantra in her head. 'I am Hélène Rosalie St Clair and I am not afraid.' But faced with the man who had murdered

Marie-Jeanne, the words would not come. No words would come. She simply stared at him, her terror obvious in her eyes, and he grinned at her.

'Well now,' he said. 'I expect you want to get back to your papa, don't you?'

Hélène nodded wordlessly.

'That's what I thought,' he said. 'So, we need you to write him a letter. You can do that for us, can't you?'

Hélène nodded again.

'That's a good girl,' said the man jovially. 'And in the meantime, you and me can have a bit of fun. I like playing with girls like you. All right?'

When Hélène nodded a third time he said, 'I'll be back to fetch you upstairs in a while, so that you can write to your papa. Then you won't have to stay in here no more. Nicer upstairs.'

The man left, shutting and locking the door behind him, and leaving Hélène wondering what she would have to put in the letter. Would they let her go when she'd written it?

It was not long before the man returned. Again Hélène shrank away, but this time he strode into the room and grasped her by the wrist. His grip was firm and he pulled her towards him.

'Now, missy, we'll go upstairs, and you'll be a good girl and write that letter.'

Hélène followed him meekly enough – anything to be out of that cold dank cellar. Still holding her firmly by the wrist he led her up a flight of steps and into a room that had a window out onto the street. There was a table and chair by the window and a rickety-looking couch along one wall. There was no floor covering except a filthy rag rug before a fireplace, where a fire smouldered sulkily beneath a cooking pot. A pail stood in a corner, and some crocks were stacked on a shelf above it.

The man pushed Hélène down into the chair and stood over her. On the table top was a scrap of paper and a pencil.

'Now then,' he said, 'you write what I tell you, understand?'

Hélène nodded and picking up the pencil, pulled the paper towards her.

'What's your name?' the man demanded suddenly.

'Hélène St Clair,' whispered Hélène.

The man stared at her for a moment and then said, 'Say that again.'

'Hélène St Clair.'

'Is it now?' The man looked thoughtful for a moment and then went on, 'Well, Hélène St Clair, write this. Dear Papa...'

Carefully, Hélène wrote as he dictated.

'I am quite safe for now and the people I am staying with will let me come home if you give them 100 gold Napoleons. If you do not give them the money in three days they will kill me.'

The man looked at what she had written and said, 'Now sign your name.'

Hélène did as she was told and the man picked up the paper and folded it.

'Now write his name on the outside,' he said. As she did so he opened the door and bellowed, 'Francine! Come here.'

In answer to his summons the drab woman appeared at the door. 'Get that boy in here,' he said.

Hélène heard her calling and moments later Jeannot crept into the room.

'You, boy, take this letter to her father.' He jerked his head at Hélène. 'Tell him no messing if he wants his daughter back.'

Jeannot took the note and as he did so Hélène caught his eye. She was about to speak but he gave her such a fierce scowl that the words died on her lips.

'I'll tell him, Gaston,' Jeannot said, and beat a hasty retreat.

When Jeannot had disappeared Francine came back, crossing the room to poke the fire into life.

'You,' Gaston growled at her, 'get out. And don't come back until I call you.'

'But, Gaston…' she began to whine.

'Out!' He raised his clenched fist and ducking the expected blow, Francine dropped the poker and ran from the room.

'That's better,' said Gaston with a smile as he shut the door behind her. 'Now we won't be disturbed.'

Chapter 14

Hélène felt bruised all over. She was back in the cellar now, cold and more frightened than ever. The man, Gaston, had asked her some questions and when she had answered them to the best of her ability, had suddenly sat down on the sagging sofa and pulled her towards him. He had put his hands around her neck, turning her head this way and that, pushing her chin up with his thumbs before running his hands down over her thin shoulders and across her chest. Hélène didn't like it and tried to pull away, but he held her in a vice-like grip with one hand on her throat, while he explored her body with the other, pulling at her clothing, prodding, poking and pressing so that she gave a cry of pain. This earned her a hard slap across her face, making her lip bleed, and a muttered, 'Shut up, bitch, or you'll get worse!'

Hélène tasted the blood in her mouth and reached up to touch her swollen lip and her stinging cheek, but he pulled her hand away and dragged her down onto the sofa beside him.

'Now you just be quiet,' he murmured, 'and we'll have a

bit of fun. Won't hurt if you don't fight it.' He grasped her hand firmly in one of his and placed it on his crotch, his other hand still at her throat, squeezing so that she could hardly breathe.

'Rub me,' he said, his voice hoarse with excitement. 'Rub me hard.' Hélène could feel an inexplicable bulge in his trousers and, frightened, snatched her hand away, but Gaston, keeping his grip on her throat, jostled her onto his knee. He thrust his hand between her legs, and grasping himself moved her up and down, up and down, up and down against him, his breath coming in heavy, rasping gasps until all of a sudden he gave a groan and shoved her away so that she fell to the floor.

It had all been too quick and Gaston was disappointed. He'd expected more. Well, he thought as he looked down at her sobbing on the floor, she'd know what was coming next time. He'd seen the fear in her eyes this time, and the thought of her terror when he brought her up to this room again was already stirring him to harden again. Still, he'd wait. The anticipation, the building excitement was all part of the thrill. She, knowing what he was going to do to her, would try to please, to ease the pain. Next time, he'd feel her hand on his naked skin, next time his hands would be on her naked skin, exploring and probing before he took her, not a thing to be hurried, a little more each time until her childish body was his entirely. He looked down at the shaking heap on the floor and grinned. He could wait.

Leaving her where she was, he flung open the door and bellowed, 'Francine! Where are you, slut?'

Francine appeared, her young-old face a mask of hatred. 'Well, satisfied?'

Gaston grinned at her. 'For now! Take her back downstairs.

I want to give her a chance to think about next time.'

Francine had grabbed Hélène by the arm and pulled her to her feet. 'Come on,' she snapped, grasping her hair and giving it a painful jerk. 'Down with you.'

When the door had thudded closed behind her, Hélène had curled up in a ball in the corner and wept. She didn't know what she'd been part of, she didn't know what the terrifying man had wanted of her, all she knew was he'd hurt her and he was going to hurt her again.

When her sobs finally died away, Hélène thought of the questions the Gaston-man had asked her. What was her name? She'd told him. Hélène Rosalie St Clair. Had she any sisters? Yes, two, Clarice and Louise. Had she any brothers? Yes, Georges and Marcel. She'd answered readily enough, though she had no clue as to why he wanted to know all this. She didn't notice the gleam of satisfaction in his eye when she mentioned her brothers. Did they fight in the war, these brothers of hers? Yes, they did. Georges had come home already, but no one knew where Marcel was. Her mother was afraid that he'd been killed at Sedan, but they were all hoping he was a prisoner somewhere.

It was only after answering all these questions that the Gaston-man had grabbed her and begun to hurt her. Had her answers been wrong? she wondered. She had told the truth and he'd almost killed her. If he asked the same questions next time, should she answer differently, or would the answers make no difference?

As the gloomy afternoon light faded into dusk, Hélène fell into a restless sleep, but it was so haunted by nightmares, conjured from the happenings of the past two days, that she awoke with a scream, shaking with fear, and fought with her exhaustion to remain awake, lest they invade her sleep again.

Upstairs, Jeannot had returned from the Avenue Ste Anne with the ransom note still in his possession. He hardly dared tell Gaston that he'd failed to deliver it.

'There was no one there,' he stammered. 'The house was shut up. I went round the back gates, but they was locked too.'

The least he expected now was a cuff round the ear, but surprisingly Gaston didn't seem angry. He simply took the note back and said, 'Come back again tomorrow, you can take it then.' Gaston was glad to have the letter back; he'd been regretting sending it so quickly. Now the family still had no news of Hélène's fate, he could keep her longer for himself.

Delighted to escape, Jeannot hurried away, leaving Francine glowering after him. He went to the ruined house, the cellar of which he, Paul and the Monkey called home.

'He's got her locked up,' he said to Paul, 'and it's my fault. I didn't know they was still in the house. Pierre told me they was going to the country and I thought they was gone.'

Paul shrugged. 'Not your fault if they changes their minds, is it?'

'And Marie-Jeanne,' Jeannot went on miserably. 'He shot her. She was kind to me, Marie-Jeanne was, when I lived there.'

'So, go an' tell them where she is,' Paul said.

Jeannot stared at him in horror. 'I can't do that, Gaston'd kill me!'

'Well, there you are then, there ain't nothing you can do. Just give them the letter and beat it.' He headed for the door. 'I'm going out to try my luck at Les Halles. Coming?'

'Might as well,' Jeannot sighed. He'd no money and a dip in someone's pocket might provide something. Together they went out and crossed the city to the crowded, bustling market where, if there were no easy pockets, at least there might be discarded food.

When they reached the market they worked as a pair. As always they kept to the street market rather than venturing inside, under the canopy of iron and glass which covered the main wholesale market. The pickings outside could be just as rich for a street urchin and escape from angry victims very much easier. In a well-rehearsed routine, the two boys eased their way through the throng that crowded the stalls. Stalls that offered everything from fruit and vegetables, baskets of apples, strings of onions, bundles of garlic, sacks of potatoes to wooden crates of live poultry, chickens on a pole, their necks wrung ready to be plucked, pails of fresh milk, baskets of eggs, crocks of butter, rounds of cheese and bunches of flowers. They wandered among the carts and waggons of the smaller traders whose wares were displayed on stands under striped awnings in the square outside the great church of St Eustache. Here the buyers were more mixed, housewives picking over the produce, discarding damaged goods, maids sent out on errands by their mistresses, gentlemen passing through to the Rue de Rivoli, to the Rue St Honoré. Numerous folk, all intent on doing business at the most competitive rates, jostling each other, being jostled from behind.

It wasn't long before Jeannot spotted a likely mark. The man, a gentleman dressed, was standing a little apart, scanning the crowd as if he were looking for someone, and as they watched from behind a loaded cart, he consulted his pocket watch. The boys exchanged glances and grinned before strolling out into the throng and moving slowly towards him. As they approached he took a step forward, his face breaking into a smile of welcome. Jeannot followed his gaze and saw a woman walking towards him. She was dressed as became a lady, but there was something about the way she walked that said otherwise. Jeannot nudged Paul and he ran, bumping into the woman just as she reached their mark and held out a powdered cheek to him. As the woman staggered, the man reached out one hand to steady her, the other making a grab at the boy now vanishing into the crush. The man's attention was completely diverted by the stumble of his lady friend and it was the work of a moment for Jeannot to remove the watch from its pocket and to slide away into the crowd, in the opposite direction from that taken by Paul. He moved swiftly without a backward glance, and completely disappeared before the mark had realised that his watch no longer nestled in his pocket.

Paul and Jeannot met up at their usual rendezvous ten minutes later and inspected their prize.

'That'll fetch a bit,' grinned Paul, as he held the watch up to the light. 'That's gold, that is. Even Renard should give us a decent price for this.'

'We ain't gonna give this to the Fox,' Jeannot said, taking it back from him. 'I got plans for this watch.'

'Oh, yeah?' Paul looked at him with narrowed eyes. 'And what about my cut?'

'We'll get something else,' Jeannot told him. 'Plenty more doves for the plucking. Everything else we take this afternoon is yours, right?'

'See how much we get,' muttered Paul ominously.

They returned to a different part of the market and continued their nefarious work. Jeannot had the watch safely in an inner pocket Tante Edith had sewn into the lining of his jacket. When he had seen the watch in the man's hand, the germ of an idea had entered his head. Could he use it to buy Hélène's freedom?

Paul watched him carefully, determined not to let him take off with their valuable prize, but mingling in the crowd who lingered for the end of the day bargains, the boys ended their afternoon as the proud possessors of two wallets and a lady's purse.

It was a fair reward for an afternoon's thieving and grudgingly Paul agreed to let Jeannot have the watch, if he, Paul, kept all the cash. Though the watch was clearly more valuable, Paul preferred the ready cash. Jeannot could try dealing with the Fox and good luck to him.

But Jeannot had no intention of selling the watch to Renard who would only give him a fraction of its value. He wanted it gold, sparkling and valuable as a bargaining chip.

'But you remember, mate,' said Paul. 'I get first dibs next time. Right?' He spat on his hand and Jeannot did the same before they clasped hands together to seal the bargain.

Jeannot was delighted with the deal. He planned to find Francine alone and offer her the watch in return for the key to Hélène's prison. Surely it would tempt her? He didn't think he could take the key by force. Francine, for all her slatternly look, was much bigger than Jeannot, her arms strengthened by hard work, her fingers long and strong. Tomorrow he would go and collect the note and then stay hidden outside in the street until he saw Gaston go out. That would be his chance; he would go inside and dangle the watch before Francine's greedy eyes and snatch Hélène away before Gaston got back. It wasn't a very good plan but it was all Jeannot could think of.

Next morning he returned to Gaston's place, and well before he reached the door, he could hear Gaston and Francine having one of their frequent and strident rows. He paused outside, listening.

'What the hell do you want with a little girl like that?' Francine was shrieking.

'What the hell do you think?'

'She's worth far more if you sell her as a virgin!'

'And who's to know she ain't?'

'Anyone what buys her from you. Won't take him long to find out, will it?'

'But by then it'll be too late, won't it?'

'She's worth money!' insisted Francine. 'You gonna miss out simply 'cos you can't keep it in your breeches? Sell her on or send her back. Either way someone will pay good money for her.'

'I got a score to settle with the St Clair family,' Gaston said, fingering the scar on his cheek, 'and she's part of it.'

'You're stupid, you are.' This was followed by the sound of a slap and a yell, 'Bastard, Gaston Durand!'

'Stupid, am I?'

'No. No, I didn't mean it. But why this kid?'

'Tender meat!'

'But what about me?' The question came out as more of a wail than a demand and Gaston gave a harsh laugh. 'What about you?' he said. 'You ain't tender meat!'

'Bastard! You're always doing this to me...'

'An' probably always will,' came the snap reply.

'No!' Francine's voice changed, harsh and strident. 'No,

you bugger, you won't! I've had enough!'

'Christ, Francine!' Gaston gave a sudden shout of alarm before there came a bang and a crash, a scream cut off, and another curse from Gaston. 'Stupid, stupid bitch!'

Jeannot shrank away from the steps and took cover in a nearby doorway. Moments later Gaston emerged from the door and strode off down the street. From where he stood, Jeannot could see a stream of blood pouring down his face. Whatever had happened inside, Francine had inflicted some damage on her man. Jeannot shuddered. He wouldn't give much for her chances when Gaston came home again.

He waited several minutes, but Gaston didn't come back and Francine didn't come out of the house. Stealthily he crossed the street and crept up to the open door. There was no sound from inside. Silently he stepped in and peered into the room. Francine lay sprawled on the floor, her head bleeding freely from a gash above her eye, but as still as death. Jeannot stood still, holding his breath. He could see the faint rise and fall of Francine's breast and knew that she was still alive. He tiptoed over to where she lay and looked down at her. Had Gaston done for her this time? A poker from the fireplace lay beside her and now that he was closer he could see a smudge of soot beside the wound. Gaston must have hit her with the poker... or maybe, Jeannot thought with a flash of insight as he remembered the blood on Gaston's face, she had hit him first and he had turned her weapon on herself. Whatever happened, Jeannot suddenly realised he was presented with an opportunity he could never have achieved for himself. Attached to the rope belt about Francine's waist was a large key. Surely it must be the one to the cellar where Jeannot knew Hélène was being held. He paused for a moment. Suppose Gaston came back and found him trying to rescue Hélène? Then the memory of Gaston saying how he was going to make money out of her one way or another spurred Jeannot into action. This was Hélène, his brave Hélène who'd gone to the Prussian parade and thrown apples at the German soldiers. She was a spunky kid; he couldn't simply step aside and leave her to Gaston's attentions.

Looking round the room he saw a short-bladed knife beside the water bowl. Snatching it up, Jeannot approached Francine and with a swift slice of the blade, cut through her belt, releasing the key into his hand. Slipping the knife into his pocket, he ran out of the door and down the stone steps that led to the cellar. He thrust the key into the keyhole and heard it scrape in the lock before he pushed the heavy door open and went into the room.

Hélène was crouching in the corner furthest from the door, her hands covering her face as she cowered away from whoever had come in. She'd already learned that whether it was the Gaston-man or the sour-faced woman, her fate was always the same.

Horrified at what he saw, Jeannot whispered, 'Hélène! It's me. Jeannot. I've come to get you out!'

Hélène gave a scream of fear and he shushed her quickly. 'Hélène,' he cried, 'come on! Gaston may come back at any moment. We gotta go… now!'

The urgency in his voice somehow got through to her and she opened her eyes. 'Jeannot?' she said. 'Is it really you?'

'Yes,' he said, his nerve beginning to fail. If they didn't get out of here before Gaston decided to come back to see if he'd killed Francine, he'd find them and kill them, instead.

'Come on, Hélène,' he said, crossing the room and holding out his hand. 'Get up! We gotta get away. Now!'

Hélène took his extended hand and shakily got to her feet. Her legs were still wobbly from her last encounter with Gaston, but she managed to stagger across the room and follow Jeannot up the stone stairs.

When they reached the room at the top she saw Francine, lying on the floor, the blood pooled about her head. At once the memory of Marie-Jeanne lying still and staring-eyed at the top of her stairs flooded her mind and she gave a cry.

Jeannot gave her hand a tug. 'She's all right, Hélène,' he said. 'She ain't dead, but we will be if we don't get away from here.' He pulled hard at her hand and after what seemed to him an age but was really only a few seconds, she turned back to him and they both scurried out of the door and into the street.

'Where are we going?' she cried as he dragged her along the muddy cobbles.

'My place,' he answered. 'Gaston don't know where it is. Then we'll find somewhere till we tell your pa.'

They reached the corner of the next street. It was as narrow as the last; gloomy, as the tall buildings crowding in on either side restricted the daylight. Its uneven cobbles were slippery with filth and a viscous stream of excrement slid down a gutter in the middle. As they rounded the corner Jeannot saw three men hurrying along the street towards them and as he realised who they were, he heard Gaston's roar of rage. Afraid he'd killed Francine, Gaston had gone to fetch Auguste and Jules to help him dispose of her corpse. Now he was confronted with the urchin Jeannot, whom he'd used to run errands, leading the captive girl away. He gave another roar and charged along the street towards them, his feet slipping and sliding on the cobbles.

Jeannot didn't hesitate; he turned and fled back the way they had come, dragging Hélène behind him. Terror gave wings to their feet and before Gaston reached the corner, Jeannot had darted into a narrow passageway, deep in the shadow of the tall tenements that lined it. Hélène saw warm light from a tabac on the corner and then it was twilight again as they ran. It was an alley Jeannot knew well, he'd lived there during the siege, with Edith and Alphonse Berger; they'd given him shelter and he'd found them food.

The alleyway ended in a brick wall that encircled a warehouse beyond, but there was nowhere else for them to go. With luck their pursuers would rush past its narrow entrance without seeing it; if not they'd be cornered unless they could somehow scale that wall. They ran to the end and Hélène stopped, trying to catch her breath.

Jeannot glanced at the steps leading down to the Bergers' basement. Should he bang on Edith's door? he wondered. No, he dismissed the idea immediately; if it wasn't opened at once, they'd lose precious moments trying.

'Over!' hissed Jeannot, and without warning he caught Hélène round the waist and hoisted her up so she could grasp the top of the wall. 'On my shoulders,' he ordered. Wobbling dangerously, Hélène managed to stand on his shoulders, from where she climbed onto the top of the wall.

'Drop down!' he ordered.

'It's too high!' she cried in panic. 'I can't get down.'

'You must,' insisted Jeannot. 'Turn round and slither.'

There was a shout from the end of the alley and glancing up Hélène saw the Gaston-man running towards them. With a cry of terror she pushed herself off the wall, tumbling awkwardly and landing in a patch of brambles below. She heard the shouting and yelling from the other side of the wall, and out of the clamour she heard Jeannot's shriek. 'Run, Hélène. Run.'

Hélène ran.

Gaston had set off after them, determined to recapture Hélène and deal with Jeannot. He was sprinting to the end of the street when he slipped on the slimy cobbles and fell, arms flailing, into the gutter. He hauled himself to his feet, his clothes and hands filthy, his face a mask of rage, and Auguste and Jules, who had greeted his fall with a burst of ill-advised laughter, came abruptly to silence as they saw his fury and continued the chase.

Rounding the corner they saw that there was no sign of fleeing children in the street ahead. For a moment they paused, then Gaston caught sight of the mouth of the passageway and shouted, 'Keep going! They can't be far! I'll look down here.'

'All right, boss,' said Jules, and he and Auguste continued along the street, while Gaston branched off down the alley. He caught sight of his quarry at the end and realising it was a dead end and they couldn't get out, he slowed a little. He had no gun with him, but his knife was tucked into his boot, and he wouldn't need a gun to cope with the two brats he'd cornered. But Gaston had reckoned without Jeannot. Suddenly he realised that the girl was already on the wall. He heard her cry out as she vanished onto the other side and saw the boy jumping, frantically trying to catch hold of the top of the wall and haul himself up.

Gaston, walking towards him, said, 'It's no good, boy. You can't reach!'

Jeannot knew then that he was going to die and with his back to the wall, he turned to face his murderer. He slid his hand into his pocket and grasped the knife he'd stolen from Francine's kitchen. It was small, but the blade was honed and sharp, and as Gaston approached, Jeannot held it concealed at his side.

'Thought you'd steal my girl, did you, boy?' Gaston grinned at him. 'Too bad! For you and for her!'

As he made a grab for the boy, Jeannot gave a sudden fierce jab upwards with his knife, slicing the unexpected blade through Gaston's ear lobe. The man gave a bellow of pain and for a moment Jeannot thought he might yet escape, but Gaston, a veteran of all too many fights, wouldn't allow so trivial a knife-wound to defeat him. His own knife was in his hand and grasping the boy, he slashed downward at Jeannot's neck. Jeannot jerked and twisted away, and the blade sliced into his shoulder causing a fountain of blood to spray over Gaston's hands, but avoiding the death thrust intended. He was still held in a vice-like grip, but with one final effort he jabbed again with his small knife, stabbing it into the only part of Gaston he could reach: his groin. Gaston squealed with pain and flung the child from him, clutching himself in agony. Jeannot's head hit the wall with a crack and he slid to the ground in a motionless heap. Jules and Auguste, racing down the alley, heard the commotion and when they reached the wall they found Gaston with blood running down his neck and bleeding profusely from an injury inside his trousers, the blood soaking through them at an alarming rate.

Jules rushed to his aid while Auguste went to look at Jeannot.

'Is he dead?' called Jules, who had ripped off his shirt and was pressing it hard against Gaston's wound.

'He soon will be.'

Gaston, suffering the ministrations of his well-meaning mate, gave a curse. 'Kill the fucker!' he mumbled, and passed out.

Chapter 15

Hélène ran, stumbling away from the wall, towards the huge building in front of her, her one idea being that she must get as far away from the Gaston-man as possible. She knew from the sounds of fighting that he and his henchmen had caught Jeannot, but there was nothing she could do for him; Jeannot had yelled at her to run and she had.

She found she was in a walled area stacked with timber and piles of bricks. In its centre was the tall building with a large yard at the front and a cluster of old wooden sheds at the back. She could hear the shouts of men working nearby, the rumble of cartwheels, the whinny of a horse. She scurried across to the old buildings and peering out from their shelter, saw a waggon standing in the yard, the horse waiting patiently as several men shifted its load of crates and barrels into the warehouse. They shouted to each other as they passed the load from man to man, unaware of a young girl crouching among the weeds watching them. On the far side of the yard was a pair of huge gates, open to the street beyond.

Hélène glanced anxiously behind her. There was no sign of pursuit from the other side of the wall, but she was terrified that at any minute Gaston and his men would clamber over and come after her. She looked back at the workmen in the yard, a human chain between her and the freedom of the street beyond, and made up her mind. She drew a deep breath and erupted from the cover of the old sheds, running headlong across the yard towards the gate.

'Hey! You! Stop!' The cry came from the foreman who had been standing out of her sight. He ran to cut her off as she made her dash for freedom, but she'd had the element of surprise and though his fingers actually caught hold of her dress, she was able to jerk away, run out into the street and keep running. She had no idea where she was or where she was going, she simply ran, turning left or right as she came to each street corner with the idea of confusing any pursuit, but there was none and when she finally ran into a square with a fountain playing in its centre, she flopped down on its stone balustrade and gulped down cool fresh water from her cupped hands. A woman walked into the square, a small white dog on a lead prancing along beside her. She paused, looking down with distaste at the girl sitting beside the fountain. What was it coming to? Street urchins like that in this area, muddying the drinking water with their filthy hands? The dog saw Hélène and began to bark.

'That's right, Toto,' said the woman in a loud voice as she drew her skirts away. 'You tell this dirty little girl to go away.' Toto continued to bark his high-pitched officious bark until the pair had disappeared round the corner into the next street.

Hélène was too tired to get up, but she caught sight of her reflection in the water of the pool and hardly recognised herself. She saw a pale girl, with her hair loose from its usual tidy plait and a face grubby and tear-streaked.

No wonder that dog barked at me, she thought disconsolately. She reached into her pocket for her handkerchief, but that was long gone and she had to make do with dipping her hands into the water and scrubbing at her cheeks with her fingers. She brushed her hair away from her face, leaving a long smear of dirt across her forehead, so that she looked no better than she had the moment before.

A gendarme walked into the square and saw her sitting there, a small dirty figure in a torn dress.

'Hey! You! Move along there. No vagrants allowed here! Off you go… and don't come back.'

Wearily, Hélène got to her feet. If she had encountered a gendarme in her previous life as the young daughter of an upper-middle-class family, she would have approached him for help, and he would have responded by taking her home to her parents. As it was, no thought of asking him for help entered her mind. She no longer trusted any man to come near her. She wanted nothing to do with him. She ducked her head in acquiescence and limped away, out of the square, following the road that ran she knew not where. She was hungry and getting cold. It was only late afternoon, but she knew she must find somewhere safe to sleep and then, tomorrow, when she felt better, she would ask someone, an elderly woman, or some servant girl out on an errand, where she was and go home.

Even that idea frightened her. The Gaston-man knew where she lived. Hadn't he stolen her from the Avenue Ste Anne in the first place? He might guess she'd go back there and be lying in wait. But where else was she to go? Surely Papa would be waiting there for her return? She thought of the letter she'd had to write. Had Papa received that yet? Was he even now finding the money to buy her back?

She was so tired that when she came to a church standing at the edge of yet another square, she went to the door and pushed it open, slipping inside. It was warm and smelled of incense. Early evening sun streamed through a stained glass window, casting patterns of glorious colour on the flagstoned floor. Before the high altar hung a sanctuary light, softly gleaming to remind her that Jesus was present in the reserved sacrament. Hélène slipped into one of the pews and for the first time since she and Marie-Jeanne had gone upstairs only two days earlier, she relaxed a little. She attended Mass with her family every Sunday as a matter of course, but she had never felt any particular closeness to God or his Son. Now, as she sat there in the quiet of the peaceful church, she wondered if God would mind if she slept here for the night.

Almost without noticing, her head drooped and she drifted off into an uneasy doze. Immediately the evil dreams of the previous night pounced again; she saw Gaston coming towards her, grinning, his teeth showing yellow through his black beard, the black hairs on his hands as he pulled at her clothes and she woke with a cry. At that moment Father Thomas, the young curate of the parish, emerged from a carved confessional box in a side aisle of the church. Hélène, halfway between sleeping and waking, saw the man, clad in black, his head fringed with dark curly hair, walking towards her and she gave an anguished cry before she fainted away, sliding down the pew onto the floor.

The young priest rushed over to her not knowing who was there or why she had cried out, and found to his astonishment a young girl, no more than about eleven, dressed in filthy ragged clothes, unconscious on the church floor.

For a long moment he didn't know what to do. Should he try and wake her up? Should he leave her there on the floor and go for help? Should he fetch her a drink of water from the pump in the churchyard? Wine? Unconsecrated communion wine? No! He drew back in horror at that idea, wondering how it could possibly have entered his mind. Father Lenoir, the parish priest, was out. What should he do? For another moment he stood perplexed before deciding that he'd go and fetch Madame Sauze who looked after the two of them in the Clergy House. Surely Madame Sauze would know what to do. He was quite right and minutes later Agathe Sauze came hurrying back with him to discover who it was lying in a heap on the church floor.

Hélène was just coming round, her eyes unfocused and her head spinning. The young curate stood in the aisle wringing his hands as Madame Sauze slipped into the pew and knelt beside the child on the floor.

'Ah, you poor child,' she soothed as she gathered the girl into her arms and lifted her up. 'Don't be frightened. Father Thomas and I have come here to help you.'

At the sound of the gentle voice Hélène's tears started afresh and she wailed, 'I want Maman.'

'Of course you do,' said Madame Sauze, 'and we shall find her. But first we'll go back to the house and I'll find you some bread and milk. We can wash your face and hands and when you feel better, you can tell us who you are and what has happened to you.' She turned to Father Thomas who still stood at a loss in the aisle, waiting to be told what to do.

'Come along, Father,' she said. 'The poor child is exhausted. You must carry her over to the house.'

Father Thomas looked down at the grubby child now sitting beside the housekeeper, and stepped forward reluctantly. He had no wish to pick up and carry a street urchin, clearly filthy and almost certainly jumping with fleas. What would Father Lenoir say when he got home and found such a child installed in the kitchen? Giving a morsel of bread and cheese at the back door to a passing beggar was one thing, having one sitting at the kitchen table was quite another.

As he took a reluctant step forward, Hélène looked up and saw him and the matter was decided for him. She gave a cry and cringed away from him, burying her face in the comforting bosom of the housekeeper. Father Thomas jerked backwards, his face a mask of distaste.

'I cannot carry her,' he said. 'She doesn't want me to.'

Madame Sauze had to agree that it was clear Hélène didn't, and so she said, 'Never mind, we will walk to the house.' Turning her attention back to Hélène, she said, 'Now then, child, come with me. We'll walk over to the Clergy House and you can have your bread and milk.'

With a firm gentleness, Madame Sauze brought Hélène to her feet and with an arm round her shoulders led her up the aisle and out of the church, followed at a safe distance by Father Thomas. Moments later they had crossed the square and entered the big old Clergy House. The housekeeper led Hélène into the large warm kitchen at the back, and sat her down in the rocking chair beside the range.

'Now then, my dear,' she said, 'you just sit there while I warm some milk.' She took a jug of milk from the pantry shelf, poured some into a pan and set it on the stove.

Father Thomas appeared at the kitchen door and said, rather ominously, 'I will inform Father Lenoir when he comes in.'

Without looking up from what she was doing, the housekeeper said, 'Thank you, Father, and I will come and speak with him myself.'

Hélène took the cup of warm milk and drained it in one long draught, before tearing at the bread that Madame Sauze had put on a plate in front of her. Seeing how hungry the child was, the housekeeper cut a generous wedge of cheese which vanished equally fast.

'Now then, my child,' she said, 'you must tell me your name and what has happened to you.'

Hélène stared up at her with wide frightened eyes and for a moment Madame Sauze thought she wasn't going to answer. Then she whispered, 'Hélène.'

'Well, Hélène, I'm going to give you a bath and see if I can find you some clean clothes.' She looked at the girl speculatively and said, 'Have you ever had a bath?'

Hélène stared back at her for a long moment and then nodded.

'Good girl,' said Madame Sauze encouragingly. 'You will be more comfortable when you're nice and clean.'

She took her hand and led her upstairs to the tiny bathroom that had so recently been contrived out of one of the small box rooms. She still had to carry the hot water up in buckets, but the tub was big enough for a child to lie in. Once she had filled the bath, she helped Hélène to remove her filthy clothes. As she did so she noticed that they were of good quality, not the clothes of a street child. Where did she get these? she wondered, as she drew the liberty bodice over Hélène's head. But the clothes were immediately forgotten when she gasped in horror as the state of the child's body was revealed. Black and purple bruises marbled her skin, patches of dull blue, islands of livid colour in its pale whiteness. Fingers had left their shape from the pressure applied to her neck and her thighs were blotched and bruised.

'Holy Mary, Mother of God!' she whispered. 'Who did this to you, child?'

Hélène didn't answer, but tears started to stream down her cheeks as she began to sob. Madame reached for her, holding her close, feeling the shuddering body against her own.

'Never mind that now,' she said gently. 'Let's get you into the bath so you can get warm.'

Hélène did as she was told, sinking into the warm water and closing her eyes. Madame Sauze looked again at the abused body and despite her age and her knowledge of the cruel world in which she'd lived for more than fifty years, she found tears in her own eyes. How could anyone do that to a child?

Realising the girl needed her privacy, she said, 'Now you get washed and clean. And I'll go and see what clothes we have.' She put a bar of soap on the edge of the bath and quietly left the room. On the landing she opened the old wardrobe where they kept oddments of clothing to give to the beggars at the back door. Amongst the various pieces given by some of the parishioners, she found a cotton dress, some rather grey underwear and an old shawl. Not all that suitable, but they'd have to do for now while she attempted to wash and mend Hélène's own clothes. These she carried back to the bathroom along with a towel, and helped the child to get dry. She had no nightclothes to offer, but she had found an old petticoat and this she put on her before leading her into one of the small disused bedrooms.

'It's time you were in bed,' she said as she spread a sheet and some blankets onto the old mattress. 'Sleep is the best thing for you, and you can tell us all about it in the morning.' She looked at Hélène's blank expression and said gently, 'You'll be quite safe here. No one will come near you except for me, I promise you. Now be a good girl and get into bed.'

As if sleepwalking, Hélène did as she was told and the housekeeper covered her with a blanket. She was about to leave the room when Hélène cried out, 'It's dark!'

'I'll leave the lamp,' Madame said. 'You'll be fine.' She turned down the wick in the oil lamp and left it on the windowsill before quietly leaving the room.

Hélène heard her footsteps on the stairs as she lay curled up under the blanket. The pain from her bruises had subsided to a dull ache, but the ache in her mind was dark and insistent. Though the lamp had been left so she wasn't alone in the dark as she had been in the cellar, she dare not close her eyes. For the moment she knew she was safe, but for how long? What would the priest say when he got home? If he threw her out like the other one, Father Thomas, wanted to, where would she go? She thought of Maman, safely at St Etienne with her sisters. They would be worried about her, wondering what had happened to her. And Papa? Would he be angry with her? Cross because she hadn't run away when the men broke in? He would have to pay Gaston to get her back, but now Gaston hadn't got her any more, he wouldn't know how to find her.

These muddled thoughts swirled through her brain, but despite her best efforts to stay awake, no longer hungry and in the comforting warmth of the bed, she finally fell asleep.

Chapter 16

Downstairs, Madame Sauze had been called into Father Lenoir's study. Father Thomas had already reported what had happened in the church and had expressed his dismay at Madame Sauze's actions.

'Of course,' he said, 'it was our Christian duty to help the child, but I had not expected Madame Sauze to bring her into the house to stay. I'm sure a cup of milk and a piece of bread was all she needed to restore her.'

'You're probably right,' agreed the priest, 'but we'll wait to hear what Madame Sauze thinks. Now, I have to say my office. I'll see you again at dinner time.'

Father Thomas took his dismissal and went away to his own room. He was annoyed with Father Lenoir's response. Of course he was pleased that Madame Sauze looked after them so well; his meals were put on the table, his clothes were washed, mended and ready to wear, and the house was spotless, all without him having to lift a finger, but he resented the fact that Father Lenoir often consulted her on parish matters, which were, Father Thomas considered, no business of hers. Newly ordained, Father Thomas took himself extremely seriously. It was a great responsibility being a priest, and when he finally got his own parish, any housekeeper he employed would know her place and remain in it.

He heard the housekeeper's footsteps on the stairs and hastily set aside his breviary, but by the time he too reached the hall, she had been called into Father Lenoir's study and the door was closed.

'Now then, Agathe,' said the priest as he waved her to a chair, 'what's all this about a girl fainting in the church?' Agathe Sauze had been his housekeeper for over twenty years, but he only ever called her by her Christian name when there was no one else present. In front of Father Thomas, or any of his parishioners, he always gave her the respect of addressing her as Madame Sauze. 'Thomas is very concerned that you've brought a vagrant child into the house.'

'Father,' said Agathe, who never dropped the formal terms of address, 'the child is in a dreadful way. She was starving hungry, which we dealt with straight away, and filthy dirty which I would say is not her usual state. Her clothes are not those of a beggar child, but the important thing to me is that she has been badly beaten. Her body is covered in bruises and she is terrified of something or someone. It was when Father Thomas approached her in the church she screamed and fainted.'

Father Lenoir, who was well aware of his curate's intensity, gave a wry smile at this, but all he said was, 'Perhaps he appeared out of the shadows and frightened her.'

'Perhaps,' replied Agathe, 'but I don't think so. I think she has been hurt by a man, and now any man who comes near her frightens her to death.' She looked seriously at the priest and added, 'You would be as horrified as I was if you saw the bruises on that child.'

'But a street child…' began Father Lenoir thoughtfully.

'I don't believe that she is a street child,' Agathe said firmly. 'I don't know who she is or how she comes to be in the state she's in, but I'm sure there's a lot more to what's going on here than a simple case of a hungry beggar.'

'And I respect your judgement, Agathe,' the priest said. 'Where is she now?'

'Upstairs in Claudine's old room, and I hope, asleep.'

'Then that's where she'll stay until the morning when we can talk to her properly. Did she tell you her name?'

'Hélène.'

'Hélène? Hélène what?'

'So far just Hélène,' replied Agathe. 'She didn't give a surname and I didn't ask her. One thing at a time. She's a very frightened child.'

'And how old?' Father Lenoir knew that there were plenty of child prostitutes in the city and was already wondering if this Hélène was such a one.

'About eleven, I'd say. Not developed,' she added as if reading his thoughts and knowing she could never have made such a comment to young Father Thomas.

'Fair enough,' said the priest, still wondering if the girl had been sold into prostitution by her parents. 'We'll see what she says in the morning.'

Hélène woke early from a restless sleep. There were no curtains at the window and the pale light of dawn crept into the room well before the rest of the household was awake. She lay in bed listening to the stillness, the silence of the house.

Gradually there were sounds of a new day from outside her window, life awakening in the square below, and Hélène slipped from her bed to go and look out. She found she was on the second storey of the house, from where she had an excellent view of both the square and the street leading into it. A cart was rattling by, laden with barrels on its way to market, an errand boy ran past with a satchel on his back and a tall woman crossed the square, a large basket balanced on her hip. The houses enclosing the square were the homes of the prosperous and the well-to-do. They had steps with railings up to their front doors, polished brass knockers and windows still curtained against the early light. Hélène felt a stab of recognition; she could be looking out of her window in the Avenue Ste Anne. The houses in both were well cared for, the people in the street could be those who passed her house every morning, neighbours going about their business. She felt her heart lift a little. Perhaps she was near home after all. Perhaps the kind woman who had looked after her yesterday could tell her the way to Avenue Ste Anne. To Maman and Papa. Her mind still refused to think of Marie-Jeanne.

She went back to bed and pulled the blankets round her shoulders as she waited for someone to come. Sounds came up from below in the house as the sun rose over the rooftops and the light outside grew stronger. Hélène wanted to be up, but she didn't dare venture downstairs on her own, she was afraid she might meet the man from the church, so she sat on the bed and waited. All she wanted was to go home.

When the two priests had come back from early Mass and were eating their breakfasts in the dining room, Agathe Sauze went up to the child's bedroom and quietly opened the door. She discovered Hélène, dressed in the clothes she had found for her last night, sitting patiently on the bed. She got to her feet as the housekeeper came in. In the borrowed clothes which fitted nowhere, she looked even more of a ragamuffin than she had the previous day.

'Ah, I see you're awake,' said Madame Sauze. 'That's good, you can come down and have some breakfast now. Are you hungry?'

Hélène nodded, and Madame said, 'Good. Let's go downstairs.' She paused at the head of the stairs and said, 'Father Lenoir and Father Thomas will be having their breakfast too. You know you're in the Clergy House, don't you? So you must expect to see them and not be frightened.' Hélène nodded again, but still said nothing. 'Don't worry,' the housekeeper went on, 'they'll be in the dining room, you and I will be in the kitchen.'

Settled at the kitchen table, Hélène made short work of the hot chocolate and fresh croissants that Madame Sauze gave her. She felt much better than the day before and even remembered to say 'Thank you,' and give a shy smile when Madame refilled her cup. Her politeness reinforced Agathe Sauze's view that this foundling was not a child of the streets.

'When you've finished that,' she said as she cleared away the plates to the scullery for the maid-of-all-work, Nina, to wash up, 'we must go to say good morning to Father Lenoir.' Ignoring the flash of fear she saw on the girl's face she went on, 'He is the priest of this church, and he is very kind. He wants to meet you and you will like him.'

Ten minutes later Agathe was knocking on the door of the priest's study and when he called to her to come in, she led a very reluctant Hélène firmly by the hand into his room.

'Good morning, Father,' said Agathe, as if she had not seen him three times already this day. 'This is Hélène who we found unwell in the church yesterday.' She turned to Hélène and prompted, 'Say good morning to the father, Hélène.'

The child murmured, 'Good morning, Father.'

The priest smiled at her and replied, 'Good morning, Hélène. Come and sit down.'

A chair had already been placed in front of his desk and Madame guided her to it before taking a seat in the corner behind her.

'Now then, my child,' began the priest, 'tell me your name.'

'Hélène,' came the whispered reply.

'But that's not all of it, is it? What is your full name?'

Hélène shifted uncomfortably. 'Hélène Rosalie St Clair.'

'And have you any brothers and sisters?' asked the priest, with the idea of setting her at ease.

It had quite the opposite effect. The colour drained from her face as the sound of Gaston's questions echoed in her head. How should she answer this time? What answer was this man looking for? She stared at him for a long moment, unable to speak.

'Hélène?' came the quiet voice behind her. 'Father Lenoir's asking about your family. You can answer him, can't you?'

As Hélène still didn't speak the priest tried a different tack. 'Where do you live, Hélène?'

Still Hélène did not reply and Agathe Sauze said, 'Yesterday you told me you wanted your mother. How can we find her if we don't know where you live?'

'Maman is not there,' Hélène said. 'She has gone to the country with Clarice and Louise.'

'Are they your sisters?' asked Father Lenoir.

Hélène said nothing, but she nodded and the two adults felt that at last they were making some progress.

'And your papa?' Agathe took over the questioning as it was clear that she received answers and the priest did not.

'He went out,' Hélène replied.

'Out? Out where?'

Hélène's lip began to tremble. 'I don't know,' she whimpered. 'He didn't come home.'

'And where is home?' asked Agathe, phrasing the question slightly differently.

'I can't go home,' Hélène said. 'He might come back!'

Now they were confused. 'Who might come back? Your father?'

'He shot Marie-Jeanne.'

'Who did?' demanded the priest, all subtlety gone. 'Who is Marie-Jeanne and who shot her? Your father?'

In answer Hélène began to cry, tears sliding silently down her cheeks and the priest looked across at Madame Sauze in frustration. 'This is hopeless,' he said. 'We're getting nowhere. Is the child deranged? Why does she not answer a simple question when I ask her?'

Agathe thought for a moment. 'Perhaps it's because you're a man.'

'But I am a priest!' he answered hotly.

'Yes, Father, but you are also a man. And I think she is afraid of men.' She nodded towards the girl who still sat on the chair facing the priest at the desk, with her back to the housekeeper. 'You remember I told you of injuries.'

The priest looked puzzled for a minute and then nodded his understanding. 'Well, Hélène,' he said, 'why don't you go back into the kitchen with Madame Sauze and see if you can help her there. I'm sure there are some jobs you're able to do for her.'

'I want to go home,' Hélène said, her voice breaking on a sob.

'Of course you do,' cut in Madame Sauze before the priest could speak again, 'but your clothes have been washed and they aren't dry yet. When they are and we've mended the tears, we'll see what we can do about getting you back to Maman and...' She had been about to say Papa, when she caught herself. It could be that Papa was the man who had abused her so badly. The man she thought had shot Marie-Jeanne, whoever Marie-Jeanne was. 'Come along now, Father Lenoir has work to do and we must let him get on.' She got to her feet and held out her hand. Hélène took it, like a small child might, and together they left the room. At the door Agathe Sauze glanced back at the priest who shrugged his shoulders as if to say, 'it's up to you'.

Chapter 17

Rosalie almost snatched the envelope from Pierre's hand and ripping it open, extracted the single sheet of paper. She cast a quick eye over it and Pierre watched as the colour drained from her face. Without looking at him she read the letter again, more slowly this time, and then gave a moan of anguish.

For a moment Pierre thought she was going to faint. He reached out a hand to steady her as she sank down onto a bench as if her legs could no longer support her. Then she raised her eyes to him.

'Is this really true?' she whispered. 'Has Hélène disappeared? Is Marie-Jeanne really dead? Tell me. Tell me what happened.'

Quietly, Pierre told Rosalie all they knew, all they had been able to discover from Arlette, and what they could piece together from the evidence in the house.

'We have searched everywhere we could think of in case Miss Hélène had run away too, and was in hiding, waiting for her father to come home.'

'But you can't find her,' Rosalie said flatly. 'And Marie-Jeanne? Where is poor Marie-Jeanne?'

'She was taken to the church last night, madame, and was buried this morning. I have come from her funeral.'

Rosalie closed her eyes and crossed herself, murmuring, 'May she rest in peace.' Beloved Marie-Jeanne who had been her nurse and nurse to all her children, murdered to protect one of them. And, it seemed, died in vain.

After a moment's silence she asked, 'Where is my husband now?'

'He has ridden to Versailles to find Lieutenant St Clair. He thinks he'll be able to help in the search for Miss Hélène. He sent me here with this letter, to break the news of what has happened.'

'He should have come himself,' Rosalie said bitterly.

Though Pierre thought so too, he said, 'He was anxious to find Lieutenant St Clair as soon as possible and he thought he should stay in Paris in case Miss Hélène came home.'

Rosalie drew a deep breath and straightened her shoulders. 'Well, Pierre,' she said as she got to her feet, 'we shall take the next train back.'

'Madame,' Pierre said, 'Monsieur was most insistent that you should stay here in St Etienne.'

'Was he?' snapped Rosalie. 'That's too bad. How can I stay here when my daughter is lost in Paris?'

'Monsieur needs to know that you and the children are safe here.'

'The children are safe here, whether I am with them or not. Mademoiselle Corbine is perfectly able to look after them…' Her voice trailed off as a thought slid, unbidden, into her mind; she had thought the same about Marie-Jeanne and Hélène, and she shook her head as if to dislodge the unwelcome thought. Tears welled in her eyes and she dashed them away. There was no time for tears. Now she had to be strong.

'I have already left them with Mademoiselle,' she said. 'I was here at the station on my way back to Paris, to find out what was going on. The train is due any minute now.'

Pierre tried once more to dissuade her, but she said, 'My mind is made up, Pierre.'

Night had fallen when they arrived in the Avenue Ste Anne. The house stood in darkness, along with so many of its neighbours.

'I have a key to the coach gate, madame,' Pierre said as he handed her down from the fiacre that had brought them from the station. Together they walked round to the stable yard, where they found, to Pierre's surprise, that the gate was unlocked.

'Emile must be back,' Rosalie said as she pushed past him into the yard.

'Wait, madame,' Pierre whispered. 'It may not be him. I will go in and see who is there. Please, madame, wait here.' Leaving her hidden in the stables, he crossed the yard and quietly opened the back door. He felt for and lit the stub of candle that always stood ready just inside. As the flickering flame took hold, the shadows jumped around him and Pierre paused. He wasn't armed but as he crept through the kitchen, he caught up a knife from the block and with knife in one hand and candle in the other, he stole quietly into the house.

Emile, sitting, silent, in the unlit drawing room, heard the back door open, the rasp of the match and the cautious footsteps. He picked up the pistol that lay by his hand and walked into the hall to confront the intruder.

The street lamp, shining in through the fanlight above the

front door, gave the hall a pale, eerie light, by which he could make out the entrance to the kitchen passageway.

He saw the flickering light in the doorway and raising his pistol shouted, 'Stop! Or I fire!'

'Monsieur!' came the urgent cry. 'Don't shoot! It's me! Pierre!'

Emile lowered the pistol, demanding, 'What are you doing here, Pierre? You should be in St Etienne with Madame and the children.'

'Madame has returned with me—' began Pierre.

But Emile interrupted, crying, 'Here? I expressly said she was to stay there, in St Etienne.'

'Well, I haven't!' Rosalie had followed Pierre into the house and speaking from behind him in the darkness of the passageway, she startled both men.

'Rosalie!' Emile stepped forward, taking both her hands in his. 'You shouldn't have come. It's not safe for you here. I told Pierre you were to stay.'

'And Pierre told me!' returned his wife. 'Don't blame him. He couldn't stop me coming.'

Wishing to leave his employers to themselves, Pierre said, 'Shall I light a lamp, monsieur?'

'No,' Emile said firmly. 'I want the house to remain in darkness. If they come back, they'll think it's deserted and I'll be ready for them. I'll call you if we need you.' And thus dismissed, Pierre withdrew gratefully to his stable loft.

Immediately he had disappeared, Rosalie rounded on her husband.

'How could you?' she demanded fiercely. 'How could you let someone take her?'

'Rosalie, be reasonable,' protested Emile. 'I wasn't here when—'

'No!' interrupted his wife. 'No, you weren't here, where you should have been. No—' she corrected herself, 'No, no one *should* have been here! We should never have come back to Paris in the first place! We were all perfectly safe in St Etienne. The war was over, the armistice was signed, but Paris was still a dangerous place to be. You knew that! You should never have brought us back.'

'You're right,' snapped Emile. 'The war was over, the armistice was signed. I needed to be back here to salvage what I could of my business. Without it we have no income. No money, Rosalie!'

'But you didn't have to bring the whole family back!' cried Rosalie, her voice breaking on a sob. 'Your little girls!'

Emile's shoulders slumped. He knew she was right. If he had needed to come to Paris, he should have come alone.

'I know,' he said softly. 'I know that now.'

'Pierre says you went to your office that morning.'

'I had to—'

'No, Emile! If you'd set out at once, we'd all be safely in St Etienne. You've lost my daughter.'

'She's my daughter, too.'

'And Marie-Jeanne, what about her?' cried Rosalie, ignoring his reply. 'If you'd left first thing, Hélène would be safe and Marie-Jeanne'd still be alive.'

For the first time her tears began to flow and once started they wouldn't stop. Emile, his expression one of despair, moved to take her in his arms, but she pushed him away.

'Don't touch me!'

There was no food in the house so they went to their separate beds hungry, but before they went upstairs, Emile checked that the coach gate was firmly bolted, and he and

Pierre dragged the heavy bookcase that stood in the hall across the front door.

None of them slept well that night and in the cold light of morning things looked as bleak as before; neither of Hélène's parents knew what to do next. Pierre had gone out for provisions, so at least they had food in the house, but apart from pretending to eat the bread and cheese he had brought, and drinking coffee, they could only sit and look at each other.

Further recriminations were pointless and there was an uneasy truce between them. Hélène had disappeared, carried off by the intruders, but there had been no ransom note demanding money, giving instructions for her return. Nothing to give them any hope that she might still be alive.

It was afternoon when there was a loud knocking on the back gate and Pierre, demanding to know who was there, heard a soft voice reply, 'It's me, Georges! Quickly! Let me in.'

Pierre unlocked the gate and Georges slipped inside. He was not in uniform but as before, dressed as a common workman, with a hat pulled low, shading his face.

'Thank God you've come, Lieutenant,' said Pierre, as he bolted the door behind him.

'Come to see my father,' was all Georges said, before hurrying into the house.

His parents heard his voice and Emile stepped into the hall to meet him. He knew a moment of intense relief as he grasped his son by the hand and echoed Pierre. 'Georges! Thank God you've come.'

'I had an odd message saying that you needed me,' Georges said, adding as he looked round the hall and saw the barricaded front door, 'What on earth has happened here, Papa?' At that moment Rosalie emerged from the drawing room. Georges stared at her in dismay. 'Maman! What are you doing here? Why aren't you in St Etienne?'

'Come in and sit down,' said his father, 'and we'll tell you everything.'

Georges listened in horrified silence to the happenings of the past few days. His beloved sister kidnapped. Marie-Jeanne dead. When Emile finally said, 'So we don't know what to do. What do we do, Georges? We don't know how to begin to find her.'

'Well, there's no point in you staying here,' Georges said bluntly. 'I told you before, things are only going to get worse. You should leave at once and go back to St Etienne. There's nothing you can do here and I have to warn you... though I really shouldn't... that it won't be long before Paris is besieged again.'

Emile looked startled. 'Besieged?'

'Papa, you have no idea what's happening, have you?' Georges spoke in frustration. 'The National Guard have taken over Paris. The army is going to take it back. It's civil war! It won't be long before you can't get in or out of the city again. You must take Maman to safety...' he paused, holding his father's gaze as he added, 'before you lose her, too!'

'Georges!' cried his mother.

'I'm warning you now, Maman,' Georges said. 'Another siege is coming and if you don't leave for the country at once, you'll find yourself trapped here. You need to be with the girls in St Etienne, and you, Papa,' he turned to his father, 'you need to be with Maman.'

'But Georges—' began his mother.

'No buts, Maman,' insisted Georges. 'You must go today, now, if you're to travel in safety. Clarice and Louise need you.'

'But what about Hélène? She needs us too.'

'So she may,' Georges replied, 'but at present you don't know where she is and you can't help her.' He softened his tone a little and went on, 'I will do all I can to find her, Maman, but looking for a small girl in the turmoil around us now is like looking for a needle in a field of haystacks.' He gave her what he hoped was a reassuring smile. 'But I do have contacts and I will see what I can learn from them.'

'Contacts? Who are these contacts?' demanded Emile. 'We heard you were seconded to General Vinoy.'

'And so I am,' agreed Georges shortly. 'Indeed, I shouldn't be here as I'm on his business now. All I can do is to beg you… no, to tell you… to leave Paris at once. If you don't, your other children may lose *you*, too.'

He got to his feet and walked into the hall. 'That wouldn't keep anyone out who was determined to get in,' he remarked, waving a hand at the barricaded door. 'You're not safe here. For God's sake, do as I ask you, Papa.'

When he had sloped off down the street, passing the house without a backward glance, his parents looked at each other in despair.

'What do we do?' Emile was at a loss and looked to his wife for a lead.

'We should go,' Rosalie said. 'Clarice and Louise need us. Both of us. We should go to the station and catch the first train out.'

'And Hélène?'

'Hélène?' Rosalie blinked hard to combat her tears. 'Georges is right. We can do nothing waiting here to be trapped in the city. We must trust to him and his contacts, whoever they are.'

'We will go,' Emile said, 'but we'll go in the chaise. We still have the horse and Pierre can drive us.'

'It'll be quicker by train,' objected Rosalie. 'If we use the chaise we'll have to stop for at least one night on the way.'

'Does that matter, Rosalie?' countered Emile. 'We'll have the chaise in the country, and you can travel in far more comfort. You know you don't like trains.'

Rosalie had to admit that he was right there, she didn't like trains, but at least they travelled far faster than a one-horse chaise. She was anxious to get back to St Etienne now; she needed to be with Clarice and Louise. Once back home in the country, she vowed she would never let them out of her sight. If Georges was right, they might get trapped in Paris and not get home for months. If it meant that they could leave the city straight away, then by all means, let Pierre drive them in the chaise.

'If we can get out of the city before the gates close,' Emile explained, 'we can find an inn for the night and travel on first thing in the morning; we should reach St Etienne well before dark tomorrow.'

The decision was made and they prepared to leave. Emile and Pierre set to work securing the front door, nailing planks of wood across the frame while Rosalie packed up the remains of the food Pierre had bought that morning to take with them on the journey. Pierre harnessed the horse and brought the chaise out into the street. Emile closed and locked the *porte cochère* behind them and as afternoon slipped into evening, they drove away, leaving the house empty and silent.

Chapter 18

When Agathe and Hélène returned to the kitchen, Agathe gave Hélène some linen to fold and the repetitive action seemed to soothe her. She sat at the table smoothing napkins and pillowcases, folding towels, setting the corners exactly together, her face a mask of concentration.

Once she glanced up at the airer, suspended from the ceiling where her clothes, washed by Agathe the night before, had been hung up to dry.

Agathe caught the look and said, 'They'll be dry by tomorrow, and then you can go home.'

As they did the various chores about the kitchen and in the house, Agathe chatted to her in the hope of eliciting a little more information. Once, Father Thomas appeared in the kitchen, and as he came through the door to tell Madame Sauze that he wouldn't be in for dinner, Hélène shrank back into the corner. He ignored her entirely and having said his piece, disappeared, and Agathe could feel the relaxation in the child.

After the midday meal which they'd eaten together at the kitchen table, she sent Hélène upstairs to her room to rest and took the chance to slip back into the study to speak again with the priest.

'She has told me nothing more yet, but she is more relaxed when we are alone together. I will try and find out where she lives as the day goes on. She let slip that she has a brother, but that brings us no closer to knowing who she is.'

'Well, she did give us her full name,' Father Lenoir reminded her.

'I know, but then something made her stop. Do you really think her father killed this Marie-Jeanne?'

The priest shook his head. 'How can we tell, Agathe? I think she is a little mad. Can we believe any of it?'

'You can believe she's afraid of men,' said Agathe sombrely. 'I've seen the bruises.'

It was as they were preparing the evening meal that Hélène finally named the street where she lived. The Avenue Ste Anne. It was only said in passing, and Agathe had appeared not to have noticed it, but it was with great relief that she was able to tell Father Lenoir where Hélène came from.

'If we can believe her,' said the priest. 'If not, we can't keep the child here, she'll have to go to the sisters.'

'The orphanage?' Agathe was dismayed. The orphanage, run by the Sisters of St Luke, was a forbidding building two streets away in the Place Armand. It was home to 'Children of Shame', illegitimate babies left on its doorstep, or children left orphaned with nowhere to go. Surely Hélène didn't belong there.

'Suppose I go to this Avenue Ste Anne and see if I can find her family?' Agathe suggested. 'Perhaps her mother will be there and can come and fetch her.'

Father Lenoir shrugged. 'I suppose you could,' he said, 'but should we be sending her back to a home where you say she has been so abused? Wouldn't she be safer at St Luke's?'

Agathe Sauze, who had seen the misery on the faces of the orphans as they were brought to Mass every Sunday, didn't think so. No. It might be a place of safety from the world beyond its high walls, but it was not a happy place. She shook her head.

'I would hate to see her go in there,' she said. 'Please allow me, Father, to visit the Avenue Ste Anne first and see what I can discover.'

The old priest sighed and washing his hands of the whole thing, said, 'Agathe, you must do as you think best.'

The relief Agathe felt was enormous and she said, 'I'll go there this evening. Her family must be frantic with worry about her, and if they do live there, they'll surely be home in the evening.'

When she had fed the household, Agathe took Hélène up to her room. 'I have to go out, child,' she said. 'Can you read?'

Hélène looked a little startled and replied, 'Of course I can, madame. I'm not a baby.'

'Then I will bring you a Bible and you can read that while I am away. No one will trouble you. Father Lenoir is in his study and Father Thomas is at a meeting.'

Ten minutes later the housekeeper left the house and set out for the Avenue Ste Anne. She and Father Lenoir had consulted a map and discovered there was such a street in the Passy district and she decided to start her quest there. She hoped and prayed that she could find the family and that it was a loving one, not one where the father abused the child and the mother allowed it to happen.

She was able to travel by omnibus for much of the way, and as its horses pulled it steadily through the city, she stared out of the window at the bustle and the busyness in the streets beyond. How easily a child of Hélène's age could become lost, disorientated in such crowded streets, Agathe thought. How easily she might fall prey to someone of evil intent. She thought of the child's bruises and shuddered.

She alighted from the omnibus and walked the final mile to the Avenue Ste Anne. The evening sun was low in the sky as she paused at last on the corner. The road was tranquil compared with the streets through which she'd just passed. There were few people about, a man riding away on a horse, a couple entering a house further down, a chaise coming towards her, clattering over the cobbles, causing her to step aside from its flurry of dust. As she looked along the avenue's gently curving length, she was dismayed. Surely Hélène couldn't come from such a prosperous area. How was it possible that a child from such a place should be lost, injured and hungry? How had she come to be allowed out on her own? Surely a maid, a governess or an attendant of some sort would accompany her if she left the house without her parents. Slowly Agathe Sauze walked the length of the avenue. Almost all the houses were closed and shuttered, their owners having made discreet exits from the city as the National Guard had taken control. It crossed her mind that Hélène might somehow have become separated from the rest of her family in the flurry of a hasty departure, but surely they would have come straight back to find her. The whole thing was a mystery; none of what she knew made sense.

She walked the length of the avenue, wondering which of the houses belonged to the St Clairs, and finally decided to knock at one of the few occupied houses and ask. She took her courage in both hands and approached an imposing double-fronted house that had light gleaming through the fanlight above the front door. Her knock was answered by a maid in a black dress uniform, a spotless white apron and a starched white cap.

Agathe explained that she was looking for the home of the St Clair family which she believed was in this street. 'Can you direct me to their house?' she asked.

'The St Clairs?' replied the maid. 'Oh yes, they live at number thirty-four, but you won't find them there now. They've left Paris and the house is closed up.' Lowering her voice she added confidentially, 'Not surprising though, after what happened there, and poor Marie-Jeanne…'

'Mathilde!' A sharp voice came from inside the house. 'Who are you gossiping with at my front door? Close the door at once.'

'Do you know where they have gone?' Madame Sauze asked quickly.

The girl shook her head and with a quick glance over her shoulder whispered, 'But I saw them leave this evening.'

'Mathilde!'

Mathilde gave her a regretful smile and hurriedly closed the door.

Agathe turned away from the house, despair in her heart. They'd left this evening. She had missed them. She should have come the moment she knew the name of the street.

Still, she thought wearily, at least I know I'm in the right place.

The maid had told her which house and now she set off to find it. The family might have just left, but perhaps there was a housekeeper or some other servant still there, who would know where they had gone.

The house stood further along, on the opposite side of the road, and was similar to the one she'd approached, but it stood in silent darkness. No glimmer of light shone from its windows, but even so Agathe stepped up to the front door to pull on the bell. As she did so, she saw that the door was damaged, wedged into its frame, a sturdy piece of wood nailed across it. What had the maid Mathilde said? Something had happened? Well, clearly something had. Someone had broken in here. And she'd mentioned 'poor Marie-Jeanne'. Who was Marie-Jeanne, and what had happened to her? Hélène had said she had been shot by… someone. Was that really true? At least it seemed Marie-Jeanne was – or had been – a real person.

There was no reply to her ring, but by now she didn't expect one. She had done all she could, and with a heavy heart Agathe walked to the omnibus and made her way slowly back to the Clergy House; she had been too late.

'The trouble is,' she said when she was back in Father Lenoir's study, 'the maid didn't have time to tell me what had happened to this Marie-Jeanne. All I discovered was that the family had left this evening and the house was empty.' She shook her head in bewilderment. 'But why would they leave, with Hélène still missing?'

'Who knows?' said the priest. 'But it brings us back to the child. What are we going to do with her? We can't take her back to her family because they aren't there, and she can't stay here.' He said this last with such finality that Agathe knew he would not change his mind. 'She must go to the sisters at St Luke's. When things have calmed down a bit, no doubt her family will return from the country and we can reunite them, but in the meantime, she must go to St Luke's… You can take her there in the morning.'

Chapter 19

Alphonse Berger climbed the steps from the two-room basement he and his wife Edith called home. He was finding the steps increasingly difficult to manage, and he was looking old age squarely in the face. I'm not old, he told himself as he grasped the handrail, taking the steps slowly. Only about fifty. But that was old these days, especially if you'd lived through the siege. It was early evening on a grey day in March and he was on his way to the market to see if there was any discarded food to be had at the end of the day. Breathing heavily, Alphonse struggled up the steps, cursing the day the boy had disappeared, deserting them once the siege was over. They had given him shelter, after all, and he, the youngster, had been the one who went foraging for all three of them. But when the siege was lifted, he'd vanished, ungrateful little tyke! Still, that was boys for you.

Edith had become fond of the lad, too fond, Alphonse thought, sharing her own food with him to ensure that he had enough. But, Alphonse had to agree when he tried to take her to task for this, it was the boy who took all the risks to keep them fed.

As he emerged out into the narrow alleyway, Alphonse paused, wheezing, his breathing ragged from the effort of the steps. He peered short-sightedly in both directions to be sure there was no danger lurking in the gloom. Edith had said she'd heard voices shouting earlier and urged him to stay indoors, but as Alphonse pointed out to her, if he didn't go scrounging in the market, they would go hungry to bed.

He could see no sign of anyone and was about to set off towards the main road when something caught his eye. A heap of something, perhaps a sack, or a pile of old clothes, discarded by the wall. He scanned the alley again, but seeing no movement, he edged his way towards the heap. If it was a bag it was probably empty, but you never knew, it just might contain something worth having. Such things could be the difference between life and starvation.

As Alphonse reached down to investigate, he saw with a jolt that it wasn't a bag. It was a body. A small body, the body of a boy, face down in the mud, blood pooled about his head. He jerked his hand away and took a step back. Surely there was nothing for him there. What could a young boy have of value? He considered the small corpse for a moment and then bent down and peered closer. There was something familiar about him, but then, Alphonse decided all street boys looked the same, skinny, grubby and pale. Then he realised it was the jacket. The boy was wearing an old jacket, patched and worn and extremely dirty, but it was the jacket that Alphonse had recognised. He knew that jacket. He'd watched Edith often enough, patching it, mending it. As he bent down for a closer look he realised it was indeed Jeannot lying on the ground. He reached down a hand and touched the boy's face. It was still warm. This must have happened to him very recently. Perhaps his had been one of the voices Edith had heard earlier, shouting.

So, Alphonse thought, the boy had come to a sticky end. He wasn't surprised, Jeannot had always been one for trouble, but he found he was sorry it had ended this way for the lad, beaten and discarded like so much garbage at the end of an alleyway.

Alphonse wondered what to do. If it had just been any boy, he'd have walked away. There were plenty of bodies to be found in the back alleys these days. Sometimes they lay there, rotting in the heat, filling the air with an ever-increasing stench until, when the nearby neighbours made enough fuss, it was carted away and buried or burned to prevent the spread of infection. Looking down at the now familiar face, Alphonse didn't know what to do. Slowly he turned away but instead of going out to the market, he went back slowly down the steps to his basement.

Edith was sitting in an old armchair by the tiny fire, wrapped in a blanket for extra warmth. She looked at Alphonse in surprise as he came in.

'You're back,' she cried in alarm. 'What's happened?'

'The boy,' puffed Alphonse, out of breath.

'The boy? What boy?'

'Jeannot.'

'Jeannot? What about him?'

'Dead in the street.'

Edith stared at him for a moment and then said, 'Our Jeannot?'

'Outside, by the warehouse wall.'

'And he's dead?'

'Looks it.'

Edith got up and hurried to the door. Grabbing her shawl she went quickly up the steps. Despite the gloom she could see a shape curled at the foot of the wall, and after a cautious look up and down the alley, she crossed over to the small body lying on the ground.

Definitely their Jeannot. She knelt down beside him and carefully lifted his head, pulling him gently into her arms. Though she was considerably younger than Alphonse they had not been blessed with children, and to begin with she'd been glad. The city they lived in was no place for slum children and without doubt theirs would have been a slum child, but once they had given shelter to Jeannot during the siege, she had come to realise what she had missed. When the siege was raised and he had suddenly disappeared, she had been heartbroken, and now here he was again, dead in her arms, breaking her heart all over again. As she cradled him to her, she felt his warmth and was surprised. It was not that long since she'd heard the altercation in the alley, a matter of an hour or so, but surely he should have been colder than this by now. She pressed her face against his chest and held her breath. Was that the faintest flutter of a heartbeat?

She looked back along the alley. Alphonse had just made it to the top of the steps again. She waved at him frantically and he made his way slowly towards her.

'He's alive,' she whispered, not daring to say it aloud in case the heartbeat suddenly failed. 'Alphonse, he's alive. We have to get him home and get him warm. Then we can look at his injuries.'

'I can't carry him,' objected Alphonse.

'No, all right, but I can. If I lift him and carry him, can you take hold of his head and keep it steady?'

Edith managed to get to her feet, still clutching the boy against her. Alphonse steadied her and took the weight of Jeannot's head as it lolled onto her shoulder. Slowly they edged their way back along the alley to their basement's steps.

'I can manage him now,' Edith said, 'if you just ease him up over my shoulder.'

Alphonse helped her move Jeannot across her body so that she could hold him with one arm, leaving her other hand free to grip the handrail. Holding him as tightly as she dare, she turned and clinging to the rail, backed slowly down the steps.

'Go inside,' Edith said. 'Find a blanket and poke the fire a bit, we need some warmth. Put on another piece of wood.'

Alphonse preceded her into the house and having tossed a broken piece of packing case onto the fire, closed the door behind her. Edith carried Jeannot into the inner room and together they laid the boy down on the mattress on which they both slept. He lay there as still as the corpse they had thought him, and for a moment Edith thought she must have been mistaken, but when she rested her head against his chest, she could still feel the heartbeat, faint and weak as it struggled to pump blood round the boy's body.

Carefully Edith cut away his jacket and shirt and examined his battered body. There were two dark bruises on his torso, and a deep cut on his shoulder now crusted with blood, but from which there was still a trickle of red. One side of his face was swollen, so that the eye was closed, and he was still out cold.

'Fetch me some water and a towel,' she instructed Alphonse, 'and I'll try and patch him up.' She sat back on her heels and considered him. The bruises on his chest and side would heal in time, she knew. It was the slash on his shoulder and the head wound that worried her more.

Alphonse brought the water and the cloth and very gently she began to clean the wounds, wiping away the mud and the blood to enable her to see the damage properly. The shoulder was not as deep as she'd originally thought. Bad enough, it needed stitching, but as the older sister of four brothers, that was something Edith had long ago learned how to do. She turned her attention to his head. The skin was grazed, the face swollen and the eye socket blackening, but again when she had gently cleaned it, she could see that this was damage which would, in time, heal itself. Her fingers explored the back of his head, finding a large lump behind one ear, accounting, she decided, for his unconsciousness.

She placed a blanket over him to keep him warm and fetched her sewing bag.

'I'm going to stitch his shoulder while he's still unconscious,' she told Alphonse. 'Put some more wood on the fire, we need to get him warm.'

Alphonse did as he was asked, grumbling as he did so that he hoped she realised the wood in the basket by the fire was all the fuel they had left.

Edith ignored his grumbles as she often did these days. They would get more firewood somewhere, but it was now they needed the heat.

Half an hour later, Jeannot lay on the mattress, his shoulder stitched and bandaged, his face cleaned, his body washed from top to toe. Swamped in a shirt of Alphonse's and covered with a blanket, he was still unconscious, but his pulse was stronger and occasionally his eyelids flickered.

The thin soup Edith had made with the last of their vegetables was shared three ways, Jeannot's share set aside for when he finally woke up.

When she and Alphonse had drunk their soup, Edith picked up Jeannot's jacket, wondering if there was any way she could mend it to make it wearable again. It was muddy and bloodstained, as were his trousers, but that could be remedied. She would fetch more water from the pump in the morning and scrub them clean. It was as she laid the jacket out on the floor, smoothing the cloth with her fingers, matching the tears and cuts for patching, that she felt something hard. Quickly she searched the pockets, but they were empty. Then she remembered his secret pocket. She had sewn it into his coat during the siege, a secret place to hide his pickings. She ran her thumb along the seam and found its hidden edge. It was the work of a moment to retrieve what it contained: a watch. A gentleman's pocket watch, gold, its case gleaming in the firelight. She held it up for Alphonse to see.

'Is this what they attacked him for, do you think?'

'Looks like it.' His face broke into the first smile of the day. 'No problem about firewood now!' he said.

'It's Jeannot's watch.'

'And Jeannot will get the warmth and the food it will buy,' Alphonse replied. 'I'll take it tomorrow.'

Edith couldn't fault this logic, so she nodded and said, 'Fine, but just make sure you get a decent price for it.'

Gently, she moved Jeannot to one side of the mattress and Alphonse lay down to sleep beside him. She hoped that he wouldn't disturb the boy, but there was nowhere else Alphonse could sleep.

She wrapped herself in her shawl and settled back in the armchair beside the dying fire, but despite her determination to keep watch, alert for any change in her patient, she drifted off into fitful sleep, to awaken early next morning, cold and stiff, with a crick in her neck. She hauled herself out of the chair and poking the embers of the fire, she put on the last few splinters of wood and began to heat water for coffee.

As soon as he'd drunk his coffee, Alphonse set out to sell the watch. Though it wouldn't fetch anything like what it was worth, it would, with care, keep them in food and firewood for the next few weeks.

Edith fetched water from the pump at the head of the alley, refilling their water buckets, and set to work on Jeannot's filthy clothes, pummelling out the dirt and the dried blood before hanging them in front of the fire to dry.

Jeannot awoke slowly, surfacing as if from deep water. He tried to move, but regretted it at once. Cautiously he opened his eyes, and quickly closed them again. One hardly opened at all and his whole face hurt. His head throbbed, there was pain in his shoulder and his ribs ached like fury. He lay completely still, wondering where he was. He remembered running away, dragging Hélène along behind him, he remembered Gaston coming at him with a knife, but then... nothing. Hélène! Where was she? Gingerly he opened his eyes again, turning his head a little to see his surroundings. They were familiar, but where?

'Jeannot, are you awake?' The voice was familiar, too. He tried to concentrate.

'Jeannot? It's me, Tante Edith.'

'Tante Edith?' He managed to speak her name, though his voice was reedy and thin.

'Yes, Tante Edith. You've been in a fight, but you're all right now.'

'My head aches,' Jeannot said plaintively, 'and my shoulder. I hurt all over.'

Edith smiled. 'I'm not surprised,' she said. 'You took a dreadful beating, you're lucky to be alive. If Alphonse hadn't found you lying in the alley, you would be dead by now.'

She sat down beside him on the mattress and gave him a cup of water. 'Here,' she said, 'drink this, and if you can keep it down, you can try a little soup.'

Jeannot drank the water and then the soup and though he still ached all over, his spirits rose a little. 'Was there anyone else there when Oncle Alphonse found me?'

'No,' replied Edith. 'You'd been dumped, but don't worry, Jeannot, they didn't get it.'

'Didn't get what?'

'Your watch. That's what they were after, wasn't it?'

For a moment Jeannot wondered what she was talking about, and then he remembered the watch he'd stolen as a bribe for Francine. It was all he had in the world.

'Where is it?' he asked.

'Alphonse has taken it to sell,' Edith said. And seeing Jeannot's stricken reaction, went on firmly, 'We need money for food and fuel, Jeannot. And you won't be able to look after yourself for a while yet. Not until those injuries heal. You'll have to stay here with us until you're better, until you can fend for yourself again.'

Jeannot, about to protest, thought better of it, and relaxed back onto the mattress. Tante Edith was right, he needed to get better before he could roam the streets again; before he could go out and look for Hélène.

Chapter 20

Hélène had spent her second night in the Clergy House, and when she awoke in the morning her heart lifted. Today she was going home. Madame Sauze had said that when her clothes were dry and mended, she could go home. Well, she knew they were dry as she had helped bring them down from the airer yesterday afternoon, and she hoped that Madame had mended the tears as she had promised.

As the day before, Hélène waited for Madame Sauze to come and fetch her for breakfast, and when she heard her footsteps on the stairs, she jumped up and was waiting expectantly when the housekeeper opened the door.

'Have you got my clothes, madame?' she asked. 'Can I have them back now they're clean and dry?'

'Here they are,' said Madame Sauze, handing over a neatly laundered pile. 'I'll wait while you get dressed and then we'll go down and find some breakfast.'

Hélène scrambled hurriedly into her clothes, and feeling the clean fabric against her skin, felt instantly more like herself.

'When can I go home?' she asked as they settled themselves at the breakfast table. 'Will you come with me?'

'Eat your breakfast, my dear, and then we can make plans for the day.'

Agathe Sauze had lain awake much of the night wondering how she was going to tell this brave child who had come to trust her, that she wasn't going home after all, but into an orphanage. How was she going to explain that her family had left Paris... without her?

'Hélène,' she said as the girl drank the last of her hot chocolate, scraping the bowl with her spoon. 'We have to talk.'

'Yes, madame?' Hélène laid aside the spoon and looked expectantly at the housekeeper. She saw the seriousness on her face and the smile on her own faded.

'I have something to explain to you,' began Agathe and then paused to select her words.

'Yes?' prompted Hélène.

'Am I right in thinking you and your family live in the Avenue Ste Anne, in Passy?'

'Yes,' replied Hélène, wondering how she knew. She had been careful not to answer most of their questions, remembering what had followed those Gaston had asked her. Before she could ask, Agathe went on, 'Well, I went to see them last night, and...'

'You went to see them? Why didn't you take me?'

'I wasn't sure I had the right street,' said Agathe.

'And did you?' Hélène's eyes were alight with hope. 'Were they there?'

'It was the right street, my dear, but I'm afraid the house was shut up. There was nobody there.'

'But what about Berthe and Arlette? And Pierre? Where's Pierre?'

'Who's Pierre?'

'He's our coachman and he looks after Papa if he needs him.'

'I think Pierre must have gone to the country,' said Agathe. 'Perhaps driving your parents somewhere?' She remembered the chaise that had swept past her as she had arrived in the avenue, certain in her own mind now that it had been the St Clairs leaving. If only… But it was no time for if onlys, they had gone and she didn't know where. 'Where would they go if they left Paris?'

'To St Etienne,' came the immediate reply.

'Where is St Etienne?' asked Agathe. There were so many villages with St Etienne in their names.

'In the country,' Hélène said. 'It's in the country. That's where they'll be.' But then her face fell. 'But why did they go without me? Why didn't they wait till I got home again?'

'My dear, I don't know,' replied Agathe. And she didn't. Why had they left the city while their daughter was missing?

'So, can I go to St Etienne today?' asked Hélène hopefully. 'I know it takes a long time in a coach, 'cos we took days coming in through the snow, but now the trains are running again, it'll be quicker.'

'We'll have to see how we can get you home,' Agathe prevaricated. 'In the meantime, I'm afraid you can't stay here…'

'The nasty priest won't let me,' Hélène stated.

'I'm afraid it isn't suitable for the priests to have you here,' Agathe began.

'But you don't mind, do you? Just until I can go to find Maman and Papa?'

There was such simplicity in the question that it made Agathe want to weep. 'It isn't a question of what I want,' she said. 'This isn't my house, I only work here.'

'But you live here too,' Hélène pointed out. 'Can't I stay with you until I can go to St Etienne?'

'No, my dearest child, I'm afraid you can't. I'm going to take you to a safe place to live until we can find your parents and get in touch with them, so that they can come and fetch you.'

'What safe place?' demanded Hélène. 'Why can't you get my parents straight away? I've told you where they are, now.'

And if only you'd told us when we first found you instead of refusing to answer any questions, you'd be back with them now, thought Agathe, but she didn't put her thought into words. There was no point in upsetting the child any further.

'The trouble is,' she said carefully, 'we need to get a message to your parents, to tell them where you are, and that may take time. Until we can do that and hear back from them, you need to be somewhere safe.'

'But I'm safe here!' Hélène's voice became a childish wail.

'I'm sorry, but it's not appropriate for you to stay here,' Agathe said.

'So where am I going?'

'I'm taking you to St Luke's,' replied Agathe.

'What's St Luke's?' asked Hélène suspiciously.

'It's a home that looks after children who have nowhere else to live,' answered Agathe, getting to her feet and holding out her hand. 'Now, come along, my dear, it's time we left. I have to be back to get the fathers their luncheon.'

Hélène didn't move. 'It's an orphanage,' she said flatly.

'There are orphans who live there,' conceded Agathe. 'But there are other children as well, children who only stay there for a short while, until they can go home again. Children like you.'

Ignoring Agathe's outstretched hand, Hélène stood and walked out of the room. In the hall she met Father Thomas coming out of the dining room and she stopped dead. He paused, looking her up and down, a look of surprise on his face. In her clean clothes, with her hair washed and neatly plaited, she looked nothing like the child he had found in the church three days ago, but even so he wasn't pleased that she was still in the house. As Agathe followed her into the hall, Father Thomas turned to her and said, 'I thought Father Lenoir told you to take this... person... to the orphanage, Madame Sauze. Why haven't you done so?'

Agathe Sauze could hardly contain her anger. 'Even you, Father, must allow her some breakfast first. It's the *Christian* thing to do.' And with this sally she took Hélène by the hand and led her up the stairs, leaving the young priest standing, scandalised, in the front hall.

Father Lenoir emerged from the dining room behind him and speaking very softly, said, 'In future, Father Thomas, I'll thank you not to interfere with matters that don't concern you.'

The young man's face reddened at the reprimand. 'I'm sorry, Father,' he stammered. 'It was only my intention to—'

'The way to hell is paved with good intentions, my son,' said the older priest. 'It is a saying worthy of your attention.'

As Agathe led her through the streets, Hélène's brain was working overtime, considering feverishly whether she could make a run for it, race off down a side street before they reached this St Luke's place, wherever it was. If she did, Madame Sauze would never catch up with her, she would be free again, in the city, but with nowhere safe to go. She didn't know her way back home, though she was sure she could get there in the end, but Madame had said it was closed up.

There'd be no one there, and the Gaston-man might come for her again; after all, he knew where she lived. But if she didn't go home where else could she go? She could try and find Jeannot, but she only had the vaguest idea of where he'd taken her when they met up with Paul and the Monkey, and she remembered the sounds of the fight, of Jeannot shouting at her, and didn't even know for sure that he had escaped. She still hadn't made up her mind what to do when they rounded a corner and Madame Sauze led her to a pair of heavy wooden double doors set in a high, grey stone wall. Hélène looked in dismay at the blank face of the forbidding building. Surely Madame wasn't going to leave her here? Panic rose in her chest and she took a step backwards, but Madame took a firm hold of her arm before she could break away. One half of the door opened almost at once and a small nun looked out at them. Seeing Madame Sauze, the nun stepped aside to let them enter. Hélène looked over her shoulder for a last glimpse of the busy street outside before the door closed behind her with a heavy thud. She knew now her chance of escape had gone. She had left it too late.

Chapter 21

Marcel St Clair had been accepted into the National Guard and had been assigned to a troop who were on duty in the Place Vendôme. He had not been there on the fateful day when the guards had opened fire on the Friends of Order who were demanding peace, and for that he was grateful. He had no wish to open fire on ordinary citizens, even ones who seemed to be challenging the National Guard. After what was being called 'the massacre' in the Rue de la Paix, the mood of the city had changed to one of edgy anxiety. Marcel's corps of guards were now patrolling the city walls, checking who was passing, both in and out, through the gates, watching for anything or anyone suspicious, on the lookout for army spies.

When the elected national government had left Paris for Versailles, organisation in the city had disintegrated. The Central Committee had called its own elections and as soon as they'd been held, proclaimed themselves a Commune. The newly elected members were installed in the vacated Hôtel de Ville. News of the Commune was greeted by the underclass of Paris with delight. Crowds gathered outside the Hôtel de

Ville in the spring sunshine to hear the official proclamation, to cheer the battalions of the National Guard as they marched past, to hear the bands play, to sing 'La Marseillaise', to cry 'Vive la Commune!' It was a new era! Now the workers could take hold of power and everything would change. It had been a day of rejoicing, a day of hope, but the joy had been short-lived. The proclamation was virtually a declaration of war with the government, and the threat of civil strife loomed large.

Despite the jubilation, it was not long before things began to go wrong for the Communards. They were disorganised, with many dissident groups each with its own agenda, and some out to settle private scores. Overall control rested with men who, though full of revolutionary fervour, were ill-equipped to lead such a disparate group and soon the Communards were falling out with each other over what should be done. One of its first actions was to repeal the rent act, the act that insisted back rent from the time of the siege must be paid to landlords, and this was greeted with delight. The abolition of conscription to the regular French army was popular, but its replacement, that all the able-bodied men must join the National Guard, was far less so, and quietly, more of the middle classes began to disappear from the city.

Already now a National Guardsman, Marcel was promoted to corporal and then sergeant as his experience was clear, and he and his men were moved out to patrol the wall from the Porte d'Auteuil to the Porte Dauphine. It was a section of the wall near the Avenue Ste Anne, and though he was not prepared to go there and announce his return to his family, he found, as the days passed, that he wanted just a sight of the house which had been his childhood home.

When his men were relieved one afternoon and he had

some time to himself, he set out for the Avenue Ste Anne. The street was quiet, just a few people going about their daily business. He was unrecognised, his uniform ensuring that no one queried what he was doing there; people hurried past him, eyes averted. It wasn't safe these days to come to the attention of the National Guard and this suited Marcel extremely well. He passed by the front of the house and seeing the shuttered windows and the boarded up front door, he paused for a moment wondering what had happened. Then turning the corner and walking down the lane, he glanced up at the back of the house. Here too the windows were shuttered and when he tried the gates he was unsurprised to find them locked. Clearly the family had left the house and were, as he'd hoped, safely at St Etienne. Marcel cast a quick glance down the narrow lane that served as a carriage entrance to several of the houses on that side of the avenue, most of which were also shuttered and closed. The lane was empty and so, unobserved, he hoisted himself up and over the wall, dropping down into the stable yard beyond. A quick glance into the stables and coach house reassured him that his family had left and he heaved a sigh of relief. He tried the kitchen entrance to the house, but the door was locked and he had no key. He went back into the stables and climbed the ladder that led to the hayloft and the two small rooms that were Pierre's domain. Though some of Pierre's possessions were still there, it was clear that the place hadn't been used for several days. There was a single bed, unmade, heaped with blankets and a pillow, a table and chair, a dirty plate, a knife and fork and a half-full glass of water. A bowl and jug stood on top of the chest set under the tiny dusty window, the drawers of which contained some underclothes. It seemed to Marcel that Pierre had left in something of a hurry, but that he did expect to be coming back. In the meantime, Marcel thought, he could make good use of the place. He looked about him with satisfaction. He had already decided that when things got too hot in the city he might need a refuge. The war between the Versailles government and the Commune was only a matter of time, he knew, and if he should need a bolthole, Pierre's loft would serve very well.

He went back down to the yard and walked through into the garden. It was clear that this had not been tended for some long time. Crossing to the garden gate that gave onto the lane, he unlocked it and pocketed the key. It would be far better to slip in and out through the small gate than to leave the main gates unlocked or hoist himself over the wall every time he wanted to come here. He would provide himself with some provisions and move his few possessions in here. Maybe, later, he'd break into the house and collect stuff from his old bedroom and a few creature comforts.

Since his parents had finally left, Georges St Clair had kept a watchful eye on the family home. The boarded front door was undisturbed, but whenever he was in Paris he would pass by, just in case there was any sign of Hélène having returned. What would she do if she got home and found nobody there? He had put the word out that his sister had been abducted and was still missing, but he'd heard nothing back and was beginning to accept that after so long there was little chance of finding her alive. His undercover work for General Vinoy prevented him from organising any real search for her, but at least much of the time now he was within the city walls and not stuck outside at Versailles with the rest of his corps.

When Georges had heard how the last few government

ministers had made their strategic withdrawal from the Hôtel de Ville to Versailles through an underground tunnel, it reminded him of something, something from his childhood that he thought would interest his commanding officer, General Vinoy.

It was a school friend of his, Martin Dupont, who had once mentioned that there was an old tunnel from the cellar of his house in a street just inside the wall near the Porte d'Auteuil. It led, he said, to somewhere on the outside, but he didn't know where. Maybe somewhere in the Bois?

'It was used in the Revolution as a way to get aristos out of the city before they met Madame la Guillotine,' he said. 'D'you want to see it?'

Georges certainly did and the two boys had crept down into the cellar to have a look.

'We have to be quiet,' whispered Martin. 'If my father knew I was showing you, we'd both get a leathering.'

The cellar was in two parts and Martin led the way to the back section. 'Under here,' he said, pointing down at the flagged floor. 'That stone in the middle lifts up.'

It wasn't as heavy as it looked, being sliced thinner than those about it. Together they heaved on the ring set into its centre, managing to raise the stone and slide it sideways. Both boys peered down into the dark hole it revealed.

'There's rungs set into the wall,' Martin said, 'so's you can climb down.'

'Have you been down?' asked Georges.

'Yes, just to the bottom,' Martin answered. 'It's like the bottom of a well and from there it runs sideways, under the wall.'

'Shall we look?'

Martin shook his head vehemently. 'No,' he said, 'it isn't

safe. My father says it's nearly a hundred years old and the roof could collapse at any time. Anyway,' he added as a relieved afterthought, 'we'd need a lamp, so we can't.'

'A good escape route though,' Georges said as they slid the stone back across the opening.

The secret of that tunnel was a secret worth knowing and Georges wondered if it could still be used. When the army was ordered out to Versailles, Georges had taken the secret to General Vinoy and was immediately sent to explore.

When he reached the Dupont house there was no sign of occupation; like so many others it was closed up.

The family must have left the city, thought Georges as he surveyed the shuttered house. But it should be easy enough to break in.

So it proved, and armed with a lantern, Georges went down into the cellar to open the tunnel. He peered into the darkness, and then feeling for the rungs of the iron ladder with his feet, he climbed down. Martin's father need not have feared collapse; the tunnel, though damp underfoot and smelling very musty, showed no signs of subsidence. Holding the lantern in front of him, he began to edge his way along. It was so narrow in places that Georges had to turn sideways to squeeze through, and in others the roof dipped so low he had to crouch, but the passage continued in front of him for what he judged to be well over two hundred metres until he found himself standing in a circular space similar to the one he had climbed down to at the other end. He raised his lantern and saw there were iron rungs set into the stonework, and hooking the lantern onto his belt he climbed up until his head came against the top. Feeling with his fingers he realised that it was not stone above him this end, but wood, a wooden trapdoor of some sort. Martin had said the tunnel came out somewhere in the Bois, but where? In the open? In another cellar? Would he be seen coming out? It was, he decided, a risk he would have to take, and bending forward, he put his shoulders against the wood above him and pushed. At first he couldn't move it, but by stepping down and then pushing upward again several times, he felt it shift a little. He heaved at it again and again, until all of a sudden it lifted and he felt a draught of cold air on his face. He eased the wood away and climbed out to find he was still enclosed in a circle of stone. Above him, silhouetted against the moonlit sky, was a winding handle and a small wooden roof, and he realised he was standing at the bottom of a dry well. Clearly it had not held water since the tunnel had been dug from its floor. It was dark outside and Georges doused his lantern before emerging into the night. He could only hope its light hadn't been seen as he'd raised the trapdoor.

He hauled himself up over the well's stone parapet and found himself in an overgrown garden. The shell of a house stood in the pale moonlight, stark against the night sky, but there seemed to be no other buildings close by. He left the lantern inside the well and once his eyes became accustomed to the darkness, Georges made his way through the garden, pushing through brambles, weeds and shrubs that had run wild. The house was derelict, its windows without glass, its roof open to the sky. No one had lived here for years, and he presumed the secret of its well was long forgotten. Having established exactly where he had emerged, Georges returned to the well and closing the trapdoor over his head made his way back through the tunnel to the Dupont house.

He returned to General Vinoy who was delighted with the information. The army now had a back door into Paris; too small for the movement of troops, but perfect for the introduction of spies. Georges, now promoted to captain, had been permanently seconded to the general from then on and had been coming and going through the tunnel ever since. The house at the far end had been put under army observation so that no one should discover the secret of the well by accident, but when entering or emerging from the Dupont house within the walls of Paris, Georges had to take his chances.

Last night, Georges had been out to Versailles to report the placement of the guards on the city walls and had just returned. As always he walked slowly past the St Clairs' house, casting a sideway glance at the boarded front door, but nothing seemed to have changed. He'd heard nothing from his parents since they had, he assumed, arrived at St Etienne more than two weeks ago. He wasn't worried about that as all communication was fraught these days and many letters never reached their destination; he had no news for them either. He walked down the alley to the *porte cochère*, still chained with a padlock, and he was about to turn away when he noticed that the small gate set into the garden wall was not quite closed.

Was someone in the garden, some intruder trying to break into the house? Georges drew the pistol that he carried tucked into his belt and gently pushed the gate a little wider. He expected to hear the familiar creak it always made, but it moved silently and Georges realised that its hinges must have been oiled. Who would break into the garden and then oil the hinges?

Once inside he left the gate open behind him for a speedy exit should he need one and crept forward into the stable yard. Glancing across at the kitchen door, he could see that it was still closed. Of course, someone might already be inside the house, but he decided to check the coach house and stables first. Pistol in hand he stepped silently across the yard and peeped in through the stable door. He could see no one, but he could hear someone moving about up in the loft. Pierre's loft. Had Pierre returned from St Etienne? He was about to call out when he saw some feet beginning to descend the ladder, feet in heavy army boots. He stepped back outside and stood ready, covering the stable door with his gun.

As he heard the man, whoever he was, move towards the door he cocked the gun and said, 'I have you covered. Come out very slowly or I'll shoot.'

The footsteps stopped for a moment and then a familiar voice said, 'You'd better not shoot me, Georges, Maman would be most upset.'

Georges, still holding the pistol extended in front of him, couldn't believe his ears. 'Marcel?' he said. 'Marcel? Is that you?'

'Better believe it, brother,' came the cheerful voice. 'Promise not to shoot if I come out?'

'Just come out where I can see you.' Even though he recognised his younger brother's voice, his typical insouciance, Georges still kept the door covered with his gun.

Marcel emerged, a smile on his face, his hands up in mock surrender. 'Surprise!' he said.

Georges was indeed surprised; after all, they'd thought him dead. The surprise was greater as Marcel was dressed in a National Guard's uniform. He stuck his pistol back in his belt and the brothers grinned at each other before they clasped hands and embraced.

'What are you doing here?'

'When did you get back?'

They both spoke at once and then laughed.

'You first,' said Georges.

'Can't get into the house without breaking in,' Marcel said. 'So I'm dossing down in the stables. The family's in St Etienne, I suppose.' He turned back inside and Georges followed him.

'They are now,' he said, 'but the most awful thing's happened and I've been trying to find any news.'

'What?' asked Marcel sharply. 'What's happened?'

Quickly Georges told him about Hélène and poor Marie-Jeanne.

'And Hélène's still missing?' asked Marcel.

'I think so. I haven't heard from our parents that they've found her.' Georges stared at him. 'And let's face it, Marcel, she's been missing for a couple of weeks now. She's not going to be found. I've put out feelers in the city, but have heard nothing of her or of any child who might have been her. If it was kidnap, the kidnappers would have been in touch by now asking for money. I think we have to accept that she's almost certainly dead.'

'I've been back a while now,' Marcel admitted. 'I'm in the National Guard,' he looked down at his uniform as if surprised to see it, 'I can ask about. We hear things in the city. We're the eyes and ears of the Commune.'

'But why?' asked Georges, wanting the answer to this question. 'Why are you with the National Guard and not back with your regiment?'

Marcel made no answer to that but said, 'I see you're in civvies, so I could ask you the same.'

'Couple of days' leave,' Georges said. 'Compassionate, to look for Hélène.'

He wasn't quite sure why he had prevaricated, lied, except that despite their reunion, Marcel, wearing the uniform of a National Guard, was now on the opposite side of the divide.

Marcel looked at him speculatively. 'All right,' he said, 'I won't ask you any more, except to say that I suppose I'm classed as a deserter and I'd prefer you didn't mention seeing me or turn me in.'

'Turn you in?' Georges shook his head. 'You're my brother!' He shook his head in confusion and went on, 'I should, I suppose, but you're one of hundreds, so what does one more matter? But why? Why have you deserted to the National Guard?'

'Sedan. Camp of Misery. The whole bloody war. You must agree that the conduct of the war was a complete disaster and our generals were utterly useless! I'm fighting for the average man now, not some elite who sacrifice men from the safety of castle walls!'

'Were you at the camp too? After Sedan? I looked for you, but it was hopeless.'

'That's what I mean,' returned Marcel.

'But what about our parents? You must tell them you're alive and well. Maman's been desperate about you, mourning you as dead.'

'But I sent them a note to say I was alive, just not able to come home yet!'

'They never got it,' Georges said. 'Where did you send it?'

'St Etienne, of course. I never dreamed that they'd come back into Paris so soon.'

'No,' agreed Georges with a sigh, 'neither did I. And they shouldn't have, but at least they've gone again now.'

They had been sitting comfortably on straw bales in the stable but at length Marcel stood up. 'Better go,' he said. 'Be careful, Georges. We're on the lookout for people like you.'

Georges nodded in acknowledgement. 'Do your best to find out what happened to her,' he said earnestly. 'The people you're with are more likely to hear of something like an abduction than I am.'

Marcel gave a rueful smile. 'You're probably right,' he said. 'I'll put the word about. How shall I reach you if I hear anything?'

'I'll come back here… soon. If you have any news leave me a note in the stable. I'll do the same. If there's any possibility she's still alive we must find her. She's only eleven, she'll never survive on her own out there.'

The two men parted. Each going his separate way, each keeping his own secrets; neither prepared to ask questions of the other to which they didn't want to know the answers, neither with any real hope now of finding their little sister. But at least in that they were both on the same side.

Chapter 22

As soon as the door clanged behind her, Hélène knew she should have run. The nun led her and Madame Sauze to a small, dreary waiting room furnished with a table, two upright chairs and a sagging sofa, and saying Reverend Mother would be with them shortly she left them there to wait.

When they were alone they sat down on opposite sides of the table. Hélène looked across at Madame Sauze with wide frightened eyes. 'Please don't leave me here, madame,' she pleaded. 'I don't like it here. I want to go home.'

'I know you do,' replied Agathe, 'and you shall just as soon as I can find your parents, I promise.' What else could she say?

It was nearly ten minutes before the door opened and Reverend Mother came in. She was a large woman, seeming taller and broader in her black habit, a girdle knotted about her ample waist and the starched white wimple standing on her head like the wings of a bird. She had a narrow face and close-set eyes above a sharp beak of a nose. She paused just inside the door, casting an assessing gaze over her visitors before stepping forward to meet them.

Madame Sauze stood up at once and performing a sort of half-curtsy, said, 'Good morning, Mother.'

'Ah, Madame Sauze, is it not? A blessed morning to you,' replied the nun. She looked across at Hélène who had remained seated and said, 'Stand up, child! Have you no manners?'

Reluctantly Hélène stood up, but looking down at her feet, said nothing.

Reverend Mother turned back to Madame Sauze and asked, 'Who is this girl? And why have you brought her to me?'

'This is Hélène St Clair,' Madame Sauze replied. 'Father Thomas found her collapsed, alone in the church. Her family are not in the city just now and she needs a place to live. Father Lenoir asks that you take her in for a few weeks until we can contact her parents and they can come for her.'

Reverend Mother eyed Hélène with disfavour. 'She doesn't seem the sort of child we should be giving a home to,' she said. 'Our home is for destitute children, we cannot give shelter and food to children who have simply been lost by their parents.'

'Father Lenoir suggests that when her parents come to fetch her, he's sure they will be more than happy to defray any costs you might have had to meet in caring for her.'

The nun's eyes flashed briefly, but then she said, 'But what happens if they *don't* come? What happens if they never come?'

'Then,' replied Madame Sauze with some spirit, 'she will be just the sort of child you care for, because she will be destitute!'

Reverend Mother pursed her lips and looking at Hélène, said, 'Well, child, what have you to say for yourself?'

Hélène looked across at Madame Sauze, a mute entreaty in her eyes, but Agathe Sauze looked away and Hélène murmured a soft, 'Nothing, Mother.'

'Just as well,' said the nun. 'Well, girl, I have decided that you may come and live here, just while Madame Sauze and Father Lenoir find your family.' She said it as if she were conferring a great favour. 'But you will have to work for your keep, as we all do.'

Hélène glowered at her, hating her in her black habit and flyaway hat. 'I don't *want* to come and live here,' she said defiantly, 'I want to go home!'

'Well, as you haven't got a home to go to, you should be grateful for the one I'm offering you,' retorted the nun. Then turning to Madame Sauze, she said, 'It's time for you to leave, madame. Sister Gabrielle will show you out. I will take care of this child from now.' She reached out and gripped Hélène's wrist, her fingers biting into her flesh. 'And you, girl, will come with me.'

She jerked hard and forced Hélène to follow her to the door. She opened it and nun and child disappeared into the orphanage. The last Agathe Sauze saw of Hélène St Clair was an agonised white face, turned back towards her, an expression of mingled misery, fear and betrayal. Then she was gone.

The portress, Sister Gabrielle, came into the room and took her to the front door.

'Don't worry about that girl, madame,' she said. 'Reverend Mother'll soon lick her into shape.'

And that, thought Agathe as she walked slowly back to the Clergy House, was exactly what she was afraid of.

It was also exactly what Reverend Mother was doing. She took Hélène into her office and made her stand in the corner facing the wall, with her hands on her head, for almost half an hour before she spoke to her again.

'Now, Hélène,' she said at last, 'I am going to speak to you as a sensible girl. Come and stand here in front of me.'

Hélène lowered her hands with relief and moved in front of the large desk behind which the nun had seated herself.

'Here at St Luke's we have very definite rules. Rules which everyone obeys without question, one of which is that you don't answer back when spoken to.' She fixed Hélène with an unwavering stare, as if daring her to break that rule now. 'You obey an instruction at once and without comment or argument. Children who break these rules are severely dealt with, so that they remember not to do so again. I hope you understand that, Hélène.' And when Hélène did not answer she picked up a small cane from the top of her desk and switched it against the wood. 'Do you?'

Hélène nodded.

'When I address you, you answer "Yes, Mother".' Reverend Mother raised her eyebrows. 'Do you understand me, Hélène?'

Hélène swallowed hard and managed to say, 'Yes, Mother.'

'Good,' said the nun briskly and rang the small brass bell that stood on her desk. Immediately there was a knock at the door and another nun appeared.

'This is Sister Marguerite,' said Reverend Mother. 'She will take you now and show you where you will eat, sleep and work. Go with her and I want to see no more of you.'

Sister Marguerite led Hélène out of the room and along a passage to a heavy wooden door at the end. 'This is the way to your part of the house,' she said. 'You will not come back through this door unless you are sent for. Do you understand?'

Hélène murmured a quiet, 'Yes, Sister.'

'Good girl.' Sister Marguerite opened the door and they stepped through to the orphanage; to a new life, if it could be called life.

The first thing Hélène noticed was the smell. It was unpleasantly strong, a mixture of cabbage, damp laundry and something she had yet to recognise. She followed the nun along another corridor and up some stairs. 'The dormitories are up here,' Sister Marguerite said, as she led the way into a long, narrow room. Down each brown-painted wall were iron bedsteads, fifteen of them. Each bed had a thin straw mattress, with a grey blanket folded on a stool at its foot. There were no sheets and no pillows.

'This is the girls' dormitory,' said Sister Marguerite. 'The boys sleep on the next floor. That's your bed,' she said, pointing to the one nearest the door.

'Why hasn't it got a blanket?' asked Hélène.

'It was Ella's bed. She died yesterday,' the sister explained casually. 'Her blanket was used as her shroud. I'll find you another one.' Hélène shrank back from Ella's bed in horror, and Sister Marguerite said, 'Don't be so stupid, girl. People die in beds all the time. Now then, we all work hard here, we earn our food and shelter, so it's time to do your share.'

The rest of Hélène's day passed in a haze. Sister Marguerite took her down to the big kitchen where all the food for the orphanage and the convent was prepared. Here she was presented to Sister Barbara as a replacement for the deceased Ella, and set to peel a bucket of potatoes. Hélène had seen Arlette peel potatoes in the kitchen at home, but she hadn't realised what hard work it could be. The potatoes in the bucket seemed never-ending and before long her hands were red and raw from the cold water and scraping with the blunt knife.

'Hurry up, girl,' called Sister Barbara. 'Anyone would think you'd never peeled a potato before!'

The midday meal, consisting of a watery soup with some unidentifiable pieces of meat floating about in it, a hunk of bread and a small square of hard yellow cheese, was served in the refectory with the sisters. It was eaten in silence while one of the novices, wearing a grey habit and a much smaller wimple, stood at a lectern and read from the Bible.

As she drank her soup and ate the bread and cheese, Hélène had a chance to look round at the community of which she was now a part. The nuns sat at tables at one end of the room, with Reverend Mother seated at the middle of a high table set up on a dais. The children were seated, twelve to a table, at the lower end of the room. The girls were all dressed in drab grey dresses, their hair tied back off their faces with scraps of grey fabric; the few boys wore smocks and baggy trousers. Their faces, pale and peaky, showed the lines of the hard and tiring life they had to live. She noticed the way they all drank their soup, never putting the bowl down before they had finished every last drop; how they tore at their bread, sometimes dipping it in the soup to soften it; how they crammed the morsel of cheese into their mouths as if it might vanish before they had a chance to taste it. Hélène made the mistake of leaving the last of her bread on the table while she lifted her soup bowl with both hands. Even as she went to pick it up again, it disappeared into the mouth of the girl sitting next to her.

'Hey!' Hélène cried, and for a moment the clatter of the refectory ceased as everyone looked to see who had had the temerity to speak, to cry out, breaking the mealtime silence. Her face flooding crimson, Hélène stared fixedly at the table and after a moment the clatter of the dining room resumed.

When Reverend Mother had said grace at the end of the meal, she paused beside her chair to say, 'Sister Barbara, please discipline the child who disturbed our meal.'

Back in the kitchen, Sister Barbara took hold of Hélène and shook her, hard. 'Stupid!' she cried. 'Stupid girl. Eat your food and stay silent! It's your first day and already you cause a nuisance. Another time and swish! You will feel my willows.' She glowered at Hélène and said, 'You understand, stupid girl?'

'Yes, Sister,' Hélène replied, guessing what Sister Barbara's 'willows' might be and not wanting to feel them. Glancing round the scullery where they were washing the dishes, she saw the bread thief, grinning as she scrubbed a saucepan.

I'll remember your face, Hélène thought fiercely. I won't forget you.

All the time they worked in the kitchen, they worked in silence, only whispering asides to each other when Sister Barbara and her junior, Sister Alice, were out of earshot. One of the girls who had been sitting near Hélène at table gave her a sympathetic grin. She pointed to the bread thief and murmured, 'That's Annette.'

Supper was similar to the midday meal, but lacking the cheese. The kitchen was then cleared and cleaned, after which all the children were assembled in the chapel for evening prayer before bed.

Back in the dormitory, Hélène saw her assigned bed was as she'd seen it before. There was no blanket laid out for her, just a coarse cotton nightdress folded across the stool. She watched as the other girls visited the toilet at the far end of the landing and when Annette took her turn, Hélène went swiftly to the other girl's bed and, observed by the startled eyes of those already in bed, she snatched up the blanket and took it. Wrapping it round her she lay down on her bed, dead Ella's bed, and pretended to be asleep.

Moments later there was a kerfuffle when Annette returned and discovered she had no blanket. There were whispers and giggles, and then a sudden silence when Sister Marguerite came into the dormitory. She saw Annette sitting on her bed, dressed in her nightdress, but with no blanket to cover her. Glancing round the room she saw every other girl had one, including the new girl in Ella's bed. Sister Marguerite realised that she had not found a blanket as she'd promised and the girl had taken things into her own hands and stolen Annette's. She should take her to task for it, but she couldn't risk another row at this time of night. Mother would blame her as much as the child. She'd known that new girl was going to cause trouble from the moment she'd fetched her from Mother's office. It was the way she met your eyes when you spoke to her; there was no humility there.

That will have to change, she thought as she sent Annette to the cupboard for another blanket. She'll have to be watched or she'll be making trouble for all of us.

Once the dormitory had settled down to sleep, Hélène suddenly felt someone sit down on the edge of her bed. Peering into the gloom, she saw the pale face of the bread thief.

'You stole my blanket,' whispered Annette.

'And you stole my bread,' came the sharp reply.

There was a muffled laugh and then Annette said, 'Yes, but you didn't get it back and *I've* got a new blanket... so I win!' Then she leaned down and put her mouth to Hélène's ear and murmured, 'Be careful, new girl, or you'll find yourself in real trouble. Know what I mean?'

Hélène didn't, but she could guess. When Annette had gone back to her own bed and the only sounds in the room were the snufflings and snorings of thirty girls, Hélène lay awake, her brain churning. How long would she have to stay in this awful place? She could feel the lump growing in her throat, the pressure of tears in her eyes, but she was determined not to cry. It would do no good and only make the other girls think she was a baby. No. She refused to cry. She would use all her energy in finding a way to escape. If Jeannot, Paul and the Monkey could make a living from the streets, then surely, so could she. She would keep a careful watch and find a way to escape this prison. She would find her way back home and hide there until Maman and Papa came back for her.

Next morning began with prayers in the chapel and then there was the same dreary round of work. All the children were assigned chores to complete, and Hélène found herself sent to the laundry. Here it was hot and steamy as the huge coppers containing the dirty clothes were brought to the boil on wide brick fireplaces. The smaller girls kept the fires going, posting dry wood into the flames so that their heat never diminished. Older girls, girls more Hélène's age, were in charge of these huge vats, and continually poked them with long poles, turning the clothes in the soapy water. Hélène was handed one of the poles and was told by Annette what to do.

'Don't get too close,' she warned, 'or you'll get splashed by the boiling water.'

Hélène was extremely careful. She was only just recovering from her bruises and she needed to be strong for her escape.

After a week of drudgery and toil, where one day was so similar to the next, Hélène had lost track of time. There was no question of schooling. When she had ventured to ask Sister Marguerite if they had lessons, she gave a bark of laughter.

'What on earth for? What use would reading and writing be to you?'

'I can read and write,' replied Hélène.

'Can you now? Well, you won't be needing it any more. Scullery maids don't need book learning,' adding as she turned her attention elsewhere, 'Reading's very overrated.'

And you can't do it, Hélène thought with a sudden flash of insight. You can't read. And for some reason the thought pleased her.

Sunday came round and the children were all given a clean set of clothes to wear for church. Hélène's own clothes had been taken away the morning after she had arrived and she was now clad in one of the grey dresses they all wore. It was rough and scratchy and made her skin itch, but it was all she had, and a pair of cotton drawers for decency.

When they'd finished breakfast and it had been cleared away, they all lined up and were led out of the back gate of the convent to form a crocodile and, two by two, they walked the half mile to the church for High Mass. Hélène found herself paired with Annette, and as they walked along the streets, Hélène looked down narrow side roads and into squares and courtyards. Surely if she was quick she could break away, disappear into the warren of streets that straggled off the main road. She wondered if Annette ever thought about escape. It seemed that they were allowed to talk quietly as they walked, and so she asked.

'Do you ever think of running away, Annette?'

Annette looked surprised at the question. 'Why would I?' she replied. 'Where would I go?'

'Home?' Hélène suggested tentatively, causing Annette to burst out laughing. 'This is my home,' she said. 'I ain't never had no other. My ma, whoever she was, left me on the doorstep in a basket.' She rolled her eyes dramatically and added, 'I'm a child of shame!'

Hélène didn't quite know what a child of shame was and not wanting to reveal her ignorance by asking, she just nodded and said, 'Oh, sorry, I didn't know.'

'Don't matter,' shrugged Annette, but said no more and Hélène was none the wiser.

When they reached the church they were herded into the back rows. Hélène could see Madame Sauze in one of the pews further forward, but the sight of Father Lenoir and Father Thomas emerging from the vestry in their robes made her sink back behind a pillar, out of sight. All through the service, the homily, the communion, her mind was racing. Could church be the place from which she could make her escape? Could she make a break for it now? She glanced round her, but saw that Sister Marguerite and the portress, Sister Gabrielle, were sitting on the end of the pews, between the children and the church door. No escape from inside the church then; she'd have to come up with something else.

As they left the church, Madame Sauze came across to where they were lined up for their walk back to the convent. She came towards Hélène slowly, not sure that she was the right child. Dressed as all the others, her hair constrained by the strip of grey, she looked nothing like the girl she had left with Reverend Mother just six days ago.

'Hélène,' she said hesitantly and was dismayed to see the pale face of the child who turned in answer to her name. When she saw Madame Sauze her face lit up.

'Have you found them? Are they coming?'

'Not yet, child, but Father Lenoir has written to several churches in outlying villages with St Etienne in their name, asking for news of them.' She gave a sigh. 'The trouble is, things in Paris are getting very difficult now with the fighting, and letters aren't getting to their destinations, so I'm afraid we've had no replies.'

Hélène's face fell, and Agathe wished she hadn't approached her; she should have stayed away until she had some good news to impart, but she'd wanted to know that the child was all right. Having seen her, she wished with all her heart that she had stood out against the two priests and kept her at the Clergy House.

At that moment, Reverend Mother emerged from the church and seeing Madame Sauze speaking to Hélène, she sailed over to find out what she was saying.

'I'm afraid we don't allow our girls to speak to just anyone in the street, madame,' she said, 'so I'd be grateful if you'd keep your distance in future.' She looked speculatively at Madame Sauze and added, 'If you have any news of the parents, please inform me, not the child. It would be so disappointing for her if the information proved to be incorrect.' She gave Agathe a frosty smile and then swept away to the front of the crocodile to lead it back to St Luke's.

As they reached the corner Hélène turned, and looking back saw Madame Sauze still standing outside the church, watching the line of children disappearing from sight.

That first week set the routine of Hélène's existence. Though she was still determined to run away if she possibly could, she found she was already getting used to how things were at St Luke's. The washing facilities were minimal and the smell she'd been unable to identify on arrival proved to be that of unwashed bodies. The food was scarce and badly cooked and all the children and most of the nuns were hungry much of the time, but gradually Hélène found that she could manage on the soup, the bread, the occasional potatoes and scraps of meat and fish that appeared at the table.

Sundays came and went; three was it, or four? But for the children living at St Luke's the world outside had no meaning. They could hear the guns, the bombardment of the city from the army that encircled it, the louder boom of the guns mounted inside the walls at the Trocadéro that returned fire, but they were never given any explanation of what was happening beyond their own walls. The curfew that had been ordered had no implication for them, they went to bed with the dusk and rose with the dawn.

Each Sunday she kept her eyes on Madame Sauze, hoping for news, but following Reverend Mother's instruction Madame Sauze didn't approach her again and Hélène soon realised that she could rely on no one but herself.

It was as she was sitting watching the nuns go up to the altar to receive Holy Communion that the idea struck her, and she realised that she did have a chance of escape from the church. As she watched the procession of sisters move through the church, the ghost of her idea grew and crystallised into a plan.

The following Sunday she made sure she was on the end of the pew, sitting next to Sister Gabrielle. She sat on the edge of her seat waiting and watching. The nuns filed up to the altar to receive the Body of Christ and at last Sister Marguerite and Sister Gabrielle rose from their places at the end of the orphanage pews and joined the other nuns.

Hélène glanced behind her. There was no one between her and the door now. It was closed, but surely it would only be the work of a moment to open it, to run outside. Once out of the church she would disappear down one of the side streets that led off the square and vanish into the city. If she moved quickly and nobody made a grab for her, she'd be out into the square so fast that they'd never catch her. She had no money, and only the orphanage clothes she stood up in, but it seemed her best chance.

Without further thought she edged to the end of the pew. She looked down the aisle to the altar. Sister Gabrielle was already turning to come back to her place. With her eyes raised heavenward, her hands clasped together in the wide sleeves of her habit, she walked slowly from the front of the church.

Now! Go now! Hélène was on her feet, heading for the door. Someone called out and people turned round to see what was happening. Sister Gabrielle's eyes flew open in time to see one of the children disappearing out of the door. She dropped her hands and ran forwards, intending to catch the child in the street outside, but as she reached the pew, another of the girls seemed to fall out of it, collapsing on the floor, coughing and spluttering and clutching her throat. It was so sudden that Sister Gabrielle almost fell over her and had to grab the pew end to remain on her feet.

'Get out of my way, child,' she shrilled, but Annette, for it was she who was writhing on the floor, clutched at her habit to restrain her, coughing loudly and wheezing, 'Help, Sister! I can't breathe!', making those in the nearby pews draw away for fear of some infection from the orphanage.

Reverend Mother appeared as if from nowhere, and almost at once order was restored. Father Lenoir and Father Thomas had continued distributing the Host, as if there were no commotion at the back of the church, and it wasn't until Annette had been taken outside and given water that she managed to stop coughing. The rest of the children were hurriedly removed from the area, and the congregation came out into the spring sunshine with something more exciting to talk about than the service, or what the priest had said in his homily.

Of Hélène St Clair there was no sign. Reverend Mother stayed at the church to speak to the priests and their housekeeper.

'Well, I hope you're satisfied,' she said angrily. 'It was Hélène St Clair who caused that furore, that commotion in the House of God! Well, I can tell you this, Christian duty or not, I will not have that child back at St Luke's.'

'Now then, Mother,' soothed Father Lenoir. 'You did all you could for the child; you mustn't blame yourself.'

'I certainly don't,' snapped the nun, 'I blame *you* for foisting her on me. She's been a disruption from the first day. She should have been whipped the day she arrived, when she disturbed the entire community, shouting out in the refectory.'

Father Thomas gave Agathe a sly smile. 'I always said she'd be trouble,' he said. 'We should have given her some food and sent her on her way.'

'Quite right, Father,' agreed the Reverend Mother. 'And now I must go and deal with Annette.' Turning on her heel she strode away towards St Luke's to deal with the girl whose unexpected coughing fit had prevented Sister Gabrielle from catching up with the truant.

Madame Sauze watched her go, knowing that young Annette was in for a tough time.

Annette knew it too, but from the moment Hélène had taken her revenge by stealing the blanket, Annette had looked at her with new respect. She hadn't known Hélène was going to make a break for it today, but when she saw her heading for the door, with Sister Gabrielle only a few metres behind her, she had acted on the spur of the moment and done the little she could to help her get away.

Chapter 23

Once she was out of the church Hélène knew that she had only moments to disappear. Sister Gabrielle would be out in a trice to grab hold of her. She darted into the first side street she came to and ran, her feet pounding on the cobbles. As she reached the corner she rounded it at speed and cannoned into a portly gentleman coming the other way. He caught hold of her, his hand grasping her arm.

'Now then, you young limb,' he began, but for the third time Hélène remembered Jeannot's shouted instruction and bending her head she sank her teeth into the man's hand. He let go with a bellow and she took to her heels, diving for cover behind a lumbering waggon and then round the corner into the next street. As before she took right and left turns indiscriminately until she was certain that she had shaken off the pursuit, and when at last she came to a wide boulevard she slowed her steps, so that it wasn't obvious that she was running away. She was free. Now all she had to do was find her way back home, but which way was it? Whom could she ask? She stood for a moment with the sun on her face getting her breath back, and then as from nowhere, it came to her.

In one of her lessons with the globe, Mademoiselle Corbine had explained that at midday in France the sun was always in the south.

Well, it's about midday now, Hélène thought, and if the sun is shining in my eyes, which it is, then I'm facing south, which must mean that west is on my right. She turned to her right and began to walk slowly along the boulevard. Home is in Passy, and Passy is at the western end of Paris. At every junction she turned her face to the sun and continued along whichever road went right. Despite the boom of distant cannon, or perhaps in defiance of it, many citizens were taking their usual Sunday afternoon promenade along the river and Hélène passed among them, just a young girl on an errand for her mistress. She was aware that she was still dressed in the dowdy orphanage uniform and that she must look out of place as she moved towards the more prosperous part of the city, but she walked purposefully, keeping her eyes straight ahead of her, never making eye contact with those coming towards her. After a while however, her strength began to flag. She'd had nothing to eat since breakfast and there'd been little enough of that, but worse was her thirst. The day was unseasonably hot, and she'd walked for several miles, but still she didn't want to stop, to draw attention to herself by asking directions. She needed to find the Avenue Ste Anne, but without anyone remembering her. She saw the green space of a small park and could hear the splash of water from an invisible fountain. Desperate for a drink, she turned in through the gate to find it. There were a few other people walking there, taking advantage of the beautiful weather, and when she had slaked her thirst at the fountain, Hélène too walked on slowly and out through the gate on the further side. That was when she saw it. The church of

Our Lady of Sorrows, its wide steps leading up to the west door above which was its square bell tower, topped with a pointed steeple; the church she and her family attended when they were in Paris. Hélène, exhausted now, could have wept for joy. She could easily find her way home from here and the knowledge gave her new strength. Until now she had thought no further than getting home, but as she approached she remembered her fear that the Gaston-man might still be watching for her. Hoping that she was unrecognisable in her grey orphan's dress, she approached the house, walking past slowly to see if there was any sign of him or his friends, but the street was empty. As she passed by she saw that the front door was barred with a piece of timber and her heart sank. The door had not been mended properly since Gaston had broken it down, so probably Madame Sauze was right, there was no one there. Still, she might be able to get in through the *porte cochère* or the garden gate and find shelter for tonight at least in the stables. Then she thought, perhaps Pierre was still there. Perhaps Papa had left him to look after the house while the family were at St Etienne. After all, he'd left Margot and Gilbert Daurier to look after the house when they'd gone on holiday last summer. Last summer. It seemed ages ago, and when they'd returned to Paris, Gilbert was dead and Margot had become quite simple, quite unable to work. Maman had sent her to St Etienne to live out her days in the peace of the country, away from the noise of the city and the painful memories of the siege.

So, Hélène thought now, Pierre might be here. She retraced her steps and turned down the lane behind the house. She saw at once that the *porte cochère* was still chained and moved on to the garden gate. She turned the handle, but to no avail. The latch didn't lift and the gate remained stubbornly shut.

Tears began to fill her eyes and she banged hard on the gate, still with the faint hope that Pierre might be there, might hear her and let her in.

She didn't hear the man approach as he moved silently towards her, but when he put his hand on her shoulder she spun round with a scream, trying to pull away. He wore the uniform of a National Guard and holding her away from him, his grip like a vice, he stared down into her face.

'Let me go! Let me go!' she shrieked, kicking out at him in an effort to break free, and to her surprise he released her and said incredulously, 'Hélène?'

She had been about to make a run for it down the lane, but hearing her name, said by a voice she loved, she paused, still poised for flight.

'Hélène?' he said again. 'Is it really you?'

'Marcel?' she whispered, looking up into his face. 'Marcel! You're alive! We thought you were dead. Oh, Marcel!' And bursting into tears she flung herself into his arms, clinging to him as he held her close, soothing her and stroking her hair.

As her sobs gradually died away, he said, 'Let's go inside, shall we?' He produced a key from his pocket and opened the garden gate and led her to the stables.

'I've been sleeping upstairs in Pierre's quarters,' he said. 'But when I have a visitor we sit down here.' He gestured to the straw bales and Hélène sat down.

'Why don't you live in the house?' she asked.

'The house is locked up and I think it's better that no one realises I'm here.'

'You said visitors?' Hélène looked confused.

'Only Georges,' grinned Marcel. 'He came looking for you and found me.'

'Looking for me?'

'Hélène, everyone's looking for you. We have no idea what happened to you, you just disappeared. Papa and Pierre came home to find you missing and… And the house broken into.' Marcel changed what he'd been about to say, not sure if his sister knew that Marie-Jeanne was dead. He reached over and took her hand. 'Want to tell me what happened?'

Hélène sat mute, her eyes wide with remembered fear.

'Never mind,' Marcel said gently. 'No need now. All that matters now is that you're safe.'

'I didn't know if it was safe to come home. He knows where I live and he might come looking for me here.'

'Who might?'

'The Gaston-man.'

'The Gaston-man?' echoed Marcel and his eyes narrowed. 'Don't worry about him, Hélène. If he shows up here, whoever he is, I'll deal with him, I promise you.'

'He's very fierce,' whispered Hélène.

'So am I,' Marcel said grimly. 'Now then, are you hungry?'

'Yes,' replied Hélène, 'very.'

Marcel went up the ladder to Pierre's rooms and returned with some bread and cheese and a couple of apples. 'Make a start on these,' he said, 'and I'll see what else I can find.'

He moved towards the stable door but Hélène jumped to her feet. 'Don't leave me,' she cried.

'Don't worry, I'm not going far.' He went out to the well at the end of the courtyard and winding the handle, drew up the bucket. He reached inside and took out a pitcher of milk and some dried meat. 'It doesn't look much,' he said as he poured milk into a glass he'd brought down from upstairs, 'but it'll help fill you up.'

Hélène certainly felt the better for some real food in her

stomach and when she sat back, she started to speak. 'They broke into the house, there were three of them...'

Slowly, as the evening drew in and the light faded, Hélène told her brother what had happened to her.

'And so they put me in St Luke's orphanage,' she concluded, 'but it was awful there and today I ran away.'

Marcel nodded, he could understand why she'd run away, but he wished she hadn't; she was far safer living with the nuns than alone on the streets.

'And this Jeannot?' he asked.

'He came and found me. We ran away, but the Gaston-man chased us. I think he caught Jeannot and I don't know what happened to him. He shouted at me to run... and I did.'

Marcel looked at her and shook his head. How had his little sister survived through all this? How had she kept up her spirits and finally managed to escape and come home? Thank God, he thought. Thank God I found her. How awful it would have been if she'd gone away again when we were so close and the city in such a turmoil.

Just last week he'd been in the Place Vendôme when amid the cheers of the Communards, Napoleon I's triumphal column had been pulled to the ground. But even as the Communards were cheering, Fort Issy, just south of the city, fell to the French army and Paris was under an even greater threat as they began to bombard the western city walls.

Hélène's not really safe here in the stables, Marcel thought, but at least she isn't out alone on the streets.

He needed to get her away to somewhere safer, away from the cannonade, for Passy could well be in the direct line of fire from both sides. He'd have to try and get her to Georges.

'Look,' he said, 'Georges was here looking for you too. We have to let him know that you're safe.'

'He's in the army,' Hélène told him. 'That's where you'll find him, with his soldiers.'

'Yes, I know,' Marcel answered, 'but the army aren't in Paris any more. They've moved out to Versailles and I can't reach him there. I can't leave the city.'

'Aren't you a soldier too?'

'Not in that army, no. But I will try to get a message to him. In the meantime, you must stay here. You can sleep upstairs in Pierre's bed, and I'll keep watch down here. I shall have to go out for provisions tomorrow, but I promise I won't leave you here alone tonight.'

He led the reluctant Hélène up to Pierre's tiny bedroom and shook out the blankets for her. 'Now you must try and sleep,' he said. 'You've had a long day. I shall be downstairs all night, I promise.'

Hélène lay on the narrow bed, not much more comfortable than the one at St Luke's, knowing that she wouldn't be able to sleep, but within two minutes she was deep in slumber.

Marcel had stayed to see her sleeping before he went back down the ladder. He could hear the incessant fire of the cannon from beyond the city walls, the answering fire of the Communards from inside. The city was under siege, civil war had begun in earnest and he and Georges were on different sides. He had no idea how he could get a message to Georges… and if he could, what could Georges do? How could he protect Hélène any better than he, Marcel, could?

He could only hope Georges would suddenly appear, as he had before, so they could decide what they were going to do with their sister. He checked that the garden gate was securely locked and settled down as comfortably as he could among the straw bales. After all, he thought as he too drifted off to sleep to the tune of gunfire, he'd slept in far worse places.

It was pale daylight when he awoke in the morning and remembered all that Hélène had told him. The Gaston-man. He felt himself go rigid with rage as he thought of the abuse his little sister had had to endure from this man, whoever he was. There must be hundreds of men in Paris called Gaston, but this one had questioned Hélène about her family, her brothers, about him? Was it too far a stretch to think it might be Gaston Durand? If he could torch a barn full of his comrades to effect his own escape, he wouldn't think twice about abducting and abusing a young girl. Marcel half hoped that the bastard would come looking for Hélène. He would castrate him.

He wondered where Georges was. He doubted if he was in Paris now, but it was possible. Clearly Georges had been a government spy, he must have had a way in and out of the city, and if so perhaps he could take Hélène to safety the same way.

But Georges did not reappear. The days passed and Marcel was at his wits' end to know what to do to protect his sister. He had to leave Hélène for hours at a time, as he and his corps were fighting in defence of the city and he knew they were outgunned. It wouldn't be long before the government forces broke back into the city and then all hell would be let loose. The thunder of the guns had become a steady accompaniment to the rhythm of life, almost tuned out, but great damage was occurring as the shells pounded away on the buildings and the walls, and Marcel insisted that she stay inside the stable block while he was away.

'Now that I've found you again,' he told her, 'I need to know exactly where you are.'

Marcel had done his best. He'd broken into the house and brought her some of her own clothes so that she could discard the dirty grey orphanage dress. He had brought out a pack of cards, some books to read, and some paper and pencils, and best of all he'd managed to keep her supplied with food. Even so, most of the time she was both lonely and bored.

'I can't stay here with you,' he explained when Hélène begged him not to leave. 'We're at war. We need every man on the barricades and that includes me.' He gave her a quick hug. 'You can hear the guns; I have to go.'

Hélène could hear the guns, all Paris could hear them, but they were not her greatest fear. Suppose he didn't come back? What would happen to her if Marcel was killed?

'You promise you'll come back?' she said in a small voice.

'Of course I'll come back,' he said, knowing it might not be a promise he could keep, but giving it anyway. Where the hell was Georges? he wondered once more. Why hadn't he come back as he'd promised? Perhaps he'd left Paris after his last visit and now the fighting had begun, he couldn't get back in. Perhaps he'd been caught. Perhaps he'd been killed. There were too many questions and no answers at all.

Hélène longed to see her elder brother, too. He would know what to do. Marcel was doing his best, she knew, but Georges would take charge. She didn't understand why her brothers seemed to be on opposite sides. They were both Frenchmen after all, both brought up in Paris, and yet...

With the resilience of youth, Jeannot made a steady recovery from his injuries. His ribs, the colour of thunder clouds, still ached if he moved quickly, but his stitched shoulder was beginning to heal up cleanly and the lump on his head had subsided, leaving only a deep scar amid his hair.

Alphonse had sold the watch and with the proceeds he had bought food and fuel. For the next weeks they'd eaten well, rather than surviving on scraps from the market floor, and this brought the flush of good health to Jeannot's face. After the first ten days or so, he began to go out into the streets. He told the Bergers that he was foraging for food, so that they could conserve the last of their precious cash, and indeed he often brought home extra fruit and vegetables that he'd managed to liberate from stalls without being caught by the angry stall-holders, but all the time he was out, he was looking for Hélène. Each evening he would slope past the house in the Avenue Ste Anne, hoping to see signs of life there, but it remained closed and dark. Had she got away from the warehouse? He hoped so and that she was hiding somewhere.

He went back to his old haunts where he found Paul and the Monkey, and from them he heard that Gaston was holed up, injured, in the tenement where he'd kept Hélène prisoner.

'He's in a bad way,' Paul told him. 'Stuck in the leg he was, and he bled like a pig and now it's gone bad.'

Jeannot decided not to tell him that he was the one who had done the sticking. It was a story too good not to spread and he had no wish for Gaston or his friends to know he was still in the land of the living and come looking for revenge.

'Francine looking after him?' he asked casually.

'Nah,' Paul shook his head, 'she ain't there no more. Don't know what happened to her.'

Jeannot thought he knew, but that was another secret he wasn't going to share with Paul. He drifted off into the city, the secret of Hélène's escape still safe.

The city was now under siege and that also produced opportunities for Jeannot and his like. Houses were damaged in the bombardment, and it was amazing what you could pick up when the dust settled. He returned occasionally to the Bergers with some of his pickings, but he had to be extremely careful. It would be the worse for him if he were caught looting, but with so many doing it, there was no real prospect of that. The National Guard were far too busy trying to keep the French army out, and the real danger was that every available man, woman and child was being press-ganged into building a second line of barricades. So far Jeannot had managed to avoid both, while providing himself and the Bergers with a few more comforts of life. 'We'll be all right,' he told them. 'Whoever wins this battle.'

It was two evenings later that Jeannot was caught. He sneaked down the lane behind the St Clairs' house and was just trying the gate when a hand grabbed him from behind, twisting his arm backwards and upwards, so that he gave a shriek of pain.

'Now then, tyke,' growled a voice. 'Thinking of breaking in, were you?'

'No,' cried Jeannot. 'I was just looking for someone, but it don't matter now, she ain't here.' He struggled to get free but his captor raised his arm a little higher and Jeannot gave another cry of pain.

'And who were you "just looking for"?'

'Just the girl what lived here, but she ain't here now. I wasn't gonna break in, honest, I was just looking.'

'Honest?' The man gave a laugh. 'I doubt if you've ever been honest in your life.'

Keeping hold of Jeannot's arm he reached past him, unlocked the gate and unceremoniously shoved the boy through into the garden. Jeannot stumbled as he was released but the gate closed behind him and there was no escape. At that moment the moon sailed out from behind a cloud and to his horror Jeannot found himself facing a National Guard. He cowered away, but the man simply grasped his arm again and led him towards the stables.

Hélène heard them coming, and hid in the straw-bale cave Marcel had constructed for her in one of the loose boxes.

'It's all right, Hélène,' he called softly. 'It's only me and someone who seems to be looking for you.'

Hélène emerged from her hiding place and as Marcel lit the lantern she saw who was with him.

'Jeannot!' she cried. 'You got away! You're alive!'

'And you,' said Jeannot awkwardly. He glanced back fearfully at the man who had brought him in.

'We're safe here,' Hélène told him. 'This is my brother, Marcel.' She turned to Marcel and smiling, said, 'This is Jeannot, Marcel. You know I told you? It was him who rescued me from the Gaston-man.'

The three of them sat together in the lamplight and Jeannot told them what had happened to him, how he'd been left for dead and how the Bergers had taken him in for a second time and looked after him.

'I'm living with them for now,' he said, 'like I did in the siege.'

'But s'posing the Gaston-man finds you?' said Hélène.

'He won't,' Jeannot assured her. 'Paul says he's back in his place, injured. Not good at all.'

'You know where that is?' asked Marcel. 'Can you show me?'

'I ain't going back there,' Jeannot said firmly.

'You just have to show me,' Marcel said. 'Point out the place, that's all. Just so's I know where to find him.'

Chapter 24

It was dark when Georges unlocked the gate and crept into the stable yard. He had only come back through the tunnel once since he had found Marcel in the stable. Then it had been for a single night to gather more first-hand information of the defences he'd seen, the numbers of National Guards, and the response of the people to the declaration of the Commune. It was information such as his, passed on by General Vinoy to his brother officers and government chief executive, Adolphe Thiers, that had suggested that the earlier attacks on the city at Neuilly, and at Courbevoie on Palm Sunday, would prove successful. That night he had had no time to visit the Avenue Ste Anne, and indeed he'd been challenged by a patrol of National Guards and was lucky to escape with his life. He wasn't expecting there to be any news of Hélène and he was loath to meet up with Marcel again so that their loyalties should be put to the test once more. But now he was back, the city was under siege, relentlessly bombarded, and he knew he had to visit his brother once more, to try and persuade him to escape with him through the tunnel and return to his regiment.

He emerged from the tunnel into the cellar and leaving the house under cover of darkness, made his way straight back to the Avenue Ste Anne. His role as spy and informant was doubly dangerous now that the full-scale attacks had begun and the streets were even more rigorously patrolled. Though he was, as always, dressed as an artisan of the people, he knew that any man found wandering the streets after dark might be shot as a spy or simply taken hostage as several prominent citizens had been; all liable to summary execution. More than once he had had to fade into the shadows as he heard the sound of marching feet and a troop of guardsmen passed by.

The fighting had been fierce, and Georges was anxious to know if Marcel had survived the attacks. He couldn't imagine why his brother had opted for the National Guard when he could have returned to his own regiment as a hero of Sedan, but it was a fact and he was afraid that Marcel might be killed trying to defend the city. He himself was taking no small risk; now that the battle was on for the future of Paris, would Marcel turn him in as a spy? Would they be able to speak as brothers and not as enemies?

He opened the garden gate and locked it behind him. He waited just inside, but there was no sound from the stables. Perhaps Marcel had left him a message as promised. As he crossed the stable yard he saw a glimmer of light under the door.

Thank God, he thought as he called his brother's name before pushing the door open. And there she was, Hélène, sitting on a straw bale, and beside her was a street urchin pointing a pistol at him.

'Hélène,' he cried, 'it's me, Georges.'

Hélène leapt to her feet and ran into his arms. Jeannot still held the pistol levelled at the newcomer, until Hélène turned and said, 'It's Georges, Jeannot, my other brother.'

'What were you going to do with that?' Georges asked as the boy laid the gun aside.

'Shoot you,' came the easy reply. 'Monsieur Marcel said just point and pull the trigger.'

'Well, I'm extremely glad you didn't,' said Georges as he walked over, picked up the pistol and stuck it into his belt. He turned back to Hélène and gave her another hug. 'Who's your bodyguard then?'

'It's Jeannot! Remember, Georges? I told you about going to the Prussian parade?'

'Yes,' replied Georges stiffly, 'I remember.'

Hélène kept a firm hold of his arm, pulling him down to sit on one of the straw bales, and went on, 'And now he's rescued me from the Gaston-man! Oh, Georges, I'm so pleased to see you. Marcel said you'd come, and you have. He said you'd take me home to Maman and Papa in St Etienne.'

'Did he now?' said Georges tightly. 'Well, between us we'll get you there. Somehow.'

'And Jeannot,' Hélène said, a statement, not a question.

'I'm not so sure about Jeannot,' Georges told her. 'It's going to be difficult enough getting you out.'

'But it was Jeannot who rescued me,' declared Hélène. 'Gaston's after him as well. You can't leave him here.'

'We'll talk about it when Marcel comes back,' Georges said repressively, wondering who this 'Gaston-man' was and hoping that Marcel would come back very soon. 'How long have you been hiding here, Hélène?'

'For ages,' answered the girl with a sigh. 'It was so boring until Jeannot came.'

'Did Marcel say when he'd be back?'

Hélène shook her head. 'No, he said he didn't know. He never knows, but he's promised he will. Anyway, I don't mind now I'm not on my own. I've been teaching Jeannot to read,' she added proudly.

Georges longed to ask Hélène where she'd been and what had happened to her, but decided to leave explanations for now. Time for all that when they had her safely out of the city. It was a great relief to find her safe and well and looked after by Marcel, but with the fighting intensifying, she wouldn't be safe here for long. He himself was only safe by keeping on the move.

He got to his feet and said, 'I have to go now, Hélène, but don't worry, I'll be back soon and you're safe here for now.'

'What about the gun?' demanded Jeannot.

'What about it?' snapped Georges. He didn't like the idea of a pistol in the hands of a boy like Jeannot.

'Your brother give it me to protect Hélène with,' Jeannot declared. 'I need it back. If somebody comes looking it's the only thing we've got.'

Georges sighed. He wasn't at all happy about leaving Hélène with this street kid, but he did have a point.

'All right,' he said, putting the pistol onto one of the straw bales, 'but you be bloody careful with it. Right?'

He was about to leave when Marcel came into the garden. Hearing voices in the stables, he approached softly, but when he recognised Georges's voice, he announced himself and pushed open the door.

While the two children slept, the brothers discussed how they might get Hélène out of Paris. Georges was determined not to reveal how he came and went, and Marcel was careful not to let him know where the guards were mounted on the city walls.

'I can't take her now,' Georges said finally. 'I'll have to make some plans, but I'll come back for her in a couple of days.'

'Don't take too long,' warned Marcel. 'Things are going to get far worse.' He looked across at Georges. 'What about the boy?' he asked.

'What about him?'

'She wants you to take him too.'

'I know,' Georges said, 'but I can't. It'll be hard enough getting her through without having another child to worry about. He's a street kid, he's well able to look after himself.'

Georges came back for Hélène two nights later, and explained the plans he had made.

'I can get her out of the city,' he said to Marcel, 'but not to St Etienne – it would take too long and I have my duties…' He let the words hang but they both knew he would be part of the final attack on the city. 'I've sent a message to Sylvie Claviet, the girl I'm going to marry when all this is over. I've asked her to come and fetch Hélène once we get to Versailles and arrange for her to be taken to St Etienne. It's the only way of getting her there and I know Sylvie will look after her in the meantime.'

'Married?' Marcel was momentarily diverted.

'Yes.' Georges's eyes softened. 'You'll love her when you meet her.'

If you meet her. If I meet her. The same thought was in each brother's mind but neither of them spoke it.

'But what about Jeannot?' demanded Hélène. 'He has to come too.'

'I can't take him,' replied Georges firmly. 'I can't ask Sylvie and her family to take in a Paris street kid.'

'A Paris street kid who saved my life,' cried Hélène in frustration.

'You say he did,' began Georges, but Hélène interrupted.

'He *did*,' she insisted, 'and was nearly killed himself. I won't go without him. You can't leave him here where that Gaston-man might find him.' She sat down stubbornly on a straw bale and looked at her brothers defiantly.

'Might as well take him,' Marcel said with a meaningful look at Georges. 'Once he's out of Paris, you don't have to send him with this Sylvie of yours. Once he's the other side of the wall, he can look after himself.' He turned to Jeannot and said, 'Can't you, lad?'

Jeannot nodded. He'd agree to anything to escape from the city, where the bombardment was getting heavier every day.

'You don't have to worry about Gaston any more, Hélène,' Marcel continued. 'I promise you. Jeannot's told me where he's living. He won't come after either of you again.'

'I won't go without Jeannot,' Hélène said doggedly, and with an exasperated sigh Georges gave in. There was no time for further argument.

'Come on then, the both of you, but listen hard. You have to do exactly what I tell you, and I mean exactly. No argument, no questions, right? You follow me and you don't speak, to me or to each other. Understood?' Both children nodded and having won her point, Hélène said meekly, 'Yes, Georges.'

Marcel shook hands briefly with Georges and then, giving Hélène a quick hug, let them out of the gate and closed it behind them. He gave them several minutes before slipping out himself and setting off after them. He wasn't going to give them away, or alert the guards to their progress, but he was determined to discover how Georges got in and out of Paris undetected. Once they were safely the other side of the wall then he would 'discover' it and it would be closed off. There'd be no more back doors for Georges or any other spies to infiltrate the city.

Georges led them silently through the back streets. The night sky was broken with cloud but occasional shafts of moonlight pierced the darkness, illuminating the streets below before another scudding cloud plunged them back into shadow. Distant, sporadic gunfire came on the night air, but Georges didn't slacken his pace. He was desperate to get to the comparative safety of the Duponts' house; when they were in the tunnel, they should be safe from discovery. Once he thought he heard a footstep somewhere close by and spun round, sweeping the children behind him, but though his eyes were accustomed to the dark he couldn't see anyone or anything and decided he must have imagined it. Keeping Hélène's hand in his, he led them stealthily through the shadows. It was past curfew and the streets were deserted, citizens obediently indoors.

Then it began, the cannonade. Guns from the far side of the wall opened fire and immediately there was return fire from the Communard cannon at the Trocadero. The return fire was badly directed and fell short, pounding into the homes on the inside of the walls. Parisians were being bombarded not only by government forces, but by their own gunners.

Georges and the children were caught out in the crossfire. None of the gunners could see them, but the shells fell about them from both sides. Masonry from surrounding houses came crashing to the ground, doors exploded open and glass crashed from windows. Fires burst into being, spreading quickly through the houses, licking draperies, catching the woodwork of the exposed roof beams. Before long, flames were leaping into the air, casting gold and red flickering light over the whole area. Panic-stricken people streamed from their houses and apartments, men running, women screaming, carrying babies, herding terrified children away from the burning buildings. Anxious to escape the smoke and flames, they rushed out into streets that, lit by the soaring flames, were now an easy target for the enemy gunners as still the bombardment continued.

'This way!' shouted Georges, but his words were lost in the roar of the cannon and still clutching Hélène by the hand, he pulled her clear as a burning beam crashed to the ground only metres away. Chaos reigned as the crowds pushed and shoved each other in their efforts to escape. Georges was forcing their way through the crush when there was another explosion close by and he gave a sudden cry, falling to the ground, clutching his leg.

'Georges!' Hélène screamed. 'You're hurt!' She dropped down beside him, trying to pull him up.

'It's not bad,' Georges said through gritted teeth. 'Just a splinter in my leg.' He got to his hands and knees and with a heave upwards from Jeannot, regained his feet.

'Come on,' he said. 'Let's get away from here.'

Even as he said that there was another salvo causing further screams and panic amongst those in the street. With great determination, Georges began limping towards the sheltering darkness of a street beyond the fire.

'Follow me,' he rasped as he staggered forwards and Jeannot grabbed hold of Hélène's hand, dragging her behind him. More mortar crashed down close by and Georges stumbled to the ground, clutching his leg.

'Get Hélène away from here,' Georges gasped. 'Take her back home, Jeannot, take her back home.'

'But we can't leave you here,' cried Hélène, crouching down beside him 'We can't leave you!'

'You must, I think my leg is broken. You must go. Tell Marcel what happened. I'll be all right, there're lots of people here.'

Another explosion rocked a nearby street and more walls crumbled in swirling clouds of dust.

'Go!' shouted Georges. 'Go now.'

'Come on,' yelled Jeannot, gripping Hélène's hand again.

Still she held back. 'But, Georges—'

'He'll be all right!' Jeannot shouted, trying to be heard over the uproar. 'He said to go! Come *on*, Hélène!' He pulled her after him, running down a twisting street, but when they reached an open square at the end of the lane she stopped short, pulling away from him and breathing heavily.

'We should go back,' she sobbed. 'We can't leave him lying on the ground.'

'If we go back we could be killed. They're still bombing. You think he wants that, your Georges? You think he wants you to go back instead of staying safe?' He took her hand again and said more quietly, 'Come on, Hélène. If he's dead he's dead and if he's not they'll find him… after and take him to the hospital. Either way there's nothing you can do about it, and we need to get somewhere safe.'

Hélène allowed herself to be persuaded and still hand in hand, they hurried across the square and set off along a narrow path that led eventually to the river. Jeannot didn't stop, but following a route of twists and turns led them towards the middle of the city. They could still hear the guns, could still see the glow of the fires and drifts of dark smoke lit in stripes of silver by the fitful moon.

'This isn't the way home,' Hélène said suddenly, stopping again as they reached a main boulevard.

'We ain't going to your home,' replied Jeannot, pulling on her hand. 'We're going to mine.'

'But we can't,' cried Hélène in dismay. 'Georges said to go back home and tell Marcel what had happened.'

'Georges weren't thinking straight,' Jeannot told her. 'Your house is right in the middle of that battlefield, innit? Next load of cannon balls could land on that and you'd be dead again.'

'But Marcel won't know—'

'No, he won't, but there ain't nothing we can do about that now. Come on.'

Reluctantly, Hélène allowed him to lead her through streets and alleys until they came to one she recognised. The one with the tabac on the corner. She froze.

'What's the matter now?' demanded Jeannot. 'We're nearly there!'

'Not down here,' wailed Hélène. 'Jeannot, not down here.'

'It's where I live…'

'The Gaston-man…'

'Is dead,' Jeannot said firmly, thinking, An' if he ain't he soon will be. 'Promise you! Come on.'

He almost had to drag Hélène the length of the street, but at last they got to the steps that led down to the Bergers' basement. Hélène hung back as Jeannot banged on the door. For a long moment she thought no one was going to answer, but then she heard the scrape of a bolt and the door eased open a few inches.

'Tante Edith,' Jeannot called into the sliver of light. 'It's me and a friend. Can we come in?'

The door opened a fraction wider and Alphonse looked out. 'Oh, it *is* you,' he said grumpily. 'Thought you'd buggered off like last time.' He stood back and opened the door wide enough for them to go in.

Chapter 25

Marcel, following them at a distance, had been some way behind Georges and the children when the unexpected bombardment started. Within minutes the streets ahead were ablaze, the crash of falling masonry combining with the thunder of the cannon. People rushed from the buildings, desperate to escape before they were crushed in the rubble. Marcel dashed forwards, thinking only of his brother and sister, but he had no sight of them in the ensuing mêlée. It was hopeless, the cannonade lasted for another half hour, by which time the whole area was devastated. Fires were still burning and many of those who had rushed to escape both fire and bombardment lay dead or wounded in the street. As the cannon fell silent, survivors emerged from where they had taken shelter, and desperate attempts were made to bring the fires under control. Marcel, still unable to see Georges or the children, concluded that they must have escaped the onslaught and were safely in the tunnel, for Marcel knew it had to *be* a tunnel, wherever that was, and he joined in the battle with the flames, filling buckets from the pump in the street, gradually reducing the fires to sporadic flares. People were moving the wounded away and it was as he helped a young woman carry her injured child back to the shelter of an almost undamaged house that Marcel found Georges. He was sitting beside the blown-in front door of an apartment building. The building itself seemed to have survived the bombardment, though it was surrounded by the broken glass from its many shattered windows. Georges was sitting with his back against the wall, his legs stretched out in front of him. His trousers were torn and blood was seeping from a hidden wound. His face was paper-white and his eyes closed against the pain of his damaged leg.

'Georges?'

His eyes flew open at the sound of his brother's voice. 'Marcel?' His voice was a husky thread of pain and he closed his eyes again. 'Is it really you?'

'Yes, it's me,' Marcel said as he crouched down beside him. 'Tell me where you're hurt.'

'Just my leg.' Georges opened his eyes again and managed a brave smile. 'Nothing much really, but I think it's broken.'

'Where are the children?' Marcel asked, looking round him for any sign of them.

'Told them to leave me here, to get away. Told Jeannot to take her back to the house and find you.'

'I wasn't there,' Marcel said. 'I was following you.'

'Hrumph,' puffed Georges. 'Thought you might be. Heard someone behind me.'

'Never mind that now,' Marcel said. 'We've got to get you home. D'you think you can walk at all?'

'Don't know till I try,' Georges said. 'Here, give me your hand and pull me up.'

Marcel, reaching down to take his hand asked, 'Which leg?'

'Left,' answered Georges with a little gasp of pain. 'Careful!'

Marcel put his arm round Georges's body, and taking his weight, eased him up onto his uninjured leg. A swift glance at his brother's face told him of the agony he was in, but Georges made no complaint as he struggled to keep his balance. Marcel looked about him and from the debris he pulled a stout wooden stave. 'Here,' he said, 'you can use this as a crutch.'

Georges took the piece of wood and leaned on it. 'Yes,' he said, 'it'll do.'

'Right,' Marcel said briskly, 'lean on me as well and let's get you home.'

They made extremely slow progress; Georges leaned on the stick and Marcel took as much of his weight as he could, but he knew his brother was in considerable pain. People were helping other wounded and no one paid much attention to the two men who struggled through the debris and began the long walk home. With numerous stops to rest, it took them over two hours to cover the comparatively short distance back to the Avenue Ste Anne and dawn was streaking the eastern sky as they turned into the avenue.

By the time they reached the garden gate, Georges could hardly move. His injured leg was dragging, he was light-headed, sweat poured down his cheeks and his pale face was a mask of pain.

'Only a couple of metres to go,' Marcel said as he swung the gate open, but for Georges it might as well have been a couple of miles. He slumped against the gatepost and in one swift movement Marcel scooped him up and carried him into the stables. Once inside he laid him on a bed of straw bales where Georges passed out.

Marcel straightened him so that he was in a more comfortable position and while he was still unconscious;

removed the torn trousers to reveal the injury they hid. The leg was indeed broken, a white shard of bone now protruding through the skin. Marcel had seen worse, far worse on the battlefields of the war. A doctor could clean and set the leg without much trouble, but without a doctor he knew Georges might not even survive his apparently minor injury. Even small wounds went bad quickly.

Marcel looked down at him. Should he try and move his brother to one of the city hospitals? No, surely that would indeed be the death of him.

In which case, Marcel decided, I'll have to get a doctor here.

He remembered his mother had always called Dr Simon to their bedsides when they were ill and Marcel wondered if he were still in Paris, or had he, too, made a hasty exit when the civil war broke out?

Georges was still unconscious, if he went now to fetch Dr Simon perhaps he could come at once and, Marcel thought, set the leg before Georges returned to the world.

Suddenly he remembered the two children. He had been so taken up with getting Georges home that for a moment he'd forgotten them, forgotten that they were supposed to be back here, waiting for him. Then he realised that the gate had been closed and locked, but surely that would have presented no problem to a boy like Jeannot. He'd have been up and over in a trice. So, where were they?

Georges gave a moan and the sound brought Marcel back to the matter in hand. He made up his mind. He would go and fetch Dr Simon and bring him back here. While he was out he'd leave the gate unlocked so that the children could get in when they got back. If they got back. The thought slipped into his mind, but he dismissed it immediately. Of course they'd get back, Jeannot was no fool and he was probably lying low somewhere until it was full daylight and they could walk the streets without fear of being questioned. Marcel wondered if he could trust Jeannot to look after Hélène, but for the moment he had to. He did not know where she was and so could do nothing for her; his present responsibility was Georges.

When he reached the doctor's house, it seemed to be shut up, but when there was no answer to his hammering on the front door he went round and banged on the back door. The windows were curtained, but he thought he could see a glimmer of light inside and he continued to knock until at last he heard movement indoors, and a reedy voice called, 'Who's there? Who is it?'

'It's Marcel St Clair,' Marcel called back. 'I'm looking for Dr Simon. My brother's been injured in the bombing and I need his help.'

There was the rattle of a chain and the thud of bolts being drawn back and when the door opened he was faced by an elderly woman, a nightcap on her head and a shawl flung over her nightgown. Marcel recognised her as Madame Yvette, the doctor's housekeeper. She, however, did not recognise him and at the sight of a man in the uniform of the National Guard, she tried to slam the door again. Marcel was too quick for her, putting his boot in the gap and saying, 'Madame Yvette, is the doctor here? I need his help.'

'You're not Marcel St Clair,' cried the woman. 'I know what he looks like, and it's not like you.'

Marcel ignored this and said, 'My brother Georges has been injured in the bombing. I need the doctor to come to him at once. Please tell him I'm here and I need his help.'

At that moment the doctor appeared behind his housekeeper and said, 'Who is it, Yvette?'

Before Yvette could answer, Marcel explained about Georges.

'Broken leg, you say?'

'Yes, it looks pretty bad.'

Dr Simon said he would come at once and having checked his bag for everything he might need, they hurried together back to the house. On the way the doctor said, 'I knew you were both in the army, but I heard you were missing.'

'I was for a while...' began Marcel.

'And now you're back,' finished the doctor. 'And in disguise, too. I won't ask what secret mission you're on.'

For a split second Marcel didn't understand what the doctor was saying, and then it dawned on him. Dr Simon was assuming he was still in the French army and only dressed as a guard as a disguise. He decided not to enlighten him.

When they reached the stable, Dr Simon went at once to Georges. He had regained consciousness and was lying on his bed of straw wondering where Marcel was; if he'd simply deserted him. And the children? Where were they? He asked as soon as Marcel appeared behind the doctor.

'I'll tell you about them when the doctor's finished with you,' Marcel said, not wanting to discuss that topic in public. 'The important thing now is to get you patched up.'

Dr Simon took off his coat, rolled up his sleeves and looking down at his patient, said, 'This is going to hurt like hell, but it has to be done or you may never walk again.' He turned to Marcel, 'Perhaps you could bring me some clean water and then come and hold your brother still.' He got to work to clean the wound and then, retrieving splints from his bag, he turned his attention to the broken bone. As he began to manipulate them, Georges passed out again, leaving the doctor free to align the bones and bind them in place.

'I'm afraid he'll always have a limp,' he said to Marcel when he'd finished, 'but he should be able to walk again, perhaps with a stick.' He looked up and went on, 'Now, who's here to look after him?'

'No one,' Marcel replied. 'My parents are still in the country, thank God. The servants have gone with them and I have to return to my unit.'

'I could recommend a good woman who might come and look after him,' suggested the doctor.

'The problem is,' Marcel said cautiously, 'that this place is… being used. The army… you know?'

'Of course,' the doctor said hurriedly, 'I understand.' He thought for a moment and then said, 'If we could move him to my house, just until he's getting better, I'm sure Madame Yvette would be happy to look after him and that way I, too, can keep an eye on his progress.'

Later that day, two men with a stretcher came and carried Georges to the doctor's house. There was still no sign of the children, so Marcel left the gate unlocked for them. He needed to return to his unit, manning the barricades hastily built to block the streets when the French army finally broke in. Marcel had done what he could. The children had vanished, he could do no more for them, Georges was in good hands and would be out of the final battle, a battle Marcel knew the Communards were going to lose. He doubted he was going to survive the fighting and there was one more thing he wanted to do before he died. On his way to his unit he went to the tenement Jeannot had shown him. The front door opened to his touch and Marcel walked into the hallway without knocking.

'Gaston's rooms is on the left when you go in. He may not be in them rooms, but watch it, he's got a cellar which is where he kept Hélène. Watch out for his wife too, if she's still there,' he'd advised. 'She'll stick a knife in you, soon as look at you.'

The door to his left was ajar, as if someone was expected.

Well, thought Marcel as he drew his pistol, he can expect me now, and again without knocking, he pushed the door open and stepped inside. The room stank, a formidable combination of faeces, urine and rotting flesh. There was a man on a cot in one corner, lying propped up against a pillow and covered with a blood-stained piece of blanket that concealed his legs. Much of the smell emanated from him. His eyes flew open as Marcel came in, staring at him and the gun which was pointing straight at him.

If he hadn't known who he was looking for, Marcel wouldn't have recognised Gaston Durand. Pale as death, there was very little left of the bullying man who was prepared to sacrifice his comrades to achieve his own freedom, or make use of a girl of eleven for his own enjoyment. His face was shrivelled, his beard thin and grey against the grey pallor of his skin, his eyes red-rimmed and watery, and there was a drool of saliva leaking from the side of his mouth.

'Well, Durand,' said Marcel, staring with revulsion at this wreck of a man. 'Have you been expecting me?'

'St Clair,' he drawled. 'Come to kill me, have you?' He sucked lips in over almost toothless gums. 'Had a lot of fun with your sister, I did. Did she tell you? Didn't always do what she was told, mind, but she learned... in the end.' For a moment he stiffened as pain shot through him, the sepsis working its relentless way through his body. 'Go on then,' he challenged. 'Shoot me! Do me a favour.'

The man shrank back as Marcel cocked the gun, but didn't fire it.

'Chicken, are yer?' taunted Durand. 'Afraid to pull the trigger on a helpless man? If someone had done to *my* sister what I done to yours, I'd shoot him like a dog.'

'Whereas I won't be goaded into committing cold-blooded murder, like you,' returned Marcel coolly. 'For what you did to my sister I'd rather let you die a long, lingering and very painful death. Why should I end your suffering? Whoever did this to you, did well.'

'Paid for it with his life, he did,' jeered Gaston. 'I got the last laugh!'

'Rot in hell,' retorted Marcel, tucking the pistol back into his belt. He had no need of it now, Jeannot had done the job for him.

As he walked back down the steps to the street he could still hear Durand screeching, 'I'm the one laughing, ain't I? I'm the one laughing!'

Chapter 26

Alphonse stepped aside to let them in and Jeannot led Hélène into the basement apartment. Edith was sitting by the tiny fire and seeing Jeannot she jumped to her feet.

'Jeannot!' she cried. 'Where have you been? We were so worried when you didn't come home again.' Then, as if noticing Hélène for the first time, her eyes narrowed and she said, 'And who's this? Why have you brought her here?'

Before Jeannot could answer, Hélène announced, 'I'm Hélène St Clair, and I don't know why he's brought me here. I want to go home.' It was not an auspicious start to their introduction.

'This is Hélène,' Jeannot said, scowling at her to shut up. 'Used to work for her family. She's all right… most of the time.'

'But why have you brought her here?' repeated Edith.

'We was caught in the bombing,' Jeannot explained. 'Had to get off the streets double quick. Nowhere else to go, and,' he added winningly, 'I knew you'd take us in, Tante Edith.' He turned back to Hélène. 'This is Monsieur and Madame Berger. Tante Edith and Oncle Alphonse. They're kind people. They took me in, in the siege.'

He gave her a nudge and Hélène held out her hand and said, 'How d'you do, madame?'

Edith looked at her suspiciously before giving her hand a brief shake and turning her attention back to Jeannot. 'Are you hurt?' she asked.

'No, we're both all right, but Hélène's brother was injured, he hurt his leg. He told us to run and we did, so we don't know what's happened to him.'

'He told us to go home,' said Hélène.

'So, why didn't you?' asked Alphonse suspiciously. 'If he told you to go there, why didn't you?'

'Too dangerous,' answered Jeannot cheerfully. 'She lives right in the middle of the sixteenth district, it's the target area. House could be bombed out an' us with it.' He gave Edith his most charming smile and said, 'We can stay here for a while, can't we, Tante Edith? Just till things settle down a bit? Don't worry about food an' that, I'll see you right.'

Edith sighed. 'I suppose you can,' she agreed reluctantly, 'but only for a few days until the bombing's stopped.' She nodded at Jeannot. '*You* can stay as long as you want to, helping us out, but not her, we don't need another mouth to feed.' Hélène flushed red at this, but at a look from Jeannot she held her tongue.

There was an awkward silence before Jeannot said, 'That's settled then. Don't worry about us, Tante Edith, we won't get in your way. We'll sleep by the fire in here.' He looked round hopefully. 'Anything for breakfast?' he asked. Seeing the anxious look on Alphonse's face, he added, 'I'll go out and find something else as soon as we've finished.'

'Are they really your aunt and uncle?' Hélène asked Jeannot in a whisper as they drank coffee and ate bread with a smear of jam.

Jeannot shook his head. 'Nah! Course not! Just what I call 'em. Told you before, I ain't got no family. I'm on my own. But we need them now, so just try and keep on the right side of them, all right?'

After they'd eaten, Jeannot left Hélène with the Bergers and set out in search of food. As he made his way through the streets he could hear the relentless pounding of the guns and they seemed to be getting louder. The war, he realised, had come closer.

Pointless going to the market if that part of the city was under fire, he thought, 'cos nobody'll be selling nothing today. 'Cept perhaps some of the small shops. It'd be worth keeping his eye open.

He changed direction and headed to his usual haunts. There was unusual activity in the streets and several times he ducked into a doorway or branched off into an alley to avoid not only the National Guards, but ordinary citizens scurrying from place to place, heads down, eyes averted. He would go and find Paul and the Monkey, he decided, and discover what had been happening while he'd been cooped up with Hélène in the stable. Things certainly seemed to have hotted up. Jeannot thought of the bombardment they'd escaped the previous night and wondered briefly what had happened to Georges. Was he still alive or had he died in the street? Well, he shrugged, not his problem.

He found his mates hiding in the old cellar they shared and crawled in beside them.

'What's going on then?' he asked. 'Something big, by the sound of it. You been out to see?'

'Yeah,' replied the Monkey, 'and came back sharpish, I can tell you.'

'The army's in,' Paul told him. 'Heard some treacherous bugger opened the gate at Pointe du Jour and let them in. There's soldiers everywhere. Need to steer clear of them. They've been streaming in since dawn.'

'Where you been, anyway?' demanded Monkey. 'Ain't seen you for days and then you turn up outta the blue an' ask what's going on! What d'yer think's going on? City's invaded, that's what!'

'I been holed up in a nice comfortable stable,' Jeannot said. 'We could hear the guns, but not close, not till now. Anyway, I thought I'd come out and find out what's what.'

'Mad to be out there,' Paul said. 'You was lucky you wasn't shot. There's National Guards and soldiers everywhere. They don't care who they kill. They been shooting anyone what gets caught in their way. We ain't going out now.'

'I can't stay here,' Jeannot said. 'I'm getting food.'

'Getting food? Then you're the only one, mate. Anyone with any sense is keeping their head down. If the government lot don't get you, the National Guards will. Saw them in the street this morning early. Prodding folks with bayonets, they was, making people go and work on the barricades.'

'Bit late for barricades, ain't it?' Monkey said. 'Saw them building one with carts and waggons and paving stones and stuff. That ain't going to keep the army out, is it?'

'Waste of time, if you ask me,' agreed Paul. 'Just going to blow their way through that shit, ain't they.'

'Good time to be picking up a few bits, though,' pointed out Jeannot, who always had an eye for a chance. 'Empty houses. Stuff lying about asking to be took.'

'You can take it, mate,' said Paul. 'I'm like Monkey. I'm going to keep my head down here. May go hungry for a few days... done that before. Don't kill yer, not like a bullet from an army rifle. They're putting sharp shooters on the roofs now, picking off people; just use anyone for target practice, they do.'

Jeannot listened to all they said but eventually left them safe in their cellar. He went back onto the streets. He couldn't stay there and miss all the excitement; he was determined to see for himself. What he saw amazed him. The artillery had finally punched huge gaps in the city walls and government troops were pouring through in their hundreds. He darted along through the back doubles, hiding in alleys, in deserted courtyards and behind walls, astonished at the damage being inflicted on the city, inflicted by both sides. Paul and the Monkey had been right. All over the city bells were ringing, the Commune's call to the citizens of Paris; to man the barricades, to keep the enemy at bay. Citizens were answering the call, too. He saw a group of women armed with rifles, carrying the red flag of the Commune, marching to one of the barricades, and ducked down behind a collapsed wall. He'd heard the women were some of the worst and he wasn't going to mess with them.

You got to be extremely careful not to get taken up by either side, he thought, as he crouched behind the wall ready to make a dash for the basement yard opposite. It was then that he felt it, something hard pressed into his ribs. A gun barrel.

'Now then, whippersnapper,' said a voice. 'We could use a likely lad like you. Come on, there's a barricade to build.' The owner of the voice, a large man in a National Guard's uniform, grasped him by the ear and propelled him unwillingly round a corner and into the next street where he found there was feverish activity, constructing a barrier to block the main road. Two heavy carts had been laid end to end across the street and beyond them several men were at work lifting paving stones and cobbles and carrying them to add strength and weight to the barricade. Beams, taken from the ruins of nearby buildings, were being heaved up to make another layer of defence.

'Right, lad, get stuck in here,' instructed his captor. 'There's some sandbags over there what wants to be brought here. If they're too heavy to carry, just drag them. Look sharp, we've plenty more of these to build.'

Jeannot moved away to where another lad was heaving at some bags of earth. He cast an eye backwards, but saw at once that there was no chance of running off. The National Guard who'd collared him was watching, rifle loaded and in hand.

'Who are you?' demanded the boy.

'Jeannot. Got you too, did they? What's yer name?'

'André,' the boy said. 'Watch out for that big bloke. He's real mean.'

Together they heaved at the heavy earth-filled bags. Gradually a wall was built across the road and on the top, behind a parapet of beams, was a firing step.

As soon as it was done several National Guards climbed up and settled down, rifles protruding over the top, preparing to hold the army at bay.

Watching them, Jeannot wondered if Hélène's other brother, guardsman Marcel, was manning a barricade like this.

Well, rather him than me, thought Jeannot as he and André were gathered up and moved on to another street where a similar barricade was under construction. Here they were set to filling the sacks, digging into the compacted earth beneath the raised paving slabs and shovelling it into the bags. To the background of thundering guns and the rattle of small arms fire, they worked under the watchful eye of the guard who had captured Jeannot. After another hour they were given some bread and strips of dried meat to eat; a pitcher of water was passed round from which they all drank copious draughts, their throats dry from the dust of their own efforts. But there was no chance of escape and Jeannot realised that he should have listened to his mates. He had made a dreadful mistake in risking the streets. The group of citizens who, like him, had been press-ganged into building defences was herded away at the end of each job, the whole time under the watchful eye – and the rifle – of their captor. As they began to move on from the second barricade, André broke ranks, making a dash for the shelter of a narrow lane that led off from the street. One of the guards raised his rifle and fired a single shot and André pitched forward, arms flung wide, as he collapsed to the ground. For a moment the other workers stared at the motionless body, but at a roar from the guard, they moved on, leaving the lifeless boy to the mercy of the city rats. No one else considered making a break for it. Even before seeing André's ill-considered dash, and the speed with which he'd been dealt with, Jeannot had decided against an effort to escape. He would wait until it was dark and then if the chance arose, he'd slip away.

The government troops were establishing themselves in key positions in the city, moving slowly but steadily through the streets and as dusk turned to dark, and Jeannot's crew laboured on yet another barrier of paving stones and bags of earth, an advance patrol came upon them unexpectedly and opened fire. Everyone dived for cover, the workers scattering into the nearby streets, some of the guards firing back from the protection of their newly created barrier. Jeannot ran like a hare, vanishing into the maze of streets beyond the

Madeleine. Once out of the immediate danger area, he got his bearings and began making his way back to the Monkey and Paul in their cellar. He'd spend the night sheltering with them and decide his next move in the morning.

As soon as Jeannot had left that morning, Alphonse jerked his thumb at Hélène who was curled up in a corner, fast asleep.

'What are we going to do with her?' he asked.

Edith shrugged. 'Keep her for a day or two, I suppose,' she replied, 'as long as Jeannot brings us enough food. If he don't, she'll have to go.'

Hélène kept her eyes closed, maintaining her pretence of sleep, but she listened to what they were saying and made up her mind. She didn't like 'Tante Edith', who looked at her with such coldness in her eyes. She didn't know why. What had she done? She hadn't asked to come here, but she knew that Edith didn't like her and didn't want her there. And what if Tante Edith went out somewhere? She might be left alone with the weird 'Oncle Alphonse', who coughed and wheezed and spat and looked at her sideways; the thought terrified her.

Where was Georges? And Marcel? They'd be worried sick about her when she and Jeannot didn't come back home as they'd been told to. She looked at the front door. It was stout with a heavy bolt drawn across it. What would happen, she wondered, if she simply got up and walked out? What would the old couple do? Would they try and stop her, or would they simply be glad to see the back of her? The trouble was that, once again, she didn't know where she was or the way home. Just as soon as Jeannot came back she'd insist he took her there.

But Jeannot didn't come back. The three of them sat in the apartment all day and waited. They could hear the continuous rumble of the guns and neither of the Bergers was prepared to venture out. Hélène thought of what Jeannot had said. Her home was 'in the target area'. Perhaps her home wasn't even standing now.

The basement apartment was dim at the best of times, with only one grimy window looking out into a tiny yard, and as twilight deepened to night, they all sat in the gloom.

'Buggered off again,' remarked Alphonse, when there was still no sign of Jeannot. 'Or killed in the bombing.'

'Oh, Alphonse,' Edith gave a cry of distress, 'don't say things like that. He must come home again. He's promised to bring some more food.'

'Promised?' sniffed Alphonse. 'What are promises to boys like him?'

'He came back last time,' Edith reminded him.

'Only 'cos I found him laying in the gutter and we brought him in.'

'He'll come, I know he will,' Edith said, but Hélène could see that her lip trembled.

She clenched her fists, determined not to cry, but Alphonse's words echoed in her head: 'Or killed in the bombing.' The rumble of the guns had been constant, all day, so people must be getting killed.

Why hasn't he come back? wondered Hélène in panic. What will happen to me if Jeannot has been killed? And if he hasn't, where is he?

Edith lit a small lamp and by its light she prepared another meal of soup. It was a great improvement on the soup they'd been given at St Luke's, hot and thickened with potatoes. She shared it out into three bowls and handed Hélène the smallest portion.

'Thank you,' Hélène said meekly. 'It's very good.'

'Not the sort of food you'll be used to, I dare say,' said Edith with a sniff. 'But when you stay with paupers you eat paupers' food.'

There seemed no answer to that and the three of them ate their food in silence, all of them listening for the clatter of boots on the steps outside, the sound of Jeannot's return.

Edith cleared away the bowls and then found a blanket which she gave to Hélène.

'We're turning in now,' she said. 'You can sleep in here in front of the fire. You'll hear Jeannot when he knocks, but don't open the door. Wake us and Alphonse will come and do it.'

There was no knock in the night and no sign of Jeannot in the morning. They could hear the battle for Paris raging across the city and they all knew that Jeannot would not be coming back.

'I'll go for food,' Edith said, putting her shawl about the shoulders and picking up a basket. 'We have to have something or we will starve.'

Realising that her worst fears were about to come true, Hélène said, 'I'll come with you.'

Edith was about to snub her offer with a brisk negative, but she caught herself in time. Perhaps they might have more luck with a child begging as well.

'All right,' she agreed. 'Alphonse, you wait here, so you can tell Jeannot where we are when he gets back.'

Alphonse grunted, but made no other comment. He was afraid to go out into streets that were a battlefield, and was glad Edith had told him to stay at home. He hoped that she would be successful in her search for food – surely some bakers were still at work, people had to eat after all – but since the government troops had been besieging the city, no fresh food had come in from the countryside. Well enough for those who had laid in supplies when it was clear there was going to be war again, but *they'd* had no money for such luxuries, living from hand to mouth, each day, every day.

Edith and Hélène climbed the steps up to the lane and set off towards the main road. Edith didn't speak to her and Hélène was pleased. She was working on a plan. It was a bright day, and the May sun was warm on her face. It was early yet, but she had already decided that when they were away from that dreadful alley where the Gaston-man had cornered them, she was going to slip away from Jeannot's Tante Edith. She hated being cooped up in the basement apartment. It was small and cold and poky and it smelled of... Oncle Alphonse. Yes, it smelled of Oncle Alphonse. She had found her way home before by keeping the sun on her face. She could do it again.

She didn't let her mind wonder what she was going to do if the house had been ruined in the cannonade.

Edith led the way through narrow streets to a boulangerie. The door was open and when she went in the baker greeted her by name.

'You're in luck, Madame Berger,' he said. 'I kept a few loaves back for my regulars.'

Although he had saved some, the price was high and Edith winced as she handed over the two francs he asked for. He reached under the counter and produced two loaves. 'Only two,' he said as she put them into her basket and covered them with a cloth.

Two francs for just two loaves of bread! Her small stock of cash was almost halved. Further on she managed to buy a cabbage and three potatoes, and a meat bone from the butcher, but the prices were incredibly high. How she missed Jeannot's talent for finding 'free' food. If he wasn't back with some soon, that girl would definitely have to go. She looked around as she came out of the butcher's, but the girl was nowhere in sight. She stood for a moment, looking along the street, but there was no sign of her.

You take the girl in and feed her and then she runs off, thought Edith angrily. Well, good riddance. With her acquisitions safely in her basket she set off for home. They would eat for another day or so, and one less mouth to feed was good news!

Hélène had watched Edith enter the butcher's shop and had made her decision. She was going home. With a quick glance through the window she saw Edith haggling with the butcher over a marrow bone and hid in a doorway further down the street. She watched as Edith came out of the shop, looked about for her and then marched off down the street. Once the old woman was out of sight, Hélène emerged from the doorway and set off in the other direction.

Chapter 27

Marcel returned only once to the Avenue Ste Anne. The district had been pounded by both sides, but even so, despite the destruction caused, once the bombardment had ceased the invading French army had been welcomed by the prosperous inhabitants of Passy. Few people in Passy and the surrounding districts had any love for the Communards, and those that had not left long ago had now come out of hiding and were trying to return to some sort of normality. The area was filled with government troops, moving openly without threat or danger. Marcel had taken the precaution of putting on workman's clothes, disguising himself as Georges had done so often before. He moved confidently along the avenue, knowing that if by any remote chance he were to be recognised, he could bluff his way out of trouble as he had when he'd taken Georges to Dr Simon. Though there was considerable damage in some of the nearby streets, it was with great relief that Marcel saw that their house seemed undamaged; at least Hélène had shelter to come back to. He continued to move with extreme caution as he approached the house, but no one challenged him and he reached the gate in the lane without trouble. He knew Georges was safe enough with Dr Simon, but he was worried sick about Hélène. Was it possible she was back now? If he could see her, or even leave a written message for her in the stable, he could at least reunite her with Georges and they would both be safe enough with Dr Simon now the fighting had moved on.

He opened the unlocked gate and moved stealthily across the garden to the stable, but when he opened the door he found it empty and it was clear that no one had been there since he had. Hélène had not been back. Where on earth were they, she and Jeannot? Had they not escaped when they'd left Georges? He had no idea where Jeannot might have taken her. Why hadn't the damned boy done as he was told and brought her home again that night? Had they been killed or wounded? How could he find out? Where could he begin to look?

For a moment despair overtook him and he sank down onto a straw bale, burying his head in his hands. The war, the siege, the renewed fighting had torn his family apart.

He sat for a long time, his thoughts bleak, his mind exhausted. What should he do? What *could* he do? Should he go back to Georges and tell him that Hélène was missing again? No point in that, he decided. There was nothing Georges could do to find her, laid up with his leg in splints; all he would do was worry.

At length Marcel got to his feet and let himself back into the house. There he found pen and paper and sitting down at the dining room table he wrote two notes – one to his parents and one to Hélène.

To his parents he explained that he had survived the battle of Sedan, but since then he had left the army.

Right or wrong, I have thrown in my lot with the National Guard. I know you'll find that very difficult to understand, but I couldn't fight any more for an emperor who cut and ran, leaving his soldiers to the mercy of the enemy and an army that squandered its men's lives so recklessly. So, Georges and I have found ourselves on opposite sides in this conflict, but we have remained brothers and have done all we can to find and take care of Hélène. I have been using the stables as a place to live, and apologise to Pierre for using all his things.

I am about to go back to my duty as a National Guard and man the barricades. I know, thank God, that I shall not be shooting at my own brother as he is safely with Dr Simon. I am extremely unlikely to survive the next few days, and if I do it will be as a prisoner, a deserter and a Communard. I expect no mercy, for I'm sure none will be given. The battle has been too long and too bloody. But I ask you to pray for me and remember me fondly, for whatever else I am, I am your loving son, Marcel.

His note to Hélène was much shorter.

Dearest, bravest Hélène.

I probably won't see you again, but if you get back to the stable and find this letter, go to Dr Simon's house where you'll find Georges, laid up with a broken leg. I don't know where you are now, but have to trust young Jeannot to take care of you as I no longer can. I can promise you that Gaston Durand will never, ever, trouble you again.

Don't think badly of me for fighting on the 'wrong' side, just remember how proud I am to call you my sister.

With my love, Marcel.

He left the letter for his parents on the hall stand where the servants always left the post and took the note to Hélène out to the stables. If she came back that's where she would look for him and he left it propped up on a straw bale. Then he took a last look round his childhood home before going back into the city to find his unit once more.

Most of the fighting was now concentrated further east. Passy was no longer under threat as the government army continued its steady progress through the city. There were short, intense battles as they came up against the hastily erected barricades. Rattling rifle fire poured into the insubstantial barriers, eventually killing almost all who tried to defend them, before the invading troops swept through and on to the next one. The government troops suffered losses too, but they were nothing as compared with the Communards who, though determined to fight to the last man, were gradually driven from behind the barricades.

Marcel and his unit defended and fell back, defended and fell back, each time losing more men, weakening their strength but not their resolve. Marcel had no illusions, he knew he was going to die, but he was determined to take as many of the enemy with him as possible. When their officer was killed, it was Marcel who took command and led his unit in retreat to survive and fight again.

It was two days later that he and his men made one final stand at Montparnasse station. Ensconced in the station buildings, they held off the attacking soldiers until, their ammunition almost exhausted, Marcel gave orders for them to fall back.

'Every man for himself,' he bellowed as, hidden inside a newspaper stand, he raked the station with steady fire, keeping the incoming troops at bay while his men made their escape behind him.

He knew his own ammunition would run out before long, and once he knew his men were clear, he used it more sparingly. There would be no escape for him, but he continued to fire at any soldier unwise enough to emerge from cover, to risk a dash towards his hideout.

At last his rifle fell silent and the attacking troops began a stealthy advance. When it was clear that they were in no further danger from the hidden sniper, several of them rushed to the newsstand, guns at the ready. They found Marcel, sitting on a stool inside the kiosk, his empty rifle across his knees, his hands in the air and an insouciant grin on his face.

It was the grin that did it. Behind them lay the bodies of their comrades, the soldiers Marcel had been picking off individually as they broke cover. The first man stared in at him, his rifle pointing menacingly at his chest, hesitating before taking the life of a man with his hands in the air in cold blood. The second man had no such qualms. He aimed his gun and pulled the trigger. At such close quarters Marcel was flung backwards, his head exploding, brains and blood and bone sprayed all over the confined space of the newsstand.

As the sound of the shot died away there was a moment's silence, then on a command, the soldiers turned, leaving Marcel's body, just another damned Communard, a bloodied heap on the floor.

Chapter 28

Jeannot and his mates lay low for that night and the next day. The dangers of the street far outweighed the need for food, but after a second night spent in the safety of their cellar, the boys emerged into the daylight. The sounds of the battle continued, but were more distant now. The battle had passed them by.

'I'm off,' Jeannot said when he'd slaked his thirst at one of the public fountains. 'Got to find something to eat.'

'Share and share alike,' Monkey reminded him. 'Meet back here with anything you've found.'

The boys disappeared in three different directions to see what they could scrounge in the way of food… or anything else.

Jeannot decided his best chance of something to eat was at Tante Edith's, and he headed back towards the Bergers' basement. This time he was even more careful than before, taking care to steer clear of any main thoroughfares, but as he zigzagged through narrow side streets and alleyways, he could see the destroyed barricades, many of them with bodies still lying where they had fallen; women and children amongst them, all dying in answer to the Commune's call to arms. He saw the body of a boy about his own age, lying on his back, his face to the sky, his eyes already missing; empty sockets left by the crows. Jeannot shuddered as he realised that if he hadn't escaped from the working party, he too could be lying dead in the street.

It was as he looked at the scattered bodies that an idea came to him. He looked round but there was no one else in sight. With slight reluctance, he crept towards the body of a man in workman's clothes that lay like a discarded rag doll across the top of the barricade; not a soldier, but a man of the people. Jeannot kneeled down and slipped his hand into the man's pocket. When he withdrew it again, he was clutching two francs. Riches!

Jeannot had few scruples about robbing a dead body. The man didn't need the money any more, but he, Jeannot, did. Those coins could be the difference between eating and going hungry. He slipped them into his own pocket and scurried hurriedly away. Others might not take such a pragmatic view of his actions, and though there was no one in sight, you never knew who might be watching.

He risked two more such robberies and though they were not so lucrative, he added another franc and twenty sous to his cash. He might not have any food to take to Tante Edith, but at least he had something to offer her.

The door to the basement was flung open even as he clattered down the steps and Tante Edith greeted him with a hug.

'Jeannot,' she cried, 'thank God. We thought you were dead. Where've you been?'

'Had to take cover,' replied Jeannot. 'Things got really hot out there.'

He followed Edith back inside and looked round the little apartment. The curtain that divided off the sleeping area was drawn back and he saw at once that Hélène was not there.

'Where's Hélène?' he demanded.

'Gone,' sniffed Alphonse from his seat in the corner.

'What d'you mean, gone?' cried Jeannot. 'Gone where?'

'Gone and good riddance!' muttered Edith.

'When you didn't come back, boy,' Alphonse said, making clear that he thought it was Jeannot's fault, 'Edith and the girl went out to try and buy some food. And she ran off.'

'Ran off?' echoed Jeannot, turning to Edith. 'Ran off where?'

'How do I know?' said Edith. 'I was in with old Felix Vellier. He had a hambone and it took me time to get it. When I came out of his shop, she'd gone.' She patted Jeannot on the shoulder. 'Forget her, Jeannot, she ain't worth it. We gave her food and then she run off.'

Jeannot forgot about the money in his pocket and turned to the door. 'I must go and find her,' he said.

'Wait!' Edith's tone was peremptory. 'What have you brought us? You promised to bring back food if we looked after that girl.'

'Well, you ain't,' Jeannot snapped. 'You ain't looked after her, have you?'

'Not our fault if she run off,' muttered Alphonse.

Jeannot paused in the doorway, and then putting his hand in his pocket pulled out one of the franc coins. 'Here,' he said, tossing it onto the floor. 'You can have that.' And by the time Edith had scrabbled for it he was out of the door and heading for the Avenue Ste Anne. He didn't know if Hélène would go back there, but it seemed the obvious place to look.

When he reached Passy he found there was a semblance of normality as a few people were out in the streets. He looked out of place in such a prosperous area and he received some suspicious glances, but no one actually challenged him and he ducked into the lane behind the house. He was relieved to find the back gate unlocked, that must mean someone was here, but when he reached the stable, it was empty.

Hélène was not there and he had no way of knowing if she had been. Nor was she in the house. The back door was still unlocked but the house was empty. But someone *had* been there, he was sure. Marcel, perhaps? Or maybe Georges wasn't as badly injured as they'd thought and he'd come back. But if so, where were they now?

Jeannot wandered round the house. In the drawer of a desk in what must be Monsieur St Clair's study, he found a small leather purse containing nearly twenty francs. He couldn't believe that anyone would leave so much money lying in an unlocked drawer, but never one to turn down such largesse, the purse disappeared into his pocket. He was sure Monsieur St Clair wouldn't miss it, and if he did, he'd think Gaston had taken it when he'd taken Hélène. Anyway, Jeannot reasoned, they owed him. He'd done his best to save Hélène and if she'd run off now when he'd got her to a safe place, there was nothing he could do about that. He was sorry, of course, he found he'd come to like the girl, admired her spunk, but he wasn't her keeper. His job was what it had always been: to look after number one. With twenty francs in his pocket, he was king of the world!

A quick search through the rest of the desk drawers revealed nothing else worth having, just papers and ledgers and such, all useless to Jeannot.

Having found the money he decided that it was time to leave; he didn't want to be caught there by any of the St Clairs now, not even Hélène. He closed both house and stable doors behind him, no need to advertise that someone had been there, then he was out through the gate and off down the street to his own part of the city. He'd share with the Monkey and Paul, but not equal shares. A man had to keep something for himself.

Chapter 29

Hélène had followed the sun as she had before, but this time it was a far more hazardous journey. She could hear the thunder of the guns, inside the city now, the rumble of destruction as buildings were shelled to clear the advancing army's way forward. She had learned something of a street child's cautious movement from Jeannot, but she wasn't prepared for the sights she saw on her way through those streets. The fighting had been fierce and the debris of buildings was strewn across the ground. Bodies lay unburied, as if tossed aside by the advancing soldiers, and the dust and the filth and the stink filled her nostrils, making her feel sick. On one corner, she found a small boy standing over the body of a young woman, pulling at her arm and weeping piteously as he cried, 'Get up, Maman! Get up!'

Hélène stopped and held out a hand to him, but he hit out at her, shouting, 'Go away!'

'You can't stay here,' Hélène said, looking round at the eerily deserted street and ruined building nearby.

But the boy kept on screaming at her, 'Go away! Go away!

Go away!' There was nothing she could do and Hélène walked on, leaving him crying for his dead mother.

There were a few other people on the streets, going about their own business, and little attention was paid to her as she worked her way westward, away from the fighting that still continued at the eastern end of the city. Occasionally she heard the tramp of feet, and from the shelter of a doorway she watched a troop of soldiers go marching by, but she didn't even know which side they were on, and stayed hidden until they were long gone.

As before, it was the bell tower of Our Lady of Sorrows that finally led her home. Hélène almost cried with relief when she saw it, still standing tall and strong, its steeple pointing straight up to heaven. She was home. Despite everything, she was home.

Afternoon was lengthening into evening as she opened the gate and let herself into the garden. She wondered if Marcel would be there, whether he'd have any news of Georges. She approached the stable, calling out as she opened the door, but the building was empty. She found some matches and lit the lamp. It was then, in its warm glow, that she saw it on a bale of straw: a folded sheet of paper with her name on it. She caught it up and held it to the lamp to read. She read it through twice, hardly able to believe what she read. Marcel had found Georges and he was now safe and cared for at Dr Simon's house; but Marcel himself had gone – gone back to the fighting and the barricades. She clutched the letter in her hand, holding it tight… a talisman. Amazingly, one brother was safe, but the other? What would happen to him? She felt a lump in her throat at the thought of Marcel fighting for his life and ending up a body on a barricade, like the ones she'd seen just that day. 'Oh please God,' she prayed, 'let him come home again safely. Don't let him be killed.'

As for Jeannot, she had no idea what had happened to him, he'd simply vanished. Perhaps he was dead too and she would never know; never discover what had happened to him that day after he'd left the basement apartment in search of food. Poor Jeannot.

Well, Hélène thought with a sigh, Marcel said to go and find Georges, so that's what I'd better do.

She extinguished the lamp carefully and made her way out into the avenue. The sun was setting now and the sky was brilliant, a rich red streaked with orange and flashes of yellow. She looked at it as she walked along the street to Dr Simon's house. What a wonderful sunset! At least the war couldn't destroy that. Reaching the doctor's house, she knocked on the front door and waited. It seemed a long time before she heard footsteps approaching on the inside. She'd been about to knock again when a voice called, 'Who is it?'

'Hélène St Clair,' Hélène called back. 'Madame Yvette, it's me, Hélène St Clair.'

She heard the bolts being drawn back and the front door was thrown open, and there she was, Madame Yvette, Dr Simon's housekeeper, a woman whom Hélène had known all her life.

Almost as if she'd been expecting her, she said, 'Come in, Hélène, your brother's in here.'

Georges was sitting in an armchair, his bandaged leg raised and resting on a footstool. When he saw who his visitor was his whole face lit up.

'Hélène!' he cried. 'Thank God you're safe. Whatever happened to you? Where have you been? We've been so worried about you!'

Hélène ran across the room to hug him. 'Oh, Georges!' she cried. 'Your poor leg! Are you all right? Will it get better?'

'Of course it will.' Dr Simon's voice came from the door. 'Well, now, young lady,' he went on. 'You're looking much better than when I saw you last. But where have you been? Your brothers have been worried sick.'

Hélène sat down beside Georges and took his hand. 'It's a long story,' she began. 'When you sent us away the other night, Georges, Jeannot was afraid that the Avenue Ste Anne was right in the target area. He said both armies seemed to be bombing Passy and so he took us to the house of some friends of his. Tante Edith, he called her, and Oncle Alphonse. They looked after him during the siege. Anyway...' Hélène explained that she hadn't known where they were, except that it was near to where she'd managed to escape from the Gaston-man over the warehouse wall.

'Jeannot went out to get some food,' she explained. 'He didn't come back and I haven't seen him since.'

'Typical,' murmured Georges, who had always mistrusted Jeannot.

'No, it isn't!' insisted Hélène. 'You never believed me, but he's always looked after me. He helped me escape from Gaston. He was almost killed by him. And he wouldn't leave me with those people and not come back... not if he could help it.' Her voice began to tremble as she said, 'Do you think he's been killed in the fighting?'

'I don't know, Hélène,' Georges answered. 'I suppose he might have been. But he's a lad who's used to looking after himself, you know.' He tried to sound reassuring. 'He's probably had to lie low for a while, but I expect he's hiding somewhere safe, and he'll turn up again before too long.'

Though goodness only knows what we're going to do with him if he does, thought Georges privately. Well, sufficient unto the day...

At that moment Madame Yvette knocked and without waiting for an invitation burst into the room.

'Oh, doctor,' she cried, 'you must come and look out of the window! All Paris is on fire!'

Dr Simon went to the window and threw back the curtains. Outside, the sky was as Hélène had seen it earlier except that darkness was falling and still the sky blazed orange and red, shot with yellow, and above were dark roiling clouds lit from below.

'It's the sunset,' cried Hélène. 'I saw it as I was coming down the road.'

Dr Simon shook his head. 'No, Hélène, I don't think so. It's to the east.' He walked away from the window and hurried out through the front door to stand in the street. Hélène followed and stood beside him as they both gazed up at the sky. Other people were coming out of their houses to stand and stare at the amazing night sky.

'Paris is ablaze,' murmured someone standing nearby. 'The whole city is burning.'

'I heard they blew up the Tuileries Palace today and the fire is sweeping through everywhere.'

'Whole streets ablaze!'

News of the fire spread as fast as the fire itself. Hélène stood listening as the news was passed from mouth to mouth.

'The Palais-Royal!'

'Part of the Louvre!'

'The Hôtel de Ville!'

Dr Simon led Hélène back indoors, leaving his neighbours staring up at the glowing sky.

'What's happening?' asked Georges, frustrated at not being able to go out and see for himself.

'Frenchman is killing Frenchman,' replied Dr Simon gravely, 'and the whole of Paris is destroyed.' Hélène saw that the old man had tears in his eyes. She had never seen a man cry and she looked away, embarrassed. Was it true? Was Paris really burning out of control?

Madame Yvette reappeared and took Hélène to a spare bedroom where a bed was already made up and a nightdress laid out. She showed her the new bathroom the doctor had had installed, where hot water flowed from the taps into a bath tub so long Hélène could lie down in it.

'Now,' said Madame Yvette, 'you have a good bath and then I will come and help you wash your hair, *hein*?'

She gave Hélène ten minutes and then returned with a huge towel that she wrapped round the girl. 'Now we will wash your hair and you will feel better.'

As she leaned over the edge of the bath and Madame Yvette rubbed soap into her hair, Hélène had a sudden recollection of how Marie-Jeanne used to do it, and the tears sprang unbidden to her eyes.

Poor, dear Marie-Jeanne, lying dead at the top of the stairs. She hadn't thought of her for several days. Hardly believing she had not, her tears ran down into the bath, mingling with the dirt from her hair.

Later that night as she lay awake in bed, she remembered the little boy trying to wake his dead mother and her tears returned. What would happen to him? He couldn't have been more than five years old. How would he live without his mother? Who would look after him?

She thought of her own mother and felt such a longing for her that it was a physical ache.

Unable to sleep, she got out of bed and went to the window. The sky in the east was still alight with flames. Dr Simon had said that the whole of Paris was destroyed, and watching from her window, Hélène thought he must be right. How could anything survive such an inferno?

The inferno continued to burn throughout the night, the flames leaping from house to house, sweeping along streets, engulfing buildings, new and old, without discrimination. Government troops fought valiantly to stop the fire spreading further but there had been no rain for nearly a month and everything was tinder dry. Homes, shops and offices went up in flames. The medieval Hôtel de Ville had been deliberately torched and the fire blazed onward, consuming everything in its path.

It was two days later that the rain finally came, helping to quench the last of the fires, but the killing did not stop. Bloody atrocities occurred on both sides. Hundreds of Communard prisoners were lined up and shot by government soldiers; over fifty hostages, including the Archbishop of Paris who had been held by the Communards, were dragged out of prison and shot out of hand.

Dr Simon had been right. Frenchman was killing Frenchman and Paris was destroyed. Retribution was long and bloody but the life of the Commune was over.

During the last few violent days, Hélène and Georges had remained in the doctor's house, but all was not well there. Instead of getting better, Georges began to get worse. His temperature soared and his injured leg gave him tremendous pain. Dr Simon had to ease the bandages as it started swelling up and changing colour, from red to purple to marbled yellow. Something had gone wrong, and as the day progressed, he became delirious. Hélène watched him with frightened eyes as he raved about a battle, shouting warnings of attack one minute and begging for water the next.

'Is he going to die?' she asked Dr Simon.

'Not if I can help it,' replied the doctor, 'but his leg is infected and unless we remove it, the poison will kill him.'

'Remove it?' Hélène didn't understand. 'Remove the infection?'

'No, my child,' the doctor said gently. 'Remove the leg.'

Hélène's eyes widened with horror. 'Cut it off, you mean.'

Dr Simon nodded. 'Yes,' he said, 'that's just what I mean.'

Georges continued to babble incoherently and Hélène continued to sit beside him, keeping watch.

'I must operate at once,' the doctor told her. 'I have seen such things before, when I was a doctor with the army, and unless I take off his leg, he will die.'

'But you said he was going to get better,' cried Hélène. 'You mended his leg.'

'I mended the bone, but the wound isn't healing as it should. I'm sorry, Hélène, but there is no alternative.'

'Will he go to hospital?' she asked, at last accepting what he said.

'No. I will operate here.' He looked at Hélène, and thinking what a lot she'd had to deal with over the last few weeks, he decided to treat her as an adult and tell her the truth. 'If Georges goes to any of the hospitals here in Paris, it is unlikely he'll come out alive. Here, we can look after him. He will have our whole attention and not simply be part of a busy hospital.'

'Will you tell him what you're going to do?' asked Hélène. 'What will you do if he says no?'

'It will be impossible to make him understand in his present state,' said Dr Simon, 'but if I don't operate he will assuredly die.'

The doctor, assisted by a younger doctor and his nurse, operated that evening. Georges was anesthetised with chloroform and the operation performed in the surgery at the back of Dr Simon's house.

Hélène sat in the drawing room with Madame Yvette for company. Surely Georges wasn't going to die now, after the war was over! It seemed an age before the doctor returned to them and told them that the operation was finished and Georges was now in bed upstairs.

'You can go and sit with him until he wakes up,' he said to Hélène. 'The nurse will be close by and when he does wake, you must call for her and me immediately.'

Hélène found Georges asleep in the bed, his face pale and his breathing ragged. At first she could not drag her eyes away from the blanket that covered him, the flatness where half his left leg should be. She drew a chair up to the bed and took his hand in her own. She would wait there until he awoke when he would have to learn that he now only had one leg.

The next few days were quite dreadful. Georges awoke to find himself a cripple. His missing leg still ached and he sank into a slough of despond. Nothing Hélène or anyone else could say could raise his spirits. His physical recovery was proceeding as Dr Simon had hoped, the gangrene which had been creeping up his injured leg had been removed, and provided there was no further infection there was no reason, Dr Simon said, that he shouldn't make a full recovery. Privately, though, he was worried about the young man's mental state.

'But how will he walk?' Hélène had asked.

'We will make him a new leg of wood,' replied the doctor. 'Other soldiers who have lost a leg have learned to walk with these.'

'I'd rather have died than been left like this,' Georges told her bitterly, 'a cripple, beholden to everyone for everything.'

Once peace of some sort was restored to the city, Hélène wrote a letter to her parents, telling them that she and Georges were, at present, living with Dr Simon.

Georges has been injured and has had to have his leg cut off. He is very sad, but Dr Simon said if he had not had this operation he would have died. I am well now and will tell you everything when I see you. Please, dearest Maman and Papa, will you come and fetch us as soon as you can.

Marcel was here, but we haven't seen him since Paris fell and we don't know where he is now.

After the first few days Georges said, 'Hélène, I want you to write a letter to Sylvie for me. Remember I was going to take you to her when...'

His voice trailed off and Hélène said, 'Of course I remember, she's the girl you're going to marry.'

'Not any more,' said Georges flatly. 'I'm not going to let her tie herself to a cripple with only one leg.'

'That's stupid,' Hélène said roundly. 'If she loves you she'll want to marry you even if you have lost a leg.'

'Don't argue with me, you're only a child!' snapped Georges. 'You wouldn't understand and in any case, it's none of your business.'

Hélène looked shocked. 'Poor Georges,' she whispered, trying to imagine what he was going through. She took his hands in hers and looking him in the eye, said, 'I may be a child, Georges,' she said softly, 'but I still think you should tell her what has happened to you and let her make up her own mind. Do you think we won't love you anymore because you've lost a leg?'

Georges gave a sad laugh. 'No, of course not, but you're family. You have to put up with me, but I just couldn't bear it if Sylvie married me out of pity!'

Reluctantly Hélène wrote to his dictation, telling Sylvie Claviet that he no longer wished to marry her. He gave no explanation, fearing her pity, he simply told her he had changed his mind.

'Won't you tell her why?' Hélène tried again.

'No,' replied Georges fiercely and the subject was closed.

One of Georges's brother officers came to see him and agreed to have the two letters sent as soon as it was feasible. There was still plenty of confusion in the city, but he promised to send someone as soon as he could. He took the letters and was just leaving the house when Hélène followed him outside and handed him another.

'This is for Mademoiselle Sylvie as well,' she said. The man took the second letter, addressed to Sylvie Claviet in the same childish hand as the one to St Etienne, and put it in his pouch with the others. 'I just want her to know I'm here looking after Georges,' she lied. And the man smiled and nodded.

'Don't worry, mademoiselle, I'll make sure she gets it.'

Chapter 30

Rosalie was in the garden picking roses for the house when the messenger arrived at St Etienne. Anne-Marie the housemaid came running out to find her.

'Madame, please come at once,' she cried, her face red with excitement. 'A soldier has come from Paris with a letter.'

Rosalie dropped her basket and almost ran back indoors, calling over her shoulder, 'Where's Monsieur St Clair, Anne-Marie? Find him at once and tell him I need him in the morning parlour.'

The soldier was waiting in the hall and as Rosalie reached him, she said, 'A letter? You've brought us a letter. Is it from my son, Captain St Clair? Give it to me, quickly please.'

The man handed over the letter, saying, 'I believe it's from your daughter, madame.'

'My daughter,' breathed Rosalie, and looking at the envelope saw that it was indeed addressed in Hélène's handwriting. At that moment Emile came in.

'What *is* the matter, my dear?' he said briskly. 'I'm talking to Patrice about the orchard and—'

'Never mind about Patrice and the orchard,' Rosalie cried. 'This man has brought us a letter… from Hélène. She's alive!' She passed him the envelope and he ripped it open. He sank into a chair as he read it and then passed it over to his wife.

Rosalie read it through twice before saying, 'We must go at once!'

'And they were both well when you left them?' Emile said, turning to the soldier.

'As far as I know, sir,' replied the man. 'I didn't actually see the captain, I was simply ordered to bring you this letter.'

Emile summoned Anne-Marie and told her to take the messenger into the kitchen and make sure he had a proper meal before he went on his way.

'Well, my dear,' he said when they were alone again, 'what amazing news is this!'

Rosalie could hardly believe that two of her children had survived the dreadful fighting in Paris; that they were safe and living with the doctor. She wept tears of joy and Emile found himself fighting back tears of his own. He had long ago accepted the fact that Hélène was lost to them, and now here she was, writing to tell them about Georges being wounded and asking them to come and fetch them both. What on earth had happened to her? Where had she been all this time?

'You must tell Pierre to prepare the chaise at once,' Rosalie said. 'If Georges is injured we must bring him back here to be nursed and he cannot travel on the train. And Hélène! My darling girl, my darling, darling girl. She's alive!' The tears streamed down her cheeks and she clasped Emile's hands. 'Oh, Emile!'

They set out for Paris that very afternoon, Pierre driving them in the chaise, a basket of provisions tucked under the seat for when they arrived. They left the two girls in St Etienne with Mademoiselle Corbine and travelled alone. Clarice and Louise had jumped for joy at the news and begged to be allowed to accompany their parents, but Rosalie had learned her lesson. No other daughter of hers was going to be brought into a city still on the edge of civil war.

'We'll bring them back here to St Etienne as soon as we can,' she promised. 'We shan't be away long.'

'You will come home again, Maman, won't you?' Louise asked anxiously.

'Of course I will,' replied her mother. 'The fighting in Paris has stopped now and we'll be back in a few days.'

They stopped overnight at an inn on the way, but were up at cock crow the next morning to carry on their journey back into Paris. This time there was no National Guard on the gates to question their reasons for travelling or to confiscate their horse.

Once they reached the Avenue Ste Anne they went straight to the doctor's house where they found Hélène, sitting with Georges, reading to him. Madame Yvette led them into the room and Hélène gave a shriek and, dropping the book, rushed into her mother's arms. Rosalie held her tightly, as if she would never let her go.

Emile crossed to the bed where Georges lay, his face pale and pinched. 'My dear boy,' he said, reaching for his hands. 'Thank God you're alive.'

'Only just, Papa,' Georges replied, as he watched his mother and Hélène weeping as they clung together. 'Crippled for life. What use is a one-legged man? I might as well be dead.'

Emile looked down at him, his eyes full of compassion. 'Never say that, Georges,' he said. 'Never, ever, say that.'

When Dr Simon came home he drew Rosalie aside and said, 'Your daughter has had some dreadful experiences since she was taken. She's an extremely brave and resourceful child, but she may find it difficult to speak of them. Try not to overwhelm her with questions. Let her tell you what happened to her in her own good time. It may take days or weeks for it all to come out.' He gave a sigh. 'I haven't asked her, but I know she has nightmares. I've heard her crying out in the night. So, I know it'll be difficult, but let her take her time telling you.'

Rosalie took his advice and asked no questions, but talking to Georges when she was alone with him, she learned much of what had happened to Hélène and was horrified. She also asked about Marcel. 'Have you seen him? Where is he now?' she asked eagerly. 'What happened to him?'

'I don't know, Maman,' answered Georges. He was unwilling to tell her that Marcel had deserted the army and fought for the Commune, so he simply said, 'But I do know that he did all he could for Hélène and if he hadn't found me and brought me here, I'd be dead now.'

It was going to take far longer than a few days, but they were able to send another message to the family waiting in St Etienne to say that they were with Georges and Hélène and that all was well.

Hélène stayed at the doctor's house with Georges, but her parents went to their own home in the Avenue Ste Anne. Rosalie was extremely reluctant to enter the house where Marie-Jeanne had been killed and Hélène had been abducted, but they had nowhere else to go. The front door was still barred and they had to enter the house through the stable yard and back door. It was cold and still and she felt it was filled with the miasma of death.

In the hall, they found Marcel's letter and learned what Georges had not told them.

'That's a disgrace!' Emile had retorted. 'How could a son of mine have deserted? We shall never be able to hold up our heads again!'

'And I'm proud that a son of mine was prepared to fight for what he thought was right!' declared Rosalie.

'But we can't receive him back into the family,' Emile said. 'A Communard!'

'If he's still alive, I will always welcome my son home,' Rosalie said defiantly. 'Communard or not.' She held Emile's gaze, her eyes challenging. 'Have you forgotten that he's been taking care of Hélène? That he rescued Georges and got him to Dr Simon? I will never forget those things, even if you do.'

'Even if he wasn't killed on the barricades, he's almost certainly dead,' Emile said flatly. 'They've been shooting the Communard prisoners.'

'I know that,' Rosalie said quietly, 'and if he's dead, he died for what he believed in. No one will know he turned his coat, unless you tell them, Emile. Georges must have known and he's saying nothing. We should say nothing, too.'

Dr Simon told them it would be some weeks before Georges would be fit to be moved. Arrangements needed to be made, a suitable, competent nurse had to be found and hired, and a downstairs room prepared for Georges's habitation.

Chapter 31

Hélène spoke little about what had happened to her, and following Dr Simon's advice, Rosalie did not push her. Emile was less sensitive and it wasn't until his wife took him severely to task that he drew back.

'Emile, the child has been through a terrible ordeal. She still has nightmares, she still wakes up screaming; you've heard her! Just leave her for now and let her memories fade.'

'But we must find those men, the ones who invaded our home...' blustered Emile, his anger reddening his cheeks. 'They murdered Marie-Jeanne, for God's sake, as well as abducting Hélène.'

'I know, but they will have to wait. We can do nothing for Marie-Jeanne and our priority now must be Hélène.'

'But they must be brought to justice,' persisted Emile.

'That justice is as nothing,' returned Rosalie. 'Nothing compared with the harm they did to our daughter. If Jeannot hadn't found—'

'That tyke!' interrupted Emile. 'He knows more than he's saying. We should...'

'So please, Emile,' went on Rosalie, entirely ignoring his interruption, 'don't question Hélène any more. We can do nothing about those who harmed her, all we can do is give her the space to heal.'

Even so, more snippets of Hélène's ordeal came out over the next few days, Dr Simon filling in the parts that he knew, and it was when she heard of the kindness Madame Sauze had shown Hélène that Rosalie felt she must act.

'I think we ought to let Madame Sauze know that you're safely back with your family,' she said to Hélène one morning over breakfast. 'I thought we might go to the Clergy House and thank her for her care.'

'She put me in the orphanage,' said Hélène flatly. 'She didn't let me stay.'

'I doubt if that was her decision to make,' Rosalie replied gently. 'It wasn't appropriate for you to stay in the Clergy House and you needed somewhere safe to live, off the streets.'

'I hated it there!' said Hélène mutinously.

'I know, darling,' said her mother, reaching for her hand, 'but it was the best place for you in the circumstances.' She got to her feet. 'We'll pay her a visit this morning and tell her that you're well and thank her for looking after you as she did.'

Even as they approached the door of the Clergy House, it opened and Father Thomas came out into the street. For a moment he stared at the mother and daughter on the pavement outside without recognition, but at the sight of him, Hélène stepped back behind her mother.

'Good morning, Father,' Rosalie said with a smile.

'Good morning, madame,' he responded uncertainly. He

was impressed by this elegant woman, clearly a lady of class, and wondered why she was calling.

'Is Madame Sauze at home?' Rosalie asked as if asking for the mistress of the house.

'Madame Sauze?' The young priest sounded surprised and added, 'Father Lenoir is in his study, but I cannot say for sure if the *housekeeper*,' he emphasised her standing, 'is in the house or has gone to the market.' He straightened his back, determined not to be daunted by this woman. 'But perhaps I may be of assistance?'

'I'd rather not discuss things on your doorstep, Father,' Rosalie said firmly, 'and it is Madame Sauze we've come to see.' She stepped forward and Father Thomas gave way, opening the front door again and standing aside for her, and the child behind her, to enter the house. As he did so he had his first real look at the girl who followed her in. She was prettily dressed, her dark hair parted neatly down the middle and caught back in a clasp at the nape of her neck before waterfalling in shining curls down her back, and her skin glowed with good health. The expression on her face, however, was one of pure loathing, and it was that look in her eyes that brought recognition to his. He looked away, entirely disconcerted. Surely this well-dressed girl with the glossy hair couldn't be the street urchin they'd put into St Luke's? She'd been filthy, dressed in rags, spouting lies in the hope of being kept at the Clergy House. Madame Sauze had been taken in, and so too had Father Lenoir to a certain extent, but he, Father Thomas, had not been so gullible. And now? And now he was faced with an upper-class lady, with that same child in tow, coming to visit them. Had she come to thank them for befriending her daughter – for the girl clearly was her daughter, with the same brown eyes under lids with impossibly long lashes, the same high cheekbones, the same sculpted lips – or had she come to complain of their treatment of her, to berate them for putting the girl into St Luke's and thus seeming to abandon her, their charitable work done, another vulnerable girl off the streets?

Well, he decided with a mental shrug, whichever it is, Father Lenoir will have to deal with it. He, after all, is the parish priest. I'm only his curate, bound by his decisions.

'I will tell Father Lenoir you're here, madame,' he said. 'Whom shall I say is calling?'

'Madame Rosalie St Clair and her daughter Hélène.'

They were shown into the priest's study where Father Lenoir greeted them with a hand raised in blessing, before they were both offered seats before his desk.

'I've come to thank you and Madame Sauze for taking my daughter in when she found herself distressed and living on the streets,' Rosalie said.

'It was nothing, madame,' he remarked calmly. 'Just our simple Christian duty. No child of her age should be left to fend for herself. It was most unfortunate that we couldn't make contact with you at the time. I can assure you it wasn't for lack of trying,' he spread his hands, 'but the tempestuous state of Paris made it impossible.'

'We quite understand, Father,' Rosalie interposed. 'My husband and I would like to make an endowment to your church as a sign of our gratitude.'

'That is most generous, madame,' declared the priest, 'and something I feel able to accept on behalf of Our Lord.'

Rosalie smiled. 'Then it will be arranged,' she said. 'Now, before we go I would like to see Madame Sauze, if I may.'

She got to her feet and Father Lenoir, opening the door, called out, 'Annette! Annette! Where are you, girl?'

To Hélène's amazement, Annette, the bread thief, appeared from the kitchen. The two girls stared at each other for a moment before the priest said testily, 'Annette, please show Madame St Clair and her daughter into the parlour and then ask Madame Sauze to join them there.' He turned back to Rosalie and said, 'If you will excuse me, madame, I have parish business to attend to, but do stay with Madame Sauze for as long as you please.' Once again he raised his hand but didn't offer it, before turning back into his study and closing the door.

Annette led them into the parlour and then scurried away to find Agathe Sauze. The delight that suffused the housekeeper's face when she came into the room and saw who was there told Rosalie all she needed to know about this generous woman. Madame Sauze held out her hands to Hélène and after a moment's hesitation the girl took them and was pulled into a warm embrace.

'You're looking well, my child,' she said when they finally broke apart. 'Thank God you're safe! He heard my prayers.' She turned to Rosalie who held out her hand and the two women sat down, their heads together as they spoke softly.

Annette came back into the room and Hélène asked, 'You work here now?'

'Yes, Madame Sauze came and asked for me at St Luke's.'

'Thanks for helping me escape,' Hélène said a little awkwardly.

'Just had a coughing fit, and Sister Gabrielle nearly fell over me.' Annette grinned at the memory. 'Got a beating from Reverend Mother when we got home again. Black and blue I was, but it was worth it! One in the eye for all of them!'

'And Madame Sauze came for you?'

'She came to see Mother and said she was looking for a housemaid to train up... and she asked for me... by name. Don't think Mother was very pleased. She tried to send Amélie, but Madame said I was the one she wanted.' Annette gave Hélène a shy smile. 'Thanks to you I'm out of that hellhole.'

'It's thanks to yourself,' Hélène told her. 'I might not have made it if you hadn't tripped up Sister Gabrielle.' She looked across at her mother and Madame Sauze, still deep in conversation. 'She's very kind, Madame is,' she said.

'She is,' agreed Annette, 'and Father Lenoir is all right, too. It's Father Thomas I can't bear. He's mean as a toad. Always finding fault and telling me I'm only alive as the result of sin.'

'I hate him too,' said Hélène with a shudder.

'Lucky you, you don't have to live with him.'

Rosalie stayed for another quarter of an hour before getting to her feet and saying, 'Well, Hélène, we must go home. Thank Madame Sauze again for looking after you.'

'I'll never forget you, madame,' Hélène promised as they embraced. 'You're my good angel.' She gave Annette a quick hug. 'I won't forget you, either, bread-thief,' she murmured, 'or the beating you took for me.' She glanced over her shoulder to be sure no one was in earshot and added, 'And watch out for that toad.'

Two days later Rosalie went back to St Etienne to superintend the arrangements for Georges's homecoming, leaving Emile in Paris but taking Hélène with her. Thus, Hélène wasn't there to see the repercussions of the letters that had been despatched. Not long after Rosalie and she had set off back to the country by train, there was a knock at the doctor's front door and Madame Yvette found an unaccompanied young lady standing on the doorstep, demanding to see Lieutenant Georges St Clair.

'I'm sorry,' said Madame Yvette, looking the young person up and down with disfavour. 'Captain St Clair is indisposed and having no visitors.' She made as if to shut the door but the young lady on the step had different ideas. She placed her foot firmly over the threshold and said, 'I think you'll find he wants to see me. Please be so good as to tell him his fiancée is here.'

Madame Yvette looked mutinous for a moment but then she shrugged and said, 'You'd better come in. I'll ask the doctor.'

Dr Simon came out of his room at that moment and seeing an attractive girl standing in his hall, said, 'Good afternoon, mademoiselle, can I help you?'

'My name is Sylvie Claviet and I've come to see my fiancé, Captain St Clair.'

'Have you indeed?' answered the doctor with a smile. 'Well, I'm delighted to see you. But, before you go in, I should warn you that he's had to have his leg amputated and—'

'Oh, I know about his leg,' Sylvie said dismissively. 'Hélène wrote and told me.'

Dr Simon raised an eyebrow. 'I see,' he said, 'but you have to understand, it isn't just his leg he's lost, it's his confidence and self-esteem… as if he were now somehow less of a man. I think seeing you will do him good, but I'm just warning you to tread carefully.'

Sylvie looked at him and nodded. 'He says he doesn't want to marry me anymore,' she said.

'I'm sure that isn't true, mademoiselle, but he may well believe that he *should* not. Men like him, brave and honest, are afraid of becoming a burden on their friends and family.'

'A burden?' cried Sylvie. 'He could never be that to me.'

'And so you must convince him,' smiled the doctor, standing aside to let her enter Georges's room. 'I don't doubt that you can; he sounds like a very lucky man.'

Epilogue

Jeannot had returned to his life on the streets, sharing his home as he had before with Paul and the Monkey. Even living with the Bergers he'd found too restricting. Now that he was a man of means – he still had fifteen francs in his pocket – he wanted to be out and about, doing the business that such men do. When the fighting had ceased, the retributions over, the firing squads silent and the executions done with, the city he had known all his life picked itself up, gave itself a shake and got on with things. Not returning to a normality that, certainly in its previous form anyway, was dead and buried with the executed Communards, but country people brought their produce into town, markets were set up, people bought and sold, and wherever that went on there were opportunities to be had, and Jeannot made the most of them.

Several times he'd been back to the Avenue Ste Anne, walking past casually, watching for Hélène. He hadn't seen her since he'd left her with the Bergers and he wanted to know she was all right. He had no idea what had happened to Marcel or Georges. He didn't care about Georges, but he'd been impressed with Marcel. Had Marcel killed Gaston? he wondered. He hoped so.

One evening at dusk he had been back to Gaston's place and even as he watched, two men, whom he recognised as Gaston's henchmen, Jules and Auguste, emerged from the building carrying a sagging bundle of... something. Was it a corpse? He followed at a distance to the next street and saw them looking about them before quietly tipping whatever it was into the central drain and hurrying away. Jeannot drew back deeper into the shadows. As far as they were concerned he was dead, and that was the way he wanted it to stay.

It was several days later that he saw activity at the St Clairs' house. The front door was unbarred and replaced with a sturdy new one.

He saw Hélène and her mother returning to the house and knew a sudden burst of relief. Hélène was all right. Wherever she'd run to that day, she'd survived. He wondered if she'd been back to the priests' house, or even the orphanage, but thought either very unlikely. He watched as they went in through the front door, and as she did so, the girl looked back, glancing up and down the street as if searching for someone. It was then that she saw him, leaning against a lamp-post a little further along. He raised a hand and her eyes widened. Was it really Jeannot? With a jerk of his thumb, he indicated the back gate of the house and he thought she nodded before she followed her mother indoors.

Moments later he was at the garden gate and so was she.

'Where did you go to?'

'What happened to you?'

They both spoke at once, making them laugh.

'Is Pierre in the stables?' Jeannot asked, looking anxiously about him.

'Don't think so,' replied Hélène. 'Papa sent him off somewhere this morning and he's not back yet. Come on, we'll talk in there.'

Together they hurried across the yard and into the shelter of the stables. Hélène flopped down on one straw bale, Jeannot on another.

'Well,' she said, 'why didn't you come back for me?'

Jeannot explained about the press gang and building the barricades.

'And where did *you* run off to?'

They sat on the bales, exchanging stories as the afternoon sun streamed in through the grimy windows, motes of dust and straw dancing in its beams. Two children, so different, but each completely comfortable in the company of the other.

It was Pierre who found them still talking when he came back into the stable from his errand in the city.

'Hey, you young tyke,' he groaned when he recognised Jeannot. 'Not you again.'

'He's not a tyke,' Hélène cried, leaping immediately to Jeannot's defence. 'He saved me from...' she paused, not wanting to explain to Pierre the horrors of Gaston's attentions, '...and I'll talk to him if I want to!'

'Not sure your parents would agree,' Pierre said mildly.

'Well, I don't care,' declared Hélène, adding with a lift of her chin, 'and you're not to tell them!'

'I won't tell them,' Pierre said, 'but you'd better scram now, youngster, before they find you themselves.'

Jeannot got to his feet. 'I'll be back,' he promised. 'When you're here, I'll come to the stables and Pierre can fetch you. All right, mate?' he added, grinning at Pierre, and Pierre returned a rueful grin and said, 'All right, tyke.'

As Jeannot crossed to the door, Hélène reached out and grabbed him into a hug. 'We'll always be friends, won't we, Jeannot?'

Jeannot extricated himself from the hug and mumbled, 'Yeah! Course we will.'

'Good,' said Hélène, smiling happily, 'that's what I thought.'

Acknowledgements

Thanks to my agent Judith Murdoch and everyone at Head of Zeus for their enthusiasm and encouragement. It all keeps me going!

About the Author

DINEY COSTELOE is the author of twenty-four novels, several short stories, and many articles and poems. She has three children and seven grandchildren, so when she isn't writing, she's busy with family. She and her husband divide their time between Somerset and West Cork.